THE MURDER CLUB

Also by Nikki Crutchley

Nothing Bad Happens Here (Miller Hatcher #1)
No One Can Hear You

THE MURDER CLUB

NIKKI CRUTCHLEY

Oak House Press

For Cate and Abbie. Without you, this writing journey would never have begun.

'Evil is not something superhuman, it's something less than human.'

- Agatha Christie *The Pale Horse* (1961)

'He who can live in infamy is unworthy of life.'

- Pierre Corneille *Le Cid* (1637) act 1 sc. 5

Chapter 1

Inside the wardrobe, he held the scarf to his face and breathed in the scent. He fancied it still smelled like her, all these years on, which he knew couldn't be right. He opened his eyes wide as if the action would make him see what he could feel around him: shoes lined up in neat pairs, most of them flat, leather, sensible. Heavy winter coats and light summer dresses. He clung to the scarf, cheap nylon, a garish pattern, made to look chic all those years ago. It anchored him. He'd done this before.

He had carved out space on the wardrobe floor, pushed shoes aside and crouched in wait. The hems of dresses and trousers sat on his shoulders. The scent of her, mingled with leather, was so pleasant he found himself inhaling, eyes shut, a hint of a smile on his face.

Then a burst of light flashed behind his eyes. He held his skull, one hand on either side, scarf tickling his face. The pain was gone as fast as it had come but left him breathless, sweat on his upper lip and prickling his underarms.

He focused on the noises of her home in an attempt to recover; the roof above cracking and cooling after a day of roasting in the unseasonal November heat, floorboards creaking as she made her way around the house, taps running, dishes being done. It didn't take long. Dinner for one. He listened as she stood at the front door calling Misty, as he'd seen her do all this week, watching as a streak of ginger emerged from the bushes and ran into the house. The TV finally being turned off.

Footsteps down the hallway. He adjusted his position, rising to stand, stooped, careful not to set off an alarm of wire coat-hangers. Taps being run, gargling in the bathroom, spitting. Toilet flushing. Footsteps down the hall. Towards her bedroom. Towards him.

He had it planned out. He'd imagined it so many times it played like a movie in his head. It was almost – almost – as good as the real thing. He'd always had a good imagination.

A sliver of light appeared under the wardrobe door as she entered her bedroom. He forced himself to breathe shallowly and evenly. He felt a bead of sweat run down the side of his face and inserted a finger inside the black beanie and scratched at his head.

He knew there was a possibility she'd open her wardrobe to put something away or get clothes out for work the next day. He was ready for that. It would be fine. But not the same. He stuffed the scarf into his back pocket, hands raised in front of him.

But she didn't open the wardrobe. Another indication that this was meant to be. He heard her humming the lyrics to a song he wasn't familiar with and whispering to Misty who me-owed in return. Her only company in bed that night and, as far as he knew from talk around town, the only thing she'd had in bed with her for the last six months. He heard the light being switched off. She wasn't a reader, didn't have a TV in her room. One of those people whose rooms are for sleeping in and nothing else.

He listened as she made herself comfortable, trying a few positions, sighing, and then ten minutes later the steady, melodic sound of her breathing, telling him she was asleep.

His hands shook, not from nerves, but excitement. The adrenalin made him strong, powerful. He stepped forward and pushed open the wardrobe door. The room was only slightly lighter. He could make out the bed in front of him, the tallboy to his left; he was a murky figure in the mirror to his right. He pulled the penlight from his back pocket and switched it on. It wasn't bright enough to wake her, but enabled him to see where he was going, not trip on an abandoned pair of shoes and give her a chance to fight back or run. He'd thought of everything.

Misty sat up on the end of the bed, golden eyes wide in the light of the torch.

He crept down the right side of the bed and shone a light on her face. Her eyelids flickered, and her smooth forehead creased. Pocketing the torch, he flicked on the bedside light and a ring of light surrounded them, a spotlight on the stage.

Just as her eyes opened – not in alarm, no, she didn't know anything was wrong yet – he punched her.

She grunted, gasped. Too shocked to scream.

She scrambled into an upright position, eyes wide in panic. There was that split-second moment of recognition, then panic became confusion.

He grabbed her head in his hands, it felt so small, and banged it hard against the wall behind her once – she screamed now, loud, too loud, and kicked up her legs under the duvet – twice – she groaned – then three times and she was out.

He let go of her head and her body collapsed to the side, almost rolling out of bed. He hadn't expected it to take that much force. She wasn't a big woman.

Dragging her out of bed, he ignored her nightgown riding up to her waist, showing off plain white underwear. He laid her at the foot of the bed. Misty looked on with a mix of arrogance and curiosity. Fuckin' cats. As long as they were fed and had somewhere warm to sleep, they couldn't give two fucks about their owners. A dog, however, loyal to the end. Even a yappy fluffball would be attacking his ankles right now.

He pulled down her nightgown, so it was resting just below her pale knees. The knocks to her head hadn't caused the skin to break, thank god – he hated blood. He could see her chest rising and falling. That was good. That was important. Her eyes were closed as if she was asleep. He knew her eyes were brown. On Monday evening they'd spoken briefly at the Royal. He could tell she wasn't comfortable around him, but word around town was she wasn't comfortable with males. He looked down at her now. Her lashes were so long they rested on the skin below her eyes, casting a feather-like shadow on her face.

He took the lipstick from his pocket. Removing the cap, he turned the base and watched the bright pink emerge like a flower blossoming. Maybelline Hibiscus Pop. He had snubbed Lentford's local chemist. That nosy bitch at the counter was always there, always ready for a chat – didn't matter about what or who, so long as she could spread a bit of gossip in that whisper that could be heard around the whole shop. He had gone into Hamilton to the Warehouse. The bargain chain store was always busy, people buying everything from clothes to fishing rods to groceries. A man buying a lipstick might cause a sideways glance from the cashier, but he knew he'd soon be forgotten once the homeless guy approached, next in line, buying a box of crackers for ninety-nine cents and smelling like the inside of a rubbish bin, or the teenage girls in aisle eight were caught shoplifting. He could've shrugged and made some comment to the cashier about his girlfriend or wife sending him out to buy her cosmetics, but couldn't be bothered – the less said the better. No need to give them a reason to remember him.

The application of the lipstick forced her lips up into a kind of grimace, or maybe a lopsided smile. It was harder than he'd thought it would be. He dabbed on a bit more. The garish pink a tattoo across her pale face. She was one of those women who wore giant straw hats in summer to save their complexion, a few minutes of sun turning her as red as a cooked lobster.

In one elaborate flourish he withdrew the scarf from his back pocket, not unlike a magician. He lifted her head to slide the scarf around her neck. He tied the scarf and then started to pull at each end. The silk slipped against his gloves, which caused him to slow down even more. Skin gathered in small folds as it was forced together. It was so peaceful. But he had broken out into a sweat. The power he felt was immense, and when he watched her chest fall for the last time the satisfaction and relief were one of being set free. He released his hold on the scarf and let it fall, its silky ends bright stains on the worn carpet.

He was done. Rising, he looked around the room. The scarf would stay. It would be wrong to remove it. He pushed the lipstick into his back pocket, where it sat snugly with the penlight. Travelling light was key. He walked out the bedroom door, turning for one last look, imprinting the scene on his memory. No photos, no keepsake – keepsakes were what brought you down. He watched Misty circle her owner, sniffing, then she leapt onto the bed, circled the area by one of the pillows and curled up in a ball. Selfish.

He made his way to the back door and stepped out into the cool air. He was smiling now. A proper smile. Not that painted on one he wore every day, the one he had to drag up from within. Genuine happiness engulfed him. He felt alive. Free. Powerful. There was no greater feeling on earth.

He walked down the quiet street, his lips forming a whistle, a tuneless sound of nonchalance. The lack of streetlights hid him from view, not that there was anyone watching. On

Thursday nights everyone in this hick town was either asleep or watching TV.

He was sick of hiding. Sick of being a no one. She always said he wouldn't amount to anything, but she was wrong. He was going to be remembered. This peaceful country town, building up to Christmas, in the middle of a freakish springtime heat wave, was about to wake up. They would start to feel unsafe in their houses. They would double-check windows and lock their doors at night. Something that was rarely done. And all because of him. He was about to make his mark. Go down in history. She was wrong. He would be remembered. Just watch. This Christmas he was going to be bigger than Santa.

Chapter 2

It wasn't often Miller Hatcher regretted her daily run, but at 6 p.m. the sun still beat down as if it was midday. It had been no cooler down by the river, but she kept on going, knowing the harder she pushed herself now the more likely she was to sleep tonight. She only had a couple of kilometres left back to her house. She crossed the footbridge onto the other side of the river, left the river path and crossed into Powter's Bush. She had stumbled upon the piece of bushland six months ago when she was exploring the town on her first run. The small expanse of native trees and shrubs planted on the edge of Lentford was named after one of the first families who settled in the area. It was thick with kauri, kahikatea and rimu, nikau palms and ferns. The rough path was crisscrossed with roots the size of her wrist and she had to concentrate as she picked up her speed. Ten minutes later the track opened up to the manicured expanse of Lentford Cemetery. A month out till Christmas and it looked brighter than usual. People making their annual pilgrimage to graves that were otherwise forgotten. Miller, veering from her path, touched her hand to her lips and deposited the kiss on her mother's headstone. 'Hey, Mum.'

She jogged through the once ornate gates, which were now rusty, any white paint left gradually shedding, and headed straight down the road. Rounding a corner, she heard her name and the rapid approach of footsteps.

'Miller! Wait up.'

Miller turned and jogging on the spot, waved to Ash – otherwise known as Sergeant Aisling Wirihana to most people in Lentford.

They continued running together, getting into a rhythm. Miller shortened her steps to match those of Ash, who was a head shorter, but then found herself increasing her speed to keep up.

'You should've rung and we could've run together,' Ash puffed, her normally pale, freckled face flushed. 'We haven't been out running in ages.'

'I thought you might be working. Next time,' Miller promised. 'You up to anything this weekend?' She gulped in the humid air. She wasn't used to talking and running, but Ash seemed to do it effortlessly.

'I'm not rostered on, so I'll just hang out with Zach – if he wants to.' Zach was Ash's teenage son, a source of equal pride and stress in the single mother's life. 'I'll probably try and get out in the garden. You?'

'Nah, no plans. I'll probably meet up with Kahu.'

They reached the corner where Ash turned off towards her house. 'Have a good one,' she shouted, waving. 'Proper catch up at mine, soon. I'll cook.' And she was off, her bobbed hair plastered to her scalp, muscled legs pumping even faster now that she wasn't with Miller.

Miller continued along for another few metres and turned right into her street. There were a few cars about, people getting in from work. Kids were still out playing, some running through sprinklers in their front yards. She heard mothers shouting 'Dinner!' and watched as children at the park across the road had one last slide or swing, and others abandoned bikes and games on front lawns, and headed to their various houses. She slowed down to a walk as she approached her driveway, noting the hedge out the front needed trimming. She was hopeless at gardening, something her mum had always been good at, and she didn't want to be *that* neighbour; her house bringing down the tone of the tidy neighbourhood. She smiled. Six months earlier she wouldn't have cared about her neighbours, didn't even know them except for a nod in the hallway of her and Nat's apartment in Auckland. But when she'd moved into her mum's old house in the small town of Lentford, her mother's reputation preceded her. Miller realised she had a lot to live up to. It had been a hard few weeks when she'd first moved in, people passing on their condolences even though her mother had died almost two years ago. The funeral had been in Lentford, but Miller was in and out in two days. The grief she had felt at her mother's death then, so fresh and raw, was not to be shared with a group of strangers. She heard a car horn and waved at Greg, her next-door neighbour, returning from work. She heard the onslaught of his three children when they realised their dad was home.

Walking up the driveway she saw bird shit on her Triumph which was parked under the silver birch in the shade. She really needed to start parking the car in the garage, but the old wooden sliding door proved too much of an effort every morning when she was leaving for work. Maybe she could get a new door installed.

Unlocking the front door, she was met by a wall of heat. She walked into the lounge and threw open the windows, stopping for a minute and withdrawing an LP from her mother's collection. Roy Orbison tonight. She turned it up loud enough so she could hear it from the back deck. She smiled at the familiar intro: drums, guitar and then Roy's soulful voice singing 'Pretty

Woman'. One of her dad's favourites. A slippery memory, one she wasn't sure was real or imagined, of him serenading her mother in the kitchen of their old house. Her mum flushed with pleasure. His hands, always stained with car grease, nails black, wrapped around her waist.

She made her way down the short hallway and into the kitchen where she opened the doors that led out onto the deck. She tapped the answering machine in the office off the kitchen. Nat's voice, always loud, bubbly, echoed from out of the office. 'Hey, Mills. Just ringing to check in. See how you're doing. Catch up with you later.'

Nat, her old flatmate, rang once a week. Miller had thought when Nat moved down to Wellington that they'd lose contact. But they were still just as close. And for that Miller was glad. The machine beeped and Kahu Parata's deep voice came from the machine. She smiled as he stumbled over his words. He hated answering machines. 'Hey, Miller, it's me. It's Kahu. Still on for tomorrow? Meet you at the high school at ten.'

She smiled, looking forward to their weekend catch up, and headed to the shower, peeling off her sweaty shorts and singlet as she walked down the hallway.

After her shower, she towelled her dark blonde hair dry. She eyed her mother's toothbrush sitting in the cup next to hers. She picked it up then put it back down again. Her head had started to pound. It was the combination of the unseasonably hot weather – it had reached twenty-eight degrees today and it was officially still spring – and pushing herself too hard on her run. But she felt weary, a good sign for the night ahead.

She wiped the condensation off the mirror. Her index finger ran down the scar on the right side of her face. It was definitely fading, but still visible. The doctors had said it would never fade completely. She traced her finger from the edge of her eyebrow curving out to her cheek to just below her ear lobe. It was a good reminder. Touching that scar did more for her than any counselling session ever could. It conjured up regret and guilt and an uncomfortable ache in her chest, and the need for a drink dissipated – mostly. She wondered if the day would ever come when the touch of that scar wouldn't be enough. She had a feeling it might. It was always at the back of her head as though something was looming, and she could do nothing to stop it coming.

She got dressed in clean shorts and a singlet and while trying to think about something else, put one of Len's ready-meals on a plate and microwaved it for five minutes. She poured herself sparkling water and grabbed a lemon from the bowl on the bench. She cut a wedge, squeezed the juice into the glass and dropped the wedge in. She thought of a cold, crisp sav or a frothy beer, but almost as instantly as the thought came, she physically shook it from her head.

'Day one hundred and sixty-five.' She looked at a framed photo of her and her mum: she'd been in her final year of high school, her dad was gone and she and her mum were happy. The days of sobriety were counted as if she were a child, checking off the days till Christmas. She couldn't help thinking that once she got to a certain number, she could treat herself. That she would be cured. That she could have one – just one – glass of wine and that would be it. A reward for her abstinence. She knew this was all kinds of wrong, but it still didn't stop her from thinking it. Every single day. And it annoyed her that after everything she'd been through, everything she'd put herself and her friends through, alcohol was always front and centre in her mind, it was still a massive part of her life even when it wasn't in it.

She took the plate and glass out to the deck and sat down

on one of her mum's old Cape Cod chairs which she'd recently sanded and repainted white. The food was gone in minutes, vegetarian lasagne this week. Len, the local cafe owner, didn't take orders. He made two dishes a week – like it or lump it. It filled her stomach in the comforting way good home-cooked food does.

She put her feet on the matching footstool and looked out across the yard. Her mother's neatly done-up old state house, pale-yellow with the obligatory orange tiled roof, was on a generous quarter-acre section. The backyard was bordered by every fruit tree you could imagine: lemon, lime, feijoa, plum, apple, quince, loquat and orange. Some her mum had planted when she'd moved to Lentford over seven years ago, others were probably as old as Miller.

She put her dishes in the sink and scooped up the mail she hadn't had a chance to open at the office today. Taking it back to her seat she flicked through it. She placed the *New Zealand Herald*, the *Waikato Times* and a couple of other magazines in plastic sleeves on the deck beside her. She eyed *First Look*, the magazine she used to worked for, and tried not to think about the stories her old colleagues were covering. With the *Lentford Leader*, a weekly publication, she never really had as much time as she wanted. And the readership wasn't overly interested in the big issues. They cared about who won the senior rugby game on Saturday, or if a new, highly praised fertiliser was working on someone's farm. Tearing open one of the three envelopes, she could almost tell what they were before she opened them – letters from supposedly well-meaning members of the public, often elderly, who weren't interested in using email, so stated their opinion on lined, white paper usually reserved for writing to the grandkids. Often unsigned.

One was written in a shaking hand, telling her how much

she enjoyed the article in last week's *Leader* on the high-school kids pitching-in in Lentford, helping the elderly with gardening, cooking or just keeping them company, and asked if she could feature more uplifting articles like that: *Miller, dear, I fear your stories are sometimes too serious.* It was signed with kind regards from Mildred Pope.

The second one was also written in an unsteady hand. He had read her article last week on period poverty. Ngaire, the editor, hadn't taken much convincing but had warned Miller there would likely be a bit of backlash. This person wrote to Miller that no one wanted to read about 'so-called' period poverty: *That kind of thing should not be mentioned in public. In my day you never heard about it. Women went about their business and we men were none the wiser. In a local newspaper, I don't believe you should be going on about teenage girls and their time of the month. Disgraceful. I've lived in Lentford for over forty years. I love our local paper but will not continue reading it if you intend to keep going down the path of such undignified subject matter.*

Miller grinned. She was proud of that piece. Explaining period poverty – that teenage girls often took days off school when they got their period as they couldn't afford tampons or sanitary pads – was the kind of story she loved working on, bringing out into the light an issue that had been in hiding. And it wasn't something she got to do often when writing for the *Leader*. She was used to dealing with the negativity now. She'd covered an equal-pay demonstration in Hamilton last month, one that many local Lentford women attended. She'd interviewed a couple of the women, one accountant and one lawyer. Some guy had written to her saying she was: *a feminist lesbian bitch who didn't have the right to use a perfectly good local paper as her personal soapbox.*

The last envelope had no stamp. Hand-delivered. She

hummed along to Roy's 'All I Have to Do is Dream' and opened it. The paper was cream, heavy, almost cardboard. It threw up images of a lavender-haired woman, perfectly coiffed and drowning in rose-scented perfume, sitting at a table writing letters to friends and family.

The date in the right-hand corner was 29 November. Yesterday. The handwriting looked rushed, ten words scrawled in blue pen, the unruled paper causing the writing to gradually slope. Miller frowned and read out loud:

Miller, tonight it begins. I look forward to the journey.

Miller stared at the note, unable to make sense of it. She refolded it and pushed it back into the envelope. In the spare bedroom she filed the letters away in a box she kept in the wardrobe. She'd been working as a journalist for almost a decade now and had kept everything anyone had ever sent her. The threats, the thank yous, the opinionated letters telling her she knew nothing. It was an odd mixture of all her years of writing, what she cared about passionately and how people had reacted to every one of her stories. With most of her stories there was a reaction, at least to the stories she used to write. That's what she wanted – people to discuss what she'd written. She wanted people to argue, disagree, stand up for what they thought was right. She wanted to bring issues to the forefront, challenge people, maybe even educate them a little. Hell, she knew for sure some were never going to change their opinions. But she'd always try. Again, she thought of *First Look*. After Castle Bay, she'd got her dream job, her promotion. A couple of years later, she lost it all.

Roy's serenading had come to an end and a heavy silence filled the house. She started the record over, carefully pulling the arm and resting it in the first groove. Walking back to the spare bedroom, she took the boxing gloves from the corner and slid her hands into them. Slapping the leather together twice, she stood facing the freestanding punching bag positioned in the middle of the bare room. She started with a few combinations, the slap of leather on vinyl, music to her ears. She went through her routine, her breathing becoming more laboured as she continued. She turned side-on, fists raised and spun a leg towards the bag, connected, spun back and repeated. A grunt escaped her lips. She gritted her teeth, frowned, got angry.

This was the only time she allowed herself to be overtaken by the anger. She set her feet facing the bag again, knees slightly bent, and gave the bag a left hook, over and over again. She squeezed her eyes shut tight, feeling her fist move the bag. She crouched over, fists curled, head down and battered the bag as fast as she could. What was done, was done. Lentford was exactly where she deserved to be. Any ambition she held was now buried by past failures and mistakes.

Chapter 3

'Cassie, today's the day. Our last session. How are you feeling?'

Cassie chewed the inside of her mouth, where a sizeable lump had formed. This was a new habit. One that had begun when she entered The Oaks Treatment Facility. It was something to do while she thought. There were always so many questions.

Fenella Gibbs, manager of The Oaks, looked at Cassie from behind her desk. She scratched at the end of a white square of gauze that covered her forehead. When she saw Cassie looking, she shook her head so her hair fell down to cover it. The pen in her hand was poised to note down everything Cassie said and did. She felt like a scientific experiment: *What was the crazy girl about to do?*

If Cassie had to say how she was feeling one more time she was pretty sure she would leap across the desk and slap Fenella senseless. No. She'd punch her. That would feel a million times better. She'd punch her right in the nose. Blood would pour out, down her perfectly ironed white collared shirt and onto her beige pencil skirt.

'Cassie?' Fenella tucked a straightened honey-blonde piece of hair over her ear. She looked as if she could be in her thirties, but Cassie knew she'd just turned forty-five. They'd had a cake for her last week in the staff room. 'Happy birthday' had rung out down the halls. While Cassie was eating a dry bran muffin, the staff tucked into chocolate gateau.

Cassie looked up and smiled. She released the skin from her teeth and said, 'I'm fine.'

'How long have you been here, Cassie?' Fenella asked, head tilted.

Cassie knew the answer to that. She'd been crossing off the days since her father had dropped her off. Left her. Abandoned her. 'Three months, two weeks and two days.'

Fenella's perfectly lined lips turned up into a smile that lasted half a second. 'Then you should know "fine" doesn't cut it here, Cassie. I want an answer. I want a considered, honest answer.'

Cassie's fingers traced the outline of the Roman coins hanging from the copper bangle on her right arm. She knew she needed to get this right. She was getting out in a couple of days, all going well. This answer held her key to freedom. If she didn't answer properly, they'd keep her longer. Her tongue poked at the large lump on the inside of her mouth. She could feel a small piece of loose skin. It was long enough that she could swirl it around her tongue.

'I do feel good,' she said, meeting Fenella's stare. She wondered if Fenella had ever stepped out of line. Looking at the framed diplomas and degrees on the white walls behind her, Cassie didn't think so. 'I feel like my mind is clearer compared to three months ago. I know now I don't need drugs or alcohol. And I know that was making me do things which weren't acceptable.'

Fenella nodded, placing the pen down and squirting sanitiser on her hands.

This is exactly the shit they want to hear. It had taken her a while to realise that's all they wanted. Tiff had taught her that. Cassie knew the counsellors were decent people, most of them, just doing their job. Fenella could only go on what Cassie told her. How were they to know if it was truth or bullshit? 'I know once I get out of here, I can start fresh. Forget the last eighteen months. I feel I've matured in here. I've left that confused girl behind.'

Fenella nodded again, leaning back in her leather swivel chair. 'Good. And Karl Taylor? Tell me how you feel about that situation.'

Cassie felt her heartbeat increase. This was where she could ruin it all. She bit down on her cheek and tasted blood. She reached across the desk for the glass of water and drank deeply.

Stay calm.

'I was wrong. I know that. I think I always knew what I was doing was wrong. As you've taught me, it was a way to deal with Mum's murder. The wrong way to deal with it.'

'You know now that you're not a one-woman vigilante? You know the police will do everything in their power to find this Karl Taylor. You know it's not your responsibility to find him?'

Cassie nodded. 'I do.'

'What else?'

She knew how this part went as well. At the start, she refused to admit it. That's why she'd been here so long. 'I can't obsess over every Karl Taylor I come across.'

'Just because the police have the name of the man who murdered your mother, doesn't mean every Karl Taylor out there is a murderer.'

Cassie nodded.

'Cassie?'

Bloody hell, they always needed verbal answers. A nod of the head was not acceptable. 'Yes.'

'Excellent, Cassie.'

Tiff was right all along. *Tell them what they want to hear.* She'd been stubborn at the start. She fought them. Didn't think anything was wrong. Still didn't. Her mother was murdered almost fourteen years ago. Eighteen months ago, her body was found right here in Lentford, at the disused dairy factory just out of town, in the opposite direction of The Oaks. The name Karl Taylor was thrown into the media as 'a person of interest in the murder of Margaret Hughes' and so the search began. But he was a ghost. The police had found nothing. And so, Cassie had made it her mission to seek out every Karl Taylor she could find. No luck as yet. The last one had been a mistake. A man living in Tauranga, her home town. He was probably too young to fit the profile of the 'real' Karl Taylor, her mother's murderer. But it didn't stop her from concocting her wildest plan yet. She'd stalked him; saw that he frequented a local pub a couple of nights a week; saw he was flirty with every woman he came into contact with. She'd struck up a conversation with him. He'd taken her back to his place. He was on board with being tied up to the headboard. She could see the anticipation in his wide smile. But when she started talking about her murdered mother, how he had done it, the smile dropped from his face and he began to squirm. She demanded a confession. He laughed at her, then called her a crazy bitch, so she punched him, then punched him again. This went on for an hour, and as her alcohol and drug buzz wore off, she came to realise he wasn't the one. He talked her into untying him with promises of not to tell but of course, he did. And that's how she'd ended up here. It hadn't been the first time. Her dad, the cops, they had been unaware she'd done it before, sought out these Karl Taylors, but this time she'd taken it too far.

Fenella signed her name at the bottom of Cassie's release form in an artful flourish. 'You're free to go Monday morning.'

Cassie rose from her chair, smiling. 'Thank you so much.'

'All the best, Cassie. You've done so well here. Your mother's death ...'

Murder, Cassie corrected Fenella in her head.

'... was a tragedy, but I'm thrilled to see your progress. You're moving on, and that's important.'

Bloody moving on. Why is moving on so fucking important?

Cassie said goodbye and left the office. Like hell, she was moving on.

Chapter 4

Lentford on Saturday morning was humming with activity. The farmers' market was set up in what was known as the village square, an expanse of lawn leading down to the Piako River from the main street. Oak trees loomed over strategically placed picnic tables, where people sat drinking coffee and eating everything from corn fritters to blueberry waffles. Oak trees were to the Waikato what palm trees were to Florida. Many were over a century old, standing tall in fields where cows grazed or, annoyingly for some, in their backyard. Many were protected by the council and so homeowners put up with the hundred-year-old giants, their leaves dropping every autumn, showering backyards and clogging gutters with their detritus.

Miller walked down Victoria Street after parking outside the *Lentford Leader* office. Some of the shops opened on the weekends – the cafe, the bakery, the bookshop and one of the clothing stores; others shut up, as they had done for decades, not wanting to adopt the modern practice of opening seven days a week. She said hello to a few of the locals as she headed to the high school on the other side of town. The school's basketball court was on the edge of the school property. Kahu's six-foot-plus frame was stretched out on the court, a ball at his side.

'Took you long enough.' He stood up, bouncing the ball on the spot. 'I live in Hamilton, almost half an hour away and you live five minutes away.'

'Yeah, yeah,' Miller smiled. 'But I also don't have the need to be ten minutes early to every appointment I make.'

She walked up to Kahu and gave him a quick hug. His T-shirt, yet another worn-out piece of clothing at least a decade old, hung from his muscular frame. 'Really?' Miller pinched the thin fabric of the sleeve between her fingers. 'Might be time to splash out and buy a new one.'

'Nah. Trina bought this one for me.' He looked down at it and the smile left Miller's face. 'It was a joke. She didn't think I'd wear pink. Actually, salmon is what she called it.' His smile didn't reach his eyes.

Miller waited for Kahu to say more. But he never did. Trina, his wife, had died just over a year ago from breast cancer. Kahu hadn't lasted long in Castle Bay as the sergeant after that. He'd never spoken to Miller about it, but she knew him well enough to understand that the pain of staying in a place he and Trina had loved, had planned to spend the rest of their lives in, was too much. And so he'd rung her one day six months ago, not long after she'd moved to Lentford, telling her he'd transferred to CIB in Hamilton and was now a detective sergeant, having completed his training earlier in his career. The Kahu that Miller had first met when she arrived in the small coastal town of Castle Bay to report on the murder of British backpacker Bethany Haliwell was not the same man she now met every weekend. He was still fun, they still talked, mostly about each other's work, they played basketball, had a coffee, but not once had he spoken about losing Trina. Miller got it and she wasn't about to force him to talk, but she knew he'd feel better if he did.

'Let's play,' Miller said, grabbing the ball off him. The pall of grief dissipated and Kahu's broad smile was back.

They played half a court, one on one. They were equally fit, and even though there were a lot of laughs they took the game seriously. After half an hour Kahu collapsed to the ground, arms spread. The ta moko covering his arms, now glistening with sweat, were a work of art. Kahu had explained it to Miller one evening in Castle Bay after Trina's funeral. It was something else to talk about. He'd avoided discussing Trina from the very beginning. He told her about the manawa lines which represented his life and his journey and time spent on earth; the main korus coming off the manawa lines represented people and groups; the smaller korus were based on tiny growth shoots on the New Zealand fern and represented new life and new beginnings. Kahu had added new korus over the years to his manawa lines, which signified adding people close to him.

'Which is Trina?' Miller had asked, hoping to engage him. Kahu responded by rolling down his shirt sleeves and staring out at the sea as the surf rolled in and broke on the shores of Castle Bay.

'By my count that's twenty-four, twenty-two to me,' Miller now said, prodding Kahu with her foot. She lifted the edge of her T-shirt and wiped her face. 'Coffee's on you.'

Outside the Kowhai Cafe a couple of pairs of Red Band gumboots stood at the door. Most shops in Lentford at any time of the day had an abandoned pair left out the front: it was a sign of politeness not to trek in whatever you'd brought in on your gumboot soles from the farm.

Kahu and Miller stood at the counter. Len, the owner, appeared from the kitchen. Mid-fifties but trying hard to look younger, he dyed his hair a dark shade of black which made his face look too pale, especially at this time of year. A small grey patch grew on his chin, not big enough to be a goatee, more of a soul patch, which he didn't bother to dye. This, to Miller, defeated the purpose.

'Great dinner last night, Len,' Miller said.

Len winked at her. He did that a lot – to every female customer. 'Carbonara and ratatouille on the menu for next week.' He winked at her again. He did it so often it looked more like a tic.

'Li in today?' Miller asked. Her neighbour Li, a university student in her early twenties, had just completed the last year of her bachelor degree and worked part-time for Len. Miller had heard stories from her that hadn't put Len in the best light – Len was controlling, argumentative and, Li was sure, a closet racist, having referred to a group of Japanese who came in for lunch as 'your kind'. Li was Chinese, and this had been his undoing as far as she was concerned.

'Not today, skiving off. Probably hungover. Bloody students.'

Li was one of the hardest-working people Miller knew. She was not the typical partying kind of student. Her parents put paid to that by buying a house for Li in Lentford instead of Hamilton, where the Waikato University campus was, plus a reliable Toyota to get her to and from classes.

'Two lattes please, Len,' Miller said. 'You eating?' she asked Kahu.

'Always.' He pulled his wallet out, scanning the blackboard menu on the wall and rubbing his non-existent belly. 'Big breakfast please, mate. Eggs fried, hold the black pudding, hate that shit, but double mushrooms.'

'Got it,' Len said to Kahu, no wink. 'By the way, love the ink, bro.'

Most could pull off 'bro'. Len couldn't. And when it was paired with 'ink' he came off looking like a try-hard.

Kahu was polite as ever. 'Cheers, mate.'

They took a seat in the corner, up against the faux brick wallpaper. Len had decorated the cafe to look like a trendy inner-city coffee shop. He'd done a good job, but it looked overdone and contrived in rural Lentford.

Kahu plucked his sweaty T-shirt from his frame. 'It can't get any hotter, can it? First of December, it's officially the first day of summer today.'

'They say it's going to get worse, much worse,' Miller teased.

'That's one thing I miss about Castle Bay,' Kahu said, thanking Len as he came over with the coffees.

Just one thing? thought Miller.

'The sea breeze. No matter how hot it got, there was always a breeze. Always a chance for a quick dip in the ocean before work.'

'And now you live pretty much as far away from the ocean as you can get in New Zealand,' Miller said. She didn't really miss Auckland's hectic pace, but she did miss being a short drive from a beach. The Piako River, which wound its way through Lentford, was broad and fast-flowing, but west towards Hamilton, a few minutes out of Lentford, it branched off and created a smaller river where grassy banks met the water. It was often packed during summer. The deepest point was only waist-deep which made it a safe place for everyone to swim. There was also the public pool, but you couldn't pay her to swim there among the giggling nappy-wearing babies, where stray hairs attached themselves to slick bodies, and plasters, along with half-drowning insects, floated on the surface.

Len appeared five minutes later with Kahu's breakfast and Miller's blueberry muffin.

'How's the paper?' Kahu asked, glancing at her from the corner of his eye.

'It's fine, I guess.'

'Fine, eh?' Kahu said.

'I don't know. I'm waiting for it to get better.'

'Still early days,' Kahu said. 'Give it time.'

'The locals don't trust me. They don't talk to me.' Miller was well aware she sounded whiny and checked herself. 'It *is* good. My workmates, on the whole, are fantastic. And some of the locals have been really friendly.' She thought of her friendship with Ash.

'Len seems to like you,' Kahu said, giving her an exaggerated wink.

Miller smiled. 'It'll take time. It's just—'

'I know,' Kahu said, wiping his mouth with a paper napkin. 'It's not where you wanted to be at this stage in your career. But what's done is done, mate.'

He was right. She knew it was time to get on with it. Lentford was her home now. She had a good job and should be grateful that after what had happened, someone was willing to give her another chance. She needed to rid herself of the idea that working for the *Leader* was a giant step down.

More of a sideways step, she thought. Just because working for a small-town paper didn't figure in the plan didn't mean it was a bad thing.

'I still get to write interesting pieces,' she said.

Kahu nodded, chewing.

'I get to choose my stories, mostly. Ngaire's good like that.'

'There you go,' Kahu said. 'And you know what? This shouldn't make you any less ambitious. Look at it as a challenge. You're a journalist. You have a job at a newspaper. Work with what you've got, I say.'

Miller smiled at him and rolled her eyes. He was right again, of course.

'Your work okay?' Miller asked, tired of talking about herself. Work seemed to be all Kahu did these days. She didn't know how big his circle of friends was. She met him once or twice a week, usually in Lentford. She'd been to his house on the outskirts of Hamilton once when he moved in. It was a bachelor pad, scarcely furnished. There was a photo of Trina and Kahu on their wedding day in pride of place on the mantelpiece, but other feminine touches were missing.

'Busy,' Kahu said, shovelling fried egg into his mouth and chewing. 'Finally got that serial rapist.'

'Really?' Miller said. The case had been open for months, with five women reporting the same man assaulting them. 'How did you get him?'

'He chose the wrong woman this time.' Kahu rested his knife and fork on his plate as he told the story. 'She was walking home from after-work drinks. It was dark and she cut across the grounds of Girls' High, right in the city, when he jumped her. She's a brown belt in judo. He came at her from behind, but she was ready. Pulled some move which she called a...' He paused, trying to remember. 'An ippon seoi nage. Got him on the ground, kicked him a few times, cracked a couple of his ribs.' Kahu grinned. 'Piece of shit deserved a whole lot more than that.'

His phone chirped on the table between them. He looked at the screen. 'Sorry. Work.'

Miller sipped her coffee and listened to Kahu's side of the conversation. 'Okay. How long? Where?' He looked at his watch. 'I'm already here. Be there in five.' He ended the call and gathered his wallet and keys. 'Sorry, have to cut this short.' He grabbed a piece of toast and what was left of his bacon.

'What's up?' asked Miller.

'Work. As always. Catch up later in the week, okay?' Kahu touched Miller's shoulder. He strode across the cafe and out the door, his phone pressed to his ear.

Chapter 5

Miller parked her car outside the *Lentford Leader* offices on Victoria Street on Monday morning. At 8 a.m. Lentford was still waking up. It was quiet enough to hear the river cascade down the small waterfall where the Piako River shrank from nine metres wide to only three, a hundred metres away from the western end of town. She walked to the Kowhai Cafe. Len had been open since 7.30 a.m., catering to the few early birds. She walked in and breathed in the smell of caffeine.

'Look, Li,' Miller heard Len's voice out the back in the kitchen. 'I employ you. I'm the boss. You're five minutes late and there's going to be a rush on soon.'

Miller looked around the cafe. There was one person sitting in the corner reading the newspaper.

'Len, it was five minutes. I'm early every other day.'

'I don't want to hear it. There are a bunch of people here who would kill for your job, you know that?'

'You're not serious? It's not exactly some high-flying career, Len. Settle down.'

Miller smiled. *You tell him, Li.*

'Consider this your first warning!' Len's voice rose and got higher in pitch as Li walked out the kitchen door and appeared behind the counter.

She rolled her eyes at Miller. 'He actually thinks I need this job,' she whispered.

Miller knew Li's parents back in Shanghai supported her financially. She'd told Miller she'd taken the job to be more independent from them. Miller didn't bother reminding Li that they had bought her a house and a car.

Li took a deep breath. 'The usual?'

'Yes, please.' Miller took a seat on one of the high stools by the window and watched as Li expertly worked the coffee machine, grinding beans and frothing milk, squinting as it hissed and steamed.

'Heard the news?' Li asked, eyes wide, when she was done.

'News?' Miller asked, assuming that by *news* Li meant gossip.

Len, obviously overhearing the conversation, came out of the kitchen and came over to Miller, almost skipping in his excitement to be the first to tell.

Li brought Miller's coffee over, determined not to miss out. She struggled onto a bar stool, her short legs, clad in cut-off denim shorts, freely swinging inches from the floor. She looked over at Len, ignoring his look implying she should get back to work.

Len shook his head in annoyance, but Miller could tell this was big. 'Someone's been murdered,' Len whispered.

Miller sipped her drink. 'Murdered?' This was Lentford. A tractor breaking down in the main street was considered news locally, or maybe a dog being run over on the main road into town. But this was actual, proper news. 'Who?' Miller asked.

'Tamara Jenson,' Len said, with Li nodding next to him, their fight forgotten in their shared knowledge of prime gossip.

'They found her Saturday morning,' Li said, taking over.

'Where?' Miller asked. She still didn't quite believe them, and didn't know Tamara Jenson.

'At her home. On Gifford Street,' Len said.

'How do you know all of this?' Miller asked. There'd been nothing on the news or in the papers that morning.

'Tamara's neighbour, Hank Lille – his wife owns the fabric shop down the street – wandered over when a friend was there Saturday. Apparently, she'd missed her shift out at The Oaks.'

'She worked in the kitchen there,' Li said, filling in the blanks.

'Anyway, after a lot of knocking and peering in windows, the friend tried the front door. Unlocked apparently. Hank stayed outside, didn't want to intrude, he said. Anyway, there was a god-almighty scream – his words – and the woman came out white as a ghost. Said Tamara was dead inside. Sergeant Wirihana was first at the scene, but CIB arrived early afternoon.'

Miller thought of Kahu leaving suddenly on Saturday morning. She hadn't heard from him since then. And Ash had been first on the scene. Miller needed to make sure she was okay. But knowing Ash she'd be taking it all in her stride.

'Can't remember the last murder we had here,' Len said, his thumb smoothing down the patch of hair on his chin. 'That woman was found, out at the old dairy factory eighteen months ago, but she wasn't a local.'

Like it doesn't count, thought Miller. *God help anyone who isn't a local.*

'There was that young girl, Amelia Dodds. Murdered on her parents' farm. But that wasn't really Lentford.' He disappeared behind the counter as the news came on the radio. 'Listen up,' he said, as customers entered the shop.

Miller watched him serve Lou the lawnmower man, who was standing in his thick woollen socks, his work boots left at the door. He took his cap off, grey hair stuck up at odd angles, and shoved it under an armpit and fished out his wallet.

'Hey, Miller.'

Miller turned towards the voice and smiled as her stomach

flip-flopped. It was Jay, who managed the small printing press where the *Leader* was printed. As he sat down beside her she breathed in his scent, shower-fresh. Whenever she saw him, he was always wearing the same thing. Dark blue jeans for weekdays, board shorts for weekends, and a polo shirt of varying colours. Today's was pale blue, which made his blue eyes even more startling. He always sported a bit of stubble, not overgrown, but not designer – a happy medium.

'Heard the news, I guess.' He ran a hand through his thick black hair, which was never styled and, Miller thought, gave him a dishevelled look which he wore well.

Miller nodded, then Len shushed everyone into silence as the newsreader mentioned Lentford.

'The body of Tamara Jenson was found early Saturday morning in the small farming town of Lentford in the Waikato. Ms Jenson lived on her own and had not turned up for her shift at The Oaks Treatment Centre on Friday afternoon. A friend went to the victim's house on Saturday morning to check on her, which is when the body was discovered. In a short statement Detective Sergeant Kahu Parata said there would be a press conference this morning, where more details will be given. Cause of death is unknown at this time, but Detective Sergeant Parata has said they are treating it as suspicious.'

Miller watched the shock on the people's faces around her. The news item had answered her question. Kahu was on the case.

'Jesus,' Lou said, rubbing at his hair and then trying to flatten it into place, without any luck. He turned to Jay. 'Ain't no one safe anymore, eh?'

Jay shook his head and moved to the counter to order his coffee.

'Anyone know her?' Len asked.

'She used to come in every now and then,' Li said.

'Really?' Len said, eyes wide.

Miller could see the cogs of his brain turning. She knew that everyone who came in from now till the foreseeable future would be told that Tamara Jenson had been a regular at the Kowhai.

Len turned the radio down as Dave Dobbyn started singing about a slice of heaven.

'Thanks, Len,' Lou said. 'The bloody town might be on its way to hell but I still gotta get these lawns done.' Lou nodded at Miller. 'How are ya, Miller? Keeping well?'

Miller smiled at him. 'Yeah, good thanks, Lou.'

'Got you booked in before Christmas,' he said. Lou did her lawns for her once a fortnight. 'Although with this bloody weather it's probably not needed.'

Miller nodded, thinking of her parched back yard.

'Anyway, let me know if you want to cancel.'

He disappeared out the door, followed by Jay.

'Thanks, Li. I'd better get going.' Miller left five dollars on the counter. 'Catch up soon, okay?'

Li smiled back at her. 'Sure thing, Miller. Have a good day.'

Miller knew this was going to be big news. Lentford took care of its own. She was still looked upon as an outsider and needed to be here a lot longer to gain any kind of trust from the locals. And when her job happened to be a journalist, that automatically tacked on another year of suspicious glances and polite hellos in the street that never led to anything else. She took her phone out of her bag and texted Ash. 'Just heard the news. Are you ok?'

Miller walked up to the *Lentford Leader's* office. She felt the familiar feeling in her stomach. A churning mix of butterflies and excitement. The beginning of a good story. Ngaire had to let her write this. Kahu might be able to give her a bit of inside information. Ngaire wouldn't give the story to Eric, and Cody was only a junior reporter.

She arrived at the office, her step lighter at the prospect of a newsworthy article to write. She walked around the high front desk that partially blocked off the staff area. Apart from the receptionist's desk at the front, there were three other desks and Ngaire's office in the back-left corner. To the right was a door that led to a minuscule, windowless tearoom and a toilet beyond that. The back door led out to a small gravel area and alleyway.

Miller dumped her satchel on her desk and placed her coffee cup down. Ngaire's door was closed, which meant she was in already. She looked over at Eric. He was always here early, not because he was a hard worker but because he was a fifty-something who lived with his ailing mother. He came in to play online poker – everyone knew it, even Ngaire. Miller often wondered why Ngaire, a workaholic and perfectionist, kept him around. But Miller knew he did the work that was expected of him. When she had asked Ngaire about Eric, his attitude, the gambling that she turned a blind eye to, Ngaire said, 'This newspaper is hard work, Miller. Good journalists are hard to come by. Eric writes well – well enough. That's all I need. And, hey, that's why you're here, to give the paper a bit of balance. And I know his long-suffering mother.'

Eric and Miller had clashed from the beginning. He was forthright in the most annoying and rude way, his first words to her being, 'How'd ya get that scar?' When Miller refused to tell him he then asked, 'Got anything to do with why you've chucked in a job with *First Look* and are now slumming it at the *Lentford Leader*?' He'd grinned at her, not expecting an answer, and she could tell he enjoyed watching her squirm. Miller resented him; he made what could've been a pleasant office environment toxic. And, she had to admit to herself, if he did find out what had happened back in Auckland, he'd spread it all over Lentford – a ripe titbit for the locals.

Eric looked up from his desk opposite hers. His thick greying hair looked like it had been cut by his mother, the short fringe uneven, tufts sticking up at the back. He smiled, his teeth crooked and crowding in on each other as if trying to escape his mouth. 'So what brought you here?' He raised his brows twice and turned back to his computer.

He had asked the same question of her every Monday since she'd started. She never answered and he never pushed. Miller was waiting for the day he got off his useless arse and dug into what had happened in Auckland. Anyone could find out if they wanted to.

Eric looked up again and, obviously having moved on, said, 'Pretty grim, eh?' He'd heard the news.

Miller nodded. 'Did you know her?' She knew he would. Eric had lived in Lentford his whole life. A 'stayer' as Hine, the receptionist, called those who were born in Lentford and never left. They stayed for familiarity, friends, family, jobs or, on the flipside, laziness or the inability to realise there was so much more out there than what their small town offered.

'Yeah,' he said, his chest pushed out.

Here we go, thought Miller.

'She frequented the Royal a bit,' Eric said. 'Nice girl. Good looking.' He scratched under one armpit and complained about how hot it was. Miller averted her eyes from the yellow-stained armpits of his shirt and flicked on her desk fan. Many of the buildings along Lentford's main street were built just after the war and some of their owners hadn't bothered with the cost of upgrading to air conditioning.

'Had a few problems with a boyfriend a few months back. Bet it's murder,' he said.

'You'd bet on anything.' Miller turned on her computer and gulped the last quarter of her lukewarm coffee.

Eric guffawed, his laugh too long and too loud to be genuine. 'I'd say it's the boyfriend.'

Always cocksure, no matter what kind of proof he had. Miller ignored him as she went through her emails.

'Billy Luft. That's who she was with. You know.'

Miller didn't.

'Farmhand. Works on the Smiths' place. Anyway, time will tell. We're gonna have the big boys in town for this.'

She heard the bells and whistles come from Eric's computer. He'd moved from poker to the pokies. He methodically tapped the keys, setting the virtual machine in motion. Every now and then he swore or let out an excited hiss.

After a few minutes, he looked over at her. 'What are you covering this week? More of your *serious* stuff?' He emphasised the word as if it was a joke. His job at the *Leader* consisted of the rural section, often with a bit of help from Miller, and the sports page, which was pretty much high-school rugby, netball and hockey, along with the Lentford Lions rugby team in winter, always in the lowest pool. And anything he could rustle up in summer – usually touch rugby, cricket, cycling or a swimming carnival that school kids were competing in.

Miller ignored Eric's jibe and went on to tell him about her article on bullying. She'd interviewed year nine and ten students from Lentford College and it would be in the paper tomorrow. 'It's important stuff,' Miller said, hoping to convince him, knowing she wouldn't, that she was wasting her breath. She didn't bother telling him what she planned for this week.

'Yeah, yeah.' He smacked the wad of chewing gum in his

mouth. 'The sooner you realise this is a backwater local rag and not some full-on national magazine like *First Look* the better.' He turned away and went back to his pokies.

'Sounds interesting, Miller.' Cody's voice came from the other side of the small open-plan office. She hadn't even seen him walk in.

'Thanks, Cody. What are you working on this week?'

'The opening of the new playground at the primary school, and a piece about the vandalism at the play centre last Friday.' Cody ignored Eric's chuckling. Miller knew this was exactly where Cody wanted to be – for now. He clearly loved his job, but the newly graduated twenty-two-year-old was destined for bigger things.

Miller's phone dinged and she read the text from Ash. 'Not my usual Saturday morning on duty, that's for sure. CIB have taken over now. Helping where I can, but not a lot I can do. Catch up soon.'

'Mail call!' Hine's voice trilled loud and clear as she entered the office with a pile of mail from the post office, her first port of call before the office every weekday morning. She walked around the small office on dangerously high pastel-pink heels and a matching tailored miniskirt. Miller had no idea what Hine was dressing for each day, but she obviously had her sights set further than Lentford. She deposited magazines and newspapers on everyone's desk along with envelopes of varying sizes.

'Thanks, Hine.' Miller put the magazines aside for later and looked through the letters. One caught her eye. Stiff off-white envelope, no stamp, hand-delivered. The *Leader* had a mail slot in the door, a throwback from the old days. They sometimes got hand-delivered mail, often abusive, never threatening (so far), but always, Miller thought, from people who had far too much time on their hands. Eric, the first in, normally dumped anything on Hine's desk instead of taking a few minutes to distribute the mail to its intended recipients.

Miller opened the envelope, trying to remember the contents of the one she'd received on Friday. Something about it beginning, or let the journey begin.

'Miller!' Ngaire's husky voice barked from her office in the back corner.

Miller put the letter down, knowing not to keep Ngaire waiting.

Ngaire had lived in Lentford most of her life. She'd attended university in Auckland and had lived in London for a few years where she met a Kiwi farmer. She was almost a stayer, but not quite. She got engaged and moved to Lentford where, with help from his parents, they bought a dairy farm. Ngaire worked for the *Leader* and became editor a few years ago when the previous one moved up north and opened a cattery. In Ngaire's words, 'Good riddance to her and good luck to those cats.'

Miller tapped on Ngaire's door and entered. The smell stopped her from reaching the chair in front of Ngaire's desk. 'What on earth is that?' she asked.

Ngaire waved a silver pen-like instrument that was wedged between her index and middle finger. 'I vape now.' She rolled her eyes. 'I know, I know, I look like a wanker. My niece brought it for me on the weekend. Supposed to help.'

Ngaire had given up a pack-a-day habit cold turkey almost two weeks ago and they had all paid for it – she was grumpier and sterner than usual. She'd blown up at Eric, which Miller had enjoyed, but she'd also never seen Ngaire like that before. Her office was now heavy with the smell of citrus – but instead of fresh and light, it was cloying, trying to be something it wasn't. Miller wasn't sure what was worse, this or the second-hand cigarette smoke that used to hang around Ngaire wherever she went.

'Lemon cupcake, apparently.' Glasses sitting on the end of her nose, Ngaire eyed the small bottle of vape juice in front of her. 'Sit down.' She inhaled, a sucking noise emitting from the vape.

She was dressed in a beige shift dress today, the large tattoo above her forearm on show. 'His name was Jake,' she'd told Miller when she had stared at it the first time, trying to figure out the name that had obviously been inked over with a blood red rose, its stem full of thorns. 'Misguided youth.' And nothing more was said.

'What's up?' Miller said, clearing her throat of lemon cupcake.

'Good weekend?' Ngaire asked, leaning back in her chair, wincing as it creaked.

'Not bad,' Miller said. The question was only for show. Ngaire wasn't one for small talk, especially the day before the paper was due out. Miller knew to keep it short and sweet. She owed Ngaire a lot.

Six months previously Miller had been jobless. She'd driven down to Lentford on a whim to go through her mum's house that had been sitting empty since her death almost two years earlier. She kept promising herself to clear out the house and sell it, but it was too hard. It was like a final farewell to her mother that she wasn't ready for – felt she'd *never* be ready for. She'd gone through her mother's stuff, looking at throwing things out or donating to the local second-hand shop, but couldn't bring herself to do it. Taking a break, she'd flicked through the local paper and found an advertisement for a senior journalist for the *Lentford Leader*. Back then she wanted to be as far away from Auckland as possible. Self-imposed exile. She walked into the office the next day and sat down with Ngaire. She had told her she wanted a fresh start. She'd said while her job at *First Look* was a fantastic opportunity, she felt she needed to be somewhere else right now. It wasn't a lie, exactly, but she omitted a few things that, as her prospective employer, Ngaire probably had the right to know.

Ngaire had sat back in her leather chair and listened without comment. The next day Miller got the call. She had the job. She was moving to Lentford. Miller didn't speak to her former editor, George, any more, but she'd sent up a silent thank you. George had always said he'd give her a good reference, no matter what had happened, but she wasn't sure he'd keep his promise.

'You hear about Tamara Jenson?' Ngaire said, taking another suck. Her long fingers were still discoloured the dirty yellow of nicotine and Miller wondered when they'd return to normal.

'Yeah. Horrible,' Miller said. 'Do you want me to cover it?' She tried to keep the excitement from her voice.

'Let me think on it.' Lemon cupcake fumes were released into the air as Ngaire exhaled. 'I know her. Tamara. Knew her,' she corrected herself. 'I'm friends with Lorraine, her mum.'

'Shit. I'm sorry,' Miller said.

Ngaire waved away Miller's condolences. 'I might do it myself. I don't want some sensationalist story. I want a story on Tam.' She picked up the vape juice and inspected it, then removed her glasses and placed them on the desk. 'Not that I'm saying you would sensationalise it. I didn't mean that. It's just that things like this, in this town, in any small town, need to be handled sensitively.'

'I understand,' Miller said. 'But let me know if I can help.' She tried not to act too desperate, but her stories for the coming week were made up of an interview with a high-school student who was off to an American college next year, and sitting in on the weekly council meeting. Covering Tamara Jenson's story would give her something to sink her teeth into. She knew she'd do a good job of it.

'The paper's already gone to print, so it's going to look a bit strange that we haven't even covered it.'

'Can't be helped. People will understand,' Miller said, but she could sense Ngaire's frustration. 'The grapevine does a pretty good job at keeping people up to date.'

Ngaire rolled her eyes. 'The bloody Lentford rumour mill.'

'We can do something next week,' Miller said. 'Front page. We'll have all the details by then. There's not much info out at the moment anyway.'

'Yeah. Okay,' Ngaire said. 'Good work on that bullying piece. Perfect. I sent it over to the principal. He's really happy, wants to start up some kind of initiative around it for next year.' She exhaled a cloud of vapour. Miller felt a headache coming on from the sickly scent. 'I've got a story for you. Beatrice Dodds. Know her?'

'No,' Miller said. As much as her work took her around Lentford, there was still a lot of people to meet.

'Pretty well-to-do. They own a couple of dairy farms. One just out of Lentford plus one down south towards Taumarunui. The Dodds family have lived in the area for over a century. Beatrice and her husband are retired now. Left the running of the farms to managers. They bought the old Boyd property up on The Hill a few years back. Dilapidated old villa dating back to the early nineteen-hundreds. She's thrown a shitload of money at it, renovated and rescued the place, had the grounds landscaped. Anyway, she's been on at me for months to cover it in the paper. Every time I see her at the Royal or the bloody supermarket, she's in my ear about it. We'll make it a feature. Everyone's desperate to see the inside of the house. Lots of photos, cover a bit on her life before and now, lots on the house. The readers like to know about that shit – the builder and landscaper, where she bought the fucking curtains and throw rugs from. You know the drill.'

'No problem,' Miller said. All in all, not the worst assignment.

Ngaire started tapping away at the computer, flicking a piece of wiry black hair from her eyes as if it was a fly. This was Miller's dismissal and she left the office.

Back at her desk she picked up the envelope and slid the letter out. She eased herself into her chair and read:

> *Miller, her name is – was – Tamara Jenson. But I guess you know that by now. You journalists are good at uncovering stories like this, aren't you? And this is Lentford – so of course, you'll know by now.*
> *She was killed on Thursday night. In her house. I killed her.*
> *I read the piece you did on the Castle Bay tragedy. I want you to do the same with me and my story. I want everyone to know me. I want everyone in this country to know I was the one who killed these women.*
> *The next one won't be too far off.*

The letter wasn't signed. Miller stared at it, her hands shaking. She felt her jaw clench and her teeth grate together.

Tamara Jenson's murderer is writing to me? Is this some kind of joke?

She looked around the office. Cody and Hine were chatting in the corner by Cody's desk, and Eric was finally getting his arse into gear and was on the phone. She relaxed her jaw but thirty seconds later a headache spread across her forehead, a band tightening, which made her clench her jaw again.

She refolded the letter and slid it back into the envelope. Out the window, Lentford was coming to life on a Monday morning. Was this really the person who had killed Tamara Jenson? Surely it was a hoax. She thought of the other letter sitting at home in the wardrobe. She thought of her article that ran in *First Look* a couple of years ago after what had happened in Castle Bay. She'd won awards for it. It had been deemed 'an eye-opening piece of journalism, raw. Hatcher did not hold back'. And she hadn't held back when she wrote it. It was her first piece as senior writer for the national magazine. George pushed her to make it personal, to tell the readers what she'd been through. And she did – anything for a good story. She'd got emails and letters from people telling her how brave she was. Then there were the others who told her she was using the unfortunate deaths of two young women to bolster her career. She remembered one from a woman, signed only as 'Kay': *It was your choice to make yourself a part of what went on in Castle Bay. But, remember, those women had no choice. You got to walk out of there. Two women are dead and you're busy making a name for yourself.*

She took today's letter out and read it again. She needed Kahu.

Chapter 6

Three months ago, it had been the start of spring, Cassie's father had driven her up the oak-lined drive of the aptly and unoriginally named The Oaks Treatment Centre. A privately-run facility which over the last couple of years had been doing a roaring trade since the government-run institutions were drowning, inundated with people desperate for help but there wasn't enough money, resources or professionals.

Cassie had sulked all the way from Tauranga, but her father and more importantly, her lawyer, said it was this or the possibility of jail time. Her dad, before this run-in with this particular Karl Taylor, had pleaded with her to stop. Said that the police were looking into it, that they'd find the Karl Taylor who murdered her mum, that it wasn't up to her. When pleading didn't work, he threatened. He told her he'd confiscate her credit cards (after the death of her mother, he'd thought by giving her and her sister everything they wanted – apart from their mother back – their lives would magically return to normal). He told her he'd stop paying for her flat and make her move home where he could keep an eye on her. This was when she was splitting her time between working at an Italian restaurant down on the Strand and seeking out Karl Taylors – which felt like a full-time job in itself. But nothing had worked, and then she'd crossed the line with this particular Karl Taylor. She could still remember the way her dad looked at her when her law-yer had told him what she'd done. Disbelief. Shock. The lawyer told her (as if she didn't know) that there was a possibility she could be charged with assault. But her dad's chequebook had done its job. Three months ago Karl Taylor's bank account in-creased substantially and Cassie was on her way to The Oaks Treatment Facility, located on the outskirts of sleepy Lentford. She had undergone counselling, many years too late, and help with what they called her 'alcohol and drug addiction'. A bit of binge drinking and a toke on a joint every now and then or a pill at a nightclub didn't call for this kind of intervention, she thought, but she went with it. She could admit now that she'd been shocked at how far she'd taken this Karl Taylor. How far her obsession had escalated. She wasn't in her right mind. She knew that now. The counsellors had helped, but it didn't take away the fact that her mother had been murdered by Karl Tay-lor and the police were no closer to finding him. She couldn't sit around and do nothing – unlike them.

She wouldn't be sorry to leave this place. It was too quiet, which made her wonder what was going on behind closed doors. The staff all spoke softly, their smiles not quite reaching their eyes, so they seemed as if they were high on something.

Cassie sat in the waiting room, expecting Tiff at any moment. She'd told her father yesterday afternoon that she wouldn't be returning to Tauranga, to his house, as was the original plan three months ago. 'I'm better, Dad. I need to make a life for my-self,' Cassie said, intent on making him believe her.

'You're better?' The relief in her father's voice was hard to miss.

'Of course. The counselling's been great. And I've actually met someone.'

'You have?'

'Her name's Tiff. She's means a lot to me, Dad. She was in here the same time as me. We really hit it off. We've decided to live together.'

'Isn't that a bit soon?' he asked. Cassie could tell he was trying to keep her happy, didn't want to send her off the deep end, but this worried him.

'I don't think so,' she said, challenging. 'She's good for me. We know what each other has been through. We've got the right tools now to cope with …whatever.'

'And Karl Taylor?'

'Finished, Dad. I promise. But you'll keep on at the police. Won't you?'

'Of course, I will. But, honey…' He hesitated. 'You know there's the possibility we're never going to find him.'

'We will. I know we will.'

The sigh was quiet, but it travelled down the phone and into her ear, speaking volumes. She knew she was a disappointment, a burden to him. Her younger sister Fiona had dealt with their mother's death cleanly and precisely, and with as little emotion as possible. Pretty much the way she handled everything in life. She was now up in Auckland studying engineering. Cassie hadn't spoken to her since she'd entered The Oaks and had no need to any time soon.

'Have you got somewhere to stay?'

'We're going to stay in Lentford, Dad.' Cassie held her breath, waiting for it.

'Lentford? Why would you do that? You told me you were moving on.'

'I *am*.'

'I don't call choosing to live in the town where your mother's body was discovered moving on.' His voice was choked.

'Dad. It's got nothing to do with that.' Not true. 'Tiff's sorted it all. She's going to get us a house. Renting is heaps cheaper here.'

Her dad paused, then another sigh came down the phone. 'Let me know if you need anything. *Anything*. Okay?'

'I will, Dad.'

'What are you going to do for a job? I don't mind paying your rent. But that's it. I want you earning money, doing something productive. Not sitting around all day, not going out and...'

He left the sentence hanging. Cassie knew that 'going out and finding Karl Taylor' was what he'd been going to say.

'I'm looking at doing a childcare course, at the polytechnic in Hamilton,' she said. 'It's only half an hour away. Starts in late February. You know I've always wanted to do it. Tiff said there are a few jobs going in Lentford over summer, so I'll pick up a bit of work. Promise.'

'Why don't you just live in Hamilton? Job opportunities would be much better. I don't mind paying extra rent.'

'*Dad.*' Tiff couldn't stand Hamilton, where she'd lived with her parents, and needed to get out.

Her dad dropped it. 'This Tiff. She's all right? A good influence?'

'Of course, Dad. I promise. Look, when we're settled you can come and check her out yourself.'

Cassie looked through the floor-to-ceiling glass that fronted The Oaks where patients were walking over the manicured lawns and gardens, some stiff-legged in a world of their own, others pacing like wild animals, eager to get out. It wasn't as though there was anything really stopping them. But they always found you. Always brought you back. Cassie had seen it.

She noticed the red Honda coming up the driveway too fast. The person parked right outside the doors and got out, the driver door still ajar. Tiff, dressed in cut-off denim shorts, a white singlet, no bra, her red hair a mess of curls and knots, walked up to the automatic doors.

'Dad, I gotta go. Tiff's here.' Even she could hear the excitement in her voice.

'Take care, love.' She chose to ignore the resignation in her father's voice. She knew he wasn't happy – not with any of this – but this was her life. And at this instant *she* was happy. That didn't happen very often.

She ended the call and grabbed her bags. Tiff had only just got in the door when Cassie launched herself at her. Tiff grunted and returned the embrace. Cassie looked around to the reception desk. The woman there glanced at Cassie and Tiff and looked down at her computer with a slight shake of her head.

Cassie stepped back from Tiff, creating space between them. 'It's been so long!'

'I saw you last week,' Tiff said, but Cassie could tell she was just as pleased to see her.

Tiff smoothed back Cassie's loose curls from her face and kissed her softly on the lips, making Cassie tense. 'Ignore her,' Tiff whispered then stepped back. 'Your carriage awaits.'

Cassie squealed with joy. She knew she sounded immature. But she was free, she was with the woman she loved (she was yet to tell Tiff that), she was in a new place ready to start afresh, and not any place, it was the place they'd found her mum's body.

Is he here? Is this where he lived?

'Let's get you the fuck out of this prison,' Tiff said, throwing Cassie's bag in the back seat. The car started on the second attempt. Tiff revved the engine and sped down the tree-lined concrete driveway and out onto the road.

Cassie gazed out her window at the cows taking shade under giant oak trees. She turned and looked out the windscreen, the heat haze making the road look like shimmering water. She tapped her hand on her knee, ignoring the song coming from the radio. The name Karl Taylor was stuck on repeat, like a song she'd heard a million times and couldn't get out of her head.

Chapter 7

Miller walked down the main street to the police station. Her stomach churned and she held a hand to her chest to steady her breathing.

She noticed Jay walking towards her. 'How's it going?' he asked, coming to a standstill in front of her. His cologne made her inhale before she'd even realised she'd done it.

Jay was a few years older than Miller. He was one of the first people she'd met when she'd moved to Lentford. They'd struck up an easy conversation at the Royal one night, speaking of the perils of moving to a small town where you weren't a local until you'd lived there for at least ten years: 'I've been here for two years, so we can be outsiders together.'

Miller had liked him straight away and had decided if he asked her out, she'd say yes. But he never did, and so whatever spark that may have existed had been doused and they had become more than acquaintances, with snatched, easy conversations around Lentford, but not quite friends. Although as much as she tried, she couldn't deny her attraction to him.

'Hi, Jay. I'm good.'

His tanned brow furrowed and he touched a hand to her arm. 'You don't look good. Everything okay?'

'Yeah, fine.' Miller tried to relax her features.

'Bad luck with the timing of this murder, huh?'

'What? What do you mean?' She was finding it hard to concentrate on the conversation, knowing what was in her bag.

'I'm just about to start the print run for tomorrow's edition.' Jay looked confused. 'You won't be able to get an article in.'

'Oh, right, yeah. Bad timing.'

They stood for a few seconds; the silence awkward. Miller was fully aware she should make conversation. On a good day she found herself tongue-tied around Jay, and today wasn't a good day.

Jay smiled again. 'I'd better let you go. Have a good one.' He walked away before Miller had a chance to say anything. *Nice one, Miller*, she admonished herself.

But Jay was soon forgotten as she walked into the lobby of the Lentford police station. Purpose-built eight years ago, it had a reception area that led back to a wide hallway. On the left was an open-plan office for the four constables; further along was Ash's office. On the right there was a tearoom and a large meeting room, and at the back a cell which was used mainly on Friday and Saturday nights to dry out the drunks who frequented the Royal.

'Hey, Bull,' Miller said, walking up to the high desk. Dominic 'Bull' Jenkins had gained his nickname because of his size – six-foot-five and built like the proverbial brick shithouse – but also because back in primary school (Lentford Primary, Bull was a stayer) he was, without fail, the winner of bullrush every time, the schoolyard game which started with one player in the middle who tackled players as they ran past, heading for the safe zone. If they were brought down, they had to join the players in the middle until everyone else was caught. Bull was never caught.

One of Miller's weekly jobs was to put together the 'Crime Watch' column which involved Ash or sometimes Bull telling her what had happened during the week in Lentford. Over the past six months, the most serious transgressions were two young men stealing a quad bike off a farm and taking it for a joy ride, and a man being fined four hundred dollars for illegally dumping rubbish on the side of the road. The weekly report was often made up of drink-driving convictions, shoplifting and altercations that had broken out at parties. This week would be different.

'Hi, Miller. You hear the news?' Bull tried his best to lower his deep voice into a whisper, but it still sounded like a megaphone, reverberating off the walls of the lobby.

'Yeah, that's why I'm here. I guess you have CIB in?'

'Sure have. They've been arriving over the last couple of days. There's a Detective Sergeant Kahu Parata in charge. I think they're finishing up at Tamara's house today.'

'Where are they setting up?'

'Out back, in the meeting room.' He indicated with his thumb in the direction of the double doors.

Miller could see a few unfamiliar faces gathered down the corridor outside the meeting room. 'Is Ash around?' she asked.

'You've just missed her.'

'Can I go back and speak to Kahu? I mean, Detective Sergeant Parata,' Miller corrected herself.

'I'll ring through,' Bull said, picking up the receiver. He spoke to someone, thanked them and hung up. 'He'll be down soon. Take a seat if you want.'

Miller sat down on the cushioned bench seat under a window, expecting Bull to continue with whatever he was doing. But he asked, 'Any ideas, theories, who it could be?'

Miller refrained from rolling her eyes. He was probably gagging for a bit of action, even if it meant gossiping with the local journo. 'No idea, Bull.'

'You know Sergeant Wirihana was first on the scene?'

'So I heard.'

'Sounded pretty grim,' Bull said. 'We'll be pushed out now that these guys have come to take over.' He shook his head in regret, as if he would've had the chance to lead the investigation.

'It's their job though, isn't it,' Miller said.

'Yeah. I don't know, they just come in here, acting like they're here to save the day—'

'Miller,' Kahu said as he came through the doors, cutting Bull off, who jerked his head down and started shuffling papers.

'Hi, Kahu. Can I have a word, please?' She glanced at Bull. 'In private.'

Kahu pushed one side of the double door open and ushered her down the corridor. 'Sorry, probably can't let you in there,' he said, walking past the meeting room.

Miller glanced in. There was a whiteboard set up on the far wall with photos attached and scrawled black writing in columns; officers sat at four desks, eyes focused on laptops.

They took a seat in the tearoom around a stained Formica table. There was a faint smell of burnt toast in the air. The small window on the far wall had been opened as wide as possible but wasn't doing much to dissipate the odour. Dirty mugs and plates littered the bench. On more than one occasion Ash had told Miller her four constables were hopeless at cleaning up after themselves. 'And there's no way I'm going to be mothering them,' she said. Although she also said she'd given in on more than one occasion when the smell and lack of mugs was too much to take.

'I've been meaning to call,' Kahu said. He checked his cell phone's screen and placed it down on the table. 'I guess the town grapevine's doing its job?'

Miller thought he looked tired, more so than usual. 'Yeah.

And it's all over the news.'

'I bet. I'm doing a briefing in ten. What did you want to see me for?'

Miller could tell Kahu was preoccupied so got to the point. 'I need to show you something. It's important. Connected to the murder.' Miller rifled through her satchel.

'Did you know her?' Kahu asked.

'No.' She smiled. 'Small town, but not small enough that I've met everyone in the last six months.'

Kahu shook his head. 'Nice girl by all accounts. Murdered in her home. Always figured this town was pretty peaceful, not much happening.'

'Same could have been said about Castle Bay. Then something like this happens and the illusion is shattered.'

Kahu nodded. 'What's up?'

Miller withdrew the two letters from her bag. She'd already been home to get the other one she'd received on Friday.

'Take a look at these. That first one I opened on Friday night, but it's dated the day before. I didn't really think much of it. Just another crazy. This one here,' she said, handing over the other envelope, 'was hand-delivered to the office by the looks of it. Not sure when. Probably last night when the office was closed or early this morning. I guess it could've been delivered over the weekend.'

Kahu read the letters, a frown developing on his face. 'Shit,' he said, laying the letters on the table.

'You think it's him?'

Kahu was silent for a while, his left foot bouncing up and down. 'Could be. Could be a hoax, someone looking for some attention. I'll take them for fingerprinting. The fact he's contacted you and mentioned, though in a cryptic way, something's going to happen...' He looked at the first letter again. '"It begins tonight" – it fits, the timing. Shit. Look, I'm certainly not jumping to conclusions here. But I'll look into it. And, you need to keep this quiet. Okay?'

Miller nodded. 'He wants me to write a story on him, Kahu. He's killed someone – if this is the guy – and he wants me to make him famous. How fucked up is that?'

'Well, you've done it before,' Kahu said.

Miller felt the sting of Kahu's insult. He knew she was a journalist, knew why she'd come to Castle Bay. Her article on what had happened was still a contentious issue between them, not really discussed, like the death of Trina.

Miller ignored Kahu's comment and said, 'I don't know why he's chosen me.'

'Of course you do,' Kahu said. That tone was still there.

'Yeah, right. But I mean, he's going to be getting a hell of a lot of publicity with or without me.'

Kahu was silent for a moment. 'Miller, you're well known because of Castle Bay. The article you wrote about that has obviously got his attention. We need to be careful. He might have some kind of infatuation with you. Was there anything else?'

'What do you mean? Like did I see who delivered the letters?'

'I wish,' Kahu said. 'I don't know.' He lowered his voice. 'I haven't worked something like this before. The first case I had in this job was gang-related. The murder was …a bit easier to stomach. I could tell myself he'd brought it on himself. His way of life. The drugs. But Tamara is – was – a seemingly innocent thirty-year-old woman. No criminal history, clean as a whistle. From what the family's said she's almost a saint – although I know by now not to believe that. We're still digging.'

'Any suspects?' Miller asked. 'Or is it too early?'

'We've been told about a violent ex. We're looking into him. Looking into work colleagues. She worked in the kitchen at The

Oaks, that treatment facility just out of town. We'll see.' He rose from the seat, letters in hand, and Miller took the hint to go.

'You okay?' Kahu asked. 'About this?'

'Scared the shit out of me, to be honest. But as you said, it's all a bit cryptic. Hopefully I won't receive any more.'

They were both silent, both thinking the same thing – there would be more. And if there were more letters, there would be more bodies.

Chapter 8

Cassie always went from deep sleep to alert and awake. There was no drowsiness, nor any violently assaulting the alarm clock to get ten more minutes, or sculling a cup of coffee to kick start her system. When she opened her eyes, she threw back the covers and got up. Bed wasn't a haven where she felt the need to spend the day. It was the place her body rested for seven hours and that was it. She had been like this for as long as she could remember. Or, more to the point, since her mum had gone missing when she was ten. The time before that, good memories and bad, seemed a dream and she was always unsure if those memories could be trusted. The sleep thing she was sure started when her mum disappeared. She waited for years for her to come back. It was the last thing she thought about at night and the first thing she thought about in the morning, before her eyes even opened. For all those years she would open her eyes every morning, throw herself out of bed and run into her parents' room to see if her mum had returned.

Cassie rolled over and came face to face with Tiff.

'Morning,' Tiff said, placing a hand on Cassie's, auburn hair tumbling down onto bare skin.

'Morning,' Cassie croaked, then smiled. 'God, it's good to be out of that place.'

'Being woken at six-thirty, every morning, even on the weekends.'

'Group counselling before you're even properly awake.'

'Shit coffee.'

'The group counselling did have one benefit,' Tiff said, sliding a hand up Cassie's thigh.

Cassie smiled and kissed her. 'Agreed.'

'Did you sleep well?'

'The best. Great bed,' Cassie said, easing herself up onto an elbow.

'So you don't mind the townhouse then?' Tiff asked. 'Because you didn't seem too happy when we got here yesterday.'

'It's fine,' Cassie said.

'Fine?' Tiff said. 'Come on or I'll start counselling you like Jade back at The Oaks.'

'It's just when we were talking about getting a place, I said I didn't want to live right in town. I like backyards, and trees and …space.'

'This is Lentford. All there is is space,' Tiff said. 'It's not like we're smack bang in a city. And, hey, look at this view.' She jumped out of bed and pulled the curtains.

The main bedroom and lounge room looked over the river, and to what was known as The Hill beyond, a couple of dozen palatial homes atop one of the only hills surrounding the flat Waikato farmland. Mount Te Aroha could be seen in the hazy distance, and right on the front doorstep was Lentford. But there was no outdoor space. Apart from a small balcony off the lounge that overlooked the river, there was nowhere to go outside. Cassie felt trapped and said so.

'I thought you'd like it,' Tiff said, hazel eyes downcast. 'I did it for us. We have everything on our doorstep.'

'I know. It's beautiful, but when we talked I said I'd love a backyard, somewhere we can sit out and have barbecues, invite friends around —'

'What friends?'

Cassie was taken aback by the question. 'Our friends. Your friends...' she trailed off, confused at the look in Tiff's eyes.

'Well, I've lost most of my friends after my wee stint in the crazy house.'

'Tiff.' Cassie put out an arm to placate her.

'You were only there for three months. I was there for six months, forgotten about. No visitors.'

Cassie had heard it all before. Tiff was an addict and her family had given up on her. She'd had a stint in jail a few years back. 'Possession,' she'd told Cassie. 'But it wasn't mine. So-called friend stitched me up.'

'Your family love you,' Cassie said, although she had no idea. In her experience that's just what families did. 'They'll come around.'

Tiff shrugged, sulking now. 'I did it for us. It feels like you're the only person I have right now. I just want to make you happy.'

Cassie didn't want to bang on about the townhouse. It was fine. 'Let's get some breakfast,' she said, wanting to defuse the situation. 'Then we need to sort out rent, bills, stuff like that. And I really need a job. Dad's happy to cover rent, but I need to work.'

'Good old Dad, forking out for you, eh?' Tiff's top lip turned up in a snarl. 'Wish my family gave me a handout.'

'It ... it's not a handout,' Cassie stuttered, surprised at Tiff's harsh tone.

'Well, what else is it?'

Cassie was silent. Her back teeth found the raised mound of skin on the inside of her mouth and she started chewing. Tiff was right. She was twenty-four years old and she still relied on her dad.

'Sorry,' Tiff said. 'It's just the green-eyed monster. It's always been hard for me, you know. My parents never gave me anything.'

Cassie felt like saying life had been hard on her too. She'd lost her mother when she was only a child. Surely you couldn't get much worse than that. But if she said anything it would sound like a competition – my life's worse than yours. 'I get it,' she said. 'Look, how about I pay the rent?'

Tiff looked up, brows raised. 'You don't have to do that.'

'Dad will give me more than enough. And I know for you getting a job will be tricky,' Cassie said as diplomatically as possible.

'Yeah, that pesky drug conviction,' Tiff said, making light of it. 'Cass, I don't want to leech off you. I'll keep looking. I promise. Something will come up. I went to the Royal last week. The guy there's looking for a barmaid. He seemed pretty cool, refused me, but maybe you could go for it? I'll probably apply for the dole for now. At least then I can contribute.'

'Okay,' Cassie said. 'But don't stress. I can cover us till the money comes through from the benefit. And I'm sure you'll get something here, Tiff. Small towns are good like that.'

'Perfect. You're the best.'

Cassie breathed a sigh of relief. Everything was sorted. If Tiff was happy, she was happy. That sparked a thought – of her mum: 'Cassie the peacemaker,' she used to say. She'd say that Cassie would do anything to make people happy. It was supposed to be a compliment, but as Cassie had grown up she felt compelled to make people happy. It felt more like a curse than a blessing, something she couldn't remove herself from, a personality trait that was stuck fast, cemented there; a memory from her dead mother, something she had to live up to – and if she didn't, she'd be doing her mother a kind of disservice.

Chapter 9

On Tuesday afternoon Miller shook off all thoughts of anonymous letters on her way to Beatrice Dodds' house. That morning's *Waikato Times* and *New Zealand Herald* had articles on Tamara Jenson. Interviews with her mother and quotes from Detective Sergeant Parata saying that at this stage they had no further comment, as they were waiting on autopsy results. Stuff like this always brought up memories of Castle Bay. It was hard to avoid, but it would do no good to drag that up again. They all floated around in her head, locked down most of the time, a cast of ghosts, vying for her attention, which she rarely gave them, mostly for self-preservation.

She drove slowly, winding up Tui Road. The houses built on The Hill all took advantage of the view of the river, the sprawling farmland and the town of Lentford. She located Beatrice Dodds' house and turned into the driveway, the wrought-iron gates open wide. To her left and right was the quintessential English garden. Dogwoods lined the boundary against neatly trimmed hedges. There was an organised chaos of chrysanthemums, begonias and dianthus, and many more she didn't know with her limited gardening experience. In front of her was a separate three-car garage. A white van with 'Lou's Landscaping and Lawn Care' stencilled across the side was parked off to the side. Down the left side of the garage she saw Lou on a ride-on mower. She spun around to the front of the house, a circle of grass and an ornate fountain in the middle turning the driveway into a roundabout. She parked her Triumph pointing up the drive and got out. Lou looked up from the ride-on, smiled and waved. She waved back and looked around. On either side and running along the front, facing the road, eight-foot hedges shielded the property from prying eyes. The house, a two-storey villa, was painted stark white with pale-grey trim. The porch ran along the front, with pale-pink miniature roses climbing up the porch railings. Miller walked up the three steps to the front door, dodging the water dripping from hanging baskets where pansies and sweet peas had just been watered, and rang the doorbell. She heard it echoing through the old house, and then heels on floorboards.

The door opened wide, and she was greeted by a woman in her sixties, with short curly hair dyed two shades too dark and an eager smile on a red face.

The smile fell away and she said, 'Hello. How can I help?'

'Hi, Beatrice? My name's Miller Hatcher. I'm from the *Lentford Leader*.' Miller hoped this would be explanation enough, but Beatrice's face told her otherwise.

'Oh. I assumed Ngaire would be doing the article,' Beatrice said, looking past Miller as if expecting Ngaire to appear.

'You have me instead,' Miller joked. Beatrice sniffed and asked Miller to follow.

The inside of the house smelt of baked goods and coffee with an underlying headache-inducing odour of fresh paint. 'Excuse the smell, and mind your clothes,' Beatrice said. 'The hallway's last coat was only finished yesterday. I wasn't happy with the original colour, too dark for the space.'

Miller followed her down the long hallway laid with some kind of varnished wood.

'The floorboards are rimu.' She turned back to Miller as if reading her mind. 'All original. I wanted to save as many of the original features of the house as I could.'

They entered the kitchen and dining room at the end of the house. Miller thought 'country kitchen' would be the best way to describe it. White wooden cabinetry throughout, an island in the centre with a wooden butcher's block on top. Pale-blue curtains framed the small windows that looked out towards the garage.

'The dining table's oak. The wood was rescued from an oak we had felled when we got here. Please take a seat.' Beatrice moved into the kitchen. 'Ngaire's been on at me for months about getting the house in the paper, so I finally caved. It really isn't my thing,' she said, when everything about her, from her blow-waved hair to the manicured nails said this most definitely *was* her thing.

Miller sat down and took in the view. French doors opened out onto a large patio with grey slate tiles that gave way to the greenest, lushest lawn Miller had ever seen. Silver birches stood sentry, lining the left and right of the back yard. The garden tapered off into a steep gully leaving the view of the river and Lentford below them.

'This is beautiful,' Miller said, getting out her notebook.

'Thank you. It was a lot of hard work. It took us almost three years to complete. Coffee?' Beatrice asked, holding up a white coffee pot.

Miller nodded, noticing that Beatrice's ring finger on her left hand had at least four rings forced past the knuckle. Biting into her skin, they looked as though they hadn't been removed in years.

Miller sipped on her coffee and let Beatrice speak. It was always interesting interviewing people. She never knew who she was going to get, depending on the person and the story – shy, angry, opinionated, sad, chatty. Beatrice was definitely the latter. She had obviously got over the fact that Miller wasn't Ngaire and pointed out cornices, flooring, artwork and drapes, naming where she'd got them from, often with a little anecdote to go with it. 'That piece of artwork there. I saw it in a restaurant up in Auckland. I noted the artist's name down and when I got home, I looked her up on the internet and you wouldn't believe it, she lives just out of Lentford. A bit of a recluse. So I commissioned her to do a few pieces. She wasn't too keen to start with, but I managed to persuade her,' Beatrice said, winking at Miller.

Money talks, thought Miller.

She turned towards the French doors at the sound of footsteps. An older man, bald apart from a fringe of grey around his ears, tramped in the door. He stopped short when he saw Miller.

'William!' Beatrice shrieked.

'Jesus, woman, calm down. What's wrong?' he said as he walked into the kitchen.

Miller screwed up her nose before she could stop herself. Beatrice looked at her, a mixture of shock and embarrassment on her face, and then looked at her husband.

'You've brought that smell in with you!' She turned back to Miller. 'He's been out to one of our farms.' Her heavily powdered face glowed pink and her décolletage turned bright red. 'Get those filthy gumboots off my polished floors. What is wrong with you?'

Standing in the pristine kitchen in his shit-caked Red Band gumboots, William looked as out of place as Beatrice would in a cowshed. He rolled his eyes and backed out the door where he removed the offending gumboots.

'You can see we have company.' Beatrice's voice had changed to sickly-sweet. 'This is Miller, from the newspaper. Now please, go and make yourself more presentable.' Beatrice's hand fluttered around her chest.

'You're the one doing the interview. I don't need to put on glad rags.' He looked down at his Swanndri fleece, T-shirt and shorts. 'I'll just make myself a cuppa and get out of your hair.' He turned to Miller. 'Nice to meet you.' He turned to the jug, switched it on and went about making his tea.

Beatrice caught Miller's eye. 'I'm so sorry. This won't be in the paper, will it? I'm very well known in this district and I'd hate for you to report on William's behaviour.'

Miller choked back a laugh. 'Beatrice, I'm not here to do an exposé on you,' she said, wondering what Beatrice was expecting from the article. After all, it was only the *Lentford Leader*, not the social or gossip pages of *OK* or *Hello* magazine. 'I'm here to write about your beautiful home. Now, can you tell me a bit about how you came to move here?' Miller asked, wanting to get the interview back on track. 'I understand you were on a farm not far from Lentford?'

Beatrice lowered her voice. 'William's arthritis. It got so he couldn't manage – that's not for the paper, by the way.' She tapped the table where Miller's iPhone was recording. Miller looked over at William, who looked fit and well, with tanned muscled legs and broad shoulders, but his hands grasping the newspaper, while large and strong, were misshapen. 'It was a tough decision, one that took a lot of persuading him. Becoming a townie was never a part of William's plan.'

Beatrice sipped her coffee. 'We decided it was time to retire. We've been working the farms for almost forty years. One just out of Lentford, where we've come from, and another in Taumarunui. We have two very capable managers. When I saw this beautiful old home come up for sale, I felt it was a sign. I'd always wanted to do a refurbishment, and this was perfect – plus it's close to town. I'd had enough of living out in the country. I love that I can walk down the hill and into town to the shops. The beautiful location is a bonus.'

William, sitting in a leather armchair in a corner of the room let out a cough, his mug noisily clattering onto the glass coffee table.

'I thought you said you were going to leave us in peace?' Beatrice snapped.

William swiped at his mouth and at the spilt tea on his lap. 'Well, you're about to give the grand tour so I thought I'd stay here out of your way.' He peeled off his woollen socks and put them up onto the coffee table.

Beatrice let out a low strangled sound. William sighed and put the socks on the floor.

'Let's go out into the garden,' Beatrice suggested.

Miller followed her, smiling at William as she left. He winked at her, obviously a little more relaxed than his wife.

They stood on the patio and looked out at the grounds. 'I'm actually not much of a gardener. Love the trees.' She waved her bejewelled hand at the silver birches. 'But I never took to gardening. I have someone who comes each week to take care of the lawns and the gardens. Plus, William and my son, Logan, love the vegetable patch.'

Miller looked to the left. Along the boundary, under the perfectly pruned hedge, were two long rectangular raised vegetable beds, neat lines of leafy greens sprouting in the sunshine.

'Come on upstairs and I'll show you the bedrooms.'

There were a total of five bedrooms, each with their own ensuite because 'who would want to share a bathroom these days?'

At the top of the stairs on the way down they passed a closed door from where Miller could hear 'Save a Prayer' by Duran Duran playing. The song finished and immediately started up again.

'I used to love that song,' Miller smiled.

'It was my daughter's favourite,' Beatrice said. 'Come on in.'

Miller followed Beatrice into the room. It was different from the others she'd just seen. No pastel wallpapers, no king-sized beds with duvets that complemented the wallpaper, no filmy net curtains at the windows. This bedroom had posters of Madonna and Prince hanging above the single bed covered by a purple candlewick bedspread, soft toys leaning up against the ruffled cushions. The wallpaper was off-white with vertical lines of soft maroon roses. The whole room was totally different from the muted country-chic palette of the rest of the house. Miller didn't know what to say.

'William said I was being silly recreating her room. It's exactly as it was back at our old farmhouse. It allows me to remember her as she was before...'

'Before what?' Miller asked softly.

'Amelia, my daughter, was murdered when she was fifteen. She'd be forty-three now. You didn't know? I thought you journalists always researched people you were interviewing.'

Miller wasn't sure why Beatrice Dodds thought this article was so much more than it was. 'I'm so sorry,' Miller said. She was completely taken aback.

'Thank you. She was such a special girl. Her death hit us all very hard. William and I haven't been the same since, and neither has Logan, our son.'

Miller realised that was the other room they hadn't been into.

Beatrice sat on the bed as the song faded out, a pink panther soft toy in her hands, stroking the matted fur. Miller wondered how often she came up here, to this shrine.

The song started playing again and it snapped Beatrice out of her trance. 'Sorry.' She placed the soft toy back in its pile, taking longer than necessary positioning it, and left the room. Miller followed, closing the door behind her.

'You won't put that in the article, will you?' she asked, her blue-grey eyes wide in the dim hallway as if suddenly realising she'd done something she shouldn't have. 'Not that it matters. Everyone knows about it. It's just that it wouldn't be …right.'

'No, of course not.' Miller was shocked that Beatrice had thought she would.

'William is very private. Of course, it was covered back then by the media. Such a shock to the small community. But we don't need it dragged up again, do we?' she said to Miller. 'That's Logan's room there.' She pointed to the room opposite Amelia's. The sound of jazz – trumpet and bass guitar – was doing its best to muffle Duran Duran.

Miller wondered how many times the poor kid had heard that song. She then realised the 'poor kid' would be a man now – in his forties, she assumed. It was then she realised how odd it was that he was still living at home. Helping out his parents?

Beatrice led the way downstairs. 'This is William's room. They call it a man cave these days, don't they?' She stood aside so Miller could see inside.

The room was small, three metres by three metres with a high window on the far wall. There was a La-Z-Boy chair in one far corner, one arm with stuffing erupting; a tarnished brass table sat to one side, a full ashtray on top. A buffet was in the other corner, gin and whisky bottles atop with a tray holding a couple of glasses. The old bookshelf, cheap MDF, was filled with books on farming and war.

Miller got the feeling this house was all Beatrice. She'd

dragged Amelia's ghost along with her and by the looks of it, William was forced to come and given one room in which he would feel comfortable.

Back in the kitchen Miller made sure she'd got everything she needed while Beatrice cleared away the coffee mugs and William sat in the corner hiding behind the *Waikato Times*.

'Mum, they'll be here soon.' The man stopped at the entrance to the kitchen when he saw Miller. 'I thought she'd be gone by now,' he said accusingly. 'You said she'd be gone by now.' His deep voice had a whiney note to it. More like a toddler complaining to his mother than a grown man.

'I'm just leaving,' Miller said, closing up her note pad and putting it in her satchel.

'Miller, this is my son, Logan. I apologise for his rudeness,' Beatrice said, wiping her hands on a tea towel. 'Logan, say hello to our guest, Miller.'

'Nice to meet you,' Logan said. He brought his thumb to his mouth and started chewing on the nail.

He was the spitting image of his father, but where William was still trim and muscular, Logan had a bloated face and a thick layer of fat around his middle. His dark-brown hair had already begun to recede. 'You too, Logan.' Miller put her hand out, but it was left unshaken. Miller watched as Logan withdrew his thumb from his mouth and noticed a small smear of blood on his bottom lip. Beatrice handed him a tissue and he pressed a tissue to his bleeding thumb.

'Sorry, Logan doesn't shake hands with other people. Do you, love? The …all of this.' She waved a hand in Logan's general direction. Miller noticed his jaw moving almost imperceptibly and realised he was chewing the bit of skin he'd just removed from his thumb. 'It happened when Amelia died. No, that's not the right word, is it?' she let out a laugh and then pressed her hands against her mouth. 'When Amelia was *murdered.* Logan took it very, very hard.'

'Jesus, Bea, she's come to do an article on the bloody paint colours and kitchen appliances. She doesn't need our life story,' William said folding the paper vigorously and slapping it onto the coffee table. He crossed over to the kitchen to make himself another cup of tea.

Miller nodded, not sure what to say, suddenly feeling like an intruder. Logan's right thumb and forefinger were rubbing together in a circular motion; his left hand, thumb wrapped in a tissue, was still.

'Mum, my meeting.'

'Yes, Logan. I'll get a pot of coffee brewing and all the food's ready. It just needs to be put out.' Beatrice brushed down his shirt, wiping briskly at both shoulders to remove dandruff and hair, and reached around to tuck the label of his shirt back into his collar.

Logan squirmed and frowned. '*Mum.*'

'Logan holds a meeting once a month,' Beatrice explained to Miller.

'It's the True Crime Enthusiasts Club,' he said proudly, his eyes just above Miller's right shoulder.

'Oh?' Miller said.

'Logan has a special interest in murder cases and what makes the person do what they do,' Beatrice explained.

William stalked out of the kitchen and onto the patio, muttering, 'The damn Murder Club.' He sank into one of the chairs outside, shaking his head.

'*Dad,*' Logan whinged again. 'Mum, tell him.'

Beatrice whispered to Miller, 'William doesn't really approve. He's nicknamed Logan's group the Murder Club, which,' her voice rose so William could hear, 'is not helpful at all.'

'Did you know Jeffery Dahmer murdered seventeen men?' Logan asked Miller.

'I— No, I didn't.'

'He had a relatively happy childhood but blamed the break-up of his parents for putting the evil thoughts he'd been having for years into action.'

Miller didn't know what to say. Logan was still looking just past her, avoiding her eyes. He was now nibbling on a fingernail that had been bitten down so short it was almost non-existent.

'We have a huge amount of murders in New Zealand. Really interesting ones, even around the Waikato and in Lentford. I'm starting a new venture. It's called True Crime Tours. I'll take people around the district and show them where people have been murdered and tell them what happened, about the victims, the murderer, the trial.'

'How... interesting.' Miller was in turn repelled by the idea and fascinated. What would the people of Lentford think of this? 'Logan, can I give you my card? I'd be interested in talking to you a bit more about this.'

Logan nodded and took the card. 'Where did you get that scar?'

'Logan!' Beatrice said and turned to Miller. 'I'm sorry—'

'No problem,' Miller said quickly, turning away from Logan. 'Could I get a quick photo of you three? Out the back maybe?'

'Yes, of course,' Beatrice said.

Miller dragged the digital camera from her bag. They all did their own photography at the *Leader*. They didn't have a budget for a photographer. Miller was getting better at it, slowly.

As Beatrice arranged the men, Miller snapped the kitchen and the patio. She'd already taken one of the over-styled master bedroom. She took a couple of shots of the three Doddses together. Beatrice was perfectly poised in the middle; William was squinting so much in the first shot it looked as though his eyes were closed, and in the second his eyes *were* closed. In all the shots Logan looked as if he was staring at something behind Miller. Beatrice had to repeatedly tell him to stop chewing his nails. If the worst came to the worst, she could just crop the men out.

The doorbell sounded and echoed out through the patio doors. Logan lumbered onto the patio and into the house at a slow jog.

'Would you do an article on him?' Beatrice asked, apologising again about Logan's intrusive question about her scar and all the while staring at it.

'Maybe. It's very… interesting,' Miller said, fighting the urge to raise a hand to her face, still unable to find the right word.

'He's very knowledgeable about it all,' Beatrice said. 'It's not gory and disgusting. A lot of people are really interested in his meetings, plus he has an online forum. It's not all about the violence, it's also about why those kinds of people do what they do.'

Miller nodded, undecided.

'Here, let me show you out.'

Already there was faint murmuring coming from the front lounge room.

'Would you mind if I stayed and listened in for a few minutes?' Miller asked.

'No problem. He might get a bit shy knowing you're listening, so best just stay by the door,' Beatrice said. The doorbell rang again and she left to answer it.

A few groups of twos and threes milled around the lounge, helping themselves to coffee and cake. A young woman turned from a conversation with two people, gave Miller a wide smile, then turned back to them. *Li.* What on earth was she doing here?

Logan was in the corner of the room reading a piece of paper. She watched him inspect his thumb, ball up the tissue and put it in his pocket. A couple in their mid-thirties arrived, greeted Logan and joined another group.

At the sound of the grandfather clock in the hallway striking two, Miller listened as Logan brought the meeting to order. Most of the talk was on the development of the True Crime Tours: which murders Logan was going to include and why. Miller looked closer at the people present. Twelve in total. There was a wide array of society. Young and old, men and women, different cultures. Apparently, the Murder Club – the True Crime Enthusiasts Club, she corrected herself – had something for everyone.

She spotted Jay. She hadn't seen him crouched down in the back corner of the room taking pamphlets out of a brown cardboard box. He stood and walked over to a side table by Logan and set them down. Seeing Miller, he smiled and walked over. 'Jesus Christ,' he whispered, shaking his head as they both stood at the door looking in. 'That bunch in there are pretty weird. Holding a meeting on murderers.'

Miller smiled. She tended to agree. 'So what are you doing here, then?' Miller asked, teasing.

He handed her one of the pamphlets. 'Delivering these. Just printed them up for Logan.'

Miller took the pamphlet, headed *The True Crime Enthusiasts Club*. She scanned the inside. Meeting time and location, what they would discuss, informative websites and forums. And on the back an advertisement for the True Crime Tours.

'See that?' Jay said. 'True crime murder tours. I mean, come on. Makes you wonder if poor Tamara will make the cut.'

Miller was silent.

'Sorry,' Jay said, sheepish, shaking his head. 'That was in bad taste.'

'I guess it depends how he's going to handle it,' Miller said, playing devil's advocate.

Jay shrugged. 'Each to their own, I guess. In a town this small... I can't see it happening without protest. I'd better get going.' He smiled at Miller and they both walked out the front door. She watched him leave in his black SUV with 'Lentford Print' on the door. *Another chance wasted.*

Walking to her car she cursed as she realised she hadn't left the windows down.

'Miller!' She turned to see Logan coming after her. 'You're Miller Hatcher! The journalist who wrote that story about Castle Bay. You're *that* Miller Hatcher.' He stood on the paved drive-way bouncing on his heels like an excited child. 'It only came to me as I was in there speaking. Kind of just clicked into place.'

Miller stood still, unable to comprehend his excitement. When most people spoke to her about Castle Bay they tiptoed around her, afraid she'd fall to pieces if they brought it up. This was refreshing. 'Yes, that's me.'

'So cool,' he said.

'Well... I'd probably have to disagree with you there.'

'Oh, yeah, sorry. Hey, where *did* you get that scar? Castle Bay?'

'No, something else entirely.' Miller's hand automatically brushed the side of her face and her jaw clenched.

'Oh, okay. You'd be quite pretty without it, but it still gives your face a bit of character. I'd better get back.'

Miller stood by her car for a full minute trying to recover from the onslaught that was Logan.

Chapter 10

Cassie smiled at the couple and passed them their order, one Heineken and one house white. They called it house white, but really it was the *only* white wine on the limited drinks menu at the Royal; along with the house red and 'champagne', which was using the term very loosely considering that Tane, the owner, bought it by the caseload for less than fifty bucks. It was the couple's third drink and it was only two o'clock on Thursday afternoon, but hell, she wasn't one to judge.

Cassie wiped down the bar, which she could never get clean. No matter what she did, it always remained sticky and stained.

'Don't worry about it, love,' Tane said coming out of the back room and filling the fridge with Heineken. 'Waste of time. You're polishing a turd.' He stood up, groaning as he arched his back, and pulled his jeans up onto bony hips. 'Getting too old for this shit. Where the fuck's Johnno?' He rubbed a hand over his mouth, smoothing down his thick greying moustache.

'Not sure, sorry,' Cassie said. 'Haven't seen him.' She'd been introduced to Johnno on her first day. He'd been shipped down from Auckland six months ago by Tane's great-niece and her husband, to be 'sorted out'. He was nineteen, a good-looking guy, albeit sullen, obviously put out that he was spending the foreseeable future in Lentford. From what Cassie had seen he was keen to man the bar when there were women to flirt with, but other than that she hadn't seen him lift a finger to help his great-uncle.

'Lazy little prick. Both his parents are lawyers, live in la-de-da Remuera – they shit money, and still the kid has issues,' Tane said, bending over again to finish his job.

Tane was a good boss, helped out at the busy periods and left her to it when it was quiet. 'As long as you don't have a police record,' he'd said, 'all good with me. Got stung a few years back by a prick. Cleaned me out of my weekend takings, never saw him again. I was told – too late, of course – he'd been in the clink for armed robbery. Anyway, ain't no jailbirds working here. Too risky.' But the best part was he didn't have too many questions about where she'd come from.

'I'm out back if you need me,' he said. He gathered the empty beer boxes and disappeared out the back door to the kitchen and storage room, the receding sound of his jandals smacking the linoleum as he reached his office.

Cassie grabbed her cloth and attacked the spirits and liqueurs that lined the back wall of the bar underneath an old advertising banner for Lion Red. Most of them, the more exotic ones like Galliano, Chambord and Chartreuse, hadn't been uncapped in years, the dusty bottles hiding the syrupy contents. Most of the patrons drank only beer, wine, gin, vodka or whisky, as far as she could tell.

She'd been working at the Royal for two days now. She'd gone in and spoken to Tane the day after she got out of The Oaks and he gave her the job on the spot. It was mostly bar work and waitressing and would do for the summer before she started at Wintec.

The couple at the bar sipping their drinks were getting progressively louder. Cassie moved away from them and started going through the box of Christmas decorations Tane had told

Johnno to put up yesterday. 'Tart the place up a bit,' he said. Johnno had rolled his big brown eyes at Cassie, flipped the bird to his uncle's retreating back, grabbed a beer out of the fridge and sauntered out the front door. Cassie hadn't seen him since.

'Did you hear about Tamara?' the woman said, taking a large sip from her drink.

'Yeah. Do you know her? Kev does.'

'Really? Scary. Sounds like the ex. Heard on the radio he's been brought in for questioning. Sad, really. The family's distraught.'

'As you would be,' the guy said, taking a swig of his Heineken.

'Such a tragedy. Oh, did you hear what happened with Mel at work the other day...' And so, they chatted on.

Cassie tuned out. She had never developed into one of those people who discussed murder cases. Murders weren't that common in New Zealand so when one did happen it took over the entire media. When a discussion about a murder began, she felt as though she was being backed into a corner with no escape.

Most people she knew took an interest in who did it, why they did it and where it happened. Theories were bandied about as if they were all expert witnesses. Every now and then someone knew the person who had been murdered, or a friend of a friend or their parents knew the parents of the victim. She had become one of those people eighteen months ago. At first, she was the poor young girl whose mother had disappeared. Then she was forgotten. Then her mother's body – no, correction, bones – were found and she became one of those people others were eager to know. People treated her differently, her friends looked at her differently, and soon *she* became the name on her friends' lips when they told others with great excitement their 'best friend Cassie Hughes is Margaret Hughes' daughter, you know, the woman whose remains were found in that small town at the old dairy factory'.

She thought about her counsellor at The Oaks. She'd opened up to her, couldn't help it. At the start she was the proverbial closed book, but there was something about her counsellor that prised her open over those three months, and Cassie ended up telling her things she never thought she'd tell anyone, things she'd never really thought about. She knew she hated being alone; she didn't need a counsellor to tell her that. She knew she often suffocated the friends and girlfriends she'd had as a teen and later when she moved out of home. She couldn't really remember what she was like before her mum disappeared. Her whole personality had been developed by a mother who had vanished one day – and every now and then she wondered who she might have been if it hadn't happened. It was worse that her mother's body wasn't found straight away. If she'd been murdered and her body found days or weeks later, it would've been horrible but there would've been no waiting, the years of her life where she was constantly on the look-out for her, wondering where she could be. At the start she would not even entertain the idea that she could be dead.

Tiff understood all this. Tiff didn't mind her clinginess. She had a feeling this was it, that Tiff was the one. The idea made her happy for the first time in years. Her last full happy memory, one that wasn't tainted with her mum's disappearance, was her tenth birthday. A month before her mum left one weekend to pick up fruit and vegetables from the farm down the road and never returned. Her dad had set a tent up in the back yard and they'd roasted marshmallows over a small fire. Mum had growled at Dad when he told them a ghost story scaring them witless. When the moon rose full into the sky they spotted satellites and planets and wished on shooting stars. They fell asleep, all four of them, closely ensconced, as it should've been.

'Hello?'

Cassie looked up and saw Tiff standing in front of her.

'You skiving off?' she asked. 'What were you thinking about?'

Cassie looked around and saw the pub was empty, Johnny Cash on the jukebox in the corner the only sound. 'Nothing,' she said. 'What are you up to?'

'Not much. Missed you. Thought I'd come for a visit.' Tiff smiled sweetly and leaned over the bar to kiss her. Cassie's stomach flipped, and she automatically looked around, checking to see who noticed.

'There's no one here, silly,' Tiff teased, knowing how she felt about public displays of affection. But for Cassie the inevitable looks of disgust or anger and snide comments from others made her feel uncomfortable kissing her girlfriend or even holding her hand. Tiff was the exact opposite, her attitude being: 'Fuck 'em.'

'Hey, why don't you go to the supermarket and do the groceries and I'll meet you back at the house after I'm done here.'

Tiff shrugged and sat at the bar stool. 'Think I'll hang around.'

'But I don't finish till six. That's another four hours. What are you going to do?'

'Just hang. Chat with you. Not exactly busy, is it.' She looked around the pub.

'Up to you. I'd better serve this guy.' Cassie walked to the end of the bar and served the man who had just walked in.

He sat at the bar sipping at his beer and started talking to her. She was being chatted up, which always amused her. She'd known very early on she was gay and all through her teens she'd felt as if she had it stamped on her forehead for all to see, but obviously that wasn't the case.

She was very polite, answered all his questions, including 'Do you have a boyfriend?', and laughed at his work stories.

'I'm a developer, commercial and residential. There's a vacant lot for sale just down the road that I'm looking at.'

Cassie knew the place. It was right next to her and Tiff's townhouse. He was obviously expecting a reaction, so Cassie made all the right noises.

'Thought the least I could do was check out the local,' he said. The look on this face told Cassie he wasn't impressed. He finished his beer and asked her what time she finished and if she was busy.

'I'm off at six, and sorry, but I'm not interested.'

He ran a hand through his thick black hair and said, 'You win some, you lose some.' She wondered how many townhouses he'd had to build to pay for his perfect smile.

When he walked out of the pub Tiff came over. 'What the hell was that?'

'I know, hard-case, eh?' Cassie grinned and then stopped. Tiff's face was red. 'What's wrong?'

'*You*. Bloody flirting with him. Jeez, you were salivating over him.'

'Tiff!'

'I was sitting right over there. I heard everything you said.'

'Well, if you heard everything I said you'll know I was just being polite.'

'Whatever. I'm out of here.' Tiff turned on her heel and marched out.

'Tiff, don't go. I'm sorry,' Cassie called. 'He was an idiot. We could both see that.' She felt her stomach drop as if she was on a rollercoaster. She felt sweat prickle her armpits and her teeth started gnawing at the inside of her mouth. She had four hours of her shift to go, four hours till she saw Tiff. She hoped she'd have calmed down by then. She was stupid. She should've just given the guy his beer and gone back to talk to Tiff. That's what she'd tell her tonight. Tane didn't expect her to entertain the punters. She was here to serve booze and that was it. She would go grocery shopping on the way home and pick up all Tiff's favourite foods and cook her a beautiful meal and apologise. Then everything would be okay again. Cassie tasted blood from gnawing the inside of her mouth and poured herself a beer from the tap. She drank deep and slow, rinsing the copper taste from her mouth.

Chapter 11

Miller pulled up in the pot-holed, gravel car park of the Royal at 7 p.m. on Thursday night. She walked towards the front door which from the moment it opened at 11 a.m. to closing at 10 p.m. was propped open with a red brick. If this wasn't done, the Royal would look as though it was closed pending a builder's report of possible destruction. The roof, on the far-left corner, was devoid of a sheet of corrugated iron, where a storm the past winter had ripped it off and deposited it further down the main street opposite the Kowhai. The windows were set high around three sides of the rectangular building, leaving the place in permanent dimness. It swallowed up time: it could be midday or 9 p.m. The only way to tell was to look up and out for a strip of blue or black sky. Glass-paned double doors out the back opened up to a high-fenced concrete courtyard. Those doors were open all year round so the inside of the Royal always smelt of cigarette smoke, and occasionally marijuana late on a Friday or Saturday night, as it wafted in from the smokers' corner.

But this was what was on offer in Lentford. It was either the Royal or the stuffy, overpriced bar and restaurant at the Riverview Hotel. The Royal was where the locals congregated and so that's where Miller often found herself. The irony was not lost on her that she, an alcoholic, had made the local pub her hangout.

On completing her first week of work, Hine and Cody took her out for drinks along with Ngaire. Eric abandoned them after his first drink in favour of the darts board. That night every part of her had wanted to head home. She didn't feel the need to socialise, or for her colleagues to know her better. She didn't want them to know what had brought her to Lentford. The mistakes she'd made.

Miller walked through the door and smiled as Ash walked towards her. 'Hey, stranger,' she said.

'Hey. Sorry, it's been a hectic few days. I keep meaning to call. Are you meeting someone here?'

'Don't worry about it,' Miller said. 'I'm actually meeting Kahu.'

'Ah yes, the famous Detective Sergeant Kahu Parata,' Ash said, looking to her right. Miller followed where she was staring and saw Kahu looking back at them.

Miller raised her hand, her index finger pointed, telling him she wouldn't be long.

'I finally got a chance to meet him,' Ash said. 'Although the circumstances could've been a bit better.' She screwed up her freckled nose.

'Is it going okay?' Miller asked.

She shrugged. 'I've got CIB in my station, closed doors and lots of whispering in the tearoom. I'm not privy to any information, and don't expect to be. I'm just helping out when I can. Local knowledge. Providing scene guards for the victim's house while they do what they need to do. Detective Parata seems pretty decent, respectful.'

'He is,' Miller said, relieved her two friends were getting along.

'Look, I better get home to Zach,' Ash said. 'How about

dinner Sunday night at mine?'

'Sounds good.'

Ash left and Miller waved in Kahu's direction, indicating if he wanted another drink. He shook his head, holding up a half-full handle of beer.

'Hi, Johnno,' Miller said, surprised to see Tane's nephew behind the bar.

'Hey...' said Johnno.

'Miller,' she reminded him.

'Yeah, right. What can I get ya?' He flicked his long black fringe off his face with a jerk of his head.

Miller ignored the brown eyes that drifted from the scar on her face down to her breasts. 'A Coke and two roast meals, please.'

'You got it.' Johnno moved to get Miller's drink. Every move was done with the least amount of effort possible. He was constantly in slow motion.

Tane came out of the back room and raised his eyebrows in Miller's direction, then said, 'Jesus Johnno, get your arse into gear, would ya?'

Tane moved to serve a man sitting at the bar in shorts, a singlet and woollen socks, his gumboots having been left at the door, who had just drained the last half of his beer. 'Another one, mate?'

'Yeah, go on. The missus isn't expecting me back for another half hour. Ya hear about Tamara Jenson?'

'Yup. Nasty business.' Tane reached for a clean glass.

'It'll be someone she knows.'

'Ya reckon?' Tane said, eyes on the beer he was pouring.

'Yeah, always is. Abusive boyfriend, jealous ex. Always someone they know. That's who they're going to be looking at first.'

'Well,' Tane said, depositing the froth-tipped beer onto a cardboard coaster, 'if it is someone she knew, good luck to them trying to hide out in Lentford. Damn near impossible. If I can't get my sixty-year-old rocks off with Edith from the supermarket without the whole bloody town knowing and commenting, then there's no way in hell some other fella's gonna get away with murder.' Tane banged the bar, laughing, and the farmer joined him.

Johnno returned with Miller's drink and her change.

'Thanks.'

'No problem. Hope to see you again soon.' He smiled at her and walked out the back, his job obviously done for the night.

Miller walked over to Kahu's table. 'I've ordered us dinner,' she said, raising her drink. 'Cheers.'

Kahu's glass touched Miller's. 'It's been a week.' He took a long drink from the handle.

The Royal wasn't particularly busy, just a few regulars propping up the bar, three couples eating dinner in the far corner and a group of rowdy young ones at the leaners at the opposite end playing darts and pool. Miller waved at Lou and Jay as they entered. Miller could feel her cheeks redden as Jay's eyes met hers and he returned the wave with a smile. *Get a grip.*

'I met Sergeant Wirihana on Saturday. She was first on the scene. Did what she was supposed to do. Freeze, control, preserve. I don't mean to sound condescending but that's not always the way. I've had a couple of crime scenes that have been compromised by well-meaning officers. You've talked about her once or twice before.'

'She's a good person,' Miller said. 'Good at her job.'

'Yeah, appears to be.' Kahu looked at the door Ash had disappeared through five minutes ago.

'She's impressed with you. The way you're handling this.'

'I'm glad she thinks so. But we've got nothing.' Kahu smiled at Tane who placed their food down in front of them. Roast pork, crackling, roast potatoes, pumpkin, kumara and peas.

Miller started eating as Kahu continued. 'The ex, Billy Luft, has an alibi. A good one. Was in Hamilton the night she was killed, got drunk and slept on a friend's couch. Left their place at six the next morning, was back on the Smiths' farm before seven. It wasn't him. I thought maybe she didn't know the guy. But how did he get in? There was no sign of a break-in. Nothing. The front door was closed but not locked when the friend went in. So did she invite him in? If she did, surely she must've known him, or was he posing as some kind of handyman or door-knocker selling something? The neighbours didn't hear a thing. Although one's an elderly couple and the other is a single mum with a teen who's blasting Metallica every hour of the day. They weren't much help. The first thing anyone knew of it was when Tamara's friend turned up on Saturday morning and discovered the body.'

In the months Kahu had worked for CIB he often used Miller as a sounding board. Miller sat back and let him speak. She wasn't expected to answer, just listen. She knew it was easier for him to talk through his theories, whatever was bugging him, instead of letting it race around inside his head in confusing circles.

'How did he do it?' Miller asked, half-curious, but also feeling she might regret the question.

'Strangled her with a scarf. Ligature strangulation is the official term. Although it appears she was unconscious when it happened. The autopsy showed she had abrasions on the back of her head and bruising under her scalp, so she was probably knocked out before being strangled. The scarf was left in place, plus there was a pretty good ligature and petechial haemorrhaging.' Miller had stopped chewing. 'Sorry, too much information?'

'No, that's okay. The poor woman.' Miller pushed her half-eaten dinner away.

Kahu took a sip of his beer and placed the handle on the wooden table. Miller's eyes followed it, watched it settle and then vibrate, causing ripples on its frothy surface to pool out in the glass.

'Sorry, I shouldn't be drinking—'

Miller looked up, startled, not realising she'd been staring. 'No. Don't say it. You deserve a bloody beer or three after the week you've had. I'm fine,' she said, angry at herself.

Kahu loaded his fork with food. In the background Creedence Clearwater Revival's 'Bad Moon Rising' was playing. Kahu finished his mouthful and said, 'She was such a nice person, Miller. I know that's not the best way to describe her but it's true. It sounds like she was one of those genuinely nice people. She was a good girl, as her mum put it. And she really was. She'd suffered with that shit of an ex, but she left him and was good. Happy. Good job. No record, never involved in drugs, not even a speeding ticket. Never been in trouble, period.'

'You'll get there. Did the letter give you any clues?'

'No fingerprints. Would've been wearing gloves. He's not an idiot. We got the manufacturer of the paper. Pretty fancy stuff. It's only stocked in ten places in New Zealand. Three in the North Island. Wellington, Whangarei and Hamilton. All of them are quite specialised places, selling expensive stationery, pens, pencils, notebooks, art supplies that kind of stuff.'

'That must be a good thing?' Miller asked, trying to be positive.

'I guess. I went into the Hamilton shop yesterday. It was a lot bigger than I expected. The woman has really good records and had CCTV cameras installed a few months ago after someone made off with a two-hundred-dollar fountain pen.'

'And?'

'We got a list of people who'd bought that exact paper in the last year. There are at least a hundred on the list. It's going to take a bit of time tracking them down and going through the CCTV. Especially when we really don't know who or what we're looking for. So far, no luck.' Kahu drained his glass. 'Who knew people bought stuff like that these days? It's sold in a pack of ten sheets and costs fifteen bucks.' He shook his head and Miller smiled. Kahu was not one for extravagances.

'So no fingerprints?'

'Wouldn't that be great. No, nothing. Few bits and pieces of trace that need to be tested. We might get lucky. At the moment, though, we have nothing.'

'You're going to get him. I know you are.' Miller was confident. That's what Kahu did. Caught the baddies.

'Hey, you know you need to keep these letters quiet. I mean, tell no one, not even Sergeant Wirihana. We need to keep everything under wraps, release information to the public as and when I say so.'

Miller nodded. Realising how hard it would be to keep something like this from Ash.

'So no more letters?' Kahu asked. He drew his finger around his plate, wiping up the last of the gravy.

'Like you need to ask,' Miller said. 'You'll be the first one to know. Trust me.'

'Maybe he's done,' Kahu said as he wiped his mouth with a paper napkin. It was a wish, a prayer – they both knew the killer wasn't done. And all they could do was wait.

Chapter 12

'Another excellent Thursday night,' Michelle slurred.

Emmeline and Kelly looked at each other. It had been their usual Thursday night ritual. Cocktails at the Riverview Hotel and then dinner in the restaurant. It was the best Lentford offered for a night out, the other option being the Royal. And, not being a weekend, none of them could be bothered going into Hamilton. Michelle had imbibed a bit more than usual, but they couldn't blame her. A break-up will do that to you. There had been a lot of chat, and lots of putting down of the ex who, up until last week, they'd all adored. But Michelle had decided he wasn't for her and so they made sure they agreed. Emmeline didn't bother telling Michelle that she'd thought he was the one. Didn't tell her that she thought for sure there would be a ring on Michelle's finger by the end of the year.

The three of them lived close enough they could all share a taxi. Emmeline told the driver where they were headed. Lentford was small enough to walk home and they'd all be home in under half an hour, but taxiing was easier – and safer after the news of Tamara Jenson last week.

'God, I'm going to be hungover for school tomorrow,' Emmeline said, the motion of the taxi making her realise how much she'd drunk.

'Jesus, a room full of screaming kids and a hangover. No

thanks,' said Kelly.

'They don't scream,' Emmeline said, standing up for her kids. 'Well, not all the time.' She loved her job as the special educational needs co-ordinator at the local primary school.

'To be honest, just a roomful of kids puts me off,' said Kelly, winding down the window and breathing in the humid air.

Emmeline smiled. Kelly had always been determined she was never going to have kids. Emmeline, however, had wanted kids since she was one herself. It was finding the man that had always been the problem. She'd started seeing a teacher from work – not totally professional, she knew, but he was lovely. He taught the Year Five and Six class and all the kids loved him. She hadn't told Michelle or Kelly yet, hadn't even mentioned it to her mum or sister. She would. But for now, it was a fun little secret to have. Getting up in the morning had become exciting, knowing she'd see him. Cheesy but true. On Saturday they were planning a walk around Hamilton Gardens and a picnic.

The taxi slowed and pulled over. Kelly opened the door and turned. 'Night, ladies. Michelle, you're going to be fine. Fuck him. Catch you next week.' And with that she marched down her driveway and through the gate to the unassuming house on the other side with its beautiful view of the river.

Michelle laughed. 'Fuck him,' she said. 'He actually didn't do anything, Em.' As the taxi pulled away, doubling back to cross the bridge, streetlights highlighted tears on her cheeks, making a trail through her thick foundation.

Emmeline grasped her hand. 'No, he didn't. But you've made the right decision. You've said so yourself.'

Michelle nodded. 'Did you know Tamara Jenson? She was our age, roundabouts.'

Emmeline had been reading about the murder in the papers. First, they thought it was the ex, but it looked like he'd been cleared. 'Yeah, kind of. Remember the pool comp at the Royal a few months back? You and I played against her and Louise from school.'

'Holy shit, we did too,' Michelle said, horrified. 'She was great fun.'

'Yeah, she's really good friends with Louise... who's taking it really badly. As you would.'

The taxi made a left after the bridge and then right into Michelle's street.

'Just here's fine,' Michelle said. The driver pulled over. 'See you next week, hun.'

'Bye. Text me when you get in.'

'Will do.' Michelle slammed the door shut and walked the few hundred metres to her house. The driver did a U-turn and carried on to Emmeline's house.

Michelle, Kelly and Emmeline had all moved to Lentford for different reasons. It was Michelle's home town; Kelly had bought a house here five years ago as she couldn't afford one in Hamilton where she worked; and Emmeline, after her OE and a failed relationship, needed a new start away from Wellington. She loved small towns and had managed to find the right job and that was it. It had been easy to meet people through school and at the Royal – where she'd met Kelly and Michelle at a disastrous speed-dating event. The three women joked that they hadn't found the loves of their lives but had found a different kind of soul mate in each other.

The driver indicated, pulling over. Emmeline handed him the cash.

'Thanks. Have a good night, love.'

Emmeline looked at her watch. It was only ten o'clock. Her mum would still be awake. Maybe she could give her a ring and tell her about Adam.

She crossed the quiet street. It was darker around here with streetlights only about every twenty metres, so she pulled her phone out and turned the torch on. Walking up her driveway the houses on either side of the low hedge were in blackness, as well as nosy Mrs Bleakly opposite her. Adam had stayed the night for the first time last weekend and the next morning, after he'd gone, Mrs Bleakly had come over on the pretence of asking about the rubbish service over Christmas and then tried unsuccessfully to wheedle information out of her about Adam.

She rummaged in her oversized handbag for her keys, cursing as she grabbed at bits and pieces, mostly junk, till she came across them. Hearing footsteps behind her she swung around, keys in her fist, making for a pretty pitiful weapon.

'Oh, you startled me!' she said, hand to her chest. 'Are you okay?'

Chapter 13

Cassie had completed her usual search on the internet. Google, White Pages, LinkedIn, Facebook. There were a few Karl Taylors in the area, as she knew there would be. Most were outside the age limit the police put on Karl Taylor.

'How are you going?' Tiff asked, coming up behind her and resting a hand on her shoulder.

Their fight in the Royal last night hadn't come to anything. Cassie's plan of cooking Tiff dinner and apologising had worked, and they hadn't spoken of it since.

'I'm okay.' She shut the laptop. 'A few possibilities.' She picked up her pen and pad, slipped it into her handbag and sighed.

'You're *not* okay,' Tiff said, hauling her up and enveloping her into a hug.

Cassie's head rested on her chest. She felt Tiff's heartbeat and steady breathing. 'I just wonder...'

'What?' Tiff asked, drawing her back gently to look at her.

'I know what I'm doing is crazy. No, not crazy, just stupid, pointless. This was the whole reason I ended up at The Oaks. Doing reckless stuff like this.' Her mind threw up an image of Karl Taylor tied to his bed, her fist meeting his nose, the satisfying crunch. And then later the sickening realisation that she had the wrong man.

Tiff placed her hands on either side of Cassie's face. 'You are not crazy. You are not stupid. You want to find out who killed your mum and this is your way of going about it. Those dickhead cops are the stupid ones. All those resources, all that money, and still, after all this time, they've given you nothing.'

'Thank you,' Cassie said. She tilted her chin and Tiff bent slightly to kiss her.

When Tiff was like this, supportive, kind, Cassie knew they'd be together forever. Tiff *got* her. 'You know what my counsellor would call you, right?'

'Hang on,' Tiff said, 'I know this one.' They often used counsellor-speak on each other, a way to make each other laugh, taking the piss out of the people who'd tried to help them at The Oaks. 'I'm an enabler.'

'Got it in one.'

'You want me to come with you? I've got nothing else to do,' Tiff said, dropping onto the couch.

'That's okay. I'll do it on my own. You don't need to be a part of this.' Cassie regretted her words as soon as they were out and she saw Tiff's face fall. 'No, wait. I didn't mean it like that. I love that you're supporting me, but I have to do this on my own.' *Please let her be okay*, she thought.

Tiff nodded. 'Hey, have you got fifty dollars I could borrow? I owe Eric for that weed we bought the other day. He said if he doesn't get it today, he'll stop selling to us.'

Eric worked at the local newspaper and from what Cassie had learnt from Tiff he lived with his elderly mother and did a bit of drug-dealing on the side. Nothing too full on, a bit of weed, pills. Cassie didn't bother reminding Tiff that it was she who smoked the weed. 'Of course,' Cassie said, keen to pacify her. She took out her wallet. 'I've only got forty. Is that okay?'

Tiff got off the couch and took the money. 'Thanks, hun.

Good luck. I'll see you later.' The front door slammed behind her, the faint smell of her spice-laden perfume and marijuana lingering.

Cassie got in her car, a bright red Mini that they'd driven over to Tauranga to collect yesterday morning. Her dad had been at work, so she'd texted him and let him know she'd been by. He'd been put out that she had visited when he wasn't there, but she wasn't ready to see him, to introduce Tiff. She was enjoying this new life and wasn't ready for her old one to intrude.

She let Google Maps guide her. Lentford was tiny but she still had no idea where anything was, except the Royal and the supermarket. Five minutes later she pulled into the cul de sac that led to Shady Oaks Rest Home.

A couple of days ago Tane had approached her, and in a roundabout way brought up her mother. 'I remember when they found her. And then the whole Karl Taylor thing. Did you know there's an old fella out at the rest home called Karl Taylor?' Cassie's face must have betrayed her as he rushed on. 'Sorry, didn't mean anything by that. It's just a coincidence. He must be in his late eighties.' But it was all Cassie needed. She had to go and see him for herself.

What is it with this town naming things after oak trees? she thought, as she turned left and slowed to park on the side of the road. A long driveway led up to Shady Oaks. Shady *Oak* would've been a more apt name, since just one oak tree stood at the start of the driveway. She got out of the car, slowing her pace under the tree to take in the shade where it was a few degrees cooler. In the corner by the full parking lot stood three stumps, fresh sawdust scattered on the neatly trimmed grass.

'Cut them down a few weeks back.' A tinny voice sounded from the entrance door to the right.

Cassie walked over. The man, easily ninety, skin buckled

and gnarled like the oak at the entrance, smiled at her with a mouthful of gums. 'Powdery mildew.' His voice rattled with phlegm.

She nodded politely and tried to move on to the doors.

'The trees.' He waved his flannel-clad arm in the direction of the fallen oaks. 'Powdery mildew. It's a fungus that settles over the leaves during spring. Stops the trees from photosynthesising.' He nodded, smacking his lips together.

'Oh, right.' Cassie moved towards the door.

She wouldn't have thought it possible, but it was even warmer inside the rest home than outside. The wall of heat that greeted her had her perspiring and breathing heavily by the time she got to the reception desk. She breathed through her mouth, trying to mask the ever-present stench: a stomach-churning combination of urine, cooked meat and industrial-strength pine scented cleaner.

'How can I help you, love?' The nurse, in her mid-fifties, had a name tag attached to her pale-purple shirt.

'Hi, Joan. I'm here to see Karl Taylor.' She tried to be friendly, casual, but every time she had to say that name she grew rigid and could feel her throat closing.

'Take the first left here.' She pointed to the main corridor. 'He's Room Eleven, on your right. Oh, and if you could just sign the register, please. Just so we can keep track of who's coming and going.'

Cassie hesitated, thought about using a different name and then changed her mind. She printed her name, signed and noted the time. She was sure this Karl Taylor was going to be a dead end. There was no point in covering her tracks. She wouldn't be here again.

She thanked Joan and walked down the hallway, her head turning left then right, taking in the varied tableaus of each room. Some of the residents were sitting in easy chairs, others lying in bed, eyes closed. Some with visitors, faces animated. Some sitting staring out the window at the butchered oaks.

The door to Room Eleven was closed. She heard a female voice inside. A nurse maybe? Hopefully not a relative. She would find it hard to explain why she was here. If there was a problem, she could just say she had the wrong room.

She was just about to turn the handle when she heard footsteps approaching. She stepped to the side and continued walking down the corridor. She turned to watch a woman leave Karl's room and walk down the corridor in the opposite direction. Once the woman had rounded the corner, Cassie went back. She took a deep breath, knocked once and opened the door.

A man – Karl Taylor, she assumed – was sitting in an armchair upholstered in a yellowish-green fabric. He was looking out the window. In profile, his wrinkled skin hung off razor-sharp cheekbones. A copy of Stephen Ambrose's *Band of Brothers* was lying open on a chair opposite him. Cassie cleared her throat and the man turned. He didn't look surprised to see her. His brown eyes were glazed, confused, as if she had just woken him.

'Excuse me. Sorry to bother you. Are you Karl Taylor?' she asked, hearing the shaking in her voice.

'What's it to you?' His voice was clearer and sharper than she'd expected.

Cassie had no answer and floundered.

'Who are you?'

'My name's Cassie Hughes.'

He stared at her, then shrugged shoulders encased in a short-sleeved shirt that hung off him like a sack and turned back to the window.

'A man named Karl Taylor murdered my mother.' Cassie sounded ridiculous, even to herself. Did she really think this man murdered her mother? No, of course not. He was the wrong age, obviously. This was *all* wrong. 'I'm sorry, I shouldn't have bothered you. It was stupid of me to come. I just wanted to see you—'

'So you've seen me.' He turned back, his eyes narrowed. 'You think I killed your mother?'

'God, no, of course not!' Cassie felt her tight T-shirt stick to her stomach. She peeled it away. 'This was a mistake.'

'Sure as shit it is. I can barely make it to the bathroom on my own, let alone knock someone off.' He laughed at his crude joke, and Cassie was taken aback. 'So you just go around stalking Karl Taylors, hoping you'll come across the one who killed your mum?'

Got it in one. He seemed more onto it now, the dazed look in his eyes dissipated. He seemed years younger.

'I guess so,' Cassie admitted.

'Stupid,' he grumbled. 'The police looking into it?'

'Yes'

'When did it happen?'

'Fourteen years ago.'

He let out another guffawing laugh. 'Shit, lass, I'd say you're up shit creek. The case isn't cold, it's in fuckin' Antarctica, frozen in a solid block of ice.' He slapped his sun-spotted hand on his knee.

Cassie bit down on her lower lip. He was an old man. He didn't know anything. 'He's out there. He's still out there.'

'Who the fuck are you?' His eyes flicked left to right and then landed on her again. 'Who are you and what the fuck are you doing in my room!' His voice had turned into a bellow. He was trying his best to get out of his armchair, but arms as thin as toothpicks refused to support him and he dropped heavily onto the cushioned seat again. 'Get out of here! I don't know you! You shouldn't be in here!'

'Shit,' Cassie muttered, backing out of the room. He was going to bring half the staff in if he didn't shut up.

'Okay, okay, I'm sorry.' She raised her arms to placate him, turned around and ran into the woman she'd seen leaving the room earlier. The glass of water the woman was holding ended up down the front of her black top. 'Shit!' Cassie said. 'I'm so sorry.'

The woman looked from Karl to Cassie. She didn't look angry, more confused. She closed the door, walked over to Karl and murmured to him as if talking to an upset baby. She settled him back in his chair and in less than a minute he was staring out the window again.

'I'm really sorry,' Cassie said quietly, realising too late she should have made a run for it.

'It's okay. What happened? Do you know Karl?'

Cassie considered lying but couldn't be bothered. 'No, not really.'

When Cassie didn't offer up anything else the woman said, 'So what are you doing here?'

Cassie ignored her question. 'Are you his family? How do *you* know him?'

The woman briefly touched the scar on the left side of her face. 'My name's Miller. I come in and read to some of the residents here or keep them company. Karl doesn't have a lot of family. Or at least none who visit.' She smiled. 'Can you tell me your name? You're not in trouble or anything. It doesn't take much to set him off, unfortunately. He gets confused easily.' She patted the man's bony hand. He grabbed at it, and Cassie watched as Miller's other hand rested on top.

'I'm Cassie Hughes. I was...' She couldn't bring herself to say it. Not to this woman who seemed kind and normal and would think she was crazy.

'Cassie Hughes?' Miller looked over at her. Quiet. Her forehead furrowed. 'You're not Margaret Hughes's daughter are you?'

Cassie stepped back. It had been a while since anyone had connected her with her mother. At the start, when she was still a child, when her mum had gone missing, it felt as if everyone was looking at her and talking about her and her family – which they were. That carried on for a few months and then, nothing. When her mother's body was found, the whole circus started again. But even a dead body becomes old news at some stage, and again she was forgotten.

She nodded.

'Your name and Margaret's ring a bell because I'm a journalist. I moved here a while back and the reporter in me was interested in the town. I remember coming across your mum's case.'

'Miller Hatcher,' Cassie said. 'I know you.'

Miller smiled.

Cassie shook her head. 'No, sorry, I don't *know* you. I know your writing. I liked the piece you did on Castle Bay.' She remembered how well Miller had dealt with the victims, telling their story without any hint of drama or gossip. She'd got to know the victims through their families as well as she could, and it showed in her piece.

'Thank you.' Miller stood. 'We should probably go. After he's had one of his meltdowns he disappears for a bit.' She turned back to the old man. 'Bye, Karl. See you next week.'

Cassie followed her to the desk where they signed out, then walked with her to the car park. They stood by Miller's car.

'Can I ask what you were doing in Karl's room?'

Cassie felt her face flush. 'Karl Taylor.'

Miller's face was blank. Cassie took a deep breath. 'A man named Karl Taylor is the main suspect in my mother's death.'

'Of course, I remember now. The police have never been able to track him down.'

'I just thought... I don't even know why I do this anymore. The police, though, they're hopeless. Mum's case is still open but nothing's happening. I just thought if I could hunt down as many Karl Taylors as I could, kind of cross them off my list, and maybe find—'

'Find the one who did it?' Miller placed a hand on Cassie's shoulder. 'I get it. I'm sure the police are doing all they can.'

Cassie snorted.

'I'm sorry, that doesn't help at all does it?'

'You could help me, couldn't you?' Cassie said before she had time to think.

'What do you mean?'

'Couldn't you do an article or something? You could interview me. I wouldn't mind. We could get Mum's name out there again. People have forgotten. They bought out that identikit sketch ages ago. He looked pretty ordinary – dark hair, brown eyes, average height. The newspapers published it for a few weeks. But it's like he's disappeared off the face of the earth.'

Miller was silent for a moment. 'The *Lentford Leader* hasn't got the largest readership. I'm not sure how helpful an article would be.'

'Please. I'll tell you everything. I won't hold anything back. No one's ever done an article on Margaret Hughes's daughters. Dad protected us from all that. All those women's magazines harassed us a few years back wanting to do a 'Where are they now'. That fucked me off. People want to hear about me, Mum, our story. Maybe we can guilt someone into coming forward?'

'Okay,' Miller said. 'We can do that if you'd like.'

'Really?'

Miller nodded and handed her a business card. 'We can catch up next week. How's that?'

Cassie watched Miller drive away. She opened her bag and pulled out her notebook and looked at the list. All of a sudden she felt weary. The name Karl Taylor swam before her eyes. It was a fucking waste of time. But Miller would help her. She had a feeling deep in her gut that this article would make all the difference. She had to believe that because if she didn't, she was out of ideas.

Chapter 14

Miller sat out on the deck, adjusting her chair to take advantage of the pitiful easterly breeze, although it felt more like a fan heater. She sipped on her soft drink, thinking of Cassie Hughes. Tonight's pick playing on her mum's old record player was *The Essential Beatles*. She hummed as Paul sang about yesterday and how his troubles seemed so far away.

Cassie looked so fragile, so haunted, and Miller wondered what the poor girl had gone through over all these years. She pulled out her notepad and started writing questions down. Ngaire had given her the go-ahead for the interview. Cassie was living in Lentford, and it was always thought Karl Taylor had been from the Waikato. 'Focus on the girl,' Ngaire said. 'People like to know how victims like her – and they are victims, the people left behind – get over it, get on with their lives.'

'I'm not sure if she really has got over it,' Miller said, thinking about Cassie's visit to the rest home. 'She's desperate to find this Karl Taylor.' Miller didn't bother telling Ngaire that Karl Taylor would feature prominently. Cassie wanted his name out there again, wanted him in the public's minds. She needed to talk to Ash. She assumed Ash, or at least one of her constables, would have been first on the scene when Margaret Hughes's body was discovered out at the old dairy factory last year.

'Knock, knock,' trilled a voice down the side of the house.

Miller stood and smiled as Li appeared dressed in an impossibly short pair of denim cut-offs and a white shoestring singlet. Her bichon frise, Patsy, sat in her arms.

'Hey Li, how's it going?'

'Excellent!' Li brandished a bottle. 'Delayed celebration for end of exams!'

'Congratulations!' Miller said. Li had been studying sociology and was in her last year.

'Grab some glasses, would you?'

Miller looked at the bottle as if it was a snake about to strike.

'Don't panic, it's grape juice. Give me some credit.' Li winked. 'This weather!' She fanned herself, her porcelain complexion tinged pink, her straight black hair sticking to the side of her face. She sat down and Patsy leapt off the deck into the backyard.

'To you,' Miller said as they clinked glasses. She sipped her drink, the bubbles played on her tongue, the sickly-sweet flavour making her crave a glass of dry chardonnay. She put the glass down. 'So what are your plans now?' Miller asked, concerned she was going to lose her effervescent neighbour.

'I'm going home to Shanghai for a couple of weeks. Then I'm back again to do my masters.'

'Impressive,' Miller said. 'What on?'

'Society and our obsession with true crime. Focusing on cases in New Zealand over the last ten years.' She grinned. 'What do you think?'

'Interesting. Is that why you were at the Doddses' on Tuesday? For the Murder Club – No,' Miller corrected herself, 'The True Crime Enthusiasts Club?'

Li laughed, a loud cackle. 'Yep. That Logan.' She shook her head. 'He's something else. Interesting stuff, though. I thought, if it all goes ahead, I could, maybe, chat to you?' She peered over her glass, hopeful.

Li knew all about Miller's time in Castle Bay, although they'd never talked about it in detail. Miller knew Li valued their friendship too much to pry. When Miller first moved into her mother's house, she had cleaned out her mother's liquor cabinet, took all the bottles into the kitchen and decanted each one down the plughole. Baileys, Glayva, five bottles of wine, a bottle of vodka and three bottles of whisky. The kitchen had smelt like a pub at closing time. She'd thrown open the windows and hauled the green recycling bin to the footpath outside. Li had been doing the same. They introduced themselves and Li had glanced at Miller's stash. 'Big party?' she'd teased.

'Bit of a clean out,' Miller said. And as much as she wanted to keep that part of her life to herself, she'd learnt Li was the kind of person you could open up to, trust.

'Miller?' Li asked. 'Could I?'

'Could you what?'

'Could I maybe talk to you about Castle Bay?' Li asked, squirming uncomfortably in her chair.

'I'll think about it,' Miller said, smiling. She didn't want to say no straight off, but she couldn't think of anything worse than sitting down with Li and rehashing the violence and terror she'd gone through in Castle Bay and then having all of that published in a thesis. 'Are your parents excited about you coming home?'

'Oh, yeah, I guess,' Li said. 'My brother's going to be there too. They're always more excited to see him. The golden son.' She rolled her eyes.

'What does he do?'

'Works in New York. Finance.'

'They must be proud of you, though?'

'Sure.' Li shrugged. 'They didn't want me to study sociology.

Told me it wouldn't get me anywhere. What kind of career could I possibly have studying society?' she asked, arms wide, some of the grape juice tipping over the side of the glass and spilling on the deck. 'They're probably right, but I love it. It's interesting.'

'Good on you. And how's Liam?' Li's boyfriend of a year had been a regular visitor next door.

'Fine.' Li averted her eyes, studying Patsy who was digging a hole under the lemon tree.

'Really? Doesn't sound fine.'

'I broke it off with him. I told my parents about him a few months back. We even Skyped and I introduced him. They were horrified, as I knew they would be. A freckled, ginger Kiwi studying English Lit was not quite what they had planned for their only daughter.'

'Li, I'm sorry. Couldn't you keep on seeing him?'

'I was going to, but god, their voices are always in my head. They're over ten thousand kilometres away but they might as well be next door. I didn't want to break up with him, but they'd never accept him. It's just easier this way. The communication with Liam wasn't great. They can't speak very good English and Liam knows zero Chinese. They want to be able to rely on my future husband when they get old – and when they saw Liam that didn't inspire the greatest confidence.'

'I'm sorry.' Miller leaned over and squeezed her hand that had fingernails painted neon orange.

'I'm bracing myself to be paraded around when I get back. They'll have a line-up of suitors, no doubt. And they always think they're being so clever. Inviting family friends over for lunch and they just happen to bring their son, or going out for dinner and we 'accidentally' meet a nice young man they know so *must* introduce me.' Li rolled her eyes. 'I come back January fifteenth. I'll get off the plane in Shanghai and will be counting the days till I get back on!'

'You'll survive, then you can crack on with the year ahead.'

Li nodded. 'Right, better go. Me and some friends are going out for dinner. Just to the Royal. Want to come?'

'Not tonight, thanks.' Miller's phone beeped. 'You have a great night. You deserve it. I'll see you before you leave anyway, at the Kowhai probably.'

Li jumped up and called Patsy. 'The Kowhai, that's one place I won't miss,' she said. 'Do you want this?' she asked, picking up the bottle. Miller shook her head.

Li skipped down the steps, jumping the last two, the half-full bottle of grape juice sloshing onto the grass. 'See you later. C'mon, Patsy.'

Miller threw the contents of her glass onto a limp rose bush and looked down at the text from Kahu. The four words cooled her sweating body and goosebumps erupted over her skin: There's been another one.

Chapter 15

Miller pulled up outside Ash's townhouse on Sunday night just before seven. She parked on the road, the driveway having enough room for only one car. The new townhouses, a row of four, were divided by six-foot-high fences. The properties were small, each with a paved area out the front and a small patch of garden out the back.

Ash opened the front door before Miller got there. 'Come in, come in! I'm so glad we're doing this.'

Ash's copper hair was tied up in a stubby ponytail and she was dressed in black shorts and a T-shirt. She always looked younger than her thirty-four years when she was out of uniform.

Miller flicked off her jandals at the door and followed Ash inside. Zach was sitting on the couch, his gaze locked on the TV, Xbox controller in his hands. 'Hey Zach,' Miller said, depositing the mud cake she'd bought from the supermarket on the bench in the kitchen.

With no response from Zach, Ash said, 'Zach! Show a bit of respect.'

Zach started at the sound of his mum's voice and turned to look at her and then Miller.

'Hi, Miller.' He gave her a genuine smile that reached his eyes, which were identical to Ash's. Zach was all Ash, from his sense of humour to his pale skin and dark copper hair – inherited from Ash's Irish mother. Ash's *Mam*, as she called her, had left her homeland almost forty years ago after marrying the Kiwi lad who had worked behind the bar at her local pub in Galway.

'Five more minutes. Then you can come and grace us with your presence,' Ash said, as she and Miller walked out to the patio. Zach un-paused his game and the sound of gunfire followed them outside.

'An early Christmas present from my parents.' Ash rolled her eyes. 'He thinks it's the perfect excuse to hole up inside over summer. But he already promised me months ago,' she raised her voice and turned her head towards the door, 'that he would find *a summer job!*'

She pulled a chair out for Miller. 'Take a seat.' Ash poured her sparkling water out of a jug, added a wedge of lime and then poured one for herself. 'I was going to do a roast but it's too hot to be cooped up in the kitchen, so I've done a few things on the barbie.' She lifted the lid of the hooded barbecue and showed off steak and kebabs already cooked. 'Zach! Dinner.'

Ash put the meat onto a platter, jogged inside and returned with a salad and foil-wrapped garlic bread. Miller sat back and let Ash fill her plate. It was no use telling her she could do it herself. Ash always looked after others.

'Garden's looking good,' Miller said, looking at the thriving vegetable garden in the corner. Flower beds bordered the back and left side of the house; rich weed-free dirt held a rainbow of perennials.

In the space of a few minutes, Zach had wolfed down his dinner and was asking to be excused.

'Really?' Ash said, exasperated. 'You haven't even spoken to Miller.'

Zach turned to Miller. 'School's going good. Almost finished for the year. Looking at blueberry picking over summer to earn a bit of cash. We're not going away for Christmas as Mum's working Boxing Day. But we're going down to Wanaka for New Years to see Nana and Pop.' He dazzled Miller with another smile then went inside.

'Smart arse. Don't have them,' Ash said, shaking her head but smiling. 'Kids. Just don't.'

Miller laughed, knowing it was all for show. Zach was Ash's world. She had him when she was nineteen. The father, an Englishman working on the Wanaka ski fields at the time, was due to leave the day she found out she was pregnant. He got on the plane and she never heard from him again. Miller knew that Ash's parents had been a huge help, supporting her in her twenties as she did her police training and completed her degree in criminal justice. Ash and Zach had been in Lentford for almost three years, after Ash was transferred to Lentford, her first job as sergeant.

'Do you know much about Margaret Hughes?' Miller asked. 'I take it you were involved when her body was discovered last year.'

Ash nodded. 'Yeah, we were called out there. The site's been abandoned for over fifteen years. It went on the market a couple of years ago. Not much interest. But there were a few developers out there last year having a good poke around and one of them came across her body, which was really just a skeleton. Why are you asking?'

'I'm interviewing her daughter, Cassie, this week.'

'Really? About the case?'

'Yeah. She sounds frustrated about how nothing's happened since the discovery of the body. She thought I could help get word out again.'

'Good idea. It got a hell of a lot of attention when the body was found, but nothing really ever came of it. I really feel for the family.'

'Speaking of which, I heard there's been another one,' Miller said. 'Were you at the scene again?'

Ash frowned. 'How did you know? Nothing's been released yet.'

Shit.

'Did Detective Parata tell you?'

'He— I— yeah, he did.' She might as well be honest about this part. 'He didn't say who the victim was.' *Like that makes it better.* She hadn't heard anything else from Kahu at all apart from the text yesterday.

'I don't know if he should be sharing that information with you,' Ash said, standing and pushing leftovers onto the platter. 'It's really sensitive stuff, and with your job...'

Miller realised she'd put her foot in it. There was no way she could tell Ash about the letters, that she was a part of this investigation whether she wanted to be or not.

'You're right, he shouldn't have,' she said, desperate to make peace. 'He often talks to me about his work. I'm a bit of a sounding board, you know?'

Ash nodded, but still didn't look happy.

'The cases he works on aren't usually so close to home, though.'

'Yeah.' Ash looked out to her garden. 'I don't mean to sound patronising, Mills, but what's happening in Lentford at the moment is horrible, tragic. It's a really big deal. The media are going to be all over it, all over this town, hungry for any bit of info they can get. Please, just don't put the investigation at risk.'

Miller looked into her lap. She hated that Ash would think she would put the investigation in jeopardy. 'Of course, I won't. I'd never do that. I hope you know that.'

'I do. Now,' Ash said, picking up a pile of plates. 'How about some of that mud cake for dessert?' She took the plates inside, leaving Miller to collect the cutlery and sauces.

Miller couldn't believe she let slip about Kahu's text. What was she expecting? For her and Ash to have a cosy conversation about the murder cases? She was well aware that Ash was on the outer in this investigation. She was the local cop used for local knowledge and guarding crime scenes, and that was it.

Miller walked into the kitchen where Ash was loading the dishwasher. 'I'm sorry,' she said.

'No, I'm sorry. You know what I'm like, Miller. I follow the rules. It's what I do best. And without sounding too much like a sheriff in a western, this is my town. I feel responsible for everyone's safety. I guess the fact that something so shocking is happening while I'm in charge is a bit hard to take.'

'You know none of this is on you, right?'

'I know. Of course, I do. And I know that Detective Sergeant Parata is your friend. I get that. I just don't want anything to go wrong with this investigation. I know the women who have been killed.'

Miller didn't bother asking her about the latest victim.

'I want everything done by the book so we can find this piece of shit and put him away.'

Miller nodded. *Me and you both.*

Chapter 16

When Miller walked into the *Leader* office on Monday morning, she had just heard on the radio news that Emmeline Porter's body had been found in her home on Friday afternoon. No other details were given.

Both she and Kahu had known there would be another one, had known this was no ex-boyfriend. Did the women know each other? Was there some kind of connection? In a town this small, surely there would be.

'Miller Hatcher,' Eric said as Miller dumped her bag on her desk.

Miller looked up. Eric was staring at her, his face smug. He leaned back in his chair, arms supporting the back of his head, yellow-stained pits on show.

'What?' Miller said. The man only had to utter a couple of words and it sent her day spiralling.

'I know why you're here.'

'Yeah, to work – unlike some others.'

'No, Miller. Why you're here in Lentford. Why you ended up working in this backwater when you had your whole career in front of you.'

Miller lowered herself into her chair, refusing to meet his eye. She'd known this was going to happen one day. It was just a matter of time. Especially with jealous tossers like Eric who had nothing else to do.

'Miller here yet?' Ngaire's husky voice shattered the silence.

'Oh yeah, Ngaire wants to see you,' Eric said, turning back to his computer with a knowing smile that Miller was tempted to punch right off his face.

Miller walked into Ngaire's office and closed the door, even though every part of her wanted to leave it open for a breath of fresh air. Today the office smelt of sickly-sweet strawberry.

'Article on the Doddses' home looks good,' Ngaire said. 'How was she to interview?'

'She was fine. A little bit uptight.' Miller took a seat, trying to forget what Eric had just said. Was he teasing her, like he had been doing for the last six months? Or did he know something?

'Yeah, uptight is an understatement. Did you hear there's been another murder? Emmeline Porter. I've done a story on Tamara. Front page tomorrow. I've put something in on this latest one. I wasn't given much when I talked to Sergeant Wirihana, and the CIB wouldn't even talk to me.'

Again, Miller felt bad, knowing what she knew and not sharing it. But Kahu had told her not to tell anyone about the letters. She didn't want to put herself in a position where Ngaire forced her to give up information that was confidential. But she also thought it was a way for Ngaire to hand over the story on the murders to her.

'Two murdered women. Surely there's some kind of connection,' Ngaire said.

'You'd think so.'

Ngaire lowered her voice. 'It's going to make for some good pieces, Miller. I'll get you to write the next one. Try and get in with CIB, okay? And you know Sergeant Wirihana, don't you? You're friends? Not sure how much she's involved but she could be a good source. Although at the best of times she's tight-lipped. A by-the-book kind."

Miller prickled at Ngaire's description of Ash but nodded, excited at the prospect.

'But remember. This is a small town. People know these women. They're their friends and family. This isn't some big sensational story. Well, actually, it is, but let's not do that. Cover the story with empathy. Got it? The last thing I need is grief-stricken families banging on my door because of the way we've covered the story.'

Miller nodded. She got where Ngaire was coming from, but it was a whole different outlook from *First Look*.

'Right. Other stories for next week's issue. The murders will obviously be front page. What else do you have?'

'I'm talking to Cassie Hughes tomorrow. And I'm following up with the high-school counsellor about the bullying story. And... one more thing. I'm going to see Logan Dodds this afternoon.'

'Logan Dodds? Beatrice's son?' Ngaire sucked on her vape.

'Yeah, he runs a true crime enthusiasts' group.' The words *Murder Club* still rang in her ears.

Ngaire paused mid-inhale, her lips puckered.

'He and a group of people discuss and research crimes – murders,' Miller explained. 'They have a real interest in it. What made the murderer do it, who their victims were, that kind of thing. Anyway, Logan is putting together a True Crimes tour around the district here. Taking people to historic murder sights. Giving them the low-down about what happened. I figured this would have a lot of people divided. Some would be interested, some would think it's creepy-as-fuck, some would think it's wrong, abhorrent.'

'Jesus Christ,' Ngaire said. 'Who knows about this?'

'Well, the people in his group for starters. All locals, I think.

Plus, I ran into Jay and he's printed up pamphlets for the club and the tours. Logan's pretty serious about it.'

'What do you think about the whole thing?' Ngaire asked.

'Undecided, leaning to the creepy-as-fuck side.'

Ngaire nodded. 'And you want to do a piece on this?'

'Yeah,' Miller said, deflating at Ngaire's expression.

'Look, Miller, I know that where you've just come from this would be a feature. Something that would definitely divide people. But in Lentford...'

Ngaire didn't have to finish. Miller knew she had to toe the line. Stick to local issues, sports, schools, council, community service. 'I know,' she said. 'It's just with the murders and now this, I thought it would be an interesting piece. I won't make it over the top. I'll stick to the facts, explain what he's doing. I don't think you give the people of Lentford enough credit.' Miller held her breath. Had she spoken out of turn?

'Is that right?' Ngaire said. Miller took comfort in the smile that tugged at the corners of Ngaire's mouth.

'I don't think they need protecting. And yeah, of course there's going to be people who disagree about what he's doing. My article wouldn't say it's right or wrong; just tell people the facts. I'm sure they'd want to know about it.'

'Okay, okay,' Ngaire said, inhaling and then screwing her face up. 'Strawberry, apparently.' She threw the vape onto her desk in disgust. 'Write the story. It can go in the last issue before our Christmas break. And god help all the letters to the editor – I'll send them your way, right?'

'Deal,' Miller said, her left leg jiggling in excitement.

As she rose to leave, Ngaire said, 'Does Logan know about you?'

'What do you mean?'

'Castle Bay.'

'Yes, doesn't everyone? Why's that?'

'I'm sure you're very interesting to a guy like him. A guy obsessed with murder and murderers. I bet he feels like he's won the lottery. Make sure it's you asking the questions – not him.'

Miller nodded and walked back to her desk, excited about the fact she was covering something with a bit of substance for a change.

'See there's been another one?' Eric said, giving her that same look, the cat that got the cream.

'What do you mean?' Miller was deliberately vague.

'Another murder. A woman; early thirties. Found in her house: Emmeline Porter.'

'Doesn't mean it was the same guy.' Miller was fully aware she was disagreeing with Eric just for the sake of it.

'Of course it was. How dumb are you? Two murders within a week in our little town.' Eric shook his head at Miller and turned back to his computer.

Hine's high-heeled walk sounded outside, followed by Cody's quick steps. 'Morning all,' Hine sang, dumping the pile of mail on her desk.

Cody sat at his desk, smiled at Miller and said good morning. He was a breath of fresh air after looking at Eric's weathered, aggrieved face. Neatly shaved – Miller wasn't even sure if he could grow facial hair – with tidy clothes, slicked back hair and freshly showered. It helped combat Eric's body odour and the smell of weed he was always draped in.

Hine sorted the mail in record time and walked around the office dropping envelopes, newspapers and magazines on the desks. 'Did you hear there's been another one?' she said. 'God, I don't feel safe in my house any more. I'm glad I've got a flatmate.'

'Yeah, you'll be fine, Hine. Both of them lived by themselves,'

Cody said.

'How do you know?' Eric asked. 'You've done one of them, have you, mate?' He laughed.

Cody coloured. 'I knew Emmeline. She worked at the school. I did a story a few months back and interviewed her.'

'Ah, go on mate, be honest, no need to be shy!' Eric continued baiting Cody.

Miller could see Cody's jaw tighten. Cody was gay, something all but Eric in the office knew. Cody preferred it that way, and Miller understood why.

'Cody, I'm busy here,' Miller said, trying to relieve the tension and get Cody away from Eric. 'Would you mind making me a cuppa?'

Cody broke his stare with Eric and took himself off to the tearoom.

Miller flicked through her mail. The off-white envelope, only a corner showing from the pile, might as well have been a bright orange flag. Grabbing it, she ignored the other envelopes that fell to the floor and stood up, taking the letter and her satchel to the toilet.

She locked the toilet door, closed the toilet lid and sat down. The naked bulb overhead illuminated the small room, which was painted the same pale green as the rest of the office. She slipped on one of the pairs of latex gloves Kahu had given her last time they'd talked and opened the envelope. She swallowed back a feeling of nausea, but was also curious about what he had to say.

Hi Miller

Yes, another murder. One won't do it. I'd be yesterday's news before I know it. I'd be forgotten in a flash. I want people to remember me. I want people to

Miller's hands shook as she put the letter back into the envelope, removed the gloves and returned to the office.

'I'll be gone for the rest of the day,' she told Hine. 'You can reach me on my mobile.'

Leaving her car parked out the front of the office, Miller walked down to the police station. There was no one on the front desk in the lobby, so she walked through the double doors. The door to her left was open; Bull was talking to a colleague with his back to her. Ash's door was closed. There were three people down the end of the corridor going into the tearoom. Miller hovered outside the door to the meeting room, unsure if she should enter. She knocked once and went in. She saw Kahu and walked towards him, her eyes drawn to the whiteboard which was fuller now than when she first saw it. There were various photos of the two victims' pale faces, scarves, abhorrent in their brightness, wrapped around their necks. No one noticed her as she walked in. Two people tapped away on laptops, another couple were on the phone

Kahu walked towards her, crossing the room in four long strides. He took her by the arm and guided her to the door.

'You shouldn't be in here,' Kahu said and led her out into the corridor.

Miller got it. As Ash had pointed out, Kahu told her a lot, more than he probably should. But he was right that she shouldn't be privy to what went on in the investigation room.

There were dark rings under his eyes and pale-yellow patches under his white shirt. 'When did you last sleep?'

'Got the call about Emmeline on Friday afternoon. Boyfriend found her. She hadn't turned up for work and wasn't answering her phone. They'd just started seeing each other. He was really broken up about it. I haven't slept much since then, to be honest.'

'When was she killed?'

Kahu looked around, his voice low. 'They've put time of death late Thursday night, early Friday morning.'

'Thursday night again,' Miller muttered.

Miller handed over the letter. Kahu took a visible breath as he pulled on a pair of latex gloves that he retrieved from a desk drawer. He scanned the letter, shaking his head. 'I don't think we're going to find anything. The last one brought up zilch. He's careful. No DNA, no trace.'

'Are you okay?'

'Nope.' His smile faltered. 'We knew there would be another one, didn't we? But I honestly thought we might be able to find something before he did it again.'

'Have you got anything at all?'

'Not a lot. Emmeline's a similar age to Tamara. They both lived alone. Tamara was knocked out and then strangled by a scarf. Same with Emmeline, as far as we can tell. Her autopsy's this afternoon. Emmeline's boyfriend tells us she and Tamara knew each other. Had played pool at the Royal together. So we're not sure if that loose connection is something we can build on.' Kahu stared down the corridor.

'Where does he get the scarves from?' Miller asked, thinking that could be a lead.

'Yeah, looking into it. We think they're old. The manufacturer label says *Milton's* and it seems nobody makes them anymore. Looks to be a brand back in the Eighties. God, I think I even remember my aunty having them.'

The label was familiar to Miller as well.

'I gotta get on, Mills. Thanks for bringing the note in. Are you okay? This can't be easy. Getting dragged into all this, whether you want to or not.'

'I'm fine. But he's not done yet, Kahu.'

'I know. Be careful. This guy knows you. The letters have been delivered or posted to your office so he may not know where you live, but in a town this small—'

'I know,' Miller said. 'He could easily find out where I live.'

Just then the door to Ash's office swung open. 'Miller. What are you doing here?' Ash looked from Miller to Kahu, frowning.

Miller looked at Kahu, unsure what to say.

'I better get going,' he said. 'Call me if you need anything.' Kahu returned to the meeting room and closed the door, leaving Miller to handle Ash.

'Miller?' Ash's tone was icy.

'I just wanted to ask Kahu about the investigation. My editor wants me to cover it.'

'And did he give you information?' Ash folded her arms, stood up taller as if to intimidate Miller, but still came up a head shorter.

Miller hated this. 'I... No, nothing important, just what's being said at the press conference.'

'You promised me you weren't going to interfere with the investigation.'

'Ash, I'm just doing my job.' Miller knew she should back down.

'Yeah, right. I hope you're telling me the truth. If Detective Parata's passing on sensitive information, information that could make or break this case and you publish it, whatever you write could potentially stuff up the investigation.'

'Kahu hasn't given me anything, I swear.'

'I could take this to his superiors, you know. He's putting the investigation at risk.'

'No, please don't do that,' Miller said, alarmed that Ash would take this so far.

'You're not leaving me with a lot of choice. Just make sure you stick to what's said at the press conference. No breaking stories.'

If only you knew.

Ash gave Miller an apologetic smile and put her hand on Miller's arm. 'Just keep your distance, please. There are rules we have to follow. Don't make it harder for Detective Parata to follow them.' She closed her office door and walked down to the lobby leaving Miller standing in the corridor.

Chapter 17

It may have been Miller's imagination but the closer she got to the river the more it seemed to cool down. It was 9.05 a.m. and the temperature was already well into the twenties. She crossed over the bridge and wound the window down. The weather person who came on after the news told her to prepare for a high of thirty-two. As she wound her way up The Hill the heat returned, and as she turned off the ignition outside the Doddses' house an ad informed her there were only fourteen days until Christmas. She wondered if all of this – the murders – would be over by then and if Lentford would even feel like celebrating.

She stepped out of her car, deafened by the cicadas and birds chirruping in the surrounding trees, maybe the only ones happy about the weather. A black cat eyed her from its shelter under a terracotta birdbath in the corner of the front garden.

She walked towards the imposing front door, noticing Lou's gardening van in the driveway again. No wonder the house looked so immaculate, she thought, the Doddses must fork out a huge amount of money on their garden. She rang the doorbell, pressing down hard, trying to eliminate the nerves she felt in her stomach. She was sure it was nothing to do with Logan Dodds. She'd done stories covering every subject imaginable for almost a decade. It was him, this murderer, who had a need for infamy. He was in her head even if she thought she was doing a good job of compartmentalising him. She'd got good at that. Pushing down her experiences, talking about them only if and when necessary. Nat, her old flatmate, had told her it wasn't healthy. Her counsellor told her it would cause more harm than good in the end. She listened to neither. She was good at compartmentalising. It worked for her, for now.

Logan must have been standing at the door waiting for her arrival. She'd only just pressed the doorbell and the door swung open. The nervous, jittery Logan Dodds of last week had disappeared. In front of her was a man with a wide smile, his brown eyes meeting hers. Only for an instant did they flick to her scar, causing her to touch her face briefly.

'Hi, Miller. Can I call you Miller?'

'Of course.'

'Come on in. Mum's set up the lounge with coffee and snacks.'

'Is she around?' Miller followed him into the room where he had held his meeting. The chairs from last week had been replaced with two leather couches facing each other, a solid wooden coffee table between them with a coffee plunger, mugs, pastries and muffins on top.

'I normally have my meetings in here. We usually push the couches out of the way and bring the chairs in. Can fit more people in that way.'

Miller nodded and asked again, 'Is your mum home?'

'In the garden with Lou talking about planting or something. I like the veggies, but the flowers and shrubs are boring. No point.' He sat down heavily next to Miller, ignoring the other couch. 'I've been really excited about this. I've told everyone on the forums I'm on.'

'You belong to forums?' Miller got out her notebook.

'Yeah, heaps.'

His enthusiasm reminded her of a five-year-old boy talking about racing cars or dinosaurs, not a forty-something man speaking about murders. She looked at his hand as he reached for a muffin. Close up she could see the damage he'd done to his nails, cuticles and skin around his fingers. Dried blood caked some, the cuticles red and raw.

'There are a lot of true crime forums and blogs. I have my own, Kiwi Crimes. Lots of forums are visited by people from all over the world. There are people on the forums who live next door to John Wayne Gacy's house, people who used to go to the same church as Dennis Rader, otherwise known as BTK. There's even a cousin of Ivan Milat on one – he gets lots of attention,' Logan said. The jealousy was plain.

'What do you talk about on these forums?' Miller asked.

'Murderers and the murders they commit mostly. Everyone has their favourite.'

Miller's face must've betrayed her.

'I know, I know. Dad thinks it's pretty stuffed up. Maybe "favourite" isn't the right word. Most interested in.'

'And who's your... favourite?' Miller asked.

'Samson Tatler.'

Miller didn't need any further explanation. Samson Tatler shot and killed his wife, her parents, and his three kids, on a dairy farm just outside Invercargill twenty years ago. It was one of those cases New Zealanders would always remember. She reached for the coffee plunger.

'Here, I'll do that for you.' Logan poured the coffee and slid it over to her.

Miller nodded her thanks. 'These people you're so interested in have hurt people, killed them, ruined others' lives. I must admit I struggle a bit as to why you treat them like... celebrities.'

Logan nodded, still smiling. He wiped muffin crumbs from

his stubbly chin. 'I get it. Dad thinks the same thing. He thinks I'm a bit,' he tapped his fingers to the side of his head, 'crazy. But it's so interesting. Why these people from all different cultures, countries and backgrounds choose to take a life. I find it fascinating.'

Miller was getting angry. 'Let's change tack a bit, shall we?' she said. She took a sip of coffee. 'Can you tell me a bit about your childhood? I know your sister Amelia was murdered. Do you feel that had something to do with your fascination?'

At the mention of his sister's name, Logan's face didn't change. 'For sure it does.' He slurped at his coffee and picked up a pastry. His belly strained at his T-shirt as he leant forward.

'You were living just out of Lentford at the time? On your parents' farm?'

'Yeah. I was twelve when she was killed. Amelia was fifteen. I went to a mate's place after school that day. The school bus dropped her off as usual, just down the road from our house. Mum and Dad were out on the farm. It was calving season and really busy, so we never expected them in till around five. Later that afternoon I biked home from my friend's house who lived a few kilometres away. I hated taking the bus. Biked, even when it was pouring down.' He paused. Miller wasn't sure what she was supposed to say about this inane bit of information so she just nodded.

'I was biking up the driveway. It was long, not concrete or anything, gravel, long grass on either side, paddocks to the left and right. I remember seeing her legs first. I knew it was her because she had these white Adidas sneakers that Mum had bought her. She'd wanted them for ages. Dad said it was too much money, but Mum had bought them anyway. Bit of a silly purchase when you live on a farm – cow shit and dirt and dust everywhere. Anyway, I remember thinking, what the hell's Amelia doing. Thought she was playing a prank on me or something – she was like that. Quite hard-case. I remember riding up to her with a smile on my face. But it wasn't a joke.'

He shook his head and looked at Miller, making sure she was listening. 'Her face was all bloody. If it wasn't for the shoes, I wouldn't have known it was her. I stood there for a bit. Confused, I think. And,' he whispered, 'I was kind of... fascinated. I'd never seen a dead body before. Not even grandparents in a coffin – they were all long gone before I was born.'

Miller lowered her head and took notes, unable to speak.

'Anyway, I got back on my bike and called out to Mum and Dad. Of course, they weren't around. I got myself something to eat and waited for them but after about half an hour I thought I should call the cops. They arrived at the same time as Mum and Dad got in from the farm.'

'Your poor parents,' Miller said, hoping to inject some kind of sympathetic feeling into Logan.

'Yeah, they both took it really hard. I think it kind of ruined them. Their relationship. They probably shouldn't have stayed together.' He shrugged his hunched shoulders and nibbled on a forefinger. He turned his head and spat out whatever he'd nibbled off.

A nail? Skin? Miller tried to hide her shudder. 'And you? How did *you* handle it?'

'Mum would tell you I didn't. She's probably right. I thought I was okay but then the doctors told me I suffered from PSTD. No, that's not right Post-Traumatic Stress Disorder,' he said, carefully enunciating each word. 'PTSD. I guess I shut down a bit. My school work suffered, I lost friends – I got in trouble for doing my Year Eleven project on her murder and the guy who killed her. Matthew Freedman was his name. Sharemilker from down the road. Married. He was twenty-five. Went to the police station and confessed the next day. Told the cops he fancied Amelia. Told them she was a tease. Said they'd had a few conversations, that they were going to meet up. He said that day she rejected him; said he was too old and she wasn't interested. Said he got angry and hit her. And then just kept on hitting her. He was sentenced to sixteen years. Committed suicide before he'd been in prison a year. Couldn't handle it, I reckon. Crime of passion. Not planned. He wasn't really a killer. It was just the circumstances.'

'So did you get on okay, after being diagnosed with PTSD?"

'Not really. Couldn't focus. Couldn't hold a job down. Mum was really supportive. Let me stay at home. I took over the veggie garden. Not like this little patch we have here.' He put his index finger in his mouth, and when he brought it away there was a drop of blood coming from his torn cuticle. Miller winced.

He ripped a tissue from the box and held it to his finger. 'I had forty square metres. It became my job. Dad thought I should get a proper job, said I was a bludger, a no-hoper. Once told me it should've been me that died, not Amelia.' He shrugged again. To Miller it looked as though he didn't disagree.

'We just fell into a pattern. When they moved here last year, I came with them. I help Mum out a lot. Plus, the club's keeping me busy and now the tours.' He sat up straight.

Miller felt as though she'd been bombarded. Logan's attitude was alarming. The way he talked about his sister's death was so off-hand, so calculated, just another murder to talk about on his forum.

She flicked through her notes. As sick as she felt, this was going to be one hell of an article. 'Logan, can you tell me about these tours?'

'Okay, so it's not like our district's the murder capital of the world or even of New Zealand, but it's where I am, so I'll make

it work. Anyway, murder happens everywhere. You'd be surprised.' He discarded the tissue on the coffee table, the small
bloom of blood stark against the white background, and picked
up a muffin. 'These small towns where everyone feels so safe,
there's always a history of violence. I mean just around here –
my sister, the discovery of Margaret Hughes's body last year
and now Tamara and Emmeline. And there's more, a lot more.
Nowhere has a clean slate, even if the people there believe they
live in the safest town in the world. I mean, look at Castle Bay.'

Miller looked up from her notepad. He nodded knowingly
at her. 'The way it works is that I take groups of no more than
eight around to the more famous areas where people have been
murdered. I give them all the details, the murderer, the victims,
if they were caught, how it happened.'

'Are people really interested in this kind of thing?'

'Sure are. I've been advertising it on the forums. I already
have three bookings for January. Two lots from America and
one from Australia.'

Miller was surprised but shouldn't have been. The world
was made up of all sorts.

'Next week I'm doing a practice run. I'm taking a few of the
club members out, plus a master's student who wants to do her
thesis on me.'

'Li Chen?'

'You know her?' Logan's smile widened. 'Great girl. Really
interested in what I'm doing. Doesn't think I'm a freak.'

Miller took the hint. 'She's a friend of mine,' Miller said,
choosing not to reveal that they were neighbours, nor to correct
Logan about Li's topic.

'Huh, coincidence. Would you like to come? You're more
than welcome. Might give your article a good angle.'

He's right about that. Miller sipped her coffee, cold now, and grimaced.

'Fresh cup?' he asked.

'I'm fine, thanks.'

'I really can't believe I'm sitting here talking to you. I've read a lot about what happened in Castle Bay, of course. I can't believe you went through all of that. Came into such close contact with someone like that.' He leaned forward, wanting more.

Miller remembered Ngaire's warning: Make sure it's you asking the questions – not him.

'Do you write a lot of these types of stories?' he asked, obviously not noticing Miller's discomfort. 'Your Castle Bay one was great, by the way. I have it in a scrapbook.'

'Sometimes. Not really,' Miller answered, happy at the slight change of subject. 'I'm actually doing an article on Cassie Hughes, she's the daughter of—'

'Margaret Hughes.' He stared at the ceiling and began to recite. 'Murdered, body discovered last year, here in Lentford, but was killed fourteen years ago. Karl Taylor's wanted in connection to her murder and is still at large.' He nodded. 'Wow, Margaret Hughes's daughter. She must be... early twenties now?'

Miller nodded, fearing she shouldn't have mentioned Cassie, but she'd been desperate to move the subject away from Castle Bay.

'She doesn't live in Lentford, does she?' Logan asked. 'I know her family's from Tauranga.'

'Just moved here,' Miller said. She needed a break. 'Can I use the toilet?'

'Sure,' he said, jumping up. 'Down the hall on the left just before you get to the kitchen.'

Miller took herself off to the toilet and locked herself in. The small room was adorned in pale-blue wallpaper with a white floral pattern. There was a toilet in the far corner and a bidet.

Who the hell puts a bidet in their house these days? There was a basin to the right with a large expanse of gleaming white bench top. On top was an array of soaps, moisturisers and even perfume. She checked the cupboard underneath: nothing but toilet paper. She splashed her face with water and picked up a neatly folded rose-coloured hand towel from the pile and pressed it against her face.

Time to get out of here. She put the towel into the cane basket, thinking it was more like a restaurant or hotel than a home. Her mind was already working the angles of this article. She would be hard-pressed not to make Logan out as crazy, damaged from his sister's murder all those years ago. Maybe she could take the sympathetic angle. Then she could leave it up to the good folk of Lentford to judge – and judge, they would.

When she walked back into the lounge, Logan looked up, eyes wide, but still that same smile.

'What are you doing?' she demanded.

He slid back in his seat, away from her open satchel. 'Sorry, nothing. Your phone was ringing. Sorry.' He jammed a thumb in his mouth, and she could hear teeth grinding against nail.

'It's fine. Look, I'd better go.'

'Do you have everything you need?'

'Yes, for now.' Miller picked up her satchel, glancing in to make sure everything was there.

'And you'll do the tour next week? I can pick you up if you want.'

'That's okay. I can just meet you here.' There was no way she wanted him knowing where she lived.

They said their goodbyes, and Miller waved to Beatrice who was still in the front garden with Lou. Beatrice waved back, walking over, removing a pair of floral gardening gloves and wiping a smudge of dirt from her linen shorts. 'How did it go?'

she asked.

'Great,' Miller said.

'Oh good.' Beatrice smiled. 'I know he can be a bit... odd. William didn't want him to do it.'

Miller wondered what 'it' was, the interview or the tours. Probably both.

'He has a real passion for this true crime. I would hope you would show him in a positive light.' It wasn't a question. 'I know it seems a bit strange, but there's a whole community of people who take a real interest in this kind of thing. I'd hate to think the article would make him a laughing stock.'

'No, I would never do that,' Miller assured her. 'This is a serious topic. I'm just not sure how the rest of the community will take it.'

Beatrice nodded. 'I understand. Thank you, Miller. He said he was going to ask you to come on his trial tour. I wasn't sure if you'd be keen, but Logan was adamant he was going to ask you. He thinks you're a bit of a kindred spirit because of, you know, what happened in Castle Bay.' Her eyes flicked to Miller's scar and back.

How easy it would be if I'd got the scar in Castle Bay. Miller nodded. There was no way she thought of herself and Logan Dodds as kindred spirits. The way he idolised these monsters was as if he endorsed what they did.

'I'd better get back to the garden,' Beatrice said. 'It's a full-time job, and in this weather, we have to keep an eye on all the new plantings so the poor things don't perish in this dreadful heat.'

Miller got in the car and pulled out her phone. No missed calls. No texts. Logan had been lying. Of course he was. Her wallet, keys and notebooks were all still there. What had he been looking for?

Chapter 18

Later that afternoon Cody grabbed Miller's hand and dragged her from her desk. 'Come on, you'll need a drink after today.'

She'd given Cody and Ngaire a broad account of Logan and her interview with him that morning. 'Okay, okay,' she laughed, grabbing her bag and joining the others.

Ngaire, Cody, Hine, Eric and Miller all walked down to the Royal on the corner of the main street. As they reached the pub Miller saw Ash and Zach coming in the opposite direction. Ash was still in uniform, Zach loping along beside her, taller than his mother already. As they filed past, Ngaire and Hine both greeted Ash and she smiled and said hello back, asking how the paper was going to be put out if they were all at the pub.

'Hey, Ash,' Miller said, uncertain how Ash would be after their encounter at the police station that morning. She slowed, unsure if she should stop.

Ash gave her a tight smile but kept on walking. Miller stood in the middle of the street and gave Zach a wave as he turned around, looking as confused as she felt.

Miller had never divulged to the others that she didn't drink. She usually ordered soda water with a wedge of lime to make it look like she was drinking gin or vodka. Yes, she could've told them. Yes, she could've said she didn't drink and made up a reason. But she hadn't. And now, six months on, it seemed too late to offer one up.

They ordered drinks from Johnno at the bar. Miller saw his eyes light up as Hine walked over to him. Sitting at their table Miller and the other three looked on as Hine giggled, flicking her long black hair and reaching forward to touch Johnno's hand.

'Watch out, Hine,' Miller said, noticing the hungry look in Johnno's eyes.

'More like watch out Johnno,' Cody said, and Miller joined in the laughter.

'So, Miller,' Eric said when Hine had settled herself at the table after telling them all she was staying on for a drink with Johnno that night. 'I got an interesting email today. From a Randall Hopkins.'

Miller stared at Eric, unable to speak. *This is it.*

Ngaire, Cody and Hine turned to Miller. 'Who's Randall Hopkins?' Hine asked.

'No one important,' Miller said. 'Believe me.'

'Oh, I beg to differ.' Eric took a sip of his beer, sat back and folded his arms.

Miller sat still. He was enjoying this. She should just go. But part of her knew it was going to come out one day. *Might as well be now. Get it over with.* She regretted not being honest with Ngaire from the start. She should've told her everything and now she was going to find out from this greasy leech. She bowed her head as Eric started talking.

'So, Randall Hopkins is at *First Look* magazine where our Miller here used to work.'

Miller could feel the others' gazes on her. She felt her jaw clench and a tight band compress her forehead. She tried to un-clench her jaw, but it felt wired shut.

'Randall told me that Miller, who was their senior writer up until a few months back, was tasked with interviewing Prisha Anand, the lawyer defending Cherie Banks.'

Eric didn't need to explain. Everyone in New Zealand knew Prisha Anand and her client Cherie Banks. Prisha had saved Cherie from a hefty prison sentence after she killed her husband. Prisha had woven together a case that told the story of an abused woman, frightened for her life, trapped in a marriage, for the last ten years totally cut off from friends and family. A lot of the trial had been aired on television and it was widely covered in the media. Prisha soon became the face of domestic violence in New Zealand, standing up for those who couldn't stand up for themselves, taking on the case pro bono as Cherie didn't have a cent to her name.

'Now, we all know an interview with Prisha Anand would've been the hottest ticket for any kind of media. And she agreed to grant one interview at the end of the trial.' Eric waved a hand at Miller. 'Miller, however, chose the night before the interview to get wasted. She turned up to the interview at Ms Anand's office hungover, smelling of booze, and it's likely she was probably still drunk. Ms Anand, defender of the downtrodden, took one look at her and turfed her out of the office. She ended up giving the interview to *First Look's* competition.' Eric clapped his hands together as if he'd just offered up a punchline.

Miller scraped her chair across the ground. She couldn't look at anyone, especially not Ngaire. She heard Cody comforting her, reaching out to her; she heard Hine telling Eric to shut his mouth, but she grabbed her bag and ran out of the Royal, Eric's cackling loud in her ears.

'Miller!' Ngaire was right behind her and stopped her in the car park.

Miller stopped but didn't turn around. 'I'm sorry,' she said. And she was, about all of it.

Ngaire came to her side. 'Come on. Let's walk back to our cars.'

They dodged kids in the car park playing with a half-deflated football, packets of chips and cans of Coke in their hands, waiting on their parents, and walked down the main street.

'There's more. No doubt Eric's letting the others know – and anyone else that's listening.'

'Yeah, he was warming up when I followed you out.' Ngaire winced. 'He's an idiot, Miller.'

'I know he is, but nothing he said back there was untrue. I was still drunk when I went to Prisha's office that day, but I thought I had it under control.' She shook her head. 'Nothing about that time in my life was under control.'

They reached their cars parked out the front of the *Leader* office. Most of the main street was empty, the shops long closed, no need to hang around in town on a Monday night unless you were at the Royal or picking up takeaways for dinner. Ngaire pulled her vape from her bag and clicked it on.

'That night, after the non-interview, I hadn't even told my editor, George,' Miller said. 'I was a coward and was waiting to do it the next day. My flatmate, Nat, had her going-away party. Apart from my slip-up the night before the interview – and boy, was it a slip-up – I'd been sober for almost a year. Anyway, I drowned my sorrows that night at Nat's party and ended up driving home drunk. I took a corner too fast. Overcorrected and collided with a tree. I don't remember much, woke up in the emergency department of Auckland hospital a few hours later. I suffered a concussion and abrasions to my hands and face, one particularly nasty one that left me with this.' She touched her scar. 'My permanent reminder. No one else was hurt, thank god. I couldn't cover up the fact I was in the hospital, but back at work I lied to my editor. I admitted fault with the Anand

interview, apologised profusely but also told him the car accident wasn't my fault.

'Randall made it his business to find out. He told George, my
editor, along with his uncle who owns *First Look* and a bunch of
other papers and magazines, what had happened, and George
had no choice but to fire me – and so he should've. I was dis-
honest and unprofessional. I was charged with careless driving. I lost my licence for six months and was given community
service. I go out to Shady Oaks Rest Home once a week or so to
help with the residents there.'

Miller turned to look at Ngaire who was looking at her, a sad
smile on her face.

'I understand that you'll need to fire me,' Miller said.

'Why?'

'For not being straight with you.'

'I knew all of this, Miller.' Ngaire turned her vape off and
threw it into her bag.

Miller stared, mouth open.

'What? You didn't think I'd ring George and suss you out?'

'Of course, I did. I just wasn't sure what George told you,'
Miller said, still shocked.

'He told me what happened. He was on your side. Said you
were a good journalist but that you needed to get your head
straight. He thought this would be a good job to enable you to
do that. And from what I've seen, you've worked your arse off
ever since you got here. You've run circles around Eric, which
he hates. You know that, right? The only reason he bothered ex-
posing you was because he feels so threatened by you. There's
no doubt what you did was stupid. But I'm one for second
chances, and sometimes third and fourth.'

Miller stared at the ground, blinking rapidly, knowing
Ngaire wouldn't deal with tears. She remembered George's

exact words when he fired her: 'I believe in you, as a journalist, you've written great pieces, but there are others like you out there, Miller, others that have the ambition, the talent, minus the baggage. When the time comes, I'll give you a good reference.'

'Go home, Miller. I'll see you tomorrow,' Ngaire said. She unlocked her car. 'Jesus, I could do with a cigarette.'

'I've been sober ever since,' Miller blurted out. She needed Ngaire to know. 'Day...' She calculated in her head. 'Day one hundred and seventy-six.' She could hear the desperation in her voice.

Ngaire nodded, winked at her and climbed in her car, leaving Miller alone on the main street. She liked Lentford. It felt like home. She had friends, a decent job, but there was still the fact she was here, a journalist in a small country town, because she stuffed up. She wasn't reporting on big life-changing issues, interviewing people who were changing the world or making it a better place – all because she'd made that mistake. This was on her. She refused to wallow in pity, but the shroud of guilt she wore daily – for the mistakes she'd made, the trust she'd lost, the disappointment she'd caused – almost brought her to her knees.

Chapter 19

On Tuesday morning, when Miller couldn't stand Eric's snide comments or Hine and Cody's looks of pity any longer, she left the office and walked north up Victoria Street. She'd talked to Nat on the phone the night before when she got home, telling her her secret was out. Nat, Kahu and Ash were the only people who knew everything about her: her struggle to get over her mother's death, Castle Bay, losing her job, the accident.

'What's the worst that can happen?' Nat asked.

'I don't know,' Miller said sulkily.

'It sounds like you have some good mates there, Mills. Maybe it's a good thing they know. Ever thought of that?'

Nat was always one for putting things into perspective. They went on to talk of Nat's job at the hospital and her new boyfriend, and half an hour later Miller got off the phone feeling better. Part of her wished she was sitting outside on Ash's patio, Zach's music blaring from his room, telling her what had happened. But she hadn't seen or spoken to her since yesterday. Miller didn't like how they'd left it. She knew Ash was pissed at her but didn't know what else to do, other than completely clear the air and tell her what was happening with the letters – then she'd understand. But she couldn't. It wasn't her place to tell.

Ngaire had made it clear that morning that it was business as usual. Hine and Cody nodded solemnly, glancing at Miller, and Eric had snorted and turned back to his computer. Ngaire had told Miller she'd have to let it blow over. 'Unfortunately, Eric's not going anywhere anytime soon, and I want you to hang around for as long as possible. So just deal with it, okay?'

Nothing like a pep talk from Ngaire. Miller could handle Eric, but Hine and Cody were her friends – and as much as she wanted, no matter what Nat said, she couldn't get past the fact they now knew her dirty secrets.

Miller slowed as she passed the village green, the expanse of grass in the main street between the library and the fish and chip shop that ran down towards the river. Three men in high-vis jackets were putting up a Christmas tree. The deep green of the fake ten-foot tree looked unnatural against the yellowing grass of the village green and the long grass that grew along the banks of the river. She carried on, noting the posters in shop windows advertising the Christmas parade next weekend.

Miller couldn't believe it was only thirteen days till Christmas. Maybe she could just let it slide this year. She wasn't sure what Kahu was up to. He'd mentioned visiting family in Gisborne. Li wouldn't be around, and she wasn't sure what Cody and Hine were up to. Nat had invited her down to Wellington. She'd said she'd think about it but preferred to sit at home and... drink, she told herself honestly. That's what she really wanted to do.

'For fuck's sake, Miller,' she muttered.

Her phone was constantly dinging, Twitter alerts related to him, who had now been dubbed the Scarf Killer. Kahu had held a press conference that morning. He'd said the two murders appeared to be related – which was obvious to everyone, they'd just been waiting for the cops to confirm it. The women, both living on their own, had been strangled in their homes.

There was a call to the public for help. They needed to know the women's movements before they were killed. Family and friends were asked to come forward. Neighbours had been questioned, asked to remember the smallest of details. No mention was made of the letters that had been sent to Miller, for now, of which she was glad. She was happy to write the news; she hated being the news.

There were new people in town. Some looked lost, consulted phones. Others stood in groups of two or three, well dressed, ready to film a piece for tonight's news. Little Lentford had been cast into the spotlight – just as Castle Bay had been – and this time Miller was on the inside. This was her town now. A town being held under the microscope by the rest of the country, questioning who could have done such a thing. There was talk around town, of course there was. In the pub, the cafe, over the counter when buying groceries, whispered gossip, but that's all it was for now – gossip.

She passed two women standing in the middle of the foot-path and walked around them, dodging a toddler twirling in circles, biscuit in hand, and a pushchair.

'Strangled in their bedrooms, I hear,' one woman said. 'What are we supposed to do? Who's next?'

'They've both been single women, younger than us. I would guess we're safe,' the other said, grabbing the stumbling toddler by the hand and smiling at Miller.

'I say lock up your house.'

'God, when was the last time any of us did that?'

Miller crossed the road when she saw Cassie's townhouse on the right, just after the bridge. The buildings were beige-coloured plaster, somewhat plain and ugly, but she knew these were the backs of the houses. Their fronts looked out onto the river. She opened the black wrought-iron gate to number four and walked into a small courtyard, a suntrap that made her already perspiring body prickle. *Sweat on top of sweat.* On either side leading up to the door were gardens filled with river stones and succulents, thriving in this weather, and Miller wondered how they handled the cold and damp Waikato winters. The door was slightly ajar, and through the small crack she could see through to the lounge and dining area and out onto the small balcony.

She raised a hand to knock but stopped. The shouting from behind the door sounded as though someone was standing right on the other side. The other voice, quieter, sad, sounded slightly further away. Cassie?

'There's no point to it, Cassie!' the voice by the door shouted.

'Well, I think there is. It can't hurt. I get my story out there. People are interested in me.'

'You sound really up yourself.'

'Tiff!' Cassie sounded hurt. 'I just meant I know people are interested in my story. I don't really want people knowing about me, but if it helps people to start thinking about Mum again...' The voice faded away and Miller couldn't hear any more.

She was about to knock when the other voice said, 'Why her? This Miller Hatcher?'

'Tiff, I've told you, you don't need to be jealous.'

'I'm not fucking jealous. Do what you fuckin' want. You always do. I thought this was supposed to be a relationship!'

Miller heard a door slam inside the apartment. She looked down at her watch, waiting as the second-hand did a full rotation then took a deep breath, knowing this interview couldn't possibly go smoothly, and knocked.

After about thirty seconds she knocked again. After waiting some more she thought about leaving, but then Cassie opened the door. Her eyes were red-rimmed and one cheek was a deep red.

'Hi, Cassie,' Miller said. 'Are you okay?'

'Hi, Miller. I'm fine. Come on in.' Cassie's voice trembled as she tried to sound cheery. 'Take a seat. I'm just fighting a bit of hay fever at the moment.' She grabbed a tissue from the coffee table. 'It's the season for it.' She laughed, but it sounded hollow and she stopped abruptly.

Miller knew not to push it. She didn't even know this woman, but felt an instinct to protect her.

'Can I get you a coffee?'

'Something cold would be great if you've got it.' Miller sat in an armchair.

'I guess it's a bit early for a beer,' Cassie said going into the kitchen which was separated from the lounge dining area by a vast island made of white marble, shot through with grey. 'Juice or water?'

'Water would be great, thanks.'

'Have you been here for long?' Miller asked, taking in the new furniture and bare walls.

'No, not long at all. Only moved in the beginning of last week. The place came fully furnished.'

Miller turned as a door opened from what she guessed was a bedroom. The woman, leaning against the door frame, looked to be just as tall as Miller, in her mid-twenties, auburn hair tied up in a high ponytail. She wore a denim miniskirt and a white singlet over a hot-pink bra. She walked over to Miller and stood over her, so close Miller couldn't rise. 'I'm Tiff, Cassie's girlfriend.' It was said like a challenge.

'Nice to meet you,' Miller said smiling, taking the glass of water from Cassie.

The two women sat on the black leather couch opposite Miller. Miller took a sip and placed the glass on the coffee table between them.

'So, Cassie. I'm not sure how you want to do this. I know it's important for you to get the Karl Taylor message out there, help jog people's memories, but I'd also like to know how you're doing, what you're up to, what life was like for you back when your mum disappeared. I understand you've never given an interview before?'

Tiff and Cassie were sitting so close they appeared joined. Tiff put her hand on Cassie's knee. Miller saw Cassie visibly stiffen and then relax.

Miller took out her notebook and iPhone. 'Okay if I record this?'

Cassie nodded. 'There was heaps of media attention when Mum went missing. Dad did all that stuff – talking to the TV people and newspapers. He didn't want us girls – I have a sister – involved in any of that. He tried his best to protect us from it all. I'm not sure how much more harm it could've done us, though. It was a real horrible time. Even when everything died down and the police weren't getting anywhere with finding Mum, we'd get women's mags pestering us with blood money to get our story. Dad always said no.'

'Can you give me some background on your mother's disappearance? You were quite young at the time. But I guess you know the details?'

'I was ten,' Cassie said, her voice quiet. She cleared her throat. 'It was Saturday morning, like normal. She'd been into town to get groceries and go to the post office. We lived on a lifestyle block about half an hour out of the city, towards Katikati. She was sending Emily, our cousin, a birthday present. She was turning five and Mum had bought her a new lunch box and drink bottle for school.' Cassie looked up with a sad smile. 'Sorry, not relevant. Funny, the things you remember.'

Tiff got up, went to the fridge and brought back two beers. 'Never too early for a beer, eh Cass?'

Cassie left her beer untouched on the coffee table and continued talking as Tiff drank. 'She got home about eleven and said she was going down to the orchard. There was a farm-gate kind of shop about two k down the road. We lived on a quiet country road, so it was a nice walk, and Mum liked buying our fruit and veg from the McAllisters. Said it was fresher and cheaper.'

Miller knew stalling when she saw it. She could tell Cassie didn't want to get to the next part.

'And that's the last time I saw her. We know from the shop owner she was there. She didn't talk to anyone else but him; just bought what she needed and left.'

'Can you tell me what happened after that?'

'It was a nightmare. There weren't really any suspects. There was nothing. She'd vanished. Dad didn't tell us what was happening at the start. When Mum didn't come home after a couple of hours, he rang the McAllisters. They said she'd been and gone hours earlier. He called all her friends. Then by dinner time he called the police. They said there wasn't anything they could do so early on. A neighbour looked after us while Dad and a few of his mates went looking for her. The place we lived, there were small farms, orchards, a bit of bush. I remember going to bed that night feeling confused, but more than that, scared. And I stayed scared and confused for years.'

'And how did Karl Taylor's name come to the police's attention?'

'You know Mum's body was found last year – at the old dairy factory here?'

Miller nodded, remembering what Ash had told her the other night. It had been big news at the time. A cold case that was on its way to being solved. But over a year later, there was still nothing.

'There wasn't much... left... of Mum,' Cassie said, gulping a sip of her beer. 'But they found her watch and bangle with the old Roman coins. Two of the three coins were missing from the bangle.' She held up her right arm, the coins running together to create a tinny jingle. 'Mum found these bangles at a gypsy fair one year. My younger sister Fiona thought they were ugly, so Mum bought one for me and one for her. We wore them all the time. They're not expensive, just tatty rubbish, but meant a lot to us.

'Anyway, it was reported on the news over a few weeks. The police asking for the public's help, showing a picture of Mum and a photo of the coin they found, saying where she was last seen, where she was found. There were two coins missing and I think the police hoped someone would come across them. I think they thought he – Karl Taylor – had taken them as a souvenir. There wasn't a lot to go on, but they hoped someone could help. A guy came forward, Gary Vogel. I've never met him. He's a builder in Tauranga and had a labourer called Karl Taylor. Karl had been working for him for a few months. Gary told police he was hard-working, kept to himself. He and the other guys didn't really get to know him. Gary remembered Karl had taken the work truck on the Saturday Mum went missing, to clean up at a job they'd finished the day before. Our next-door neighbours had had an extension done. Karl was supposed to get the truck back to Gary by noon, but he never showed. He tried contacting him on his mobile but he never answered.'

'Gary did well to remember all this, fourteen years after the fact,' Miller said.

'That's what we all thought. But he told the police he remembered as he needed the truck to start a new job on another site that afternoon. He almost missed out on the job because of it.

Karl turned up early the next morning with the truck, apologising, saying his mum was sick. He'd headed straight to Hamilton to visit her. Gary let it slide and didn't think much more of it.'

Cassie took a deep breath. Miller could tell this was hard on her. She glanced over to Tiff who was staring back at her. *What is her problem?*

'The next weekend Gary was cleaning his truck and came across an old coin. He had no idea where it had come from. He said he asked Karl if it was his, but he said he'd never seen it. Remembered he got a bit jumpy about it, but he had no idea then why he would. Karl Taylor resigned soon after that. Gary held onto the coin all that time, quite liked it, became a lucky charm.' Cassie shivered. 'When Mum's case came on TV, showing the coin, he put two and two together. The coin was the same, quite distinctive, not any old coin.'

She showed Miller one of the coins on her bangle, the bust of a long-haired man in profile wearing an elaborate headpiece. 'And the dates matched. So he went to the police and gave them Karl Taylor's name. He worked with a police sketch artist and got an identikit picture done. Have you seen it?'

Miller nodded. To her it looked like every second guy who passed her by. There was nothing exceptional at all about him. Average height, brown eyes, longish brown hair, unshaven. And this was fourteen years ago. Who knew what he looked like now. 'How about photos of him?'

'Nothing,' Cassie said. 'No family was ever tracked down and Gary said Karl never joined in with the others, didn't go out for a beer after work, kept to himself. I don't know about the identikit. No one's come forward yet.' Cassie sounded as if she expected someone to do so any day.

'The police have looked into all the Karl Taylors, searching by approximate age. He was thought to be mid-thirties at the time. They looked at everything. But there was nothing. Gary paid his casual labourers in cash. There was no bank account in his name. He didn't have a car. He was living completely off the grid. He's a ghost. Police were working off last known sightings and interviewing those whose houses he'd worked on. But he was a loner. Quiet. No one ever really knew him.'

Cassie buried her head in her hands. 'Shit, sorry, but this all seems so fucking hopeless as I tell it to you. A needle-in-a-haystack. They've told me it's likely Karl Taylor is an alias, but...'

The tears came now. Miller knew that if Cassie admitted Karl Taylor was an alias, all she'd done in searching for her mum was a waste of time.

'You've read the articles? About how she died?' Cassie asked, dabbing her eyes with a tissue.

Miller winced. When the skeletal remains had been found last year, police reported that Margaret Hughes had been stabbed multiple times.

'A forensic anthropologist found marks on her rib cage that were consistent with a double-bladed knife. I don't know if he killed her back home by the orchard, or if he took her and drove her all the way here to Lentford and stabbed her out by the dairy factory. Did she fight? Is that how the coin came loose from her bangle? Was she still alive when he took her in the truck? Did she remove one of the coins, leave it so someone would find it?'

Cassie was getting hysterical now. She got up and started pacing the room, stopping and looking out to the river. 'Or did she fight him, and lose the coin then?' She pinched her running nose. 'Do you know what I overheard one of the detectives saying to his partner after they'd talked to Dad? He said, "He certainly knew what he was doing." He said it with a hint of awe in his voice, as if he was impressed with him, what he'd done. The perfect crime.'

Cassie started crying again, this time heaving sobs.

'You have to leave. Now.' Tiff put her beer bottle down on the coffee table harder than necessary.

'It's okay, Tiff. It's just talking about it all. What he did to her. How hopeless this all seems. It's a bit emotional. But really, I'm fine.'

'No, you're not, Cass.' Cassie came and sat down by Tiff who put a protective arm around her, which Cassie snuggled into. 'She's upset you. Look, you can't even pull yourself together.'

Cassie looked at Miller and then to Tiff.

Tiff nodded, persuading. Cassie nodded back.

Tiff got up from the couch, clearly expecting Miller to do the same.

'Cassie, please call me if you'd like to continue the interview,' Miller said, standing up. 'We've still got a lot to talk about and I'm still very keen to do this article for you. I think I can help you.'

Tiff stepped in front of Miller to block her view of Cassie, which Miller took as her cue to leave. She walked to the door and turned. Cassie's head was in her hands, Tiff stroking her back, whispering calming words, but Tiff's eyes were on her. She mouthed, 'Get. Out.'

Chapter 20

At the Royal that night, Cassie leaned against the bar, gazing past the customers chatting, playing pool and darts, blocking out the buzz of conversation around her. She was shattered after her interview with Miller, although it had felt more like a counselling session at The Oaks in the end. She'd felt guilty when Tiff had asked Miller to leave and told her so when she had left. Of course there was a fight; Tiff saying Miller was taking advantage of her situation, trying to get a good story, and Cassie denying it, saying it was her idea. They'd made up, as they always did, before Cassie came into work that afternoon. Neither of them mentioned Tiff hitting Cassie. There was no apology, and Cassie didn't expect one. But at least things were back to normal now. She knew Tiff had done it out of frustration. Tiff didn't trust Miller. Cassie had texted Miller an hour ago, apologising and suggesting they catch up again, maybe at the Royal, away from Tiff who was just being protective.

She stood up straight, grabbed a cloth and started wiping the bar, watching the man who had just walked in, uncertain, eyes shifting left and right, taking in his surroundings. He was in his early forties, pudgy, dressed in chinos and a short-sleeved shirt; a sheen of sweat glowed on his forehead. After surveying the room, he headed towards her, the tip of his thumb in his mouth, chewing on a nail. First date, maybe?

He took a seat at the bar, picked up a coaster, put it down then started picking at his cuticles which were already red: one finger was stained with blood. He caught her staring and took a paper napkin from a pile on the bar and pressed it to his finger.

'What can I get you?' Cassie asked.

He looked at the selection the taps offered. 'Beer, please. Any of those is fine.' He waved at the taps in front of him not meeting her eye, and his thumb and forefinger joined and slowly circled.

'Sure thing.' Cassie poured the beer and placed it in front of him. 'How's your day been?'

He finally looked up at her. His dark eyes squinting, as if he couldn't see her properly. 'You're Cassie Hughes, aren't you?'

'Yes. Do I know you?' Apart from Johnno and Tane, plus Tiff and Miller, and some of the regulars, she didn't really know anyone in Lentford.

'No. I'm Logan Dodds.' He took a sip of beer, licking the foam from his lips.

'What do you do around here, Logan?' Cassie asked, polite, nothing else to do.

'I run a true crime enthusiasts' group and tour.'

'Oh,' Cassie said. *Weird.*

Logan took another sip. 'The tours are a new thing. We've had quite a few murders around the district. People who haven't lived here for long, like you, are surprised to hear that. But there are things like this going on everywhere, all over New Zealand. Even in the sleepy little towns like this.' He flashed her a lopsided grin.

When she said nothing, he continued. 'So you probably wonder what happens on the tour?'

Cassie didn't answer, picked up her cloth and moved further down the bar.

Logan picked up his beer and followed her down. 'I take a van full of people around different sites. There have been a few murders in town. Obviously, the ones that have just happened. You know. By the Scarf Killer.'

Of course I know. It's the talk of the fucking town.

'I won't cover those, though, as no one's been arrested. But there are some historical ones. My sister included.'

Cassie stopped wiping the bar, pity replacing her anger. 'Your sister was murdered?'

'Maybe I should've opened with that,' he mumbled.

'What do you mean "opened with that?"' Cassie asked, pity melting away to confusion.

He scratched his head and flakes of dandruff floated down to the bar. 'I like you,' he said. It came out as a whisper.

'You don't know me,' Cassie frowned. 'Excuse me.' She moved down the bar to serve a customer.

When she was done, Logan came back to her, picking up the conversation where they'd left it.

'And that's why I thought it would be polite to ask, or at least let you know, that your mother's murder will be featured on my tour.' He took the napkin off his finger, inspected it and left it on the bar.

Cassie couldn't speak. *Who the hell is this freak?*

'Now, I know no one has been arrested yet. But the whole Karl Taylor thing is fascinating. The police are positive he's the one who did it yet can't find him.' He smiled at her.

'You can't do this.'

'Yes I can.' He finished his beer. 'Don't be mad.'

'Mad? This is disgusting,' she hissed. 'What you're doing is sick.'

'I don't think so. That's just your opinion.'

'You have no right to use my mother's death for your own

ends!'

'Okay. I'm sorry.' He held up a hand as if surrendering. 'I kind of forget that not everyone thinks like I do.'

You reckon? 'Can I get you anything else?' Cassie asked, hoping he'd say no and leave.

'Another beer please, Cassie. And I really am sorry.' He made proper eye contact for the first time.

Cassie poured him another beer, wishing there were a few more customers so she could keep herself busy, away from him.

He sat in silence, beer in hand, taking small sips. The Royal closed at ten on Tuesdays. *Fifteen minutes to go.* She eyed the clock on the wall, willing the hands to move faster. She could feel him staring, but when she looked back at him, he averted his eyes.

Tane came out of the kitchen. 'Time to get this crowd moving.' He poured himself a handle of beer and moved around the tables, chatting and laughing, letting people know to finish up.

Looking straight ahead at the line of bottles behind the bar, Logan said, 'Have you got a boyfriend?'

Cassie was sure, even in the dim light, that he was blushing. She would normally just say no and move on, but this guy bugged her. 'No. Actually I have a girlfriend.' She waited for the reaction. Sure there was going to be one. She enjoyed the look of confusion on his face.

'Sorry, girlfriend? You don't look like one of those.'

'One of what, exactly?' Cassie folded her arms to stop herself from leaning across the bar and slapping him.

'You've been through so much with your mum, and now to have to carry this burden as well.' He rubbed his temples. 'I don't normally drink. It's gone to my head a bit.'

Cassie looked over his shoulder as Tiff marched across the bar.

'Hi,' Tiff said and then turned to Logan. 'What the fuck are you doing here?'

'Tiff,' Cassie warned.

'No,' Tiff said, turning to Cassie. 'This guy came knocking on our door an hour ago looking for you. I told him you were here. Then asked what he wanted. Told me it was none of my business.'

Logan was staring at Tiff, who turned on him. 'Getting a good look are ya, perv? Why did you want to see Cassie?'

'It's none of your business,' Logan said, draining his beer and standing up.

Cassie rolled her eyes and leaned across the bar, put a hand either side of Tiff's face and kissed her. She watched from the corner of her eye as Logan, eager to get as far away from them as possible, stumbled from his chair.

Cassie shouted to his retreating back, 'Don't bother coming in here again!'

Tane came around her side of the bar with a stack of empties, and Cassie cringed at her words and blatant show of affection for Tiff.

'Not quite the farewell I expect you to give our customers, Cassie,' he said.

'Shit, sorry, Tane.' She could feel herself blushing.

Tane laughed, an abrupt cracking sound. 'No worries. Haven't seen Logan Dodds out in a while. His folks come in here for dinner once a week. He's a bit of an odd one. Off you go. I've seen Johnno sneak upstairs. I'll drag him down to finish up here.'

'Thanks, Tane.' Cassie rounded the bar to Tiff.

'What the hell was that about?' Tiff asked.

'Some freak. This one was totally out of the box.'

Tiff stared, waiting for more, but Cassie couldn't be bothered.

Knowing Tiff, she'd hunt him down and beat the shit out of him. 'Come on, let's get out of here.'

They got burgers from the fish and chip shop. Cassie found herself looking for Logan. As hard as she tried not to be bothered by him, she was. He was fascinated with her mother, with her. He gave her the creeps. No, it was more than that. He *scared* her. He'd left her feeling exposed.

Chapter 21

Miller sat in the *Leader*'s toilet again, latex gloves on, shaking hands opening the letter. She felt sweat bead on her upper lip and licked it away. She knew what it was and couldn't believe there was another body. This town was too small to take another murder. How soon would it be until she knew one of the victims?

Hi Miller

I guess this letter gave you a bit of a fright. I bet you thought there was another one. But I think you and that Detective Parata know there's a pattern by now. You're not stupid, Miller. That's what I like about you. Why I chose you to tell my story.

Everyone used to think I was stupid. But I'm not. Look at how I've got away with this — two murders in a town where everyone knows everyone and those hotshot cops still have no idea. That's the good thing about a small town. I know for a fact the cops have nothing. People talk.

I can't wait to sit down and tell you my story.

Say hi to Detective Parata for me. I see you're good friends. But everyone knows that, after you mentioned him in your Castle Bay article. Is he just a

Miller lifted her hand to her face, felt her jaw clenching as the letter fell onto her lap. She forced herself to unclench her jaw. It was a bad habit and one she couldn't rid herself of. It had started a week after the accident. She'd woken with an aching jaw and a headache as bad as if she'd been out drinking all night. The doctor told her it could be a response to the accident and said it should sort itself out, but it hadn't. She'd tried hypnosis and herbal remedies but nothing had worked. Her doctor said it was likely due to stress or anxiety and asked how she'd coped with stress in the past. She hadn't mentioned the alcohol or pulling out her hair in moments of stress, which the clenched jaw had seemed to replace. She could do without both.

She felt sick. She took deep breaths of muggy air. It wasn't working, so she grabbed her satchel and the letter and stumbled out into the office. She grabbed a large envelope from Hine's stash and pushed the letter into it, and walked out, telling Hine she'd be back in ten.

Standing outside she bent over and took deep breaths, ignoring stares from passers-by.

'Miller?' She felt a warm hand on her back.

'Kahu.' She stood, giving herself a head rush. 'I'm fine,' she answered his unasked question.

'No, you're not. C'mon, I'm doing the coffee run this morning.'

Before they stepped into the Kowhai, Miller, one glove on, held the letter for Kahu to read. He finished it and she put it back into the envelope and handed it over. She peeled the glove from her sweaty hand and pushed it into her satchel.

They placed their order and sat down at a table in the corner.

Len was looking in her direction, their eyes met, and he

smiled. Li was working the coffee machine and had given her a quick wave. People came and went ordering coffee to go, sitting down for breakfast. The place was small and she picked up chatter – most was about Emmeline and Tamara.

'Who could it possibly be?'

'Heard that it's likely someone in Lentford.'

'Got the big guns here, but they seem to be doing fuck all while this nutter picks off women.'

Len came over with their coffees. 'Thanks, Len,' Miller said. He lingered and his eyes darted to the envelope. When nobody said anything else to him, he took his leave.

'He knows me, Kahu. Knows us.'

Kahu grunted. 'Everyone knows me. I'm plastered over the news almost every night telling the public in a different way each time that we have fuck all.'

'Have you got anything? Anything you can tell me about? You don't have to tell me if you don't want to,' she rushed to say, not wanting Kahu to think she was being nosy. *But that's exactly what I'm being.*

'You're a pretty big part of this, Miller. I don't mind sharing, and I know you won't blab.' It was said as a warning. 'We found skin under Emmeline's nails. She scratched the son of a bitch. Put up a fight. Waiting on DNA now. But that'll take a while.'

Miller looked around the cafe again, automatically looking at each male, checking for scratches. Then realised how silly that was.

'How about the paper he writes my letters on. Anything?'

'They finished up on that yesterday. Went through the list. No leads. Everyone's been looked into. No red flags.'

'Trace? From either of the women?'

'There was a bit. Not a lot. He was pretty clean. Fibres on Tamara's nightgown look to belong to some kind of fleece clothing.'

'That's good,' Miller said, hopeful.

'It helps to build a case when we do catch him,' Kahu agreed. 'But at the moment stuff like that isn't helping us catch him.'

'Do you have any suspects at all?'

'There's been a couple. But because of the letters to you, it's really just bringing them in for questioning. Tamara's ex, Emmeline's new boyfriend. Friends.'

They both sat quietly. Each with their own thoughts.

'And you still don't know how he gets in?'

'No sign of a break-in at Tamara's or Emmeline's. Which makes us think both of them knew him. We're looking into who they know, who they might've come across, some way the two women are connected. And there's always the chance... In this weather people are leaving windows open. It could just be a case of him climbing in.'

'I know they'd met before, Emmeline and Tamara,' Miller said, 'but that might be completely random. Maybe it's just the fact they live alone.'

Kahu sighed. 'Yeah.'

Len walked over to clear their empty coffee cups and Kahu ordered coffees for those back at the station. 'Getting anywhere on the murders, Detective?' Len asked, glancing at Miller. No wink today.

'Getting there,' Kahu said.

'Really tragic,' Len said, 'especially in such a small town.'

Miller thought the murder of anyone, big city, small town, was pretty tragic. Neither Kahu nor Miller answered so Len was forced to walk away.

'Always on the look-out for a bit of gossip,' Miller said. 'He's always coming to me with little bits of rumour and gossip for me to put in the paper. Like I work for bloody *OK* magazine or something.' She looked at him behind the counter where he seemed to be telling Li off for something. When he walked away Li looked over and rolled her eyes.

'Kahu, do you think he's going to come for me? The way he writes, he either expects to be caught or he's going to force a meeting – to tell me his story.'

Kahu gave her a wry smile. 'Yeah, well I'd rather catch him before he comes for you.'

'I'm not really scared. From what he's written he needs me.'

Kahu turned to face her. Their eyes met. 'You need to be careful, Miller. I know what you're like. You'll put yourself out there to help someone out, to get the story.'

Again, another dig at her covering the story.

'Will you cover it?' he asked, head cocked. 'Once it's all over?'

She didn't want to disappoint him. But she knew a story like this would be huge. 'I don't want to contribute to his infamy, if that's what you mean.'

Kahu raised his eyebrows as if he didn't believe her. 'But all of you journalists, that's what you do.'

Miller felt the insult. That's what it was, saying 'journalist' like it was a dirty word.

'Yeah, you're right, Kahu. It *is* what I do. It's my job and every other journalist's out there to get the facts, tell the public the story, especially with something like this. For people to understand the crime. Shouldn't they know the criminal? It's their right to know.'

'Is it, though? Why do they need all the gory details? Why do they need to know that Emmeline scratched and fought for her life but wasn't strong enough, so was knocked out and strangled to death? Why do the public need to know the background behind the man who did it?'

'I know you think it's too much, Kahu. I know you didn't

agree with the article I wrote on Castle Bay. But as long as there are readers out there interested, I'll be reporting it. I have to. It's my job. And you know as well as anyone, the public help. If it wasn't for them there'd be cases that are still unsolved. People need to know what's happening in their own town or city. The people of Lentford need to know there's a killer among them.'

Kahu picked up a paper napkin and folded it over and over again into a small square. 'I know all of this. I'm sorry, I just think these lowlifes should be put in jail and forgotten about, no news articles, no visits, no further education in prison. Sure, I believe in rehabilitation in some, but not all cases. Definitely not all.' He threw the napkin on the table. 'Look, the media is useful. I know it is. I have first-hand experience that not all journalists are bad.'

Miller smiled. 'Why, thanks for that.'

'Your articles have been great, you know.'

'You read them?' She felt ridiculously happy.

'Course.' He smiled back, the argument over. 'Be careful, Miller, okay? If you need me to come stay with you, I will. You just have to ask.'

Miller nodded. 'I kick-box you know. After Castle Bay, I was so angry with myself... being taken. I was so weak.'

'Miller you had no idea. None of us did.'

'I know, but now I can stand up for myself.'

They walked over to Li, and Kahu collected coffees for his team. 'See you Saturday for a game, if not before?'

Miller agreed and they said their goodbyes at the door. Neither had discussed the killer's last words, the possibility of more between her and Kahu, and for that, Miller was glad. There was enough going on without a murderer screwing up one of the few decent friendships she had in her life.

Chapter 22

The rest of Miller's day was packed. She got a phone call from an overexcited Logan reminding her about the tour tomorrow afternoon, which she'd agreed to go on. She thought of Kahu, wondered what he'd think of Logan Dodds and the article she was going to publish on him. She imagined him shaking his head, looking at her, through her, with those dark eyes, daring her to disappoint him.

'It's my bloody job,' she muttered.

Eric looked up. 'What's that?'

'Nothing.'

'First sign of madness,' he joked. 'Talking to yourself.'

'Well, I must've gone mad ages ago,' Miller said. She was uptight and angry. She knew Kahu cared about her. They were friends. But she hated that her job, or the articles she chose to write, had become such a sore point. She rolled her shoulders, trying to work out the stress that had built up. She knew what would work. A drink. Vodka, wine, beer. If there was the promise of a drink at the end of her day she could easily go on.

'No,' she whispered, earning another look from Eric.

He leaned back in his chair. 'You're pretty cosy with the lead detective, aren't you?'

'Cosy? No. He's a friend.' Miller gathered her bag and phone.

'Any news? Leads?' he asked, getting up from his desk and

walking over to her.

Miller thought of everything Kahu had told her. 'No, nothing. Not that I'd tell you anyway.' She tried to pass him but he blocked her way. He smelt of mothballs and damp.

'Can't actually believe you're still here,' he said. He was too close now, his breath hot. Miller stepped back. 'You lose a big story for a national magazine, drunk-driving, involved in a car accident where you disfigure yourself.' He lifted a hand to her face. 'You'd be pretty hot without—'

'Fuck off, Eric,' she said. It took all her will not to punch him.

He strolled back to his desk, whistling tunelessly. 'And still, you're here.'

Wanker. Miller felt the need for fresh air, but stepping out into the main street afforded her no relief. The day was overcast, which made the heat even worse. Tinny Christmas music drifted from various shops as she walked to her car. The shops down the main street were in full yuletide mode: plastic Santas, tinsel, Christmas trees and lights had been jammed into front windows along with the usual display items, depending on the shop. She looked back to the village square where the plastic tree took centre stage, decked out in fairy lights, tinsel and ornaments that reflected the sun, surrounded by staid oaks that looked down on it, disapproving of its frivolity. It all seemed silly, pointless, crass in light of what was going on.

She unlocked her car and threw her satchel onto the passenger seat. Ngaire had asked her to do a piece on the two murders. 'Link them if you can – even if it's just both of them being from here. Lorraine Jenson's happy to talk – if that's the right word. I've already talked to Emmeline's parents. They live in Invercargill. Her body was sent down yesterday. They want nothing to do with an article. They feel her death should not be publicised. Private people. They told me they're working with the police to get any information. I don't know, maybe talk to the boyfriend if you can.'

Miller drove across the bridge and wound her way up to The Hill. She passed the Doddses' house and carried on further until she pulled up to Lorraine Jenson's house. It was a well-kept modern build, tinted windows dark against the beige plaster, as if the house was sleeping. It wasn't as ostentatious as the other houses on The Hill, but nice enough. Miller thought of her mum's old state house down on the flat. She got out of the car; the only sound being the cicadas in the nearby trees celebrating yet another day of oppressive heat.

The interview was quick; she was in and out within half an hour. Lorraine Jenson, widowed three years ago and now coping with the murder of her only child, let her in and through to the lounge at the back. The windows were open, to no avail, and the house was heavy with heat, but also something else. And no matter how silly or fanciful it sounded, Miller thought, that dark, all-encompassing *other* was grief.

Lorraine wanted this interview, wanted to show people who her daughter was, wanted to celebrate her life, not speak of the way she left this world. This small woman, sitting erect, a teacup balanced on her lap, surrounded by photos of her only daughter, spoke of school days, first dates, travel and family Christmases, but the event itself weighed her down. No matter the stories she told, she was still talking to a reporter about her daughter because she had been murdered, and Miller could see the instant she realised it. Halfway through a story about Tamara's twenty-first at the Riverview in town, she stopped short, looked around the room, and burst into tears. A cat came in and leapt onto the couch next to her. She blindly reached out a hand for it and the cat moved closer as if to help where it could. It settled comfortably and purred as Mrs Jenson stroked its ginger fur. 'This is Misty, Tamara's cat. It's silly, but she knows. She knows Tamara's gone and she's been such a comfort to me.' After that, she shut down, didn't speak, and Miller took her leave.

Next on the list, after lunch, she met with Adam Potter, Emmeline's boyfriend. When he sat down with her at a corner table in the Kowhai, she could tell he regretted the decision to meet in a public place. She'd never seen him before. He was a big guy, pale face, haggard, early thirties at most. He looked around. Some obviously knew who he was. People glanced up from sandwiches and coffee, threw a sympathetic look in his direction and then looked back down again. Other tables started up conversations – the murders were never far from anyone's mind in Lentford, and now, here was someone intimately connected to one of the victims.

Len brought over their coffees. Looked like he was going to say something, but then walked away.

'It sounds so cheesy. But she was the one.' Adam stirred his coffee. 'We'd only been going out for a few weeks. You have no idea. The fact she's dead is tragic and heart-breaking and so, so unfair. But the way she was taken... I can't stop thinking about it. The fear she must've felt.' He put down the teaspoon and leaned in, his voice quiet. 'I feel sad, I feel angry, I feel guilty I wasn't there. But that's the point, isn't it? That's what the cops are saying. He's preying on women living alone. He wouldn't have tried anything if I'd been there.' His face crumpled and he looked into his coffee as if expecting to find an answer there, a reason why.

'You'd only been together a few weeks, Adam, but you knew her. Would she have opened her door to a stranger? Let him in for whatever reason?'

He shook his head. 'Not a chance. She liked living on her own, but the few times I stayed there I could tell she was conscious she was a woman living alone. She had a routine of locking up the house at night. Even in this weather, she refused to leave windows open, even a little bit. She had a fan in her room that she left on all night.'

There goes Kahu's theory.

'Did she know the other victim that you're aware of? Tamara Jenson?' Miller already knew the answer but wondered if she could get more out of Adam.

'Yeah. I knew Tamara as well. She was a good friend of a teacher, Louise Bradley, at school. Em and I had discussed her murder. We were both shocked. And here I am talking about both of them now. Em said she'd played pool with Tamara at the Royal a few months back. I met her about six months ago there. There were a few teachers from the primary school having drinks and Louise had dragged Tamara out. Louise told me Tamara had just broken up with her boyfriend so she was trying to cheer her up. I remember her being quiet.'

'What are you up to now that school's out for the year?' Miller asked. Would he want to stay here?

'I'll have been here a year in January. It sounds silly but I'd kind of planned what was next for me and Em. A year or so of dating, then I was going to pop the question. I have no doubt she'd have said yes.' His smile was weak, not cocky. 'We'd set up a life here. I'd move in with her. She really wanted kids ...'

Miller's heart ached for him. She turned off her iPhone which was recording and put a hand on his. 'I am so sorry,' she said.

He stood. 'I think I need to get out of here.' Miller wasn't sure if he meant the cafe or Lentford. 'Do you need more for the article?'

Miller shook her head. His pained expression told her she wouldn't get any more from him. She needed nothing else. These women were loved, they'd be missed, they'd left a hole in this small town. She and the rest of the cafe watched Adam walk out and the whispers became loud conversations, people joining in from other tables, about the tragedy of it all.

Chapter 23

Miller worked on Tamara and Emmeline's article for the rest of the afternoon, every few minutes peeling the backs of her legs off her leather chair and adjusting her desk fan for optimum lukewarm air, ignoring Eric, wanting to get it done before five so she could see Cassie at the Royal. The muscles in her neck were taut and she needed a run to rid herself of this day. Just past five, she emailed the story to Ngaire and walked out of the office without a glance or word to Eric. She bit her tongue when she heard him shout out, 'Well, goodnight to you, Miss High-and-Mighty.'

Tosser.

She walked down to the Royal and waved to Cassie who, by the looks of it, had just finished decorating the bar. 'Tane insist-ed,' Cassie said, rolling her eyes.

Miller looked around. Fairy lights flashed behind the bar; tinsel surrounded the doorway to the toilets and around the scoreboard next to the darts. It hung off the leaners next to the pool table.

'Not really my area of expertise.' Cassie frowned, looking at her efforts. 'It looks a bit shit.' She lifted her mass of black hair, wiping her neck.

'It looks fine,' Miller said, even though she thought it made the tired-looking Royal even more so.

Tane came out of the back office. 'Thanks for doing that, Cassie. Lipstick on a pig, but good to get into the spirit. And if I left it to bloody Johnno it'd be fucking Easter by the time he got round to it.' He walked down the other end of the bar and served a couple waiting there.

Miller sat at the bar and asked Cassie for a Coke.

'I'm sorry about the other day,' Cassie said. 'I wanted it to go better than that. The interview. But even after all this time, it's so hard to talk about.'

'It's okay. Really,' Miller said, gulping down her Coke, the fizz bringing tears to her eyes.

'Speaking of Mum, I had a real weirdo in last night,' Cassie said, looking over Miller's shoulder as if expecting him to appear. 'Some guy going on about some kind of tour. He was taking people to murder sites or something like that.' She shuddered.

'Logan,' Miller said, suddenly uneasy. 'Logan came to see you?'

'Big guy, overweight, gross habit of biting his nails?'

'That's him.' Miller realised what Logan had been doing in her bag. He'd found Cassie's details in her notebook and tracked her down. She explained to Cassie what had happened.

Cassie glanced up towards the door again. 'Is he dangerous? He knows where I live.'

'I'm not sure,' Miller said, not wanting to cause alarm. 'Maybe just a bit unbalanced.'

Cassie laughed. 'Tiff saw him. Said a few choice words to him.'

'I'm sure she did,' Miller said, unable to keep the acid from her tone.

Cassie paused. 'I'm sorry about Tiff the other day. She was trying to protect me. She's like that.'

Miller pulled out her iPhone to record. 'Can we do this here, now? I just need a little bit more about you, really. Just consider this a conversation.'

'Or a counselling session?' Cassie laughed again. 'No problem. I mentioned it to Tane. He's been great about it.'

Miller smiled. She was growing fond of Cassie, after only two meetings. She couldn't fathom the kind of life she'd had and wanted to do anything she could to help.

'When I think about it, I needed her there for so many things. I'd liked girls for ages. For as long as I could remember, even before you're supposed to get proper crushes. I remember in Year Five when I was nine, talking to friends and sharing our crushes. Mine was Lily Gardner. She had long black hair and kind eyes. I told them my crush was James someone, the first guy that wandered into my line of sight. And that's when the lying started. To my friends, and to Mum and Dad. A lie of omission, really, as my sexuality – sex full stop – wasn't talked about in our house. When Mum went missing, the regret of not telling her was so strong. And when we realised she was never coming back, I felt guilty that I'd hidden who I really was. She would never know the real me.'

Tears welled in Cassie's eyes. *This isn't the best place for a chat about this*, Miller thought.

But Cassie sniffed and continued. 'It was the hardest on us girls. Me and my sister. I know there are Mum's parents. I know people say that parents shouldn't have to bury their child, but Nana and Grandad had her for forty-three years. Dad loved her, I know. But we lost our *mother*. Not to cancer or a car accident. We said goodbye to her one day and we never saw her again, and we never knew why. For so long everything was hanging in the air – all these unanswered questions. So many what ifs.' She shook her head. 'Every child needs their mother. *I* needed her. I felt lost back then and I feel lost now. I have no direction. It's like when she disappeared she took part of me with her and now I can't function. I've lost a part of myself and I don't think I'm ever going to be able to find it.'

Miller looked down, suddenly emotional. *Pull it together, Miller.* She suddenly felt guilty about having her mother as long as she had.

Cassie turned away and served a couple who took their drinks to the pool table. She came back and said, 'Sometimes I used to imagine she'd had an affair. That she'd run away with a man. And that one day, once she had everything sorted, she'd come for me. And then when she didn't, that dream got old, rotten almost. It used to give me comfort, but then it turned – left me wondering why she hadn't come to get me yet.'

She picked up a cloth and started wiping down the bar. 'I'm not sure if I fully appreciated the fact that there was a chance she'd been taken, murdered. But as the years went by, I started to understand that she wasn't coming back. That whatever had happened, whether it was through her own decision or someone else's actions, she was gone from my life for good, and I started to fall apart. Drinking, drugs, one bad relationship after the other. As the years went on and the uncertainty built, the lack of answers, I found myself thinking I'd done it all wrong.'

Miller sipped her Coke. 'Done what wrong?'

'I'd grown up wrong. Her disappearance had broken me, and I'd put myself back together incorrectly. It's like Mum was my instruction manual.'

They were both silent. Cassie seemed fine, as though she'd got something off her chest. Not for the first time that day, Miller felt a huge sadness for what some people had to go through.

Cassie's face lit up and Miller turned to see who had walked in. Tiff. The tall redhead walked towards them. She glanced at

Miller, eyes narrowing, then ignored her. She walked behind the bar and said, 'Hey babe, thought I'd come see you for a quick fix.' She grabbed Cassie by the waist, which made her giggle, and kissed her.

Cassie pulled away, glancing around. 'Tiff,' she whispered, stepping back.

Miller was sure the performance was for her. Tiff marking her territory.

'What are you up to?' Tiff asked Cassie, still ignoring Miller.

'Just finishing up my interview with Miller.' Cassie's face was flushed. 'It's actually been really good to get some things out. Thanks, Miller.' She walked to the other end of the bar to serve someone.

Tiff leaned forward over the bar and hissed, 'Leave her alone.'

'Excuse me?'

'Leave her alone. I know all about you, Miller Hatcher. You've spent enough time with my girlfriend. She's not one of your lost causes. Not all young women need to be rescued – not by you.'

Tiff adjusted her expression for Cassie's return. 'Better go, Cass. I'll get us some dinner. See you at finishing time?' She leaned in for a kiss, but Cassie stepped back, grabbing Tiff's hand and squeezing it instead. Tiff smiled and walked away.

Chapter 24

Miller woke on Thursday morning with a sick feeling in her stomach. Her alarm clock read 6 a.m. She hauled herself out of bed, changed into shorts and a singlet and went for a run, hoping to clear her head. But the peace of Lentford at this time of the morning only made her mind race. For each of the last two weeks there had been a murder. Kahu had told her that time of death for both women had been late Thursday evening. Did two murders make a pattern? If it did, they couldn't do much about it anyway. Everyone was on high alert. Windows and doors were locked when some hadn't bothered to do so for years. Surely he couldn't get away with it again – the whole town was ready, waiting.

At home, she finished up an article for Ngaire. She'd told Logan she'd meet him at his house just before ten. She walked into the lounge and chose a record. It needed to be something light, fun, to contrast the day she was about to have. *The Essential Beatles* was a good pick but once she'd finished her coffee, got out of the shower and changed, she heard 'Yesterday' reverberating throughout the house. The melancholy ballad was not the way she wanted to start her day and she moved the arm to the next track and hummed along to 'Penny Lane' as she got herself ready.

She looked at a photo of her mum and dad on their wedding

day, running her finger along the silver frame, wiping the dust off. It had been a rocky marriage and had ended when her dad had died of liver disease when Miller was sixteen. This morning she looked at her mum, choosing not to look at her dad. 'Day one hundred and seventy-nine, Mum. See how well I'm doing?' She smiled. But she could feel the familiar pressure building. This one wasn't about a story, not really, her normal stress about wanting to get something right, this was about *him*, the letters, and whether there would be another one. This was about the fact that she knew deep down they would eventually meet face to face, but she didn't know when and she didn't know how the meeting would go down.

Just one drink. Just one drink and the pressure will evaporate. I could handle things so much better.

'No,' she said quietly, looking at her dad's face in the photo. It was yet to tell the story of his alcoholism because at that stage he was just a 'social drinker'. She thought of the times he drank to get a handle on things, to get through a week... a day.

Miller started at a knock at the door. She walked down the hallway, put the chain on – she'd never done that before – and looked through the crack.

The sight of Logan Dodds shocked her. 'Logan, what are you doing here? I thought we were meeting at your place.' She unchained the door and grabbed her bag.

He knows where I live.

'I was picking up Li, so thought it would be silly not to pick you up as well.'

Miller gave him a tight smile. 'How did you know where I live?' She hoped her tone didn't come off as accusatory.

'I'm a Dodds. We know everyone around here.' He smiled, clearly pleased with his vague answer. 'Ready?'

Miller locked up and walked to the van parked on the side

of the road.

'You can hop in the back with Mary and Joseph,' Logan said as he heaved his weight into the driver's side.

Miller let out an involuntary laugh. 'Mary and Joseph?'

'We know, we know. But you can't help who you marry,' Mary said. She would've been in her mid-sixties and wore long cotton pants, a collared shirt and a cardigan. Miller almost passed out looking at all the layers she had on.

'Sorry,' Miller muttered.

'Not a problem,' Joseph said. He was sitting next to Mary, his hand entwined with hers. He had on shorts, long socks and lace-up shoes, and a short-sleeved shirt with blooming wet patches under his arms. He wiped the sheen of sweat from his bald head that was marred with liver spots.

'Miller, I've told Mary and Joseph about the article and they're happy to answer any questions.'

Miller nodded her thanks to the couple and took the seat behind them in the van.

'Hi, Miller.' Li turned around from the front seat.

'Hi, Li.' Miller was glad there was someone normal on the bus. Then scolded herself. She couldn't go into this morning with preconceived notions about Logan being crazy.

'I've just explained to Mary and Joseph about what Li's doing with her masters. Very interesting,' Logan said, smiling at Li. 'Right, are we ready? Make sure you're buckled up.'

He pulled out onto the road. Miller could hear Li and Logan chatting as though they were old friends. She pulled out her notepad and leaned forward to get Mary and Joseph's attention. 'Mary, can I ask why you're here?'

'To support Logan, of course. We're from Hamilton so we pop across for the True Crime Enthusiasts Club once a fortnight, plus we're on a lot of the same forums. We have a real interest in this kind of thing.'

'I'm sorry to ask, but don't you think it's a bit... macabre?'

'I guess some people think that,' Joseph said. 'But really we're just normal people—'

'What's normal?' Logan shouted, a noise that reverberated around the inside of the van.

'Good point, Logan,' Joseph turned around in his seat. 'Let's put it like this. Most of us go through life following the rules of society, right?'

Miller nodded.

'Most of us are not violent, we don't hurt people – even when we think we'd like to. We're on the straight and narrow. It fascinates me that there are people out there who, for whatever reason, choose to leave the straight and narrow. There are people that were born never to walk it, but there are also people out there who are forced to leave it. That's all. It's an interest in people, our differences.'

Miller nodded. 'And you, Li?'

'I'm on the fence with this one, Mills. That's how I need to be if I'm going to look into it objectively. I think there are a lot of different reasons why people have such a preoccupation with murderers.'

Logan's voice took on a tone of authority. 'Li and I are going to have quite a few interviews. I have a lot of knowledge to share. I'm going to be her main form of information.'

Li turned and gave Miller a quick wink.

'I must admit, the murders of those two young women are horrible,' Mary said, pale hand to her chest, fingering the long gold chain that hung around her neck.

Miller saw Logan's eye twitch in the rear-vision mirror. Everyone else murmured their agreement.

'It makes me wonder if we've got a serial killer on our hands,' said Joseph. 'Unbelievably in little Lentford. Who would've thought?'

'No. He's not a serial killer,' Logan said from the front. 'He's a spree killer. Committing murders in a short space of time. A serial killer is one who commits murders over a period of time, with a cooling-off period. Looks like he does it on a Thursday. Makes you wonder if there will be another one tonight. What do you think, Miller?'

'Why do you ask?' Miller said, refusing to look at him. She looked out the window at the parched fields, thinking the landscape needed a drink even more than she did.

'You seem to have your finger on the pulse of Lentford. You know what's happening. Any ideas? ... No ideas?' If Logan knew about the letters she'd been getting, he'd be out of his mind with excitement. And then: *Could it be Logan sending the letters?*

Their first stop was just out of Lentford, at the disused dairy factory. They got out of the air-conditioned van and were greeted by a wall of heat. Miller knew what they were doing here before Logan even started his spiel.

'Margaret Hughes, mother to Cassandra and Fiona, wife to Brian, was found here on April twenty-second last year. It is thought Margaret was taken at or around the farm-gate shop she visited just down the road from her house on the outskirts of Tauranga. The body was found by a property development team scoping out the site for potential housing. Karl Taylor, a builder's labourer, was working on the Hughes's neighbour's house at the time of her disappearance and is a potential suspect in her murder. With help from Karl Taylor's previous employer, police released an identikit of Karl Taylor but so far, no luck.'

Logan spoke clearly and authoritatively, and if it hadn't been for the subject matter, Miller would have been impressed. She hated to think what Cassie would do if she knew he was out here now. Logan guided the group around the mostly vacant lot, overgrown with weeds. The old dairy factory was now nothing more than a few dilapidated buildings. Logan led them over to one that had been gutted. With his back to it he pointed at the ground. 'This was where Margaret Hughes's remains were found, in a shallow grave. The murder took place over ten years ago and so all that was left was skeletal remains. The police reported that she died from stab wounds. Not a lot else was found. Some bits of clothing and her bracelet and watch. The case is still open but from what I understand police have nothing on Karl Taylor. Feel free to take photos before we go back to the van.' He stepped to the side, waving a blowfly away, then picked at a cuticle on his left hand.

Mary pulled a small digital camera from her bag and Miller turned to walk back to the van. Li caught up with her and walked alongside her.

'Be careful with him, Li, okay?' Miller said, placing a hand on Li's back.

Li waved a hand. 'He's harmless.'

'I don't know.'

'Seriously, Miller, I've had a chat with his mum – god, that makes him sound like a teenager. But it's that, isn't it? He appears younger than he is. Vulnerable almost? He wouldn't hurt a fly. Strange interests maybe, but seriously he's the best fodder for my thesis.'

Miller walked on in silence, the sunburnt grass crunching under her feet.

They were back in Lentford within ten minutes. Logan slowed the van and said to Miller, trying to make eye contact in the rear-vision mirror while also concentrating on the road, 'I know you think this is odd, Miller.'

Miller didn't say anything.

'But what I'm doing here isn't new. There are true crime tours all around the world. Jeffery Dahmer in Milwaukee, the Zodiac Killer in San Francisco, Jack the Ripper in London.'

'I guess it's the size of the place,' Miller said, trying to explain without offending. 'New Zealand is such a small country, Lentford such a small town.'

'There's the Villisca axe murders in Iowa, small town, twelve hundred people, smaller than Lentford by over half. People pay to stay in the house where eight people were murdered. How about that?'

Miller wasn't quite sure what she was supposed to say, and the rest of the occupants of the van remained silent.

'Logan, how much will people pay for these tours?' Miller asked, wincing at her clumsy change in subject.

'Sixty dollars. The tour goes for about three hours and we visit six sites. We're doing four today. Just a trial run.'

'We got it for free since we're the guinea pigs,' Mary said, shrugging her way out of her cardigan and enveloping the van in body odour.

'And do you fear any kind of reprisals from victims' families?' Miller asked

'I don't think so,' Logan said. 'They do it everywhere else with no backlash.'

Miller wasn't sure about that. Her article was at least going to give him exposure in Lentford.

'Look,' Logan said, pulling over outside a tidy blue weatherboard house, 'how is what we're doing any different to the hordes who visit Auschwitz or Dealey Plaza where JFK was shot?'

'Logan,' Miller said, 'those events were on a world stage, a part of history, a part of politics and war. Before they were murdered, the victims here were like Margaret Hughes, ordinary people living ordinary lives.'

'Twenty-three Shelley Road,' Logan said, ignoring her. 'Come on, everyone, let's go.'

They stood on the footpath of the deserted street outside the house that was bordered by a picket fence, its khaki paint blistering and peeling in the sun. A For Sale sign had been jammed into the ground. Miller wondered if prospective buyers were told about what went on in the house.

Logan began to speak. 'In August 1987, Belinda Martin, Lindy to her friends, was murdered by Lauren Lewis. In 1987 the population of Lentford was just over two thousand. Lindy and Lauren both worked in the local supermarket and both frequented the Royal.' Logan hesitated. 'Offering their services.'

There was silence. Then Miller asked, 'They were prostitutes?'

'Yes. One night, Lauren followed Lindy home in a rage from a client's place and confronted her right here, on the street. She accused Lindy of stealing one of her regulars and demanded payment. Witnesses said later they could hear the fight. Lindy wasn't about to give up her hard-earned cash and ignored Lauren. But Lauren followed her into the house and again demanded the money. When Lindy didn't pay up, Lauren knocked her to the floor and strangled her.'

Mary got her camera out and started snapping.

'Lauren was arrested only an hour later. She didn't take into account that there was a witness. Lindy's thirteen-year-old son saw the whole thing.'

'Oh, how horrible. The poor boy,' Mary said, leaning over the fence to get a better shot of the house.

'Lauren was found guilty of murder and was sentenced to life with a minimum non-parole period of fourteen years. She was released in 2003. I've tried to track her down. I wanted to interview her for my website, but I couldn't find her.' Logan sounded disappointed. 'Right, next stop,' he said, walking to the van.

They drove through the main street of Lentford and just before they got to The Oaks Treatment Centre Logan indicated right off the main road to Hamilton and drove down to the river. There weren't a lot of houses down here, mostly farmland, and one public reserve.

The van came to a stop under an oak tree, the Piako River in front of them. They got out of the van. There were some other cars parked strategically under trees and Miller could see young children with parents playing in the shallow and teens in inner tubes floating out in the middle where the water was cooler and deeper.

Logan led them away from the screams and shouts and splashing to a line of oaks that bordered farmland. 'This is council property here,' he said. 'It's used for picnics and as you can see, is a popular place for swimming. In February 1997, Lance Hohepa, who was seventeen, was waiting here for his girlfriend Jennifer. She never showed up, but Lance was beaten to death by an older man she had also been seeing in secret.'

'Jealousy?' Joseph asked. 'Crime of passion?'

Logan nodded. 'It came out in the case that Jennifer had been trying to break up with Lance, but he wouldn't take no for an answer, and had started to get obsessed with her, following her home from school, standing outside her house at night. Jennifer got sick of it and her and this older man – Grant Lee – made a plan to get rid of him.'

Miller looked around. There was a wooden plaque attached to a small pole to the right of the last oak tree. She read the inscription: 'To our precious boy, taken too soon. You will always be in our hearts.' Not for the first time that day, Miller felt she shouldn't be here, with Logan.

'Grant Lee was older, but only in his mid-twenties. He and Jennifer had no idea what they were doing when they were planning the murder. They didn't think too much about hiding their tracks. Grant had been in trouble before, had spent a couple of years in prison for theft. The police managed to get prints off the piece of wood he used to beat Lance to death. It was found lying on the banks of the river, just here. I think he assumed he'd thrown it in.' Logan shook his head, a small smile on his face.

'Excuse me? What's going on here?' The woman had come up behind the small group so silently none of them realised she was there.

Miller turned, took in the tall woman in her late fifties, the bunch of flowers in her hand. Her stomach sank. Lance's mum. She felt as though she'd been caught doing something she shouldn't have.

Nobody spoke. Li stared at the ground. Mary stepped closer to Joseph.

'I asked what you were doing here. You,' she turned to Miller. 'You're the journalist, aren't you? You work for the paper.'

'I do, yes,' Miller said, separating herself from the group, catching Li's eye.

'This has nothing to do with Lance, does it?' she asked.

'It does actually,' Logan said, stepping forward.

Oh god, thought Miller as she watched Logan stand up straighter.

'My name is Logan Dodds and this is a true crime tour.'

The woman's eyes widened. 'A *what?*'

'This tour takes people to various sites where the act of murder has taken place. I talk about the crime and give information on what happened.'

The woman stepped back, horrified. Her mouth opened and closed, trying to find the right words.

Shit, thought Miller. *Why the fuck am I here? Why am I giving someone like Logan Dodds publicity when it causes this much pain?*

The bunch of flowers in the woman's hand trembled. Her lips disappeared into a thin line. 'You think just because my son was murdered twenty years ago it's forgotten? Like it's not personal anymore? That just because it didn't happen last week or last year it can be treated as a bit of general knowledge or trivia? You think there's a set amount of time that the pain and grief just dissipate until it was just a thing that happened all this time ago?'

Logan shook his head. 'Of course not. We also cover murders a lot more recent than your son's.'

Jesus Christ, thought Miller, *does he actually think that is her issue?*

The woman looked at Logan in disbelief, the anger gone, confusion flooding her face. She walked to the plaque, placed the flowers down, and laid a hand on the plaque – lichen-covered and split after years baking in the sun and swelling from winter rain. She took a moment and Miller saw her breathe in deeply. She returned to the group, looking at each of them as she spoke. 'We are not gossip. We are not a headline. We are not to be stood in front of and gawped at. My son was more than the way he died. I bet you know nothing about him other than the way he was killed, do you? Did you know he was beaten? It took hours to die from his injuries – out here, alone,' she sobbed, cutting her sentence short. 'You didn't bother to learn he was a loving big brother, loved reading and English and music, dreamed of being a songwriter, could play any song on the guitar. You didn't know that – did you?'

They all watched her walk back to her car. Miller turned from the others and walked over to Lance's memorial. She touched the swollen, sun-baked wood, whispered an apology and joined the others. Li looked distressed. Miller thought she could see tears in her eyes. Miller caught her eye, mouthed 'Are you okay?' Li nodded and glanced at Logan, then shook her head.

'Logan, I'm going to make my own way back home from here,' Miller said. 'Li, you coming?'

Li nodded.

'We still have one more stop,' said Logan. 'I was going to take you to where Amelia was murdered.'

'You put your sister's murder on your tour?' asked Li, incredulous.

'Of course.'

'Thanks for your time, Logan,' Miller said, uncertain how he'd react to them leaving.

'Do you have enough for your article?' he asked.

'Oh yes. Heaps.' She was now wondering if she wanted to write the damn thing at all. She had thought it would make a good story, but being a part of today had left a bad taste in her mouth. She could put another spin on it, but then she remembered Beatrice Dodds asking her not to make Logan out to be some kind of crazy.

Except he is.

Chapter 25

Madison Nilson left the cycleway and running path and turned into her street. It was too hot to run after work, so she'd left it till later. It was almost eight-thirty and only now was it starting to get dark. She reckoned she'd lost half her body weight by sweating. It was cooler down by the river. Her mum hated her running down there; she'd rung a few days ago telling her about the two murdered women, as if Madison had no idea two women had been killed in the town she lived in.

'Mum, they were murdered in their homes. Not down by the river,' she said.

'Still,' her mother argued, 'the papers are saying they both lived alone. You need to be careful.'

Her parents, both devout Catholics, Sunday church-goers, hated the fact she lived an independent life, supporting herself. Her mother had always needed a man to look after her and she couldn't understand why Madison had chosen such a 'hard road' for herself. After uni and travel, she'd wanted to stay up in Auckland, but her parents had talked her into taking an accounting job in Lentford. To her surprise, she enjoyed the more laid-back lifestyle. Plus, she'd just bought into the partnership in town, something her mother was in parts proud of and concerned about. 'It's just such a big responsibility, Madi.' Which translated to 'Wouldn't it be better to just get yourself a husband and have a few kids?'

After her shower Madison sat on the old leather sofa in her lounge and eyed up the latest Lee Child novel she wanted to get stuck into. She struck a deal with herself: *Ring your mother. Reward: Lee Child.*

She poured a glass of wine to fortify herself. Her parents were teetotal, always had been, and they thought Madison was the same. It was a silly secret to keep. But some things were easier to not bring up. It had just gone nine o'clock. Their dinner would be long over and the dishes done. The news would've been viewed with grumbling from her dad and tut-tutting from her mum. After the news the television was always turned off, because, according to her dad, 'everything else on TV is rot'. She'd been eighteen and at uni before she got a chance to watch *Shortland Street* and *Survivor* for the first time. Madison had remembered the advent of reality TV had nearly sent her father to an early grave. 'People prancing around, expecting us to care about their silly lives, broadcasting their relationships for all to see. Imagine what their parents think.'

Her dad would be comfortably ensconced in his thirty-year-old La-Z-Boy, reaching for his pipe. Her mum would've made them both a cup of chamomile tea (no caffeine after three) and her knitting would be ready and waiting at her slippered feet.

She punched in her parents' number and her mum answered on the fourth ring. As always, she was happy to hear from Madison, but the questions came fast. 'How's work? You're not working too hard, are you? You know your Uncle Richard died from a heart attack and he was in a highly stressful job like yours.'

'Mum, my job's not highly stressful, and Uncle Richard was a librarian.' She held the receiver away from her ear and took a sip of wine while her mum carried on talking.

'... supermarket today and she told me to say hello to you.'

'Lovely,' Madison said, having missed the first part.

'What's happening with those poor girls? There wasn't anything on the news about it tonight.'

'I've no idea,' Madison said. And she didn't. It was all that was talked about in town, at work, down the main street, in the pub and cafes. But it was just rumour and supposition, a chance for some people to air grievances and gossip.

'You be careful. I don't want you to wind up in a ditch somewhere.'

'Yes, Mum,' she said. 'But you know the girls were murdered in their houses, right?'

There was a loud knock at the door and Madison took it as her chance to say goodbye.

'Someone's at the door, Mum. I better go. Love to Dad.'

'Ask who it is before you open the door,' her mum said hurriedly.

'Yes, Mum,' Madison laughed and hung up.

Wine glass in hand, still smiling, she crossed the lounge and opened the door.

Chapter 26

Miller woke from a sound sleep on Friday. After her morning with Logan yesterday, she had gone back into work after lunch and finished up a story about the need for people to think before they took on pets around Christmas time – one of those stories that get churned out every year but she doubted whether people paid attention. She'd visited a place in Lentford which took in abandoned animals – mostly cats – and talked to the woman there. She didn't get home till after six. She'd had a quick bite to eat and beat the shit out of her punching bag till she lay, spent on the floor, hardly able to move.

She got ready for work, relieved it was Friday, but aware that something could have happened last night. Would there be a letter for her at work? Had Kahu already been called out? Would he let her know? He knew this was on her mind as much as his. She felt her jaw tense as the thoughts careened round her head, and she slapped it gently with both hands.

Miller walked down the hallway, satchel over her shoulder, phone in her hand, still trying to decide what to do with Logan's story. She came to a standstill a few metres from the door.

There was an envelope, off-white, lying on the mat, half-visible where it had been pushed under the front door.

She felt her legs buckle; her satchel slid down her leg and onto the floor and her phone fell to the ground with a thud.

Miller walked to the door cautiously, as if the letter could do her physical harm. She picked it up and held it in her sweating palms, the idea of fingerprints or any kind of trace being garnered from the envelope the furthest thing from her mind.

She tore it open and read:

> *Miller, surprised? I know where you live. In Lentford, everyone knows everyone. It makes what I'm doing easier. Easier to destroy families. To destroy this shithole town. I hear the gossip. I see the fear in women's eyes. And I'm doing that.*
> *Her name is Madison Nilson. Madi to her friends.*

Miller groaned. She knew Madi. Not well, but Ngaire had put on welcome drinks when Miller had arrived at the *Lentford Leader*. Tate Accountants were big advertisers and Madi had come along. Miller had chatted to her – they'd both attended AUT. She was looking to become partner and Miller knew she'd just bought into the firm. She kept reading.

> *She has the day off today. She's lonely, Miller. Go to her. Who knows? Maybe there's still time.*
> *You love to help, don't you? You love to save people who can't save themselves, the weak ones. 52 Thomson St, Miller.*

'Fuck,' Miller said. 'Fuck!' She grabbed her bag and ran out the door. She'd ring Kahu on the way.

She started her car, it coughed into life and she backed out the driveway. Thomson Street was only a couple of streets over, towards the river. The roads at this time of day were empty. With one eye on the road, she rummaged in her satchel for her phone. 'Fuck!' she screamed, hitting the steering wheel with the palm of her hand. She'd left it at home. It was too late. If there was even a slim possibility Madi was still alive she needed to get to her.

Miller swung into the driveway of number fifty-two, wincing as the bottom of her car grated over the bump. She left the engine idling as she jumped out of the car. She found herself unable to catch her breath. Taking deep breaths of stale muggy air didn't help so she charged up the terracotta steps and turned the door handle. Unlocked.

She walked straight into the lounge room and looked around.

Could he be here? Waiting for her? Was this part of his plan?

She walked through the house, footsteps uncertain, making her way through an unknown floorplan, positive she could hear her heart, slamming against her chest. Her top was soaked through with sweat. She walked down the hallway. Toilet and bathroom on her left. She opened a door on her right. 'Madi,' she whispered, her voice coming out in a rasp. She cleared her throat. 'Madi?'

It was an office, with a desk and boxes piled high in one corner.

She moved to the next door, opened it, peered around the corner.

And there she was, lying on the bedroom floor. She looked as though she was asleep, but she wasn't, of course she wasn't.

Miller put a hand over her mouth, willing her toast and coffee not to come up. Her vision blurred as she stepped towards Madi and lowered herself onto her knees. Madi was dressed in a white singlet and blue-and-white check boxer shorts. She noticed her painted red toenails but willed herself to look at her face. Her eyes were closed. Her skin looked reddish pink. As if in slow motion, Miller pushed the scarf that was wrapped around her neck so tight the skin had puckered and tried to find a pulse. Nothing. She watched her chest, waiting, expecting some kind of movement. Nothing.

Kahu's words came to mind: *ligature strangulation.*

A fly had entered the bedroom and buzzed around Miller's head. She waved at it and it settled on Madi's cheek. Miller screamed, her arms flailing. The fly took flight and landed on the curtain. Miller felt like opening the curtains and windows – as though a bit of fresh air would bring Madi back to life. But she knew she shouldn't touch anything else.

She closed the door to Madi's bedroom and made her way to the phone. With hands that seemed unwilling to work, she found the station's number in the thin local phonebook by the phone and dialled, asking for Detective Sergeant Parata, telling them it was an emergency. She was put straight through.

'Detective Sergeant Kahu Parata.'

'Kahu...' Miller said, perching on the couch before her legs gave way altogether.

'Miller? That you?'

'There's been another one. Madi Nilson. Fifty-two Thomson Street.' Miller lowered her head onto her knees.

'Shit,' Kahu muttered. 'Are you there?'

'Yeah. Can you come? Now? She's... she's dead.'

'We're on our way.'

Kahu turned up five minutes later. 'Are you okay? Are you hurt?'

Miller shook her head.

He laid a hand on her shoulder and walked up the steps to the house.

'Second door on the right down the hallway,' she called as he disappeared inside.

Kahu appeared a few minutes later, walked to the end of the

driveway and made a call.

When the rest of Kahu's team had turned up he guided Miller to a wooden bench seat to the left of the front door. 'Are you sure you're okay? You're probably in shock.' He stared down at her, his forehead creased.

'Kahu, I'm fine. It's not like I haven't seen a dead body before.' She said this as if it was no big deal, but they both knew it was.

'Just a few questions, okay?' Kahu pulled his notebook out of his back pocket.

Miller sipped on water and watched as the white crime-scene tape was stretched across the driveway of Madi's property. A uniformed police officer, one of Ash's constables, Miller didn't know his name, stood in front of the tape, clipboard in hand. Miller wondered for a second where Ash was. The officer ignored the neighbours who came out of their houses, some still in their dressing gowns, walking up to the tape, muttering between themselves, before asking him what had happened. It didn't take a genius to figure it out. Miller watched as people on their way to work slowed down in their cars, necks straining as their cars crawled past. That bright white tape with the red words POLICE EMERGENCY spread across it attracted gawkers the way a flame attracted moths, Miller thought. Astonished, worried, excited expressions met hers as eyes darted around the scene.

'How did you find out about this?' Kahu asked. 'Another letter?'

Miller nodded. 'Delivered to my house.'

Kahu swore, shaking his head as he made notes.

'He gave me her name and address. He was pleased about how everything was going. The way he was destroying families.'

'Can you tell me what you touched inside the house?'

She took another sip of water as she thought. 'The front door handle, the door handle to the office and Madi's bedroom.' She closed her eyes, back in Madi's house. 'Her neck. I checked for a pulse. I had to push the scarf away. Then maybe the walls down the hallway – I felt kind of dizzy. And the phonebook and phone.' Miller nodded, sure she'd remembered everything.

'We'll need to take your fingerprints and DNA for elimination. I need to get inside. Can I meet you down at the police station this afternoon to do that and take your statement?'

Miller nodded.

Kahu put a hand on her shoulder. 'I'll get Mark to take down the tape so you can back out. Have you got the letter?'

They walked over to Miller's car where she took the letter out of her satchel. The paper shook as she handed it over. 'I didn't wear gloves, sorry.'

Kahu took her hand and squeezed it. 'Are you okay to drive?'

'Yeah.' She clasped her hands tightly together to stop them shaking.

'See you this afternoon?'

'Okay.' Her voice was barely a whisper. It felt strange to leave, knowing Madi was still inside. She knew there was nothing she could do – never had been. 'He played me, Kahu. Tricked me, like it was a bit of fun, a practical joke.'

'What do you mean?' Kahu asked.

'In the letter. He said I should go to her. That maybe it wasn't too late. That I could save her. But she would've been dead already, right?'

'If it's anything like the other two – which I'm sure it's going to be – there's nothing you could've done, Miller.' He squeezed her arm. 'Maybe take the day off, eh?'

'Yeah, maybe,' Miller said, unsure of what she was supposed to do for the rest of the day if she wasn't working.

She watched Kahu suit up and disappear into the house. Mark waved her out of the driveway and before she drove off, she watched him shoo away the eager spectators like annoying gnats and place the cordon back up.

Chapter 27

Cassie struggled in the front door, laden down with shopping bags. 'There's been another one,' she called out to Tiff. 'Madi Nilson.' She couldn't believe a third woman had been murdered. Her heart broke for all the families involved. She knew exactly what they were going through. Did they realise that the pain, the memory of how they'd died, would never go away? Cassie was sure she wasn't alone. She was positive family members and friends of murdered loved ones carried that pain around their necks, shackled to their hearts for the rest of their lives. Many people, different people, teachers, friends, strangers, had all told her it would get easier. Like she was learning to ride a bike or figuring out geometry. Like with a bit of practice, after a bit of time, the fact that her mother was murdered would become just another event in her life, something she'd drag up from the depths of her memory and relive once in a while. How wrong they were.

'Tiff?' Cassie needed her. She needed to feel Tiff's arms around her, telling her everything was going to be okay – even if it wasn't. The town of Lentford was losing its appeal. And then she wondered if it really had any appeal to start with.

Cassie started putting the groceries away. She'd done a half shift for Tane. She wasn't supposed to work tonight, but Johnno hadn't shown – again. He'd rocked up half an hour ago, full of excuses for Tane, and wide smiles and winks for her, telling them he'd finish up like he was doing them a favour. It was almost 8 p.m. and she was starving. She filled a saucepan with water and turned on the stove.

Tiff walked into the lounge, the look on her face darkening the whole room. Cassie braced herself.

'Where have you been?' Tiff asked, not looking at her.

'I've been at work. Tane called. I had to go in. Johnno was a no-show again.'

'We were supposed to be going out for dinner, Cassie. We organised it last week.' Tiff turned to her, eyes unblinking.

Cassie looked away first. 'We were? I don't remember setting anything up. I'm sorry, Tiff.' She turned to the chopping board and started cutting up the chicken. She didn't want to fight.

'You could've told me you were going out. I got home ready for our big night and you weren't even here. I was worried.' Tiff walked into the kitchen, which suddenly felt too small with both of them in it.

Cassie leaned against the bench, wanting to get some distance from Tiff. 'I left you a note, on the coffee table,' she said.

Tiff raised her eyebrows.

She doesn't believe me, Cassie thought.

Tiff walked over to the coffee table and started throwing the magazines off the table.

'Tiff!' Cassie said, rushing into the lounge, bending down to pick up the magazines and newspapers that had slid into corners and under the couch.

'Well, I'm looking Cass, and I can't see any note. Can you?' she said. Her face had turned red and she was breathing heavily. *A raging bull.*

Cassie stepped back, magazines and newspapers in her hand. She was sure she'd left a note. Positive. She'd used a bit of the mint-green notepaper they kept by the phone.

'I left it right there,' Cassie said, pointing at the table. She began to chew the inside of her mouth.

'It's not there, Cassie,' Tiff said. 'Look, you've been preoccupied with this article coming out. Maybe you just forgot.'

Tiff was giving her an out. This was good. She didn't want to fight. She *had* been preoccupied, pinning all her hopes on Miller's article getting more exposure for her mother's case. She probably had forgotten.

'Tiff, I'm so sorry,' Cassie said, walking towards her.

Tiff took her in her arms. 'It's okay. But you owe me dinner,' she said, smiling.

'How about pasta? I'm cooking it now,' Cassie said. 'You sit, relax. Beer?' She walked to the fridge and took two out. She handed one to Tiff who sat on the couch while Cassie returned to the kitchen to finish cutting up the chicken.

'Speaking of leaving messages, your dad rang today,' Tiff said.

'Oh, great. That's the first time you've spoken to him, right?' Cassie said, happy the two got to have a chat.

'He was actually really rude. How does he feel about you being gay?'

Cassie frowned, confused. 'Fine. Always has been.'

Tiff shrugged, putting her bare feet on the coffee table. 'Well, he didn't sound like it to me.'

'What did he say?' Cassie asked, refusing to believe her dad was anything but his usual polite self.

'It wasn't so much what he said, just the way he said it. Very stand-offish, you know? I tried to make conversation. I told him about where you were working, about Lentford, the house. But I didn't really get much back from him.' Tiff drained her beer, walked back into the kitchen and put it on the bench.

'I'm so sorry, Tiff. That really doesn't sound like Dad.' Cassie stood with her back to Tiff, stirring the pasta sauce.

'Are you saying I'm lying?' Tiff's voice was low, barely a whisper.

Cassie swung around, ready to defuse the situation. 'No! God no. Look, I'm sorry he was rude to you. I'll have to have a word to him next time we speak.' She reached forward, grasping for Tiff's hand, begging not to be shut down. 'You two should really meet. I know you'd get along.'

Tiff took Cassie's hand. 'He actually mentioned coming for a visit.' Tiff kissed Cassie's knuckles. 'But I don't know, Cass. I don't need his negativity. I escaped my homophobic family and don't really want to be entering another one. Do you get me?'

Cassie nodded. She didn't know much about Tiff's family in Hamilton, but she did know they hadn't treated her well.

'Could we maybe hold off on the visit for a while? Just till me and you get a bit more settled.' Tiff leaned in for a kiss, waiting for an answer.

Cassie nodded, flushing hot as Tiff's lips grazed hers.

'Thanks, Cass. I'm going to have a shower before dinner.'

Tiff left the room and Cassie exhaled. She picked up the empty chicken tray and put it in the bin. Just as she was closing the lid, she saw the very edge of a mint-green piece of paper. She didn't need to pick it up. She knew exactly what it said.

Chapter 28

Miller sat at her mum's dining room table that stood in the centre of the small kitchen. It would forever be 'Mum's table' just like it was 'Mum's house'. They'd had the table at their old house when her dad had still been around. A photo of her mum sat in the middle of the table. Miller spooned muesli into her mouth while she chatted.

'One hundred and eighty-one days, Mum,' Miller said proudly.

She loved this photo of her mum. It was older, taken almost fifteen years ago, long before the cancer had taken over her body so abruptly and completely. She was walking along the beach, fit, tanned, healthy, her husband was dead – a good thing. She was happy. Miller could tell from the photo. She'd known her mum well enough to know when she wasn't happy, even if she was smiling. Her mum could always do the same with her.

'There's been another one. I feel responsible. And I know you'd tell me that it isn't anything to do with me, but it's me he's contacting. He thinks we're a team. He thinks I'm going to make him famous. I don't want to. I feel sick at the thought of it, and Kahu... He hates what I do, at least this part of it. He thinks these people should be locked up and never heard from again. But I've tried to tell him, the public deserves to know – don't they?'

Her teeth grazed her lip and she clenched her jaw. She took another spoonful of muesli to counter the headache that would develop if she didn't relax.

It was 7.30 a.m. and the fact she was one hundred and eighty-one days sober didn't stop the thoughts of having a drink. She felt it more now, more so than she had in a long time. It was like a wild animal trying to get free, the craving, clawing at her insides. But other times, weeks at a time, sometimes when all was going well, it lay dormant. At the moment it was like a physical pain. She knew it was the stress. She knew there was no way she could control what was going on, and she hated that. They were at the mercy of the Scarf Killer. And she hated that even more.

She took her empty bowl to the sink, rinsed it out and laid it to dry on the stainless-steel benchtop. Her mum had a dishwasher, but she hadn't used it since she'd moved in. It would take her over a week to fill it.

Would it just go on? No, she knew it wouldn't. He had a need to be known. Surely it would get too much for him. Would he give himself up? All to put his face to the Scarf Killer name? Was that what he was going to do? At the moment he was the most hated person in Lentford; hell, in New Zealand. Tamara and Emmeline's stories had been covered in one way or another in the *Leader* as well as the national papers – soon to be joined by Madi. She and the rest of the country had seen photos of fresh-faced young women, posing at the beach or on bush walks. Family and friends had been cut from the photos so the public could look into the eyes of the women who had lost their lives so violently.

Her phone rang, snapping her out of her thoughts. She grabbed it when she saw the name on the screen. 'Hi, Ash,' she said, hopeful and nervous at the same time.

'Hi.' There was a pause and Miller waited. 'I was talking to Detective Parata yesterday. He said... he said you were the one who found Madison Nilson.'

'Yeah.' Miller squeezed her eyes shut tight.

'I'm so sorry. I know how horrific that is. Look, I want to apologise about the other day. You're my friend and I treated you badly. All you were doing was your job.'

Miller wondered how much Kahu had told Ash – not the whole story by the sounds of it.

'It's okay, Ash. I'm glad you rang – I've missed you.'

'Me too.'

Miller waited for more questions about Madi, but they never came.

'Look, I'm on duty now so I'd better go. I just wanted to touch base. Make sure we're all good.'

'Yep,' Miller said, relieved. That was one less thing she had to worry about. She needed Ash in her life and the last couple of days without her had been harder than she'd have thought.

That afternoon Miller finished her article on Cassie and her mother. Kahu, despite working on the Scarf Killer case, had given her a bit more of the back story on Margaret's murder, since Hamilton CIB had the case. All of it matched up with what Cassie had told her. He'd given her a copy of the identikit that had done the rounds last year.

'Was there anything else about him?' Miller had asked. 'No tattoos, scars?'

'Not that anyone can remember. It was a long time ago.'

Miller realised then how impossible it was. She could only hope this article would jog someone's memory. There was talk that this Karl Taylor had mentioned he was from the Waikato – was it a slip of the tongue or was he already, before Margaret's murder, trying to mislead? If the *Leader* could get his name and picture out there again, maybe someone would recognise him, even if he had been using an alias.

She emailed her piece off to Ngaire for approval and headed to the supermarket. When she got home, Li was returning from walking Patsy. Miller hadn't seen her since Logan's tour a few days before. She parked the car, grabbed her shopping and met Li at the end of the driveway. The small dog danced around Miller's ankles, and she leaned down to scratch her behind the ears.

'We didn't get round to talking about Logan's tour,' Miller said. 'Do you feel uneasy about all this? Giving him this kind of attention?'

Li shrugged, but Miller could tell it didn't sit right with her. 'You're doing the same, aren't you? Doing an article on him?'

She has a point.

'He really is interesting to talk to though,' Li said, scooping Patsy up into her arms and allowing her face to be licked.

'If by "interesting" you mean crazy.'

'You must admit, he has a lot of knowledge. He's going to come in really handy for my research – especially all the local stuff.' Li put a squirming Patsy back down on the ground.

'Yeah, but he's only some, I don't know... amateur,' Miller said, struggling to find the right word.

'I know. And I'm going to talk to a lot of experts – psychologists and police detectives. But this just gives me another angle,' Li said, determined not to be put off. 'I guess you heard there was another one on Thursday night. Madi Nilson.'

'I heard,' Miller said, biting her tongue. Li would want all the details, and it wasn't something she wanted to talk about at the moment, if ever.

'You're friends with the lead detective right?' Li said. 'Parata?'

Miller could see where this was going and didn't answer.

'He used to work in Castle Bay, didn't he?' Li was looking at Miller closely, her head tilted to one side.

Miller nodded. Without waiting for the question, she said, 'He may speak to you. But not any time soon. Not while the Scarf Killer's still out there.'

Li nodded and rocked on her heels, excited.

Miller moved her shopping bag from one hand to the other. 'Li, do you think Logan...' She wasn't sure how to pose the question.

'What?'

'Never mind.' The guy was a bit odd, but she wasn't going to make the mistake of branding him a murderer. 'I'd better go in. When are you off to Shanghai again?'

'Wednesday morning, four more days.' She made an exaggerated sad face, her bottom lip protruding. She picked up Patsy, who was yapping for attention. 'I just want to get stuck into my thesis – there's so much work to be done.'

'What are you doing with Patsy while you're away?' Miller wondered if she should have offered to look after her. But she was out so much the poor thing wouldn't get enough attention.

'She's in the kennels for a few weeks. I'll be back on the fifteenth of January. Hopefully by then all this craziness has died down.' She winced. 'Excuse the pun. And our nice little town will be back to normal. I'm really hoping the news of the Scarf Killer hasn't got to Shanghai – Mum and Dad would have me out of Lentford in a shot and then who knows where I'd end up!' She walked back to her house, Patsy in her arms.

Kahu pulled into the driveway just as Miller reached her door.

'C'mon in.' She ushered him inside. 'Shit day?' she asked, taking in his creased shirt, half untucked, sleeves rolled up. He'd already replaced his shoes with jandals.

'Shit day,' Kahu nodded as they walked into the kitchen.

Miller opened the doors out onto the deck. 'Drink? Sorry, I don't have any beer,' Miller said, unable to meet his eye.

'We've talked about this,' Kahu admonished her as he sat down in the chair facing the back yard, exhaling. 'Water would be great.'

Miller got them both an iced water and they sat side by side looking over the garden.

'I've never been a big drinker, you know,' Kahu said, long legs stretched in front of him.

'I'd noticed,' Miller said. They'd been out a few times, in Lentford and Castle Bay. The most she'd ever seen him drink was a couple of beers.

'Is it because of the job?' Miller was careful not to pry too much. It had been a while since Kahu had opened up about anything other than work.

'Nah, even before then. Dad was an alcoholic.'

Miller felt her face flush. She saw Kahu glance at her and he carried on. 'I remember when I was in my teens one of my aunties telling me it was hereditary. I remember her words, after one of Dad's benders. "You ain't got a hope, boy." I don't think she was being mean. Just stating the truth. Anyway, true or not, it scared the shit out of me. I decided early on I didn't want to be like him. Sure, I drank a bit in the last couple of years of high school. Mostly because, I hate to admit it, I couldn't stand the way my mates looked at those who abstained. Back then a seventeen-year-old on the first fifteen rugby team was expected to sink half a dozen beers after the game. But I got good at hiding it. Seems silly now but back then my mates, my peers were everything to me. I cared what they thought about me. Still, I never really got a taste for it. Sure, a cold beer on hot summer's day is great, but I never felt the need for more.'

'And Trina?' Miller said, treading softly. 'I guess she knew all of this. Supported you?'

Kahu nodded, brushing a fly from his sleeve. He wasn't going to give her any more.

'My dad was an alcoholic too,' Miller said. It was easier to talk about him and his problem. 'I thought like you when I was a teen. I was the sensible one. Out of all my friends I was the one who didn't drink. I'd seen what it could do. I only started drinking when he died.' Miller touched the scar on her face. Time to change the subject. 'Kahu, Madi Nilson—'

'Yeah?' Kahu sat up straight.

'I noticed something when I discovered her.'

Kahu nodded as if he knew what was coming.

'The lipstick,' Miller said. 'Bright pink lipstick. I thought it odd. She was in her pyjamas when I found her, and I'm assuming she was killed the night before. It didn't look like she was wearing any other make-up, plus this looked like a bit of a botched job.' She remembered Madi's top lip where the lipstick had crossed over the edge of her lip onto her face.

Kahu was quiet as he finished his water and put the glass down on the deck. 'We're not releasing that part to the public.'

'It's him? Did he put lipstick on her? All of them? Tamara and Emmeline too?'

Kahu nodded, and Miller shuddered. There was something about that act that was so personal, yet disturbing, knowing what he'd done to the women.

'This goes no further, Miller,' Kahu warned.

'Of course.' She always felt put out when he warned her. *Doesn't he trust me?*

'We need to keep some details from the public. Just in case we get anyone trying to confess who didn't actually do it.'

'Really?'

'Sometimes. We have people who are well known to us. Ones that would confess to it just for the attention. By keeping this detail quiet, we can weed them out quicker. It's crazy,' he said, swiping an arm across his sweaty forehead.

'Kahu, I look at these women and they're not similar, physically. I thought he'd be going for the same type of woman. That's what men like this do, isn't it?'

'Not necessarily. It looks like his only prerequisite is women living alone. Let's face it, it's the only way he can be doing what he's doing. They are the same age, roundabouts – early thirties.'

'Did anyone hear anything at Madi's place? Neighbours?' Miller asked, wondering how someone could be murdered in their home and no one sees or hears anything. This wasn't the big city where people kept to themselves. Everyone knew their neighbours in Lentford, kept an eye out for them – mostly.

'Both neighbours are away. It's getting to be like that – school's finished for the year. People are starting to take off on holidays. The elderly couple on one side left for a cruise on Wednesday. On the other side, the family have got kids and they left for the beach a couple of days before that. I don't know if he knew this or just got lucky. There are a few people around here on our radar. Ones with records, violence towards women, done their time and live here, or moved here over the last year or so.'

'So?' Miller asked.

'So nothing.' Kahu looked at Miller. 'They've all been cleared.'

'Jesus,' Miller said, getting up to refill their glasses. 'This is just so—'

'Slow? Frustrating?' Kahu said. 'You got it. You know how it works. There's a lot we can do with the resources we have, but sometimes we have to face facts. These pricks are either cleverer than us or, more likely, have dumb luck.'

Miller thought of Cassie and her mum, how Margaret had been dead for so long and the ghost that was Karl Taylor had never been found. Is this what would happen to the Scarf Killer? Leads would dry up, tips would result in dead ends, the case getting colder and colder; one by one people being taken off the case until just one detective was working it. And when there was no more action to take, the file would be shelved; still open, but growing ever colder by the day, until the only people who remembered Emmeline's, Tamara's and Madi's names were family and a few detectives.

'I'm not giving up,' Kahu said.

Miller flinched. She knew he was doing his best. That's all he ever did.

'From those letters, I believe he's going to show his hand, and if not, these kinds of people get sloppy, blasé. He's going to fuck up, Miller, and I'll be there waiting.'

Chapter 29

Miller and Li walked into town on Sunday afternoon for the Lentford Christmas parade. Miller wanted to take a look at who was there. For whatever reason, she felt the killer would be there, and part of her felt she could identify him. If he was following her, stalking her, would she be able to tell? Ever since this had started, she hadn't got the feeling she was being watched or followed. So much for sixth sense and women's intuition.

'I love the Christmas parade,' Li said as she walked alongside Miller, her short legs struggling to keep up with Miller's long strides. Miller decreased her pace.

'Really?' Miller had never been one for Christmas parades. The annual one in Auckland took over Queen Street when half of the city turned up. She would get herself as far away as possible from it.

'Just the whole Christmas thing,' Li said.

'Did you celebrate back home?' Miller asked, uncertain of the Chinese culture.

'No! Never!' Li turned to Miller, wide-eyed. 'Definitely not at home. Shopping malls go all-out, but that's always commercially driven, make money at any cost. But I love the traditions you Kiwis have. The tree, the decorations, the food, the Christmas parade, extended families getting together – at the beach or a backyard barbecue – and don't get me started on Santa!'

Miller laughed. 'No Santa in the Chen family?'

Li's face was deadpan. 'No Santa, Miller! Can you believe it?'

'Poor Li!' Miller rubbed her back, laughing. 'So you're *really* not looking forward to going back?'

Li sighed. 'I do like seeing my parents, even if they are a bit strict. They are my parents, right? I just feel a sense of freedom here. I feel restricted at home.'

'You'll go to Shanghai, have a lovely time with your family, meet a few nice men…'

She laughed when Li elbowed her.

'And you'll be back before you know it.'

Li took a deep breath and nodded as if preparing herself.

As they got closer to town the crowd began to swell. Cars, not able to park in town as the main road had been closed, filled up the side streets. Others, like Miller and Li, had abandoned cars and chose to walk. Whining children, hot from the walk, begged for ice blocks and a swim at the pool later. Miller heard one young girl scream as her hokey pokey ice cream slid off its cone and splattered in a heap onto the steaming tar seal, where within seconds it was reduced to a cream-coloured puddle. There were hurried promises of another ice cream and muttered cursing about the weather.

Li and Miller took their place on the main street in the shade. Li chatted to the couple next to her, and Miller took the chance to look around, her eyes trying to seek out Ash. She'd be here somewhere. She knew a few people but by no means everyone. Across the road her eyes met Logan's. He was standing between his parents. William looked, as usual, out of place, and Beatrice was talking to a woman beside her, her hands flailing as she regaled her with a story. Logan wouldn't look away and waved his hand in greeting. He didn't smile. The greeting confused Miller. *Logan* confused Miller. She nodded at him and looked away, not wanting to appear friendly. She didn't want him to think they were close. She hadn't started his article yet. Didn't know where to begin or if she was actually going to write it.

Miller looked left down the street and saw Johnno, dressed in black jeans and a black singlet, saunter up to a group of teenage girls, tanned skin on show in denim shorts, miniskirts and midriff-baring tops. He sidled up to one of them, put an arm around her. Miller shook her head, watching the others swoon as he kissed the girl on the mouth and led her away from her friends, across the road to the village green.

Cody and Hine were standing with Ngaire outside the *Leader* office. The crowd's attention turned to the main street as the bagpipes started, marking the start of the parade. Cody caught her eye and waved, brandishing a camera in the air and rolling his eyes. He'd obviously been roped into taking photos for the paper. If it wasn't for the murders, the Christmas parade would have been front-page news this coming week. But now it would be relegated to page two.

The kilted bagpipers walked past, followed by fire engines and police cars, school and kindergarten floats plus various farm machinery dressed up in tinsel. Country town Christmas parades sure were different from the city ones, Miller thought. Clowns in billowing satin trousers and bright suspenders jogged along the side of the road, white paint melting off their faces, making them look more like Stephen King's Pennywise than comical entertainment. They passed out lollies to waving kids while wiping away the face paint dripping into their eyes.

'How're you going, Miller?' She jumped in surprise and turned to see Len next to her, dressed in a pale-pink short-sleeved shirt and denim shorts. He always managed to look so out of place.

'Hi, Len. Thought the cafe'd be open.'

'Got someone covering for me. I thought I'd come out and take a look at the festivities.'

Miller nodded.

'Sad news about Madi Nilson.' Len's index finger caressed the fluff on his chin.

Miller nodded. 'Very.'

'I heard you found her.'

Miller turned and looked at Len. He was staring straight ahead, a small smile on his face, looking at the local gymnastics group's float.

She felt the sweat dry on her skin and goose bumps erupt. 'How did you know that?' She knew for sure Ash would've kept it quiet. Bull?

'Miller, this is Lentford. Big news like that never stays quiet for long. You should know that by now. Must've been horrible, walking in on a dead body.'

Miller could smell him. His deodorant and aftershave were cloying.

'I ...' She had no words.

'Poor girl. She used to come into the cafe a lot. I can imagine her putting up a fight. She was pretty spirited.'

What does he mean by that?

'It's really sad,' Miller said, pulling herself together. 'Did you know her well?'

'Not really. As I said, she was in the cafe a lot. I actually asked her out once. Got shot down.' He gave a laugh that sounded more like a cough, then pointed down the road. 'Here comes the main event.'

Miller looked where Len was pointing. And there he was: Santa. His sleigh was atop a trailer being towed by a quad bike. Children gasped excitedly and the four-deep crowd surged forward, Li among them, the twenty-two-year-old unable to hide her excitement amid the pint-sized children. Small hands waved out, anxious to be seen by the big man. As the sleigh passed, Miller could see it was Lou. He was almost unrecognisable. She had only ever seen him in his lawnmowing gear: navy top and work boots, hairy muscled legs poking out from black shorts. He hadn't lost his gruff expression, and Miller smiled at the red velvet, fur-trimmed hat pulled over his wrinkled brow.

'Wonder who talked him into that.' Len was almost doubled over in laughter. 'Maggie, I'd say. I think she's on the parade committee. Along with every other committee in Lentford.'

Lou raised a gloved hand to the kids. Miller couldn't tell if he was smiling, as his mouth was hidden in the bushy beard made from what looked like a mass of glued-together cotton balls. He had a pattern of waving to the left and then to the right and then wiping the sweat from his eyes.

The crowd started to disperse as Santa's sleigh disappeared around the corner to join all the other floats. A few kids dragged their parents down the road in the hope of catching Santa. Miller hoped Lou was prepared.

Cody and Hine walked over. 'Pub?' Hine asked. 'I'm gasping.' Where everyone else looked as if they were melting, the only evidence that Hine was uncomfortable was a slight sheen of sweat on her face.

'Yeah, okay,' Miller said. The day stretched before her and she didn't want to be home alone, nothing but thoughts to get in her way. She looked around for Li, who was talking to Len. It looked serious. The conversation finished and Li joined them.

'Do you want to come to the pub?' Miller asked.

'I can't,' Li said. 'Len wants me to work for a couple of hours this afternoon. He's such a jerk. I wasn't supposed to be on and then he guilted me into saying yes, reminding me I was going to be away over the busy season, and I could at least do him a favour.'

Li looked close to tears and Miller rubbed her arm.

Len was watching them, waiting for Li. 'Better go.' She rolled her eyes. 'Catch up with you later.'

Cody, Hine and Miller made their way down to the Royal which was abnormally busy for a Sunday afternoon. Kids ran around the car park out front while parents sat in the only slightly cooler interior, knocking back beers and shandies. Cassie, Tane and Johnno – back from wherever he'd been with his latest conquest – were all working behind the bar.

Hine found a table in the corner by the window. 'My shout, ladies,' Cody said, grinning. He looked as out of place as Len in Lentford with his designer sunglasses resting on his gelled hair, but he wore it well, Miller thought, as opposed to Len.

'Thanks, Cody. Vodka tonic, please,' Hine said, brushing the seat with a paper napkin before she sat down.

'Coke, Miller?' Cody asked. 'Or juice?'

This was the first time they'd all been at the pub together since Eric had regaled them all with her past misdemeanours. She loved that Cody didn't make a big deal of it.

'Coke will do, thanks, Cody.' Miller sat down with Hine.

Cody bent down and whispered, 'Hine and I, we didn't want to say anything... make you uncomfortable. But we're here for you. You know, if you need us. And Eric's a dick. But we all knew that already.'

Miller felt ridiculously grateful. 'Thanks guys,' she said, and Cody disappeared to get the drinks.

Hine surveyed the room. 'Who're you looking for?' Miller asked.

'No one. Someone. Anyone,' Hine laughed, throwing back her head. 'I'm always on the look-out for someone. That Johnno's not too bad.' She looked over at the bar where he was busy pouring handles. Hine winked at Miller as Cody came back with Jay, who was helping carry the drinks.

'Hi, Jay.' Hine pouted as she took a sip from her drink. She'd moved on from Johnno and now homed in on Jay. 'Sit down by me.' She patted the seat next to her.

Jay placed his beer and Miller's Coke on the table. He looked over at Miller and smiled.

'Isn't this cosy,' Hine said, moving her chair closer to Jay.

Cody gave Miller a sly smile. 'Cheers, everyone.' Half of the handle of beer disappeared in several successive gulps. 'Shit, I needed that.' He slumped back in his chair.

Miller watched as Hine laughed at something Jay said, then touched his bare arm. Miller was surprised at the feeling in the pit of her stomach – jealousy. She reminded herself she'd had a few occasions where she had the chance to ask Jay out and she'd been too scared to. She turned to Cody and asked, 'Get some good photos?'

'Yeah, I think so.'

The four of them looked over as Lou entered, still in his Santa outfit – minus the hat and beard. He'd taken off the red velvet coat and walked over to the bar with it slung over his shoulder. His friends ribbed him and he smiled good-naturedly.

'Good on Lou for doing that,' Hine said, giggling at the sight.

'Maggie asked me if I wanted to do it,' Jay said, shaking his head.

'Not keen?' Miller asked.

'Hell, no. Not really my scene.'

'What *is* your scene, Jay?' Hine asked, leaning closer to him, head cocked.

He looked happy enough to be in her clutches. *What red-blooded man wouldn't be?* Miller thought.

She looked up to see Aubrey Moore, the receptionist at the

Riverview Hotel, walking towards their table, her large eye liner-rimmed eyes locked on Miller. She didn't know much about Aubrey, just that she was in her mid-thirties and an up-and-coming prospect for chief town gossip. Today she was dressed in a bright-yellow sundress, tan sandals on her feet. She approached Miller, mouth tight as if she'd just sucked on the lemon floating in her gin and tonic.

'I've heard you're doing an article on Logan Dodds.'

Miller didn't bother asking Aubrey how she knew. Lentford, like all small towns, had a group of people who made it their business to be in the know, and from what Cody and Hine had told her, Aubrey knew how to pump people for information.

'You can't do an article on that hideous crime tour he's starting. It's an embarrassment to the town.'

'Is that your only concern about it?' Miller asked. 'That it'll embarrass the town?'

'Of course not. I ran into Karina Hohepa yesterday.'

Ran into or purposely sought out are probably the same to her.

'It's ghastly. How can you give a man like that publicity? Karina was so upset when I talked to her. Logan's just dragging the whole thing up again. Just because you think it's a good story doesn't mean it should be published. This isn't Auckland, you know. People aren't interested in stories like this.'

'I understand, Aubrey,' Miller said. Aubrey's tone had got louder and higher as she spoke and other tables were looking on. 'Look, I don't even know if I'm going to write the article.'

'Yeah, so un-bunch your panties, Aubrey and go have another G&T,' Cody said, and turned back to his drink.

Aubrey glared at him, spun on her heel and walked back to the group she'd been sitting with.

'That woman knows everything,' Miller said.

'Uh-huh,' said Cody. 'Plus, Bull has a huge crush on her so

she gets all the goss from the police station as well.'

'That explains it.' Miller realised where Len got his information: Aubrey, by way of Bull. She knew that Kahu was doing his best to keep what they'd found so far confidential. And Ash was the most professional person she knew. But Bull was a different story. Soon her name was going to be connected to Madi's whether she liked it or not.

'Explains what?' Cody asked.

'Nothing,' Miller said hastily. 'Bit of an age gap isn't there, Aubrey and Bull?'

Cody shrugged. 'Ten years or so. Hine said Bull was best friends with Aubrey's younger brothers in school – has always been obsessed with her. She knows it as well. Uses him. Gets all the news about what's happening down at the station.'

It was then that Miller noticed the pub had quietened. She looked around and saw a crowd gathered at the side of the bar. Cody and Miller craned their heads to see who was in the middle of it all. Miller caught a glance of Bull in the middle of the throng, a head taller than those around him. His pale face was flushed, eyes wide, hands gesticulating. Word got around the pub quick enough.

'They've found him! The Scarf Killer.'

'Jack Jenkins, you know, started work on the Smithson's farm a few months back.'

'They've found him?' Hine said, turning to Miller then back to Jay, who just shrugged.

All eyes were on Bull, who was enjoying his fifteen minutes of fame. He was being knocked left and right with back-slapping and people grabbing at his hand to shake it, as if he had single-handedly brought him in. Miller was a hundred percent sure Bull wasn't supposed to speak of this to anyone and wondered what Kahu would have to say once he found out.

'Thank god that's over,' Hine said. 'I have a flatmate. And I know he was only after women who lived on their own. But shit, it was all getting a bit scary.' She sucked on her vodka tonic, pursing her pink lips, and moved closer to Jay. Miller noted she was almost in his lap and ignored the flip-flop sensation in her gut.

Cody nodded in agreement.

Hine got up from the table, yanked down her miniskirt which had ridden up her thighs and walked over to Bull, squeezing through the throng.

Miller and Cody watched as she flicked her hair and pressed her lips together, then she and Bull smiled at each other. Hine was doing what she did best. Thirty seconds later she dragged Bull over to their table with a fresh drink in her hand.

'So, Bull, tell us all about it. Here, sit in my chair.' She pushed Bull into her chair, looked around for somewhere to sit, then perched on Jay's lap. Jay looked as though he was in heaven. Of course he was. He was a guy in his early forties, who had the full attention of a twenty-something. Miller didn't stand a chance.

Bull coloured and cleared his throat. 'Jack Jenkins has been arrested. Just brought him in. He's been charged with sexual assault before, done time a few years back.'

'What evidence do they have?' Miller asked, wondering if Jenkins was one of the men Kahu had been looking into.

'Not sure,' Bull said, hesitant in his answer. 'Detective Parata's talking to him at the moment.'

'So he's actually been arrested? They're not just talking to him?'

Bull didn't get a chance to answer as someone listening in from the next table spoke up. 'Course it's him.' He took a long drink from his beer and wiped his mouth on his bare arm. 'You can tell he's a psycho. He's got that look in his eyes, the way he holds himself. Guilty as sin.'

Everyone around them nodded.

Trial by small-town pub, Miller thought. What this guy didn't know, what many people didn't know, was that 'the look in his eye' usually didn't come till it was too late. And that the way he held himself had nothing to do with what he was.

Miller finished her drink in silence and sent a text to Kahu: 'Jack Jenkins? Scarf killer? Bull's just let half of Lentford know at the Royal.'

Miller was surprised when Kahu replied almost immediately: 'Bloody Bull. Brought Jenkins in for questioning because of his record. He was away at his parents for two of the three murders. Have just released him.'

The atmosphere in the Royal was celebratory. The three behind the bar were rushed off their feet as people toasted to the capture of the Scarf Killer. Miller rose from her chair, said goodbye to Hine, Cody and Jay, and smiled at Bull.

Enjoy it while it lasts, she thought. Kahu, and Ash, will have your arse tomorrow morning.

Chapter 30

Miller's feet pounded against the concrete along the river path. Sweat dripped into her eyes, ran off the tips of her fingers, but she didn't stop. After Madi, then the revelations at the pub that afternoon, it was getting to be too much. He was still out there. And still there was nothing she could do. Reaching the end of the river path, she slowed to a jog. She crossed onto the small grassed area by the river, where a family was gathered around a small fire. River rocks contained the fire and they held pink and white marshmallows skewered onto metal prongs over the flames. The campervan up on the road must belong to them, she thought. She nodded to them and walked down to the river, wondering about the lack of sense of having a fire in these conditions.

The river here, away from town, close to her house, was fast-flowing and deep. There was no gradual incline into the river, just a grassy bank that dropped to the water. Miller lifted her T-shirt and wiped her sweaty forehead, then took off her shirt and wet it in the river. She squeezed it out and draped it over her shoulders, feeling her core temperature slowly falling.

She watched the dad pour a mug of water on the flames and gather his family back up to the campervan. Along the path, she watched a runner approach. He raised his hand and jogged over to her. She became painfully aware that she was standing in her crop top, her midriff bare, and dragged her T-shirt from her shoulders to cover her front.

'Miller, hey.' He took off his cap and sunglasses.

'Oh, Jay. I didn't recognise you. I normally see you in jeans and a polo shirt.' She realised she was staring at his tanned, muscled legs and raised her head to meet his eyes.

'Well, I guess I'd better make more of an effort.' He smiled, his eyes drifting to the skin on her stomach that was still on show.

Jesus, are we flirting? Miller realised how long it had been. There was a fleeting relationship in Auckland during the Castle Bay trial. Craig, an accountant, had become too needy and a little too focused on her part in the trial. It had gone on for too long and soon he was talking about moving in, when all she thought about around that time was work and whether today was going to be the day she broke her sobriety. And so she had ended it.

'I didn't know you ran,' Miller said, realising how stupid she sounded.

'Yeah, try to get out here every day. What about you?'

'Same. I'm surprised we haven't run into each before now.' She turned her head to the left, just over Jay's shoulder, where movement caught her eye. 'Oh shit!' She ran over to the abandoned fire. The mug of water on the fire hadn't been enough to extinguish it, and Miller stomped on the flames that crawled over the yellowing grass. Jay was at her side, doing the same. Miller shook out her damp T-shirt and started hitting the ground. Jay disappeared and returned with his T-shirt sodden to do the same. It was alarming how quickly it spread and they soon realised it was too big for them to handle.

'Have you got your phone?' Miller asked, panting.

Jay had already pulled it out of his pocket. Five minutes later the fire siren went, calling all volunteers to the station which wasn't far away, a block over from the main street.

Jay and Miller continued thrashing the burning ground. It had started off as only a small circle but now a large patch of grass was alight, devouring the dry ground.

Fifteen minutes later the fire truck arrived, followed a short while later by an ambulance.

The fire was put out in minutes by the group of volunteers, Lou directing proceedings. Miller recognised Tane and Adam, Emmeline's boyfriend. Aubrey, in too-big overalls and a lop-sided helmet, operated one of the hoses which she was now winding back up.

Miller watched Bull walk over to her, offering to help, but whatever she said in return halted him in his steps, so he made do with watching. They both glanced over at Miller and then continued chatting.

Miller and Jay sat in the back of the ambulance getting the burns on their hands seen to.

'This is the last thing Lentford needs, isn't it,' Jay said, holding his hand out as the ambulance officer cleaned and dressed a burn on his palm.

'Tell me about it,' Miller said. 'Eight days till Christmas and Lentford's not in the best shape. What are you up to for Christmas?' Miller asked, regretting the question as soon as it came out of her mouth. She hated it when people posed that question to her.

'No plans, really. Lou and Maggie have taken pity on me. But I don't know. I kind of feel like I'm gate-crashing.'

Miller nodded, knowing how he felt.

The ambulance officer finished up with Miller's hand. She had small burns on her knuckles, but nothing too serious.

Lou came up to them. 'You two okay?'

They both nodded.

'Any idea how this started? Looks like a campfire.'

Miller explained what she'd seen.

'Bloody idiots. Who would even think about lighting a fire in this weather? Fuckin' tourists. C'mon, you two. Miller, Bull's waiting to take you home. Jay, you can come with me if you want.'

Miller was hesitant to leave, thinking this could be her chance. But the image of Jay and Hine in the Royal that afternoon dashed the small amount of confidence she felt and she waved goodbye to Jay as he made his way up onto the road.

Chapter 31

On Monday morning Miller did the coffee run for everyone back at the office. She hadn't heard anything more from Kahu and was curious to hear what the locals thought. She knew Bull speaking out of turn wouldn't have just finished at the pub. Yesterday afternoon everyone would have gone home and told husbands or wives and friends. Before Jack Jenkins arrived home from speaking with the police, he had already been labelled a murderer.

'Morning Miller,' Len said behind the coffee machine. He winked at her as he took her order.

'Morning, Len. Li not in today?' Miller asked, glad he didn't expect Li to work today as well as her un-rostered shift yesterday.

'Little bitch bloody quit on me halfway through her shift yesterday,' Len said, shaking his head.

Miller winced at his language. 'What happened?'

'Got her knickers in a twist. Had the gall to call me a racist. Can you believe that?'

Yes, Miller thought.

'Bloody Asians came in here yesterday. Demanding this and that like we were a bloody five-star restaurant. I may have called them bloody chinks or something like that,' he laughed. 'Not to their face, though,' he said when Miller didn't join in.

Like that makes it better. 'Nothing like a bit of casual racism, eh Len.'

He looked at her, confused, then laughed again.

Idiot.

'Anyway, she had a hissy fit and walked out. She better not think she's getting paid for yesterday. She's more trouble than she's worth.' He finished up an order and took it to a table and returned to make Miller's.

'Let me know if you hear of anyone after a job, eh? Good hours. Great boss.' He winked again and Miller felt the urge to punch him right in his twitchy eye. She'd pop in and check on Li before she left for Shanghai.

'Hear about Jack Jenkins?' Len asked as he got milk from the fridge and ground the coffee beans.

'What? That he was taken in for questioning about the murders and released an hour later because he had an alibi?' Miller knew she sounded pissed off but didn't care.

'Huh,' Len said. 'Word is he's the one. He murdered our girls.'

Miller thought his choice of words odd.

'It wasn't him. Just gossip,' she said, paying for the coffees.

'Well, it's all around town. It's all anyone's talking about when they come in.'

No doubt fuelled by you.

'So if it's not Jack, who is it?' Len mused.

Miller shrugged, not in the mood to get into this with him.

'Any theories, Miller? You're good at this stuff, aren't you?' He winked again, as though they were sharing a private joke.

'Thanks for the coffee, Len.' Before she turned to leave she said, 'If you're chatting to anyone today you may want to help Jack Jenkins out and put them right.'

Back at the office Jay had delivered the latest issue of the *Lentford Leader*. Copies would be delivered to houses and shops tomorrow, but Miller wanted to take a few copies over to Cassie. She felt it was on her for the article to draw someone out who had some knowledge of Margaret's murder.

Miller walked down the main street to Cassie's house. 'Bloody Jack Jenkins,' she heard a man say, standing in the middle of the footpath talking to two others. 'Not surprising, though. I hear he's already been in the clink.'

The other two muttered their agreement.

Two women passed Miller, dressed in neon activewear and caps, talking as fast as they were walking. 'I always knew there was something dodgy about him,' one said. The other nodded emphatically.

It took all of Miller's strength not to pull them up and set them straight. She didn't even know Jack Jenkins, had never even set eyes on him. And, hell, for all she knew he was a piece of shit, but he still didn't deserve this. She approached Cassie's house, wondering if Jack's life in Lentford was over.

She knocked, and Tiff answered the door dressed in a crop top and boxer shorts. Miller could smell marijuana as it drifted out the door, joining the already oppressive heat, making Miller light-headed.

'Hi.' Miller physically braced herself. 'Is Cassie in? I brought her a few copies of the paper.'

Silence.

'Her article's in it,' Miller said, handing Tiff the papers.

Tiff took them and threw them in the corner by the door.

'She wanted copies for her dad and sister. I put a few extra copies in for... whatever. I thought she might want them. Can you make sure she gets them?' Miller hated how this woman made her feel. Awkward. Defensive.

Tiff folded her arms across her chest. 'You know Cass is taken, right? You know she's my girlfriend?'

'Of course,' Miller said. 'Look, Tiff—'

'Tiffany. Only my friends call me Tiff.' She leaned against the door, her face slack, looking bored, wanting Miller to leave.

Miller felt her lips stretch, attempting a smile, but it turned into a grimace. '*Tiffany*,' she said, placing emphasis on her name, knowing she was being petty, 'I have no interest in Cassie in that way. I've done the article. I've helped her out, I hope. She's a great person—'

'I know that,' Tiff frowned.

'And I hope something comes out of it for her.'

'Yeah, we all do. Was there anything else?' Tiff said, stepping back, already closing the door.

'No, but tell Cassie she can ring me any time if she needs anything.'

'Yeah, right,' Tiff said, closing the door, leaving Miller standing on the front step.

Miller got back to the office five minutes later. Eric's eyes were locked on his computer screen, no doubt gambling away his salary.

'How's the hand?' Cody asked. Most in Lentford knew about the fire down at the river yesterday evening. After all, Aubrey had been in attendance.

Miller clenched and unclenched her knuckles, which were still red and raw from the fire. 'Fine. I think Jay came off worse.'

Ngaire had texted her later that night telling her to write an article. She said there had been a scrub fire on a local farmer's land as well. 'Talk to one of the volunteer firefighters. Get a few quotes about the weather, the need for vigilance, etcetera.'

'Bloody hell,' Hine said, turning in her swivel chair to face Cody and Miller. 'It literally feels like we're in hell.'

'Might want to look up "literally", Hine,' Cody said.

'Well, we've got some sicko murdering women, it's so hot

the tar seal outside is melting and it seems now the town is catching fire. Feels like hell to me.'

Cody shrugged, happy to be put in his place. 'The town's not actually on fire.'

Hine screwed the piece of paper up in her hand and threw it at him.

Miller thought Hine was right, though. Lentford was not the place to be at the moment.

'What are you up to for Christmas?' Cody asked Miller from behind his desk.

'Not much,' Miller said. And by not much, she actually meant treating the day like any other. Christmas had become a major non-event. It didn't bother her too much, but she knew it bothered other people that she was so low-key about it. She didn't want anyone to feel sorry for her. She especially didn't want invites to family gatherings. Ash had texted a couple of days ago inviting her to lunch with her and Zach; she'd yet to make up her mind.

'You meeting up with family? Doing the big lunch thing?' Cody asked innocently.

As much as she liked Cody, he would be the type to invite her along to whatever he was doing, so Miller nodded and smiled.

The door from the main street opened and Aubrey walked in, dressed in her Riverview Hotel uniform of pale-blue, short-sleeved shirt and black pencil skirt. She pulled a white hand-kerchief out of her handbag and pressed it against her forehead before approaching Hine.

'Here we go,' muttered Cody, turning back to his computer screen.

Miller did the same. Aubrey would pop in every few weeks with a list of 'newsworthy' stories for the *Leader*. Ngaire would assign either Cody or Miller to the stories if they were of any value, which they rarely were. Miller hoped there was nothing important. The content for their next issue needed to be in by Christmas Eve and the paper would be put out on the twenty-seventh before their break over the new year. She already had her hands full with articles on Emmeline, Tamara and Madi, along with all the other pieces Ngaire had assigned her.

After Aubrey had spoken to Hine, she walked towards Ngaire's office, frowning at Miller as she passed.

'You're in her bad books after yesterday at the Royal,' Cody said.

Miller smiled. 'I don't even get extra points for helping to prevent the fire? I think I'm probably always in her bad books. What does she want with Ngaire? More great leads?'

Hine shrugged. 'Apparently, she has some information that could make a very good front-page story. She said if Ngaire didn't want it she'd take it to the *Waikato Times*.'

Cody and Miller rolled their eyes in unison.

Aubrey was back out of the office within five minutes, and ten minutes later Ngaire called Miller into her office.

'Sucker,' Cody teased.

'Shut the door,' Ngaire said. She pushed herself back from her desk and eyed Miller. 'Aubrey's just brought a possible story to me.'

'Oh yeah?'

'She said one of my reporters has been receiving letters from the Scarf Killer.'

Miller's heart skipped a beat. 'Fuck,' she said. Kahu was going to go nuts.

'Indeed,' Ngaire said, reaching for her vape.

'Ngaire, this can't get out. This isn't a story – well, not yet anyway. These letters I've been getting, they're a part of the ongoing police investigation. They aren't supposed to be public knowledge.' Miller felt herself sweating in the small office. She got up and started pacing, fanning herself with her hand. *Bloody Aubrey and Bull*, she thought, remembering how they looked at her at the fire yesterday. Then she realised, if Bull knew, did Ash? Surely Ash would've said something.

Ngaire held a hand up to calm her. 'I managed to get hold of Detective Sergeant Parata. He's going to have a word with Aubrey, make sure this goes no further.'

Miller nodded and sat down again.

'But it *would* make a good piece,' Ngaire said. 'Why's he writing to you?'

Miller hesitated but knew she could trust Ngaire, plus it felt good to talk about it with someone. 'He writes to me with their names, once he's... killed them. He wants to be famous. He wants me to write about him. Once he's done, I assume. He wants his story told.'

'Well, there'll be plenty of people to do that. Why you?'

'I guess because I live here. He's also mentioned Castle Bay, the article I wrote about that.'

'It would make a great piece. It would get picked up, for sure.' Ngaire's business hat was on now.

'I don't know if I feel comfortable doing it,' Miller said, thinking of Kahu.

'People want to know about this stuff, Miller. Normal people, everyday people who go about life obeying laws, being basically decent people, want to read about this other side. And who better to write it than you?'

Miller knew all of this. 'It feels like I'm doing him a favour. It's not helping anyone. It's just feeding the public's hunger. And giving him what he wants.'

'That's what a journalist does, Miller, feeds the public's hunger, whether it be for politics, violent crime, education – you name it. It's what we do.'

'Well, I can't do anything at the moment. Not till they catch him.' *Or he gives himself up.*

Ngaire was silent. Miller didn't want to fight her on it, but in the end Ngaire was her boss.

Ngaire turned to her laptop. 'You sorted with the fire article?'

Miller nodded, breathing a sigh of relief. Subject changed.

'Good. We're sorted for next week's issue with a strong emphasis on the murders, of course. I'm firming up stories for the first issue next year. You can do the interview before Christmas or after, up to you. But it will be in next year's first issue. Maggie Muller,' Ngaire said.

'Lou's wife?' Miller asked, suddenly interested.

'You know them?'

'I know Lou.'

'Lawnmower guy,' Ngaire said. 'Anyway, Maggie Muller's the president of the Lions Club here. First female president of the organisation in the Waikato – bit of a big deal. Lentford has one of the oldest chapters in New Zealand, so I wanted to do a story about that in conjunction with Maggie and her presidency.'

Miller nodded. It would be a good story and perfect for their readership.

'Maggie's expecting a phone call to set it up. They're not going away over Christmas so she's happy for you to pop in any time.' Ngaire inhaled on her vape and exhaled menthol-scented vapour into the small office. 'Good?'

'No problem,' Miller said, rising to leave.

'And keep me posted,' Ngaire said, eyeing Miller through the dissipating cloud of vapour. 'This is going to be big.'

Miller nodded, dismayed but understanding the excitement in Ngaire's voice.

Chapter 32

'Off you go, Cassie,' Tane said, coming out of the office to join her and Johnno behind the bar. 'It's past six, you're all done.'

'The place is heaving, Tane,' Cassie said. 'I can stick around if you want.'

'Johnno and I can handle it. Can't we?' He turned to Johnno who rolled his eyes. As usual, Johnno wanted to be anywhere that wasn't the Royal.

'Off you go. I see your lady friend's already here.' Tane pointed at Tiff at the pool table and handed her two handles of beer.

Cassie walked out from behind the bar and weaved through the full tables, the Eagles' 'Hotel California' battling for attention over the din.

Tiff leaned over the pool table, one lithe brown leg hard up against the table, the other stretched out behind her, arms poised, showing off a decent amount of cleavage in her singlet. Cassie smiled and her stomach did a pleasant twist, knowing Tiff was all hers. She walked towards her, smiling.

She and Tiff had had a great weekend. They'd gone down to the river on Saturday evening after all the families had packed up and gone home for dinner. They'd had a swim, and even though the sign proclaimed there was an alcohol ban, they'd drunk wine and made out on the picnic blanket under the oak trees that bordered the river. On Sunday they'd gone to the

Christmas parade which Tiff said was naff, but Cassie managed to talk her into. They'd scored drugs off Eric at the Royal after her shift and got high late Sunday afternoon. Cassie had put out of her head the incident with the note in the rubbish bin. She hadn't confronted Tiff – there was no point. Tiff would just turn it around and blame her. She was beginning to understand Tiff more and more. She'd had a hard upbringing from what little she'd shared and needed extra attention. Tiff got jealous easily, but Cassie was getting used to that, thought it was a compliment. Tiff only got like that because she loved Cassie so much, she was sure.

'Hi,' Cassie said after Tiff had taken her shot.

'Hi!' Tiff said, victorious as the eight ball smoothly entered the pocket for the win. 'Come. Sit. How was your day?' she asked as they both sat on stools, their back to the leaner, looking out across the room.

'Okay. Glad it's over. You?'

'Fine. Boring, really. Especially with you not at home.' She intertwined her fingers with Cassie's. Cassie looked around the room, and Tiff, smiling, understanding, let her hand go.

'Oh, you missed me,' Cassie said, teasing. 'Look what I've got.' Cassie rummaged around in her bag and brought out the copy of the *Lentford Leader* that Miller had dropped off that afternoon.

'Ta-da.' She turned and put the paper on the leaner, pointing at the full-page article titled *It's Not Over*. 'How does it look? The paper's not officially out till tomorrow, but Miller wanted me to get one. Here, have a read. And, look, there's the police artist's sketch of Karl Taylor, nice and big, so it can't be ignored. Don't know about the photo of me, though,' she said, cringing. She looked at Tiff, knowing the photo was pretty good, but still wanting Tiff to compliment her. She realised Tiff had gone quiet, too quiet.

'What's wrong? Is the photo that bad?' she joked, inspecting it.

'Who took it?' Tiff asked, sipping at her beer.

'Miller did. I didn't want to, not really, but she said it helps when people can put a face to the name in the article. I guess I'm going to get a few stares around here now,' Cassie said, not looking forward to questions and glances all over again, but if it helped, she would gladly put herself on a pedestal to be gawked at and spoken about.

'You have a look in your eyes. It's flirty,' Tiff accused, wiping foam from her top lip.

'Tiff!' Cassie laughed. 'It's hardly flirty. If anything, I look sad, reflective.' She angled her head to look at the photo.

'Whatever,' Tiff said. 'It's not like it's going to cause much of a stir. You do realise that in the last few weeks three women have been murdered?'

The way she said it was accusatory, as though Cassie had forgotten about the women's murders.

'Of course I do. Don't look at me like that. It's horrible what's been happening here. I just... I don't know, I just want one person to come forward, to kick start the investigation again. It's only going to take one person to remember something. Don't you think? Plus, Miller said other papers might pick up the story.'

'Don't hold your breath,' Tiff muttered.

They sat in silence, Cassie wondering, yet again, how their conversations could so easily deteriorate.

'Miller said she dropped a few copies off at home this morning,' Cassie said.

'Not that I know of.' Tiff drained her beer and walked up to the bar without saying anything else.

Cassie took a deep breath. She put the newspaper back in her handbag. She'd been so proud, but she should have known Tiff wasn't going to be excited about it. She had something against Miller and was never going to get on board with this while Miller was involved. Trying to think up something else to talk about that wasn't so volatile, she startled when she heard a voice to her right.

'Cassie Hughes?'

Cassie turned. 'Fenella. Miss... Dr...' Cassie laughed and so did Fenella. 'Sorry, I didn't expect to see you here.'

Fenella was dressed in her usual garb, pencil skirt, tailored shirt and heels. Cassie hadn't seen her since she'd left The Oaks.

'It's Fenella, please.' She tucked her hair behind her ear.

Cassie noticed the slightly puckered pink scar that ran along her forehead, just above her left eye, which had been covered by a bandage last time Cassie had seen her. Fenella noticed Cassie staring and brought her hair back to partially cover it.

'Not my usual haunt,' she told Cassie, looking around. 'Just meeting a friend here for a drink.'

Cassie nodded, thinking the Riverview Hotel would be more to Fenella's taste.

'How have you been?' Fenella asked, and then immediately said, 'Don't answer that if you don't want to. I'm not being nosy. It was just a general question.'

Cassie smiled. Fenella was nice out of The Oaks, not so uptight. 'I'm really well, thank you. I'm doing much better.'

'I'm glad to hear that. And who are you here with?' Fenella asked, looking around.

'Um, well.' Cassie hesitated. 'My girlfriend. Here she comes now, actually.'

Fenella looked to where Cassie's eyes were and they both watched as Tiff wound her way from the bar over to the table.

A strangled groan escaped Fenella's lips.

'Are you okay?' Cassie asked.

Fenella was already backing away. 'Lovely to see you, Cassie. I'd better get going.'

'Was that Fenella I just saw?' Tiff asked, eyes wide. 'What the hell was she doing here? Not really her style. Uptight bitch.' She put the beers on the table and sat down.

'She said she was meeting a friend. I swear when she saw you, she had a mini-fit,' Cassie said.

Tiff barked out a laugh. 'I guess I wasn't the most well-behaved patient at The Oaks,' Tiff admitted.

'Seriously, when she saw you walking over here her eyes bugged out of her head and she made this weird groaning sound. What the hell's that about?' Cassie asked, confused over the woman's reaction.

'Fenella, groaning, what a wonderful thought,' Tiff said, raising her brows at Cassie.

'Why would she react like that?'

'No idea, Cass. Eric's out the back. Apparently, he's been told he can't deal in here anymore. So he's gone out to Smoker's Corner. I'm not sure that's quite what Tane meant. Got some cash? Shall we go score?' Tiff asked picking up her beer and motioning for Cassie to do the same.

'Yeah, I guess so,' Cassie said, even though she wasn't really up for it. She had work tomorrow and Eric's weed made her feel horrible.

They walked out the back of the Royal where a few decrepit picnic tables and the skeletons of old sun umbrellas were piled in a corner. Cassie turned as she went outside and met Fenella's eyes. She didn't look confused or anxious, she looked scared.

Chapter 33

Miller sat in the lounge, finishing her article on Emmeline, Madi and Tamara – their early lives and their lives in Lentford, and also the safety issue around women living alone, and how this shouldn't ever be an issue. The only thing people really wanted to know was who this guy was and how or when he was going to be caught. But Miller had nothing.

She'd already told Ngaire she wasn't going ahead with Logan's article, and after explaining why, Ngaire agreed. 'I don't need the wrath of the town, especially at this time. Have you told Logan?'

'No, not yet,' Miller said. She wasn't looking forward to the task.

She looked at the list of stories she needed to get done for the last issue. Talking to a council member about the new recycling bins, the Salvation Army Christmas food drive, and an interview with one of the primary-school teachers about the school holiday programme. She sighed. 'Riveting.'

On the plus side, Ngaire had left her in charge of articles on the Scarf Killer, so she could do another article on that next, hopefully with a bit of inside knowledge from Kahu. Who knew? This time next week he could be caught, and it would all be over.

Her phone rang and she reached over to the stereo to quieten

Elton's 'I'm Still Standing'. 'Ngaire, hi, what's up?'

'Lorraine, Tamara's mother, has organised a candlelit vigil for the murdered women on the village green tonight. Can you go cover it? Photos would be good. I know you've already spoken with her, but maybe a fresh quote? Apparently the mayor's speaking as well.'

'No problem. Are you going?'

'Can't make it tonight,' Ngaire said, giving no excuse.

Miller hung up and went back to work. She wondered what the turnout would be like. Would the town want to get involved in this?

Miller arrived at the vigil just before eight-thirty. The sun was beginning to descend, the gleaming orb disappearing behind the hills, bathing them in orange and golds as it went. The vigil was scheduled for nine o'clock, which Miller thought was a bit late, but Maggie, Lou's wife, who was handing out white tapered candles, told her that Lorraine thought it would look nicer in the dark. 'The candles, you know,' she said. 'Plus it's a hell of a lot cooler now.' Maggie patted her brow with the back of her hand. 'Although not cool enough.'

She was right, Miller thought. The temperature was still well over twenty-five degrees and there was no breeze to lift the heavy heat that blanketed the small town.

'Maggie,' Miller said. 'While I've got you, shall we set up a time for your interview?'

'Oh, yes, how exciting,' Maggie said, fumbling with her candles. 'Will there be photos?'

'Yes.' Miller smiled as Maggie patted her hair which had lost a lot of its usual body in the heat.

'Well, I've got an appointment at Deidre's tomorrow first thing,' Maggie said, naming the only hairdresser in town. 'So how about tomorrow, around ten?'

'Sounds perfect,' Miller said.

Maggie gave Miller her address and walked off, all five foot nothing of her, swallowed up into the crowd, passing the candles out left and right, speaking to every second person she came across, her voice directing people where to go and what time it was starting, breaking through the subdued conversations around her.

Miller held her candle and followed the crowd into the centre of the village green. She estimated that there were close to two hundred people present. She looked around. He was here. She was sure of it. It wasn't intuition or sixth sense, she just felt he would be here. He'd be enjoying this, wouldn't he? He'd made all of this happen. Seven days before Christmas and a town was in mourning. He'd be in his element.

Miller saw Cassie and Tiff and began to walk over, but Cassie, meeting her eye, shook her head almost imperceptibly. Miller got it: she wasn't welcome. She gave Cassie a sympathetic smile, letting her know she understood.

Ash stood with Bull, who towered over her and most of the crowd. Ash looked in her direction and Miller waved out. Ash raised her eyebrows in greeting, her eyes moving away and scanning the crowd. Typical Ash. When she was on duty, she was the consummate professional. And Miller knew she would be on the look-out for him too. She'd spoken to Kahu briefly and he'd said that he'd given Bull a warning about spreading gossip about the letters. 'It's likely he was having a nosy in the meeting room and came across them.' He'd said neither Ash nor the other local constables were aware of the letters and he wanted it to stay that way for the moment. 'I had a word with an Aubrey Moore. Apparently Bull had spoken to her about the letters. Bit high-and-mighty, gave me some spiel about the public's right to know. I put her right.' Miller had no doubt.

Johnno was on the outskirts of the crowd, pacing back and forth. He looked like a caged animal, and if what Tane said was true, Lentford was his prison. A young woman nearby waved to him. He responded by raising his head once. She ran up to him, throwing her arms around his neck and they walked away, their figures swallowed up in the shadow of the oaks.

Before it got too dark Miller took her camera from her bag and took photos of the gathered crowd. Seeing Eric, she lowered her camera and watched him slowly moving forward, face blank, staring at nothing, ignoring the chatter around him. As people passed him, a space opened up and she saw him pushing a wheelchair. A woman, dressed in a thin cotton dress that looked like a nightgown, sat in the chair, a thin blanket on her lap, her bony hands resting on the back of a Yorkshire terrier that barked and snapped at anyone who dared look in its direction. The woman looked up at Eric in what Miller could only describe as adoration, her mouth moving. Eric bent down and gave her a stiff smile. The smile was gone before he'd righted himself.

Lou and Jay were standing on the outside of the crowd that was coming together.

'Hi, Miller,' Jay said with a smile, which Miller returned.

'How about a photo you two?' She raised the camera.

Lou held his hand up to his face. 'God no.'

She laughed and lowered it. 'How are your hands?' she asked Jay.

He held up his left palm, which was covered with a large beige plaster. 'Not too bad. And you?'

Miller did the same to him. 'Fine.' He inspected her knuckles, his hand lightly brushing hers, causing her to blush and change the subject. 'I'm not sure about the idea of a candlelit vigil in this kind of weather.'

Jay raised his eyebrows. 'Good point. Not sure if I'm up to putting out any fires tonight.' He smiled at Miller. 'What do you think, Lou?'

'Bloody ridiculous,' Lou grumbled. 'I told Maggie, but she said everyone would be responsible. We'll see.'

'I've just been talking to your lovely wife about her interview for the paper, Lou.'

'What's this?' Jay asked.

'Mags has just been appointed president of the Lion's Club,' Lou said, his chest pushed out in pride.

'Good on her,' Jay said. 'I remember my dad being in the Lions. Been around for a while, eh?'

'Over sixty years, so Mags tells me,' Lou said.

'Miller,' Jay said, turning to her. 'I read your article on Cassie...'

'Hughes,' Miller said, when she saw he was floundering.

'Right. Good read. Sad story, though.' He shook his head.

'Very,' Miller agreed. 'We're hoping someone will come forward with some new info.'

'Been a while hasn't it?' Lou asked. 'I remember when they found her body. Jeez, the uproar it caused. Although it had nothing on the circus of the last couple of weeks.'

'Well, I hope something comes from it,' Jay said. He looked away and over Miller's head. 'Looks like it's starting.'

'Ah jeez, I don't even know why I'm here,' mumbled Lou.

'Um, to support the community, Lou? To remember three murdered women, maybe?' Jay's tone was teasing. 'Cmon, it's the least we can do.'

The three of them walked into the crowd. Miller stood behind Cassie and Tiff. They were standing close together, bare shoulders touching. Tiff turned and noticed Miller staring. Her top lip curled into a snarl and she turned back to face the front.

There were two teenage girls standing to Miller's right. They pointed at Cassie. 'That's her,' one said in a whisper that really wasn't. 'Cassie Hughes. The one in the paper.'

The friend nodded knowingly. Miller noticed other people looking in Cassie and Tiff's direction. The whispering started: 'Margaret Hughes.' 'Murder.' 'Old dairy factory.' 'Body.' 'Karl Taylor.' 'Never found him.' As the information was passed around, Cassie was oblivious, deep in conversation with Tiff. When Tiff nuzzled Cassie's neck, Miller heard the two teenage girls giggle. One of them said, 'Oh my god! She's gay!' Cassie, obviously hearing this, stepped away from Tiff, her hands clenched at her side.

The two loudspeakers to the left and right of the small group at the front let out deafening feedback, which caused some to cover their ears and the assembled group to quieten. The mayor, Keith Walker, began to talk, welcoming everyone, especially Lorraine and Emmeline's boyfriend Adam, who were both standing at the front with him. Adam looked straight ahead, his eyes lifted, looking over the crowd. Lorraine pinched her nose with her thumb and forefinger, blinked rapidly then looked around the crowd, nodding at different people, drawing, Miller thought, strength from everyone. Miller took a few more photos and then put the camera in her bag.

Lorraine whispered something to Adam. He squeezed her hand and whispered something in her ear. She nodded and stepped forward, taking the microphone from the mayor. 'For those of you who don't know me, I'm Lorraine Jenson, otherwise known as Tamara's mum,' she said with a smile, and the gathering smiled along with her. 'My beautiful, caring girl was taken from us almost three weeks ago. The way in which she left this world was... horrific, and one that I don't wish to dwell on. Tonight we are here for her, not for the person who took her. He doesn't deserve to be in anyone's thoughts. He doesn't deserve to be known.'

People nodded and murmured their agreement.

'Tonight is for Tamara, for Emmeline.' She turned and looked at Adam. 'And for Madi. Three women taken too soon in the most violent way. We remember them for who they were and not for how they died.'

People made their way around the crowd lighting the candles. Almost immediately someone dropped a lit one. Miller held her breath as the dry grass ignited but it was dampened by a gumboot-clad foot.

'Thank you for coming tonight. It means so—' and that's when she broke down. Maggie was at her side, an arm around her as the closing-in darkness was lit with hundreds of candles. Adam stood on the other side, candle in one hand, the other on Lorraine's shoulder.

The minister from the Anglican church said a prayer which was punctuated with shouts and screams from younger kids who had been dragged along and were playing tag on the perimeter of the gathering. 'Can we please now have a moment of silence for Tamara, Madi and Emmeline.'

And after a few last shouts of laughter from the kids and a few grizzles from tired babies, there was silence, as if even they knew this was important. Miller turned and looked towards the back where Beatrice, William and Logan were standing. Logan, separate from his parents, his lit candle held close to his face, illuminating his doughy features. He was looking around, then met Miller's gaze with a glimmer of a smile.

'Thank you so much, everyone,' the minister said, and turned to Lorraine, talking in low comforting tones.

The mayor took the microphone. 'I know this is a hard time

for Lentford,' he said. 'But we need to stick together. There's no point in blaming and gossiping. It does us no good. This person *will* be found, and he *will* be brought to justice.'

Ngaire had told Miller that Keith Walker had been the mayor of Lentford for the last twenty years. He was almost seventy and had kept the job because no one else wanted it. He carried on speaking, his expressionless voice reverberating around the village green. He spoke about Lentford being held hostage. How no one was safe. Especially women. His speech had gone downhill and people were starting to murmur, uneasy.

'Women need to take precautions,' he said. 'These women were attacked in their own homes, where they should've felt safe.' He cleared his throat. 'Women of Lentford, you need to be aware of what is going on around you to keep yourselves safe.'

'So we just add that to the list, do we?'

The woman who had spoken was a few metres away from Miller, towards the front. She was in her thirties, black cropped hair, a head taller than many around her. Her voice was strong and rang out loud and clear as the murmuring stopped. 'So as well as jamming our keys between our fingers as we walk to our car or front door, checking the back seat of our cars before we get in, as well as not walking home by ourselves after dark, or going running by ourselves. As well as taking self-defence classes all to get home safely – where apparently, we should be worried about our home now too if, god forbid, we've chosen to live *alone*. We're to lock ourselves up at night in our homes. Ignore the sweltering temperatures and close every window just in case some psycho's going to break in and attack us.'

Miller heard shouts of agreement around her.

'Here's a thought,' the woman continued. 'How about the cops catch this son of a bitch so we can get our town back?'

There was a loud cheer. Miller had to admit, she was with

the woman. Lorraine walked away with Maggie and Adam towards the main street. They didn't need to hear this. They'd already lost their loved ones. No safeguarding had worked for Emmeline or Tamara.

'Well,' said Walker, looking around, a drowning man well out of his depth, 'maybe Detective Prata could come up and say a few words.'

Miller winced at the mispronunciation of Kahu's name. She hadn't seen Kahu, but he must have been close to the front as he walked forward, took the microphone without his usual easy smile and looked out into the crowd.

'Kia ora koutou,' he said to the crowd, catching Miller's eye and then moving on. 'You need to know that we're doing everything possible to catch whoever's doing this. I am well aware the process seems slow, but we have many leads we're looking into.'

Miller knew he hated doing stuff like this and wasn't about to do what people wanted: make a promise that this man would be caught. He'd never get people's hopes up like that.

'What fuckin' leads?' someone yelled from the back. 'You go on about these leads. But you still haven't got him.'

This started the crowd off again.

'I understand your frustration,' Kahu said, ever diplomatic. 'But if you just let the police do their job, we'll do our best to get this guy.'

'Fuckin' bullshit,' someone else called back.

That's when the yelling and shouting started. Anyone with any kind of grievance against the police, be it to do with the Scarf Killer or something else, started hurling abuse at Kahu. Someone threw a bottle that hit Kahu in the face. He dropped the microphone and turned away from the crowd. Ash sprinted off in the direction of the main street in pursuit of two men, and

Bull moved into the crowd, getting everyone to disperse.

Walker grabbed the microphone and in a slightly panicked voice told everyone to move on. Candles were blown out, plunging the village green into darkness, leaving the lights up on the main street to guide people back to their cars.

Miller got her phone out, turned on the torch function and made her way against the current of people leaving. She reached Kahu, who was on his feet. She shone the light in his face to check for damage. 'Are you okay?' she asked.

'I'm fine,' he said, annoyed. 'Bloody idiots.' He ran a hand over his cheekbone.

'You were lucky the bottle didn't break.'

'Yeah, lucky.'

A man in a St John's uniform came over. 'I'm Hamish Masters. You okay, detective? You need me to check you out? Our station's just a block over.'

'Thank you. I'm fine. Really,' Kahu said. Miller knew he hated the fuss.

'Sergeant Wirihana got him,' Hamish said. 'The guy who threw the bottle. Tamara's cousin, I believe.'

Kahu sighed. 'She can let him go. I won't press charges. I'm going to head back to the hotel. Thanks, Hamish.'

'I'll walk you back,' Miller said, linking her arm into Kahu's.

The Riverview was only a couple of hundred metres down the road. 'Want to come in?' Kahu said as they reached reception and nodded hello to the manager. 'Not sure if I can sleep any time soon after that.' He rubbed his cheek and winced.

'Sure,' Miller said and turned to the manager. 'Are you able to send some ice up to Detective Parata's room, please?'

The manager glanced at Kahu, clearly curious about what had happened, but nodded. If it had been Aubrey, she'd have got the whole story out of them in a minute flat.

They got up to Kahu's room and the ice arrived in a bowl soon after. Miller grabbed the tea towel on the bench and wrapped a few chunks of ice up and handed it to Kahu. They both sat at the small table in the corner of the large room. 'Nice digs,' Miller said. 'Have you been home recently?' There was a suitcase on the floor, a jumble of dirty dress shirts and trousers, and an open wardrobe showing two clean shirts and a jacket.

'Only when I need clean clothes. But there hasn't been time lately. Cases like this are twenty-four seven. I need to be here.' Kahu pressed the ice against his cheekbone. 'We found some trace. What we thought was bits of dirt on the floor in Madi's room.'

'Okay...' Miller wasn't sure how dirt was supposed to solve a murder case.

'We got it tested.'

'And?' Miller said, hoping there was more.

'It's a type of fertiliser. Pony poo basically. Used in gardening.'

'Huh,' Miller said, underwhelmed. 'And?'

'It's something. But not a lot.' He walked over to the kitchenette and got a glass of water.

'Lou,' Miller said.

'What?' Kahu said, sitting back at the table.

'Lou, who owns the lawnmowing business.'

'Oh yeah, I know him. Maggie's his wife. She introduced herself to me tonight. Pretty full on but a nice woman.'

'He does gardens, stuff like that.' Miller knew she was reaching, knew better than to do that around Kahu.

'Is that it, Miller? Do you actually know him?'

'No. Not really. He does my lawns. I know him to say hi to and have a chat.' Miller thought back to the Doddses' house, their perfect garden and William and Logan's lush vegetable beds. 'How about Logan Dodds? Do you know him?'

'No.'

Miller told Kahu about Logan's group and the true crime tours.

'Creepy,' he said. 'Doesn't make him a murderer, though.'

'He gardens,' Miller said. 'Him and his dad have a big veggie patch. He'd use fertiliser like that.'

'So because he's a gardener who uses fertiliser, he's the one who did it.'

'There's something about him,' Miller said.

'This fertiliser's just one small piece of trace evidence from Madi's house. We didn't find anything like that at the other two. You can't just grab at something and accuse someone, just because they look or act a bit funny. You know what small towns are like – the gossip, the rumour. You know first-hand how that can ruin a person's life.' Kahu took a sip of water. 'I tell you this stuff because it's what we do, isn't it. We talk about work. We bitch and we complain and then we get on with it. I don't share this stuff with you so you can start a wild-goose chase. I know you're in on this. More than anyone else because of the letters. But you've got to keep things in perspective.' Kahu wiped a hand over his face and got up to put the wet tea towel in the sink.

Miller flushed in embarrassment. 'Sorry, I just—'

'You just didn't think. You get a whiff of something and you're like a dog with a bone.' Kahu shook his head.

'I know, I know. Comes with the job, I guess.'

'Miller,' Kahu said, sitting back down at the table with her, 'we'll look at everyone. Almost anyone could be a suspect. But we do it quietly and we do it thoughtfully. No rushing head-on and accusing someone of murder when we don't have all the facts.'

'Consider me scolded,' Miller said, trying to lighten the

mood.

'I'm sorry.' Kahu shook his head, putting a hand on Miller's. 'It's just, this one's getting to me. It's taking too long. It's Tuesday today, and I'm scared there's going to be another one, and then another one after that.'

'Will you look into Logan?' Miller rose from her chair, knowing she was pushing it.

Kahu snorted. 'You really are like a dog with a bone.'

'Sometimes I'm right, though.'

'Yeah, yeah,' Kahu admitted. 'Get out of here. I've got an early start. Have you got your car? You're not walking, are you?'

'No, it's just down the street. I'll be fine.' Miller got her keys out and jammed them between her fingers, a ready weapon. 'This is Lentford, after all.'

Miller got back to her car and cursed as she turned the ignition – nothing. She loved her old Triumph but hated how temperamental it was. She tried a couple more times with no luck. She'd call Steve the mechanic first thing in the morning for a jump-start. He'd done it three times since she'd been here. Home was only a fifteen-minute walk. The main street was quiet; everyone from the vigil long gone.

She passed the Royal which looked as if it was just closing. People were scattering to cars or walking home. Fifty metres up, she turned left off the main street. It got darker here, the residential streets not as well lit. The heavy sound of footfalls came from nowhere, chasing the comfortable silence away.

She turned, her heart thumping. Two men were racing towards her. There was no doubt in her mind they were coming for her. She deliberated for a few seconds – run back to town, to the Riverview, or run home? She was closer to home. She turned and broke into a sprint, but those few seconds of deliberation had cost her. Even at a sprint, the two men were on her. One grabbed her shoulder, halting her stride, making her stumble.

'Miller Hatcher,' one of them said, standing in front of her. He was dressed in shorts, a T-shirt and heavy work boots. He bent over, panting. 'We hear you're doing some fucked-up article on Logan Dodds.'

Miller cursed Aubrey yet again. She turned to walk away but collided with the other guy who had moved in behind her. She stepped to the side, both of them in her sights. 'Look,' Miller said, arms held out in front of her, stepping back. 'I am *not* doing the article.' She looked behind at a house, its windows black. If she shouted loud enough maybe someone would come.

'Yeah, right,' the other one said. His long hair fell into his eyes, his upper lip glistened with sweat. They'd probably come straight from the Royal. He held a Murder Club pamphlet in front of her. 'What is this shit? A club about murders? Fucked up is what it is. And you fuckin' journalists think you have a good story and go for it. Never think about anyone else involved. You need to go back to wherever you came from.'

Miller walked backwards along the footpath and then turned and broke into a run again.

'Shit!' one of them yelled. 'Get her!' Again they were too fast and one of them ploughed into her, knocking Miller to the ground. Her face hit the footpath and she could taste blood. She turned onto her back as one of the men stepped towards her. She kicked out at his shins before he could get any closer.

'Bitch!' he yelled, clutching his shin.

Miller got to her feet as the other one approached. She spat out a mouthful of blood and visualised her punching bag as he came at her. She lifted her left leg off the ground and bent her knee. Her foot connected with the guy's midsection and brought him to his knees.

'Hey!' Miller turned and saw Logan lumbering towards her. His heaving mass reached her, out of breath and wheezing. 'Miller, are you okay?' he asked, surveying the scene in front of him.

The two men were on their feet and advancing on Logan. *Shit*, Miller thought. *This is not going to end well.*

'Just who we wanted to see. The town freak,' one of them said, a wide grin on his face.

Miller's bag had landed a few metres away from her. She edged towards it, her shaking hands finding her phone, and she rang Kahu. By the time she ended the call Logan had been dealt a couple of blows to the face, his T-shirt was splattered in blood, and he was in the foetal position on the footpath. Both men aimed kicks at his back and stomach. Logan shouted in pain. Miller had never been more confused about what to do. She couldn't leave him, but if she tried to fight the two men she knew she couldn't win. She wiped her mouth, leaving her hand stained with blood, and approached the two men. 'I've just rung the police,' she said. 'They'll be here in minutes.'

They stopped and looked at each other. One turned to Miller. 'Hopefully you've learnt your lesson.' A growling sound came from his throat and he spat on Logan. He pulled the pamphlet out of his pocket, screwed it up and threw it at Logan and then both turned and ran.

Kahu arrived a minute later in a T-shirt and shorts, jandals on his feet. 'Shit, are you all right?' he asked, holding her face in his hands, squinting at her mouth. 'I've rung the ambulance and Sergeant Wirihana. Here, sit.' He led her to the grass verge and seated her before going to attend to Logan, who was moaning a few metres from her.

'Why did they do this?' Kahu asked.

'The article,' Miller said.

'What? On the Scarf Killer?'

'No. Kahu,' she said, 'meet Logan Dodds. President of the Murder Club.' She lay back, feeling queasy. Closing her eyes, she listened to Logan correcting Miller and telling Kahu about the True Crime Enthusiasts Club.

Chapter 34

Miller's alarm clock switched on and the radio host blared out, way too chirpily for 6.30 a.m., that it was 'five sleeps till Santa and I hope all your Christmas shopping is done!'

Miller groaned and kicked the covers off. She didn't get to bed till after midnight and had slept fitfully, images of Santa and the Scarf Killer streaming through her subconscious.

Her mouth ached. Hamish from St John's had taken her and Logan back to their base. He cleaned Miller up and applied butterfly stitches to her cut lip. He said Logan had been lucky: a small cut above his eyebrow, bruising to his face and torso, and most likely a couple of cracked ribs.

Beatrice arrived, eyes wide at the blood spatters on Logan's T-shirt. She enveloped his large frame in a hug and whispered to him, 'Oh, I'm glad you're all right. My god, the fright you gave me.' She looked up at Kahu. 'Who was it. Who did this?'

Logan had given Ash the details. He knew both men. She was already paying them a visit.

'*Why* did they do this?' Beatrice asked.

'They were a bit upset about me writing the article on Logan,' Miller said. 'It's probably not the best idea to publish.' Miller knew it was a cop-out – she hadn't yet told Logan she wasn't doing the article, and this was a good reason, at least better than 'You're too creepy'.

Beatrice nodded. She helped Logan up and thanked Hamish.

'Miller, are you going to be okay?' Logan asked.

'Yes, Logan. Thank you for what you did.'

Logan nodded, a thumb jammed in his mouth, chewing at the skin around his nail, and let himself be led out by his mother who was still whispering in his ear.

'Do you still want me to look into him?' Kahu asked. 'Seems decent enough. Saved you from those two dickheads.'

Miller thought 'save' wasn't quite the word. But that was ungrateful. If Logan hadn't appeared, who knew what would have happened.

She lay in bed, vaguely remembering the excitement that Christmas used to evoke. Out of everything Christmassy she remembered the music, but only because her parents had rejected Christmas carols. Instead of 'Jingle Bells' and 'The Twelve Days of Christmas', Miller's Christmas soundtrack had been the Beatles, the Rolling Stones and Elton John.

She got out of bed and winced as she walked down the hallway. She'd pulled a muscle from the roundhouse kick she'd performed last night – connecting with a solid, six-foot man was quite different from her padded punching bag. As she made herself coffee, she thought of the candlelit vigil. People were getting sick of the police doing nothing. Miller knew they were doing everything they could, but to the people of a town where three women had been murdered in three weeks, it looked as if they were sitting on their hands. It was Wednesday today, and Miller wondered who was next, and where the next letter would turn up. Work? Her house? The idea that he'd slid the letter about Madi under her door while she was inside sleeping – that he knew her, knew where she lived – still sat heavy with her. Would he break into her house when he was ready to show himself? Would he turn up on her doorstep and ask to be let in? Or would Kahu and his team find him before all of that happened?

Just before ten she checked in with Kahu. Last night he'd asked her to text him in the morning. 'So I know you made it through the night,' he said, half-joking.

She didn't hear back from him straightaway and so deposited her phone into her satchel and locked the front door. She stopped on the steps and looked up. The sky for the past month had been an unwavering deep blue without a single cloud marring its canvas. But today it was the colour of the river stones found on the bottom of the Piako River. She held her hands out as if expecting rain, but it was still the same dense heat.

Maggie and Lou Muller's house was red brick with a corrugated iron roof, nothing special, which made the garden and lawn look even more spectacular. Miller parked on the strip of concrete and admired the hedges and shrubs, all pruned to perfection. There wasn't a single blade of grass out of place or a stray leaf to mar the mown lawn. But, like most sections in Lentford, the hue was brownish yellow rather than green, and crunchy underfoot.

The glass-paned front door opened before Miller reached it, and Maggie stood, coiffed and perfumed, to welcome her. She wore white linen pants, a pale-pink top with a patterned scarf across her shoulders tied in a loose knot at her chest. Miller wondered about the unnecessary second layer in this heat, but the first words out of Maggie's mouth cleared up any confusion. 'Is this okay for the photo? I had no idea what to wear.'

'You look great,' Miller said.

'Oh, you poor thing. What on earth happened to your lip?' Maggie asked as Miller followed her through the lounge and into the dining room, which still sported carpet from the Seventies, a swirling mix of browns, beiges and creams.

'I had a wee stumble last night on the way home from the vigil. It's fine.' Miller touched her lip, instantly realising she should've known better than to lie. Word about what happened last night would already be making the rounds.

Maggie pulled out a chair for Miller and began chatting about how excited she was to be in the *Lentford Leader*. 'Ngaire's done so well with the paper since she took over as editor. We used to go to school together. Did she tell you that?'

'No, she didn't,' Miller said, tempted to pry into what the young Ngaire had been like. She envisioned an intelligent, articulate chain-smoking fifteen-year-old.

'The paper's so good for Lentford. Great content. She always includes everything going on in the community.' Maggie poured tea into two bone china cups without asking Miller what she wanted and added in a heaped teaspoonful of sugar. 'Now, how would you like to do this?' she asked, patting her hair, making sure every strand was still in place.

'We can just have a chat really,' Miller said, taking out her iPhone. 'You're okay if I record the conversation?'

'Oh, yes,' Maggie said, sipping at her tea.

'Great. So tell me a bit about the Lion's Club in general, how you came to be involved with it and maybe a bit about your childhood and how you got to be where you are now.'

'Certainly – oh! Biscuits.' Maggie jumped up and went into the kitchen. Miller heard rifling around, tins being opened and biscuits being put onto a plate.

'Here we go. Not homemade, unfortunately. I'm just too busy at the moment,' she huffed, but Miller could tell 'busy' was exactly what Maggie wanted to be.

'Now I made some notes. I hope that's all right?' She reached out for a few bits of paper on the sideboard behind her and carried on talking, something about always being prepared, and then making a joke about how that was the Scouts, not the Lions.

Miller's face automatically arranged itself into a frozen smile as she stared at the paper in front of Maggie. Thick. Almost like cardboard. Off-white. She found her hand crossing the table to feel the consistency of the paper. It was exactly the same. She would know it anywhere.

Maggie stopped and looked at Miller. 'Lovely, isn't it? Although I shouldn't be using it to jot notes down. It's all I had to hand last night when I got home.'

'It's lovely. Where did you get it from?' Miller asked, trying to remember what Kahu had told her about the paper. Stocked in only ten places in the whole of New Zealand. Was Maggie's name on the shopkeeper's list they gave the police?

'I'm not sure. My good friend Alice Fenton, she lives in Hamilton, buys it for me every birthday and Christmas. I commented once how beautiful it was and now for the past five years I've been given it as a gift.' Maggie stopped just short of rolling her eyes.

'And what do you use it for? Is it just you who uses it? Or maybe Lou as well?' Miller knew the questions were ridiculous, but this was the paper the Scarf Killer used.

Maggie chuckled. 'Lou wouldn't use this, no. Not much of a letter writer.'

'But he knows you have it?' Miller asked.

'Yes, of course he does. I'm sorry, Miller, but why all these questions?' Miller could see Maggie was trying to be polite, but the questioning had thrown her.

'Sorry, Maggie. It's just really lovely paper. You don't really see such beautiful stationery these days,' Miller said, trying to cover up her shock. 'Back to you.'

Maggie spoke for the next half hour with very little prompting from Miller. On the sideboard was a large framed wedding portrait of Maggie and Lou on their wedding day, muted colours and smiling faces. On the wine rack were more photos, grouped tightly together, of vacations, young children, and those same children as adults. The carpet underfoot was comfortably worn. Miller could see into the lounge where two well-worn sofas sat side by side in front of a widescreen TV, thriving house plants on either side. A normal house for normal people, Miller thought. She needed to see Kahu.

She noticed Maggie had stopped talking. 'Thank you so much, Maggie. You've been great.' The way Maggie had been talking Miller assumed she had everything she needed for the article.

She grabbed the digital camera from her bag and took Maggie outside to stand by a camellia bush. 'Perfect, Maggie,' Miller said, hoping one of the half dozen photos she took would do.

'When will the story run?' Maggie asked as Miller packed up the camera.

'Ngaire said probably the first issue next year.' Miller thanked Maggie for her time and after calling Kahu to find out where he was, she headed straight to the Riverview Hotel.

He was in the hotel bar when she arrived five minutes later. 'Nice for some,' she said.

He smiled. 'It's only lemonade. That bloody meeting room at the station gets a bit hectic. Can't hear myself think.'

'How's the face?' Miller asked, noticing the bruising that had come out on his cheekbone.

'It's fine. More to the point, how are you?' He looked at her cut lip.

'Fine.' Neither wanted to talk about last night. 'I have some information,' Miller said, feeling herself getting excited.

'Information?' His eyes narrowed. 'Miller...' he warned.

'I wasn't sticky-beaking. I swear. I was at Maggie Muller's house—'

'Lou's wife.' Kahu shook his head. 'This isn't about the fertiliser thing, is it?'

'Hear me out. She has the paper. The paper that the killer uses.' Miller waited for Kahu to react. She was disappointed.

'Right. How can you be sure it's the same paper?'

'Kahu, I know that paper. She said she got it from a friend in Hamilton, as a gift.'

'Okay.' Kahu rearranged papers on the table.

'So?' Miller said, getting increasingly frustrated.

Kahu made a note. 'I'll get someone around there this afternoon.'

'Is that it?'

'What do you want me to do, Miller? Arrest Lou Muller? And Maggie too while I'm at it? Maybe they're in on it together.'

Miller shrugged.

'One of my officers will go round and have a chat—'

'To Lou?'

'Yes, to Lou.' Kahu's words were slow, his tone patient. She knew he was getting sick of her. 'This is good, Miller. It will be checked out. Just be patient. Let us do our job.'

She nodded. 'Today's Wednesday.'

Kahu was silent, closing up various manila folders on the table.

'Tomorrow night, Kahu.'

'I don't need to be told, Miller.'

Chapter 35

Miller left Kahu, confident that he would do something about Lou Muller. She had to trust him.

Lou had mown her lawns. She'd offered him a drink. He'd sat at her mother's dining room table and they'd talked about Maggie and his grown children. If she saw him down the street or at the pub, she'd have a chat with him. He came across as a caring, community-minded guy, albeit a bit gruff, but what did she really know about him?

Heading to Shady Oaks retirement village, the large drops, only a few at first, landed heavily, held their form and then slid down her windscreen. Then the downpour began. It was so sudden and so ferocious Miller had to pull over, her windscreen wipers unable to keep up with the torrent of water. She watched as people, caught unawares, ran for cover under trees or back into their homes. It was over as quickly as it had begun, as if a tap had been turned off. Miller wound down her window and breathed in the fresh scent of a world washed clean. The trees around her moved in a breeze that chased away the dirt-coloured clouds and by the time she got to Shady Oaks the blue sky was back; a clean palette. Miller stepped out of her car. In the carpark, the sun was already drying patches of concrete, other areas were puddles of warming water. She headed to reception to sign in.

'We haven't seen you for a while, Miller,' said Joan, the nurse who had shown her around on her first day and introduced her to some of the people who didn't get regular visitors.

Miller smiled. 'Been a bit hectic.'

'Those murders,' Joan said, dancing eyes turning worried. 'Just horrific. I know Tamara's mother. Went to school with her. Tragic.' She shook her head. 'Hello, Mr Appleby!' she called out as a stoop-backed gentleman made his way down the hall. Despite Joan's high-decibel greeting he didn't seem to hear and continued on.

'Anyway,' Joan said, her voice lowering. 'I was just saying to Stan, my husband, last night. When's it going to end? Is he just going to keep killing?' She shuddered.

Miller made all the right noises, wishing she could tell Joan that he'd be caught soon, that it would all be over by Christmas.

'Better be off, dear, got my rounds to do. Are you in to see Karl?' Joan asked as they started walking down the corridor.

'Yes, bought him in a copy of the paper,' Miller said, holding up a copy of the *Leader*.

'Oh, he'll love that,' Joan said, turning into a room. 'We get a few copies that we put in the lounge, but they all seem to go walkabout. Good afternoon, Mrs Patel! How are we today?'

Miller carried on down the corridor. She thumped on the door, wincing at the noise, but Karl wouldn't hear her otherwise. She heard a muffled noise inside which she assumed meant to come in.

The wall of heat made her stop for a second at the threshold. All the windows were closed, and the small bedroom smelt of urine and coffee. 'Karl, how are you?' Miller said, breathing through her mouth.

'Who's that?' Karl asked, turning in his chair by the window, squinting.

'It's Miller, Karl. Just thought I'd pop in and drop off the paper.' She crossed the room in four strides. 'Shall I open a window? It's a bit hot and stuffy. Let's get you some fresh air. Did you see all that rain we got before? A shame it didn't last a bit longer,' Miller prattled on as she opened the curtains wider.

'No, leave it closed,' Karl said.

'Why?' Miller asked, hand hovering by the window. 'You need a bit of fresh air in here.'

'Nope. Fuckin' cicadas.' He adjusted himself in his chair with arms so thin they looked as if they would snap.

Cicadas? Was he scared of them?

'Too fuckin' loud. They bloody plant themselves right outside there, on those shrubs.' He leaned towards the window pointing at the clouds of blue and purple hydrangeas sitting below the window. 'Bloody clicking and whizzing. They're the only bloody things happy about this heat.'

Miller pulled up the other chair to sit by him, wondering how long she'd last in here.

'Two people have carked it in the last week. They tell us its old age, heart, whatever, but it's the heat. Need air conditioning in this dump.'

Miller didn't disagree. 'Well, we could cool it down in here – you know, help with the heat – if we opened a window,' she tried again.

'No. Got my fan.' He pointed to the small oscillating fan on his bedside table that was barely causing a breeze.

'Karl, if you want me to stay, I'm going to have to open the window or I'll pass out.'

He grumbled something which Miller took for acquiescing. She opened the window as wide as she could and took a few deep breaths.

'See,' he said accusingly as if she had doubted him. 'Fuckin' cicadas.'

He was right: the buzz and click of insects drifted into the room. Miller had never minded the sound of the over-exuberant insects. She smiled and tried to change the subject. 'I brought you a copy of the latest *Lentford Leader*. Hot off the press.'

He took it from her and started flicking through the paper with gnarled hands. 'You're a good girl.'

'And,' she said, 'this.' She produced a box of Black Knight liquorice from her satchel. 'Merry Christmas, Karl.'

'Oh, you do spoil me. Thank you, Miller.' This was often the way it went with Karl – foul-mouthed and grumpy to grateful and appreciative all in one breath. He placed the box on the floor and continued looking through the paper.

'What are you up to for Christmas, Karl?' Miller asked. 'Do you have family coming to visit?'

'Nah,' he said. 'Locked up in this shithole for Christmas. They try and put a little something on but,' he waved his hand dismissively, 'it's always a bit lukewarm. The ones who are out of it don't even realise what's happening, and those of us who do would rather be anywhere but here. Instead of watery ham and mashed potatoes for lunch, it'll be dry turkey and burnt roast potatoes.' He buried his head deeper into the paper, seeming interested in an ad for the womenswear shop in Lentford.

Miller had met Karl six months ago and he'd never spoken much about family. He'd mentioned his parents once or twice and a daughter in passing but that was it. Miller wanted to know more but knew there was no point in pushing him, so her visits were made up of general chit-chat, listening to Karl whinge about the food, staff and residents at Shady Oaks, and Miller reading aloud to him.

'I know her,' Karl said, lifting the newspaper and pointing at Cassie's photo. He frowned. 'I know that face. How the hell do

I know her?'

'She visited you a few weeks back. Poor girl. She lost her mum a few years back. She – the mum – was murdered. The man who police think killed her is Karl Taylor. Same name as you.'

'I know my bloody name,' Karl muttered, and Miller considered herself chastised.

She looked closely at Karl, watching as the creaky cogs in his head began to turn.

'Yes!' he said. He began reading the article. 'Cassie Hughes, mother Margaret murdered, body found at dairy factory...' He carried on reading the story, tut-tutting every now and then.

He brought the paper closer to him. Miller watched as he studied the identikit photo.

'I'm not sure how good the likeness is,' she said. 'The witness the police have was working from a fourteen-year-old memory. I don't think I'd be very good at describing a work colleague I had that long ago.'

It seemed as if Karl hadn't heard. 'It says here police think there's a good chance his name isn't even Karl Taylor. They think he used an alias.'

'Yeah, they think he may have used someone else's name the whole time he worked in Tauranga.'

'I know what a bloody alias is, girlie!' Karl turned, his overgrown eyebrows settling low over his eyes.

Miller patted his knee. He was prone to outbursts like this. She was used to it. 'I know, Karl. I was just making conversation.'

With the paper laying across his knees, he went back to looking at the identikit drawing, trembling fingers outlining the hair and face.

'I don't want to get anyone in trouble, you hear?' he said.

She nodded, unsure of what he was talking about. He carried

on, 'But I feel bad for that girl. Cassie. She reminds me of my Amanda when she was younger.' He gazed out the window.

'Amanda?' Miller asked. *His daughter?*

'It's been over ten years, hasn't it?' Karl said, ignoring Miller's question.

'What has?'

'Margaret Hughes. When she went missing.'

'Fourteen,' Miller said. 'Why?'

A sparrow alighted on one of the hydrangeas outside, bending the flower so it dropped a few centimetres. It regarded Karl and then Miller.

'Grab that bag for me,' Karl said, leaning forward.

Miller reached for the plastic bag on Karl's dresser. It was filled with broken crackers and bread crusts. He took a crust from the bag and with some effort stood up. He reached out the window and the bird, smaller than Karl's fist, took the crust. It took flight with some difficulty and landed on the grassy area a few metres away.

'Visits me almost every day,' Karl said, proudly, handing the bag back to Miller.

Miller smiled but wanted to get him back on track. 'What were you saying about not wanting to get anyone into trouble?'

'What? Oh, well, my grandson. He's always been a bit of a bad seed.'

Miller was quiet, not wanting to break Karl's concentration.

'But... I don't know. He had a rough start. I always felt bad for him. He was... different. If I'm honest he scared me a bit.'

'Sorry, Karl, I don't really know what you're talking about.' *What's he trying to say? Is it something to do with Margaret?*

'Doesn't matter,' Karl muttered. 'It's nothing.'

'What's your grandson's name, Karl?' Miller asked.

'I'm not bloody telling you. You'll be off to the cop shop

before I know it and they'll be picking him up accusing him of murder.' He laughed at her, incredulous.

'Did he murder someone?' Miller asked, not wanting to make him even more pissed off than he was but she needed to know.

'No, course not.' He went back to reading the paper, but Miller could tell he was thrown. He held the corner of the paper and was working the page back and forth with his thumb and his forefinger until it ripped.

'You mentioned he was a bad seed, had a rough start to life.' Miller leaned forward to try and get his attention.

'No, I didn't.' He stuck out his bottom lip, sulking.

'Karl, this is really serious. Do you know something about Margaret Hughes' murder?' She could hear her voice rising and forced herself to calm down.

'It's all in the past.' He stared out the window. 'No use dragging up what's long over with.'

Miller was beginning to get frustrated tiptoeing around him. 'Karl, do you know something about Margaret Hughes' murder?' she repeated. 'Did your grandson have something to do with it?' She knew she was pushing; knew he didn't like it.

'How dare you!' He threw the paper down on the ground. 'I didn't say anything like that. It was you who wrote the bloody article, started talking about this Cassie and Margaret Hughes – not me. I just mentioned my grandson, nothing more. Jeez, I can bloody tell you're a journalist now. Jumping to conclusions.' He swiped a hand across his mouth where spit had gathered in the corners.

'Karl, I'm sorry. I obviously misunderstood.' Miller put her hand on his.

He withdrew it and turned away from her. 'You can go now,' he said.

She scanned his room. She'd never noticed any photos. A lot

of the other residents had them jammed onto every flat surface they could find – bedside table, drawers and windowsills, taking up one whole wall – a lifetime of memories from family homes being forced into one small space. She looked at the solid set of drawers sitting between the wardrobe and ensuite. She couldn't look there now, not with the mood he was in. Did he have photos of Amanda? Of his grandson?

'Okay, Karl.' Miller said, knowing she'd have to leave it for now. There was no point pushing. 'Have a lovely Christmas. I'll see you in the new year. We can start a new book.'

She got no answer. As she left she heard the window being wrenched closed and the creak of his armchair as he sat down again, tunelessly humming, as if nothing had happened.

Joan came out of the neighbouring room. 'Karl in fine form this afternoon?' she asked. 'Grumpy old bugger.'

Miller smiled. 'Joan, does Karl have a daughter?'

'I think so. He doesn't have much family. Never gets visitors, apart from you, dear.'

'He's spoken of his daughter. Amanda, I think. And also mentioned a grandson. I was wondering if I could get her details. Chat to her... maybe convince her to start visiting?'

'I'm sorry, Miller. We're not able to give out that kind of information.'

Miller knew it was a long shot. Joan was a by-the-book kind of woman.

'Maybe chat to him when he's in a better mood?' Joan said. 'Must dash, there are Christmas carols in the lounge and I'm chief conductor. See you, and Merry Christmas.' Joan marched down the hallway, calling out to various residents to come down to the lounge.

Miller stopped at reception to sign out. The young woman manning the front desk was on a call, so she flipped the book around to look at it. The book was divided into three columns: 'Name/Contact phone number/Resident visiting'. Miller read through pages and pages of visitations trying to find Karl's name. The book held over four months' worth of visitors but apart from Miller's name and Cassie's a few weeks ago, there was nothing.

Miller waited until the woman got off the phone and introduced herself. 'I've just been visiting with Karl Taylor. He gave me some money to buy his daughter a box of chocolates for Christmas,' Miller said, 'The poor thing's forgotten her address and I was wondering if you would mind giving it to me so I can deliver them to her.' She crossed her fingers.

'No problem,' the woman said. Her long nails flew across the keyboard and she noted down the address for Miller on a neon-pink Post-It. 'There we go.'

'Thank you so much,' Miller said, and left before Joan showed her face.

On the way to the car, she looked at the address. Holland Road, Hamilton. The police had always said Karl Taylor was from the Waikato. Did they ever suspect he had taken a family member's name? Probably not – it would've made the search even bigger, almost impossible. Had Karl Taylor's grandson used his name and murdered Margaret Hughes? Is that what Karl was alluding to? Did the identikit force Karl to remember someone he hadn't thought of or seen in years, someone who he'd been happy to forget about because he'd always been scared of him?

Miller got home from Karl's at five o'clock. She looked over at Li's place, noting the pulled curtains in the front rooms, only now realising that Li had left for Shanghai today. She felt guilty that she'd been so caught up in everything she hadn't even said goodbye.

Chapter 36

The noise entered Miller's subconscious on Thursday morning. She dragged herself out of sleep, opened her eyes and tried to identify where it was coming from. Not her bedroom. Not inside the house. The front door. A frantic, continuous scratching on the front door. Was it a letter? Was he standing outside her door right now?

She tried to calm her breathing as she walked out of her bedroom and stood in the hallway. No letter on the carpet, but the scratching continued. At the door she reached out for the handle. She turned the lock and opened the door in one smooth motion, ready to face whoever was out there. She looked down. Patsy jumped up the small step and started barking, dancing in circles yapping at her. Miller bent down to pat her, trying to work out what was happening. Li was in Shanghai. Patsy was supposed to be at the kennels. Why was she here?

'Patsy, here Patsy,' she murmured to the dog, trying to calm it. She crouched down, her hand outstretched. 'Come, Patsy.' That's when she saw it, on the dog's front paws, on her face, the pinkish hue on her white fur.

'What's this, Patsy?' she asked. 'What have you been up to?' But she knew. She knew what it was.

She tried to keep calm. 'Where's your mum, huh?' Miller slipped on a pair of jandals by the door, kept on murmuring to

Patsy, trying to calm the dog, trying to calm herself. She walked over to Li's place, Patsy sitting comfortably in her arms.

Miller tried the front door, knowing it would be unlocked. She stepped into the house and Patsy jumped from her arms, landing awkwardly on the wooden floorboards. She barked at Miller and disappeared down the hallway. The house already had that closed-up musty smell, along with something else, sour, but Li had only left yesterday morning.

Miller walked down the hallway, following Patsy's whimpering. Flashes of Madi's house came to her, her lounge, her hallway, her bedroom. The memory halted Miller's steps, preventing her from getting to Li, but then she quickened her pace when she realised Li might need help. She rounded the corner into Li's bedroom and fell against the door jamb. Her vision blurred and she covered her mouth from the stench – a sweet-sour rotten smell, like nothing she'd ever experienced before.

She swallowed and felt tears prick her eyes. She needed to ring Kahu but no matter how hard she tried she couldn't move. Her eyes were locked on Li's dead body.

Blood from a head wound had congealed on the floor, marring the white carpet. A navy scarf lay limp around her neck. Li's body was bloated and her perfect skin was a marbled grey-green colour; a red foam gathered around one corner of her mouth and nose. Miller couldn't work out what the low hum was at first until she spotted the blowfly alight on Li's head, joining at least a dozen others. Miller felt the bile rise and ran to the toilet to throw up.

She choked back sobs as she went into the lounge. She called the police station and asked to be put through to Kahu. It was a long wait while they tracked him down and Miller tried to calm herself. It didn't work. The deep breaths she took made her feel ill. The smell of death was lodged in her nostrils.

He'd got her. Li was dead. Was this personal? He knew where she lived, probably knew she was friends with Li. He did this because of her.

'Parata.' Kahu's voice came down the line and Miller lost it completely. She couldn't believe she was making another call like this to Kahu.

'Miller? Miller, what's wrong? Are you hurt?' She could hear the worry in his voice and tried to pull herself together.

'Li. My next-door neighbour. She's dead. He got her, Kahu. Please come...' She felt her knees give way and she fell to the floor. She couldn't be in the house any longer. On hands and knees she got herself out the front door where she gulped in the air that smelt of lawn clippings and heat. She buried her face in her knees. She couldn't believe she was here again. She was like his puppet. He killed. She discovered.

Within ten minutes Kahu arrived with his team and Ash pulled up in a patrol car. They both ran to her. Ash got to her first. She sat next to Miller on the step, a protective arm around her shoulder. Her head close to Miller's, she said, 'I was having a coffee with Kahu when you rang. Come on, you don't need to be here.' She took Miller's hand and helped her up. Ash guided her out of the driveway and back to her house. In the kitchen she made coffee and heaped two teaspoons of sugar in while Miller sat at the kitchen table. She placed it in front of Miller, who pushed it away with a shaking hand, the smell making her feel nauseous.

Miller's teeth started chattering so Ash left the kitchen and came back with a throw from the lounge and wrapped it around her. Miller heard footsteps and Kahu appeared in the kitchen. 'Sorry, just had to make some phone calls.' He took a seat at the table with them, placing a hand on Miller's and giving it a squeeze before withdrawing it. 'What made you go over?'

'Patsy, Li's dog. She was scratching at the door this morning. She had blood on her.'

'Okay,' Kahu said.

'Where is she?' Miller asked.

'Who?'

'Patsy,' she said, worried for the dog.

'Your other neighbour just came over. He offered to take her off our hands.'

'Okay, good. Greg's nice. Has kids,' Miller said.

'Just a few questions, all right?'

'Of course.' Miller took a deep breath.

'When did you last see Li?'

'On Sunday. We went to the Christmas parade together. She worked that Sunday afternoon – at the Kowhai. But Len fired her.'

'What did you touch in there?'

'Not much. I didn't touch her body.' An image of Li came to her again. 'The front door. I leaned against her bedroom door. Used her phone – her landline. I think that's it. Oh, I threw up in the toilet,' Miller said, a hand on her mouth.

'Was she safety-conscious?'

'I think all women living on their own are.'

'So she wouldn't let someone into her house she didn't know?'

'I wouldn't think so.'

'Had she mentioned anything about threats, anyone following her, strange behaviour?'

'No. But Len mentioned she quit her job at the Kowhai on Sunday. It sounded like that got a bit heated.' Miller sipped her coffee, and her hands started shaking again. She looked up at Kahu. 'How long's this going to go on for?' She took a deep shuddering breath. 'He's a day early. It's always Thursday night. He kills them on Thursday night, and I get the letter on Friday. That's how it goes. That's right, isn't it? Is he getting impatient? Are they going to come quicker and more often now?' She knew she was rambling.

Kahu was silent, his eyes on Ash. Miller looked at Ash's face. Eyes wide. Stunned.

'Shit,' Miller said, realising what she'd said.

'You've been getting letters from him?' Ash asked, frowning.

'Sorry. Sorry, Kahu. Ash, I couldn't tell you. It was part of the investigation. And Bull knows. I thought you should know. But Kahu said we should keep it quiet...'

'God, I don't care about that Mills. Shit, I can't believe you've been going through all that. Why's he writing to you?' She reached out for Miller's hand.

Miller looked at Kahu and he nodded. 'I got the first letter the night after he killed Tamara. I've received one each time he's killed a woman. He had this idea I can make him famous.'

'He wants you to write about him? Why? Everyone's already out there doing that.'

'The whole Castle Bay thing, I think. He wants to tell me his story so I can share it with the world.'

Kahu rose. 'I need to get back over there. Sergeant—'

'Call me Ash.'

'Ash, are you okay to stay with Miller?'

'Of course.'

Ash walked Kahu to the door and Miller went into the lounge and looked out the front window. She could already see Li's driveway being cordoned off – it was Madi Nilson all over again. Within minutes a crowd had gathered, edging against the cordon. The plastic tape could be broken through or ducked under, but it held the power to hold back the throng. People held cell phones in the air, recording suited and booted forensic technicians moving in and out of the house. An older woman was watching a young man who was recording it all, his head moving to the right every now and then to take in the scene in real time. She shook her head at him in disgust and turned back to the action. *You're just as bad*, Miller thought.

Kahu appeared back at the lounge door. 'One more thing. Did you hear anything last night?'

Miller was silent, thinking. 'I didn't hear anything. No raised voices, no screaming. When you told me about the other victims, I thought surely their neighbours heard something. How could something like that happen twenty metres from me and I didn't even know it?' She shook her head. 'She was supposed to go to China yesterday. I thought she'd left. I never got to say goodbye.' Miller buried her head in her hands. I don't even know when she was killed. I saw her house closed up yesterday morning and didn't think anything of it, just assumed she'd already left – but … she was in there … like that. I could've–'

'Hey,' Ash said, joining her on the couch. 'Don't blame yourself. There's only one person to blame for this. Let Kahu and his team do their thing and get some answers.' Ash nodded at Kahu, giving him the okay to leave.

'Oh god, her poor family,' Miller groaned. 'They'll be expecting her.'

'Don't worry. We'll make sure they're informed,' Ash said. 'I'll go make you a fresh cup of coffee.'

Miller lay down on the couch, pulling her legs up to her chest. Her radio alarm clicked on in her bedroom and she heard the two perky hosts halfway through a conversation, admonishing those who hadn't done their Christmas shopping yet and that there were only four more sleeps to go.

'Fuck Christmas,' Miller said in a small voice. 'Fuck it all.'

Chapter 37

On Friday morning Cassie opened her eyes and stretched. It was past nine and she wasn't due in at work till one. Tiff was already up from the sounds of kitchen cupboards being opened and slammed shut. She hauled herself out of bed and pulled the curtains.

'Another glorious day in sunny Lentford,' she thought, watching the river as it cruised past, muddy brown, on its way to somewhere no doubt more important.

She walked into the lounge to see Tiff in the kitchen, a rare occurrence.

'Sit,' Tiff said, pointing a spatula at her. 'At the table.' She turned back to the stove.

Cassie grinned and seated herself at the table where there was orange juice and a plunger full of black coffee. She poured herself a cup.

'What are you up to?' Cassie asked. Since they'd been living together Cassie had done most of the cooking, and cleaning come to that.

'A treat for my love,' Tiff said, bringing over a plate of pancakes and maple syrup.

'What did I do to deserve this?' Cassie said, beyond elated that Tiff was doing something for her.

Tiff shrugged, smiling and seated herself opposite Cassie.

'Mum always used to make us pancakes on Sunday morn-ings,' Cassie said. 'How about you? Any family traditions?' For weeks now Cassie had tried to pry information out of Tiff about her family, with no luck. A couple of days ago Tiff grudgingly admitted they lived in a 'mansion on River Road in Hamilton. River views. Flash cars. Nice clothes. Just not much love or at-tention for their only daughter'.

'Yeah right,' Tiff laughed, her mouth full of pancake and syr-up. 'We didn't have family traditions, Cass. From as far back as I can remember they didn't care about me. I had two old-er brothers, amazing at everything they turned their hand to – sport, school – then I came along, an absolute underachiever. Not worth spending any time on.'

'Tiff...' Cassie said, a hand on hers.

'So what do you think about getting out of here?' Tiff asked, shovelling more food into her mouth.

'What do you mean, get out of here?' Cassie asked, going with the change of subject. 'I've got work today. But like a weekend away?' She tried the pancakes. They were amazing, soft and fluffy, still warm, drowning in syrup.

'No, like for good,' Tiff said.

'Why? Where would we go? I've got my course starting in February. I'm guessing you don't want to live in Hamilton?'

'There's no way I'm living in the same city as my parents. Why do you even want to do the course? We could leave here. Go to Wellington or Auckland, or even the South Island.'

This was completely out of left field. 'Where would we get the money? We have no savings, even with Dad picking up the rent. We have no money to pack up and move.'

'Your dad,' Tiff said, as if it was a no-brainer.

It annoyed Cassie the way Tiff expected her father to foot the bill. 'I want to do the course because I'm sick of scrounging off

Dad and of living in the past. I need to move on.'

'What? You don't care about who murdered your mum any-more?' Tiff's tone was accusatory.

Cassie sat back in her chair, shocked. 'Of course I care. Why would you say that? It's just since Mum's body was found I've been at a standstill while I went on a ridiculous mission to find Karl Taylor. I want more. Mum would've wanted more for me. I feel I'm letting her down living like this.'

Tiff got up and took her plate to the kitchen, leaving Cassie's empty plate where it was.

'What? Your mum would've wanted more for you? Like having a job and living with your girlfriend's such a bad thing.' Tiff stood in front of her now, her face tense.

'Don't be stupid. You know I didn't mean it like that,' Cassie said, reaching for Tiff's hand.

The punch came from nowhere, and left Cassie's right cheek-bone feeling as though it was on fire. She put a hand to her face, in shock.

'Don't. Call. Me. Stupid.'

Dazed, Cassie got up and moved to the other side of the room. She felt the tears coming. How could Tiff do that?

There was silence in the room with just Cassie's sobs echoing around the lounge.

'I'm sorry,' Tiff said, walking towards her, arms out as if trying to placate a stray dog. 'Shit, Cass, I'm so sorry.' Cassie heard her choke back a sob. 'I can't believe I did that.'

Cassie looked into Tiff's eyes, seeing the hurt and confusion there. She knew Tiff didn't mean to hit her.

Tiff enveloped Cassie in a hug, and Cassie wrapped her arms around Tiff and held on. Because if she didn't, who knew where she'd end up.

Chapter 38

Miller sat at the kitchen table on Friday morning staring at the bottle of wine in front of her. She felt suitably numb. Not from the alcohol – none had touched her lips, not yet – but from lack of sleep, shock. She'd talked with the police after they went over Li's house yesterday and took away her small, lifeless body. She'd given her statement. They didn't need her fingerprints: those were already on file from last time. Madi.

She thought of Kahu, couldn't imagine the pressure he was under. The need for the Scarf Killer to be caught was taking up every part of his life, as well as Miller's. He had to be caught. Miller knew, one way or the other, it would be over soon.

She'd dozed on the couch and had woken up sweating under the throw in the lounge. Grabbing her keys, she'd driven to the supermarket, filled her basket with ready-meals, even thinking to get a special frozen roast meal for Christmas Day, which was pathetic, and found herself in the wine aisle. She'd grabbed the nearest bottle, looking left and right, as if she was shoplifting, and paid at the checkout. She'd eaten her macaroni and cheese last night with the wine in front of her. She'd gone to bed soon after, leaving the wine where it was and tossed and turned for the rest of the night, realising that this was it. She'd reached a point where the need for it was so strong, she couldn't talk herself out of it. The reasons to drink were starting to outweigh the reasons not to.

She ran her finger down the edge of the bottle. It was a pinot noir from Central Otago. A good one. Was she going to ruin the last one hundred and eighty-seven days of sobriety? They'd been so hard, every single one of them. But she'd done it and on her own. But who could blame her now? Wasn't she allowed a slip-up every now and then?

Just a glass. Just a sip.

She looked at her mum's photo in front of her. Tried to imagine what she'd say. What words of comfort would take the painful craving away, but that didn't help. She eased herself up from her seat and went into the bathroom. Looking at her reflection she ignored her cut lip, the sad eyes and the dark smudges below them and looked at her scar.

Nothing.

That little twinge of guilt wasn't there today as it had been since she'd got it.

It's because nothing matters.

Li was dead. Emmeline, Tamara, Madi. He was playing with her now, teasing her. He had total control and she was well aware she was losing any control she possessed. She ran back into the kitchen, grabbed the bottle by the neck and twisted the screw cap off. She closed her eyes, breathing in. The sweet, citrus notes made her mouth water.

There was a knock on the door, and she froze, caught in the act. Was it Kahu? She couldn't bear to see the look of disappointment on his face. She listened. Maybe they'd gone away. She looked at the bottle in her hand then started as there was another knock, one after the other, getting louder and louder.

'Fuck.' Miller put the lid back on the bottle and pushed it to the back of the pantry and stalked down the hallway. 'This better be fucking good.' She wrenched the door open and came face to face with Cassie, head down, hands playing with the bracelet on her arm.

'Cassie? Are you okay?' *Back into caring mode,* thought Miller. *Cassie's upset. You can help. It's what you do.*

'Sorry to come round like this,' Cassie sniffed as Miller ushered her inside.

'Cassie, what's happened to your face?' Miller asked, noting the red mark on her cheekbone.

Cassie touched her face and she winced. 'I didn't realise it left a mark. I just threw some clothes on and came here.'

'Tiffany?'

Cassie nodded, and fresh tears started. 'She hit me. She started talking about moving away and me not doing my course next year. I told her she was being stupid and—'

'Come on, come into the kitchen and we'll get an ice pack on that.'

Cassie sat at the kitchen table while Miller wrapped an ice pack in a tea towel and handed it to her, then put the kettle on.

Cassie sighed as Miller deposited teabags into two mugs. 'I feel like nothing's going right. Ever since I've been in Lentford I've told myself I'm happy, that Tiff's great. I didn't see what she was really like. Because, believe me, there were signs. I didn't think it strange that I'd chosen to live in some backwater where my mother's body was discovered. I knew Dad thought it was, but he let me get on – I was always good at talking him into stuff. But I've talked myself into believing all this is normal when really, it's so far from normal it's laughable. I don't even know who I am, Miller.'

She took the mug from Miller and placed it on the table. 'With Mum, and then all the craziness over Karl Taylor, then hooking up with Tiff who, I might add, I thought was the love of my life, but I've just had a bit of sense knocked into me, literally. I have no idea who I am – Cassie whose mum was murdered. Cassie who can't function without a girlfriend. Cassie whose girlfriend beats her up.'

Miller placed her hand on top of Cassie's. 'I get it,' Miller said, wondering if she actually did. 'Look, I may have some news.' She remembered Karl Taylor and her trip to Shady Oaks on Wednesday. So much had gone on since then she'd completely forgotten about what he'd said.

Cassie looked up, hopeful. 'Karl Taylor? Did someone come forward?'

'Kind of. I still need to look into it. But remember Karl Taylor from the old people's home that you visited? He read the article and I think he might have recognised the identikit. He went a bit strange, started rambling about his grandson, how he was a bad seed and he was even frightened of him. I questioned him, tried to get a name, something, anything from him, but I think he realised he'd said too much. He became worried I was going to call the cops.'

'So you honestly think this Karl Taylor's grandson could've killed Mum?' Cassie said, eyes wide.

'I don't know,' Miller said, not wanting to get her hopes up. 'I've got an address for his daughter, Amanda, so I'm going to go see her. Today,' Miller said, a plan forming.

'Thanks for this.' A wave of Cassie's hand encompassed the tea and ice pack. 'I'd better get going. I've got work this afternoon.'

'Cassie, if you need a place to stay, you're welcome here. If you need to get away from Tiff for a bit.' *Or forever*, thought Miller.

'It's okay. It was a stupid fight. I do have some things to think about, though.' Cassie got up from the table and Miller walked her out. 'Let me know what happens, would you? No matter how small, even if it turns out to be nothing.'

'I'll let you know,' Miller said.

Cassie stopped at the front door, bending down. She held an envelope out to Miller. 'For you?'

Miller froze, then frowned. She thanked Cassie and took the envelope.

'Catch up soon, Cassie,' she said, already preoccupied with what might be inside the envelope.

She grabbed a pair of latex gloves from her satchel and took the letter into the kitchen and opened it at the dining room table. This time she didn't feel scared – she felt angry. *The gall of him.* He'd delivered this letter during Cassie's visit. There were still cops coming and going from Li's house next door. Miller had always thought he'd show his hand, want to be captured at some stage, because how else would everyone know who he was. In his mind he was a criminal mastermind, managing to kill four women while evading the police.

Miller, it wasn't me. This one wasn't me. Someone's copying me. What do they say, 'Imitation is the sincerest form of flattery'? I don't buy that. It's a cop-out. Unoriginal. I've done all the work. I've certainly made myself a name – and not just in Lentford – but all around New Zealand people are gagging to find out who I am. And I know you are too. I'm done. It's over. I'm not an animal. This was never going to go on and on. There were only ever going to be three. See you soon.

Miller refolded the letter and put it back into the envelope. She grabbed her phone and satchel and set off to track down Kahu.

She entered the police station and smiled with relief when she saw Ash on the desk. 'I've had another letter.'

'Shit.' Ash's eyes flicked towards the double doors and back again.

'Is Kahu here?'

'He's... he's a bit busy at the moment, Mills.'

'Ash, you know this is important. I don't need to go back there, if that's the problem. Could he come out?'

'It's not that, it's... he's just busy.'

Just then the door opened. 'Miller,' Kahu said, glancing behind him and then looking at Ash. He stepped through the open door and closed it. 'What's up?'

Miller handed him the letter from her satchel. 'Another one.' She watched him as he read it. 'Is this right? It wasn't him? If it wasn't, who the hell would do this? Someone's copying him? Who would do that? I was thinking it was just his way of not owning up to killing Li, but he wouldn't do that, would he? He loves us knowing what he's done. That's the whole point of his fucking letters.'

Just then Miller was still, quiet. Her brain had rarely stopped throwing up images of Li's dead body for the last twenty-four hours: the congealed blood, almost black; Li's bloated face; the navy scarf around her slender neck. 'Kahu, he's right. It wasn't him. There was no lipstick.'

Kahu gave a tight smile. 'Ten out of ten,' he said. 'We've got someone in there. We arrested him earlier this morning. He's confessed to Li's murder.'

Miller almost dropped to the floor with relief. 'Who is it? Do I know him?'

'Yeah, you do. Look, you shouldn't really be here. We haven't released any information to the media yet. We've just interviewed him and he's on his way to Hamilton. He'll appear in court tomorrow.' Kahu hesitated. 'It's Logan Dodds.'

Miller dropped onto the bench seat under the window. 'Logan Dodds?'

'We figured out it's likely Li died Tuesday night.'

'The night of the candlelit vigil.' Miller looked up at Kahu. 'The night those guys were after me.'

Kahu nodded.

'Jesus. When Logan came along...' Miller couldn't finish.

'He's told us he had an interview with Li on Tuesday night before the candlelit vigil. We found notes from the interview that Li had transcribed. At the top of the paper she'd written "Tuesday 19 December 8 p.m." He did the interview, attended the candlelit vigil with his parents and then told them he was going to walk home. He went back to Li's. When he came across you and those two guys, he'd just killed her. The scarf he used to strangle Li belonged to his mother.'

The door opened again, and two detectives filed out and waited. After a moment Logan Dodds appeared, handcuffed, wearing creased shorts and jandals; his T-shirt, a size too small, left his pale, hairless stomach on display. Beatrice came up behind him, a hand on his shoulder, looking ten years older. Suddenly the small reception room felt very crowded.

'Son of a bitch,' Miller whispered, standing. Ash came to stand by her and laid a hand on her arm as if worried about what she might do.

'He told his mother last night. She brought him in first thing this morning,' Kahu said.

'Miller,' Beatrice said, trying to get her attention. 'Could you please refrain from reporting this in the *Lentford Leader*?'

'Beatrice, I think that's the least of your problems right now. You think your son can murder someone and you still get to protect your family's precious reputation?' Miller asked, incredulous.

'He's sick. Miller. You must understand. I know you un-derstand.' She reached out, an act of solidarity, friendship, but Miller shook her head and stepped back.

'That's Li's,' Miller said, her head indicating towards Beatrice's wrist.

'What?' Kahu said.

'The watch,' Miller said, voice calm. 'It's Li's.'

Any pretence Beatrice had put up now shattered. Her tanned face paled and she struggled with the gold clasp on the watch and shoved it into the hands of the detective next to her. Letting out a strangled cry she rushed from the station.

'There's an inscription: "With all my love, L." It's from Li's ex – Liam. Go on,' she said to the detective. 'Check it.'

The detective turned the watch over, then nodded at Kahu.

'It was Mum's birthday a few weeks ago and I didn't get her anything,' Logan said, speaking for the first time. The sound of his voice, soft and whiny, made Miller want to scream.

Miller turned to leave. She couldn't bear being in the same room with him any longer.

'Miller,' Logan said. She could feel his eyes on her. She looked at him then away. 'I know Li was your friend, and I'm sorry for your loss. After my sister, Amelia, I've always... wondered... what it would be like. And now I know.'

Chapter 39

Tiff wasn't at home when Cassie got back from Miller's. She'd be off getting high somewhere, Cassie was sure. That was something else she wasn't into. She did it because Tiff liked it, but it was something she could see might be a slippery slope. She didn't want to become that person again. She rang Tane, telling him she had a migraine and couldn't come in. Tane did his best not to sound pissed off, but it was a Friday, three days before Christmas.

There was only one Winslow in Hamilton in the White Pages online so finding an address was easy. She drove past beautiful homes on River Road with river views and finally found the one she was looking for. Driving down the steep driveway she parked next to a sleek black Audi. The house was weatherboard, two storeys, surrounded by thick foliage, so much so she couldn't even see the river down the side of the house.

She stood at the door, took a deep breath and used the tarnished grey-green door knocker to announce her arrival. A man in his late forties answered the door. Tiff's dad. Had to be. Tiff had his eyes, nose, hair, everything.

Cassie introduced herself. 'I'm your daughter's girlfriend. I've come to see you today because I need some information.' Even to her ear her speech sounded forced, rehearsed.

'You know Tiffany?' the man asked. 'You know where she

is? Sorry.' He stood aside to let her in. 'Come in, please. I'm Gerard, Tiffany's father.'

He ushered her into a hallway and through to the dining room and kitchen off to the right. 'Please take a seat,' he said. 'Coffee?' He walked to the bench without waiting for an answer and began to grind beans next to a gleaming coffee machine.

Cassie sat down at the long bench seat that took up one side of the dining room table, which was strewn with papers and a laptop. She waited as Gerard set about making the coffee and frothing the milk, the machine hissing and spitting.

'Excuse the mess,' he said. 'I'm an accountant and work from home occasionally. We have an office, but I like the vibe in here.' He smoothed back his auburn hair, obviously nervous.

He brought two oversized mugs to the table and sat down. 'Ah, sugar.' He stood up again so forcefully that he knocked his chair over. He went to the pantry, placed a silver sugar bowl on the table and, picking up his chair, he sat down with a loud sigh. 'I'm sorry... Cassie, was it? We haven't heard from Tiffany since she went into The Oaks. We've had a bit of trouble with her since... Well, forever, it seems. We thought it best not to upset her by trying to track her down. We've been told by countless therapists and counsellors that she's an adult, that her choices are her own, that we need to let her start living her life, not pandering to her every whim.'

Cassie was taken aback by this softly spoken man. He was nothing like the father Tiff had described. She had spoken of a brash man, uncaring, unsupportive.

'We're living in Lentford at the moment,' Cassie said. 'I work at the Royal, the local pub.'

'And Tiff?'' Gerard asked.

'She's... looking for work,' Cassie said, trying to be diplomatic.

'Can I ask you, is she off the drugs?' Gerard looked down at his half-empty coffee mug.

Cassie felt as though she was about to tell a child Santa wasn't real. 'I... No, she's not. I'm sorry.'

Gerard's shoulders slumped. 'What can I do for you, Cassie? Is there a reason you came?'

'I met Tiff at The Oaks. I was dealing with some stuff. I loved her... Love her... I don't know,' Cassie said, confused. 'She... she hit me this morning.'

Gerard looked up; the corners of his mouth dropped.

'When I think about it, she hasn't treated me right from the beginning.'

'It's who she is, I'm afraid. She uses and abuses everyone in her life. She lies, she cheats, she would do anything for money. That's how it started. Stealing money from me and her mother, even from her older brothers.'

'What for?' Cassie asked.

'At the start it was just wanting money for junk food, magazines. Then when she was fourteen, she bought cannabis from a guy that had been selling to high-school kids. He was dealt with, Tiff and a lot of other kids were suspended. Most learnt their lesson but Tiff, by then, was hooked. Large amounts of money were going missing. By sixteen she'd moved on to methamphetamine. She was running away, often we didn't see her days at a time. At first, we called the police in panic, thinking she'd been murdered, but she'd always turn up. Eventually the police, while kind enough, pretty much told us Tiff would turn up when she was ready. And, of course, she did, always looking for more money, or she'd stay clean for a few days, sleep and eat and we'd get glimpses of the old Tiffany, but then she'd disappear again. That's been our life for the last nine years.'

Gerard wiped a hand across his eyes and took the coffee mugs to the sink even though Cassie's was still half full.

'I had no idea. That's not the story she told me,' Cassie said. 'I'm so sorry.'

Gerard stood at the sink, his back to Cassie. 'She was always good at lying, sucking people in. I'm sorry you became a pawn in her little game.'

'How did she get to The Oaks?' Cassie asked.

'She'd been to a heap of treatment facilities, run away from all of them. We took her to this one, hopeful as ever. And to our shock, she stayed.'

'Why didn't you visit her?' Cassie asked, trying not to sound accusing. 'Tiff was always so sad on visiting days when no one turned up. At least that's what she said.' She was beginning to realise she needed to look at Tiff in a whole other light – her actions, what she'd told Cassie about everything.

Gerard returned to the table. 'We were told we shouldn't contact her. By this stage I believe she really hated us. Her counsellor told us it would be detrimental to her recovery. And so we stayed away. But her counsellor did check in with us, letting us know how she was doing and by all accounts, she was doing great.'

'I think she was,' Cassie said. 'I met her the first day I arrived. She scared me a bit. She was so confident, knew exactly what she wanted.'

Gerard smiled. 'That's our Tiffany.'

'I don't think I can stay with her,' Cassie said, tears coming from nowhere, which she hastily wiped away.

'Cassie, I don't believe you should. We love our daughter, always will, we can't not. But she has ripped our family apart and she leaves a trail of destruction wherever she goes. We'll always be here for her – but you're young. You shouldn't let her into your life. She'll only destroy it.'

Chapter 40

To get Logan out of her mind, Miller left for Hamilton after she'd seen Kahu. She stopped in at the Kowhai to get a double shot of caffeine. Kahu had said no information had been released about Logan, but Lentford being Lentford, word had got out. The cafe was buzzing. Aubrey was holding court, spewing information about Logan, true or not, but the crux of it was right on. Logan Dodds had murdered Li Chen. Miller waited for her coffee in the corner by the door, refusing to engage with anyone, preparing to leave as soon as Len called her order.

'Thanks, Len.' She took the cup from him. The Len standing in front of her was very different to the one she usually saw. 'You okay, Len?' she asked.

Len sighed, raking a hand through his hair. 'I can't believe it.' His voice broke. 'She was a good girl. And I was...' He cleared his throat. 'I didn't treat her as well as I should've. And now she's gone. Excuse me.' He turned and walked into the back room, away from prying eyes.

Miller hoped that Li, wherever she was, had heard him.

The address the young receptionist had given Miller for Amanda Taylor was in Fairfield. Miller turned down the street, slowing to find the right number. She parked in front of the red brick house. The neighbours, doors and windows flung open, were playing Metallica on high volume. Amanda's house was partially obscured by weeds and grass that grew almost a metre high. Miller walked down the cracked path and knocked on the door. When no one answered, she walked to the side of the house, clearing a path through grass and weeds, sending up a flurry of cabbage butterflies and cicadas, screwing up her nose at the overpowering stench of dogshit, and peered into the lounge window. Empty. No furniture, no curtains.

'Can I help you?'

Miller flinched and turned to see a woman standing a few metres away on the path.

'I was looking for Amanda Taylor,' Miller said, trying not to look guilty.

'Don't live here no more.' The woman took a deep drag on her cigarette and exhaled away from Miller, although the slight breeze blew it back into Miller's face.

They made their way around to the front of the house and walked back down the path. 'Amanda's been gone almost two years now, I think.' The woman rubbed at her chapped lips, picking at a piece of dry skin.

'Do you know where she lives now?' Miller asked hopefully.

'She's at River Village. Assisted-care facility. Had a stroke a couple of years ago. I was the one who found her.' She pointed to the front steps. 'Was on her way out grocery shopping and collapsed right on those steps there. Anyway, it left one side of her face paralysed, so she can't speak too well, has a bit of memory loss and depression. After the stroke she never came back here. Sad really,' the woman said, without looking sad.

'How about her family?' Miller asked.

'She spoke about her father sometimes. I think he's in a rest home somewhere.' She ground her cigarette butt onto the footpath with a wedge heel.

'Yes, I know her father. How about a son?'

'Never mentioned him, but I didn't really know her that well.'

Miller thanked her for her help and got back in the car.

The woman came over and knocked on Miller's window. 'You might want to let that old folks home know what's happened here. Just in case the old fella carks it and they can't track her down, although fat lot of use she'd be – couldn't organise her way out of a paper bag let alone a funeral.' She walked away, stumbling on her high wedges, and back into the house, yelling, 'Turn that fuckin' music down!'

Miller entered River Village into her phone to get directions. The drive to Hamilton East was less than ten minutes. She passed Claudelands Event Centre on her left and continued along Grey Street. She stopped at the traffic lights in the middle of Hamilton East's main street and watched people going in and out of shops that were glittering with tinsel. Cafes with chairs and tables set up outside were heaving with customers. Miller revved the Triumph's engine and eased ahead as the light changed green. She turned right off the main road and drove down towards the river.

The River Village was clean but run down. The furniture in the waiting room was tired, the vinyl covered chairs spewed out foam, and magazines over a year old were strewn across a chipped coffee table. At reception she asked to see Amanda Taylor and was taken into a large lounge room. A ranch slider was open as well as windows on the opposite wall, but it was still stifling. The two pedestal fans humming in the corner did nothing but move the heavy air around, rustling the pine needles on the Christmas tree in the corner.

'Amanda, dear, you have a visitor.' Before leaving them, the receptionist said to Miller, 'Lovely that you're visiting. It's not often anyone comes to see her.'

Amanda was sitting in a chair. Her right hand was closed into a fist, the knuckles white, as if holding onto something tight; her left hand lay limp in her lap. Her hair, a mix of browns and grey, was pulled into a lank, greasy ponytail. 'Do I know you?' she asked, her speech slightly slurred.

'No, you don't. But I know your father, Karl. My name's Miller.' She pulled up a seat close to Amanda and caught the light floral scent of talcum powder.

'I haven't seen him in quite some time.' Her already watery eyes teared up. Her right hand, still clenched, began to rub up and down her thigh in agitation.

'Please don't worry, he's doing fine. I told him I'd come and check on you,' Miller lied, 'see how you were doing.'

'Not bad,' Amanda sighed.

Miller looked around the room. Everyone looked to be at least twenty years older than Amanda, many sleeping in armchairs, covered in rainbow-coloured crocheted blankets, even in this heat.

'I couldn't look after myself at home and my doctor said it would be best to move here. They take good care of me.' She smiled, one side of her face frozen in place. 'Would you like to see my room?'

'I'd love to.' Miller helped Amanda up. Her left arm hung limp as they walked to her room, Miller holding her right forearm.

Amanda opened the door and shuffled in. It reminded Miller a lot of Karl's room at his rest home, but seemed, if possible, even smaller.

Amanda sat on her bed and lay back with her feet up. 'Take a seat.' She waved to the chair.

'Do you have any other family?' Miller asked.

'I have a son, and my father, of course. I've seen neither for a very long time.' She looked out the window which gave a view of the carpark and the road beyond. Miller felt she was losing her.

'A son?' Miller asked. 'And where does he live?' Miller made sure her voice was light and cheery.

Amanda raised her clenched fist to her mouth, rubbing her knuckles back and forth across her lips. 'I have no idea. He was always one to travel around. I have photos. Wherever he went he always used to send postcards and sometimes photos. Would you like to take a look?' Again, that lop-sided smile.

'I'd love to,' Miller said, feeling her stomach drop.

Amanda reached into the drawer on her bedside table and pulled out half a dozen photos. 'Here's one of me, Mum and Dad. And this one's of the whole family at Christmas. There's my handsome boy.' She pointed to a lanky boy of fourteen or fifteen.

Miller waited as she went through a few more photos hoping she had a more recent one of her son.

'Oh, this one here, it was sent... ' She checked the back. 'January 2005, what's that? Almost fourteen years ago. Goodness how time flies.' She handed it to Miller.

Miller took in the photo. He was standing outside a house, a construction site really, next to a truck with 'Vogel Construction' written along the side.

'He worked for a builder in Tauranga for a summer before he went globe-trotting,' Amanda said.

Miller felt an uncomfortable buzzing in her ears. The identikit was no good, really. The eyes were too close together, the hair not long enough or scruffy enough, the face shape too round. But who could blame the witness? He had put trust in an old memory when he offered the image up to the police last year.

'Jay.' Her voice was husky and she didn't recognise it.

'You know Jason?' Amanda sat up, eager, eyes bright.

'I... I do,' Miller said.

'How is he? I haven't seen him since he got back from the UK – five years ago now. He visited me and gave me some money. He's such a good boy. We had trouble with him in his teens, adopted, you see, but he came right,' Amanda said emphatically.

Karl's words 'bad seed' came back to Miller.

'You need to tell me where he is!' Amanda was up now, standing over Miller. Her change in demeanour reminded Miller of Karl. 'You need to tell me where he is!'

Miller stood and tried to calm her down but Amanda hit out with her right forearm.

'Everything all right in here?' a nurse came in, assessing the situation.

'No, it's not! She knows where my son is and she's not telling me!' Amanda backed into the corner. 'She's hiding him from me!' And then she started screaming.

'I'm so sorry,' Miller said, first to the nurse and then to Amanda. 'I didn't mean to upset her.'

'It's okay, hun, she has these episodes every now and then.' She pressed a button above Amanda's bed and within a minute another nurse came in holding a syringe. 'Time for a lie down, Amanda,' she said softly.

'No!' Amanda screamed, 'No!' She slid down the wall and the nurse injected her arm. Miller noticed her hand unclench and something roll under the chair.

While the two nurses helped Amanda onto the bed, Miller picked up the object from under the chair and held it up to the light. It was a Roman coin, a hole drilled through its centre as if it had been attached to a bangle.

'I'm sorry, but you should probably go now,' one of the nurses said.

Miller nodded, unsure what to do with the potential evidence, but she knew she couldn't take it with her. She put the coin on Amanda's bedside table and left on legs that threatened to give way underneath her.

Miller went straight to the police station when she got back to Lentford, but Ash was out on a call and no one seemed to know where Kahu was. Someone said he'd gone into Hamilton with Logan, someone else said he was following a lead and wouldn't be back till later. Miller should have told one of the detectives, but she needed to tell Kahu herself. He'd trust her and wouldn't look at her like she was some amateur sleuth, which, she realised, was exactly what she was. She couldn't stop thinking of Jay. She walked back to her car, looking at the people passing her, the cars going past down the street. He'd seemed such a nice person, friendly. More than that, she had been attracted to him. How old was he? He looked to be in his early forties, so would've been thirty, maybe younger, when he killed Margaret. He'd got away with it for all these years because a family member wouldn't or couldn't speak up.

Without anywhere else to go, she went home. She texted Kahu telling him she had important information and to call round when he was free. Pulling a jug of water from the fridge she considered calling Cassie but knew it was too soon. This news was huge, and Miller knew the police needed all the information before telling Cassie. Her stomach did a flip – this time in excitement, not nerves or fright. Cassie was going to get closure. Jay would pay for what he had done.

Out on the deck, she looked back on the last twenty-four hours. Li was dead, Logan had been arrested and she'd discovered that Jay had killed Margaret. She sighed. And still there was someone out there, murdering women. It wasn't over. Ten minutes later there was a knock on the door and Kahu shouted out, 'Hello?'

'Come in!' Miller said, rising from her seat and getting him a drink.

'You should have that door locked, you know,' Kahu said.

'I know, I know,' Miller said. 'I always make sure I'm locked up come evening. How's your day been?' she asked as they each took a seat outside on the deck.

Kahu expelled a long breath of air and looked out across the garden. 'First, there was Logan, he's been shipped off to Hamilton. And then I went to speak to Lou—'

'And?' Miller asked. 'Did you find something out? One of the detectives I spoke to when I was trying to track you down said you were following up a lead.'

'He has an alibi – Maggie. He's not the Scarf Killer.'

'Oh. Right,' Miller said.

'We talked about the women. He admitted he knew them. But that's not uncommon in a town this small.'

Miller was silent. 'So is the paper just a coincidence? It seems so unlikely.'

'I'm not finished,' Kahu said. 'Turns out Maggie and Lou have a boarder.'

'They do?' Miller asked, frowning. 'I didn't see anyone there when I interviewed Maggie.'

'They've got a portacabin out the back. Small kitchenette, room for a bed and ensuite. Jay Martin rents it off them.'

'Holy shit,' Miller said, eyes wide, suddenly short of breath.

'I asked Lou about him, and between him and Maggie they're sure he's come across the three women before – Madi's accountancy firm dealt with the printing business. Emmeline took a few kids for a field trip there last term. Maggie told me Aubrey

– you know, the bloody big-mouth,' Kahu said, mistaking Miller's horror for confusion, 'said he'd asked Tamara out, but she'd refused him.'

'Oh shit,' Miller said, realising the enormity of what Kahu had just told her. She got up from her seat and started pacing. 'Jesus Christ. What did Maggie and Lou say about the paper? He was obviously taking it.'

'Yeah. They never saw him do it, but the house is often left open and Maggie and Lou have always said to come in if he needed anything, so it's absolutely possible he came and took it.' Kahu drained his glass. 'Look, it's not a lot, but enough to bring him in and have a chat, get a DNA sample and see if we can get a match to the skin we found under Emmeline's nails. I asked Lou about the fertiliser. It's the stuff he uses on his own veggie garden, plus other gardens he works on. He told me Jay could easily have stepped in it. Neither Lou or Maggie have seen him all day. I'm getting a search warrant for the cabin and we're going around there now.'

Kahu stood. 'Sorry, you said you had something to tell me.'

'You might want to sit back down again,' Miller said, feeling as though she'd just been for a run, finding it hard to catch her breath.

She went on to tell Kahu about what Karl Taylor had said and the photo she'd seen when she visited Amanda, plus the coin. Kahu had taken out his notebook, and as he jotted down names and addresses, he was shaking his head.

'It's him, Kahu. Jay killed Cassie's mum and he's the Scarf Killer. He's got to be.'

'Now we just need to find the son of a bitch. God, I hope he hasn't got wind of something and left town.' Kahu wiped a hand across his forehead. 'I can't figure him out. His MO. Margaret Hughes was found stabbed, as far as the forensic anthropologist could tell from what was left of her body. She told us the underlying bone, her ribs and her hip bone, were scored by a knife.'

Miller shivered involuntarily.

'But Emmeline, Tamara and Madi were strangled. It's completely different. Not a drop of blood was found at any of the scenes.'

'Margaret's murder was a long time ago,' Miller said. 'Maybe he hadn't sorted out what he was doing yet. Or maybe something went wrong.'

'Possibly. But why the big gap? Did Margaret's murder satiate him enough not to do it again for all these years?'

'I guess there's the possibility he has done it again and hasn't been caught,' Miller suggested.

'I don't know,' said Kahu. 'Doesn't sound like something he'd do.'

'His mother, adoptive by the way,' Miller said, remembering, 'said he'd been in the UK. I'm not sure for how long. But she mentioned him returning a few years back. Maybe he was biding his time, and god knows what he got up to over there.'

Miller walked Kahu to the door and looked up and down the street at the kids across the road playing in the park and riding past on their bikes. 'Remember his letters, Kahu. He wants to be known – by as many people as possible. He'll make himself known when he's ready. I'm sure of it.'

'No doubt he will, Miller. I'm just afraid how he's going to do that. These letters, it's all for extra attention, on top of the murders. I have a feeling the last thing he'll be doing is walking up to the police and turning himself in.'

Chapter 41

On Friday night there was another sudden downpour that stopped almost as soon as it started and left the air feeling heavy, as if Lentford itself was weighed down by the stress and worry of what it had been through the last few weeks. Miller locked the house up as an onslaught of mosquitos, loving the hot, damp air, made for the kitchen light. She turned the fan on in the living room and slipped Neil Young's 'Time Fades Away' out of its sleeve. One of her dad's favourites.

She wondered where Jay was now, a hundred percent sure he was in Lentford or not far away. She had always been sure there would be some kind of stand-off, and the stress of not knowing when it would come was unbearable. She thought of Cassie, happy that she now had some sort of closure, and of the three women's families. She thought of Li and Logan – that might have been the hardest to take of all. Li, a good friend, murdered by someone they both knew hadn't been quite right. To halt her thoughts, the inevitable blame she put on herself, she turned the music up louder, but it didn't help. Only one thing would. She walked into the kitchen and opened the pantry, reached to the back and grabbed the neck of the wine bottle.

The knock on the door could hardly be heard over the music, and Miller couldn't be sure if she really had heard it. She left the wine bottle where it was, walked into the hallway and listened.

There it was again. She turned the music down in the lounge and, remembering Kahu's warning, asked who it was. It was almost nine-thirty and dark outside, thanks to the sudden storm.

'It's Tiff,' a muffled reply came.

Miller raised her eyebrows. This would be interesting. She'd seen her last Monday when she'd gone to drop off copies of the *Leader* to Cassie and Tiff had accused her of trying to steal her girlfriend.

She opened the door. 'Hi,' she said, on guard.

Tiff made eye contact then looked down at her feet.

After a brief silence Miller said, 'Would you like to come in?'

Tiff nodded and stepped inside, following Miller into the lounge. 'Take a seat,' Miller said, indicating the armchair while she sat on the couch.

Miller took in Tiff's drawn face and her red, puffy eyes. She began to feel sorry for her but then remembered what she'd done to Cassie. Miller waited.

Tiff looked around the room, then her eyes settled on Miller. She didn't look her in the eyes – she looked at her scar instead. 'Is Cassie here? Are you hiding her here?' Her eyes swept the room again, her neck craning into the hallway.

'No, she's not here. Why would she be?'

'I wouldn't mind if she was here. I wouldn't blame you for hiding her from me or for her doing a runner. I was horrible to her this morning and I feel bad about what happened.' The words came out in a rush and it left her panting.

Miller didn't bother to admit Cassie had been to see her. Tiff seemed remorseful but Miller still wasn't sure if she trusted her.

'She's not here, Tiffany. I promise you. Can I get you a glass of water or something?' Miller asked, noting the perspiration on her forehead.

'Got anything stronger?'

'No, I don't,' Miller said. She wanted Tiff out of here as soon as she could get rid of her.

'Water would be good, then.'

Miller went to the kitchen and came back with two glasses of water. Tiff drank hers down in two long gulps and asked to use the toilet.

'Down the corridor before you get to the kitchen.'

Miller put the record back into its sleeve and pulled the curtains closed. She stood in front of the fan, letting it dry the sweat on her skin. She heard the toilet flush.

Coming back into the lounge, Tiff sat down on the couch next to Miller. 'Sorry for intruding,' she said. 'I want to apologise about the way I've acted. I can see that I'm losing Cass. I do this. I struggle to get close to people and then when I do, I fuck it all up.'

The tears started, and Miller, after a few seconds of indecision, moved over to comfort her, half expecting Tiff to turn on her. The Tiff she'd seen tonight was a whole new person. Maybe the fight and losing her temper and Cassie disappearing was enough to make her realise she had a good thing in Cassie.

'An apology goes a long way. As long as it's sincere. Cassie's a lovely person,' Miller said, feeling sick at helping Tiff get Cassie back. She didn't think Tiff, all attitude and sharp corners, was right for Cassie, who seemed so innocent and kind and decent. But right now, she just wanted Tiff out of her house.

Ten minutes later, Tiff's tears had dried and her phone vibrated. Tiff stood and took it out of her back pocket. 'I better go,' she said.

'Cassie?' Miller asked, unsure if this was good or bad.

'No,' she shrugged. 'Hopefully she'll be back when I get home. She was supposed to work this afternoon but Tane said she called in sick.'

'Are you walking home?' Miller asked at the front door, thinking of Jay out there somewhere.

'Yeah. Don't worry, I'll be okay,' Tiff said. 'Been fighting my whole life. I'll make it home just fine. You make sure you lock up.'

All Miller could do was nod, astounded by the incredible one-eighty in personality, as she said goodbye to Tiff.

Miller thought of the bottle of wine in the pantry, but instead double-checked all the locks on the windows and doors. And in the spare bedroom, everything she'd learnt about kickboxing went out the window as she punched and kicked, no care in her stance or technique. She knew she could injure herself this way, but she felt the need to let go. She grunted and sweated for over half an hour and then lay spent on the floor, gazing at the ceiling, thinking that if she could get through Jay's capture and conviction, and Logan's conviction, she'd be okay. Christmas would come and go. It would be a new year in less than two weeks.

She took a cold shower and climbed into bed just before eleven. Throwing off the duvet and then the sheet, she lay staring at the ceiling, wishing, praying, begging for sleep. She closed her eyes and tried deep breathing. *In one, two, three. Out one, two, three.* After ten minutes she felt herself drifting.

The noise, a creak nearby, broke the silence and her eyes opened wide in the darkness. Her mother's house did creak. It was old. The roof creaked after a day in the sun; the house creaked because it was over fifty years old; the floorboards creaked from one side of the house to the other.

She closed her eyes again. She heard a shuffle close by. Footsteps? And then the definite creak of floorboards. Trying to keep her breathing even, as if she was asleep, she cursed the pitch-blackness of her room, helped by the blackout curtains hanging over the window.

There was someone in the room with her. She knew it. She could feel it.

She blindly reached for her mobile phone on the floor beside her bed where it was charging.

Her upper half hanging out of bed, she turned her phone on. The glow of its screen lit up the carpet around her. She pointed it along the floor and saw his face, only a metre from hers. He was on his hands and knees, his eyes wide, grinning.

Miller threw her phone in a panic and she heard it thump against the wall by her bed and the room was swallowed by darkness. She pushed herself up in bed, crouching, her back against the headboard and grappled for the switch of her bed-side light, a whimper escaping her lips, as she came face to face with Jay.

Jay rose to his feet, still smiling. 'I had a feeling you might not be asleep and then realised you were probably a bit of a night owl.' He picked up her phone and slid it into his back pocket. 'Especially these days, with so much on your mind.'

Miller looked across the room at her open wardrobe, where Jay had come from. How long had he been hiding in there?

'How did you get in here?' Miller asked, trying to keep calm but the question came out high-pitched, flooded in fear. Before she could think any more, she lunged for him. Having the ad-vantage of height she kicked him in the guts as she flung herself towards him from her bed. He doubled over and Miller raced from the room. She lashed out at the wall and turned the hall light on as she ran to the front door. Her hands fumbled with the deadbolt, fingers jerking from the adrenalin, refusing to grasp the small handle.

Jay grabbed her right arm and pulled her away from the door. She lost her footing and fell on the carpet. Jay grinned down at her. She fought him without a second thought. She remembered Castle Bay, her confusion, missing the chance to fight back because people who showed her one side were actually something else. She wanted to hurt him, wanted him to regret choosing her. She spun her body around and kicked his right shin. His leg collapsed and he went down on his knees. She got up, jabbed him left, right in the face and ran for the door again. It was only a couple of metres away but she felt as though she was in a dream, running in slow motion or through mud. Was this what happened with Madi and Emmeline and Tamara? Did they put up a fight? Did they almost escape? Were they this close to freedom only to have it whipped away from them?

She was breathing heavily, unable to get enough air into her lungs. She reached forward but felt a strong grip around her ankles. Jay pulled her towards him, and she dropped to the ground.

'Guess I should've known you'd be a fighter.' He picked her up off the floor. Standing in front of her, he held her arm tight with one hand and drew a finger down her scar, leaving it feeling on fire.

'Damaged, like me. That's one of the things I liked about you. When we first met. Remember? I was delivering that week's paper and you'd just started. I knew your name already, and Cody and Hine were raving about how lucky they were to have you working there. I knew then it was time to start planning. You were the final piece of the puzzle.'

Miller squirmed but he increased his hold on her, his fingers digging into her flesh. 'Let's go.' He turned her towards the front door.

'Where?' She dug her bare feet into the carpet.

He pushed her to start walking. 'You'll see. Don't scream.

Don't make a sound. I'm not going to hurt you.'

'And I'm supposed to believe that?'.

'Don't you get it? I can't have anything happening to you.
You're the one who's going to tell my story.'

Chapter 42

It was almost midnight when they turned down the deserted street. As they pulled into a driveway, the car's headlights illuminated the For Sale sign erected in the front garden. She knew this house. They'd been here on the True Crime Tour with Logan. She jogged her memory. Lauren someone had killed her friend Lindy.

'Home sweet home,' Jay said. 'Come on, round the back.'

He held Miller's hand in a firm grip and guided her around the back of the house. They walked up three concrete steps. Miller noticed a smashed pane of glass as they entered the small kitchen. 'This way,' Jay said, leading her through to the lounge. He turned the lights on. It was bare – no curtains, no furniture.

'What are we doing here?' Miller asked, looking around.

'This is where I tell you my story,' Jay said. 'Sit.'

Miller, standing in the middle of the room, lowered herself to the ground, not taking her eyes off Jay, taking some pleasure when she saw the red marks her punches had left on his face. Jay sat down opposite her, his legs crossed.

'I was returning home for lunch late this morning and saw two cars in Lou's driveway. One was a cop car. I knew then they were on to me.'

'So you're hiding out here?' Miller asked.

Jay nodded. 'I'm going to tell you my story,' he said again, pulling Miller's phone out of his pocket. 'You can record our conversation.' He handed it to Miller, and she turned the recording function on and lay the phone on the carpet in front of her. Jay rose and started pacing. He frowned and brought a hand to the side of his head. He walked over to a backpack and got out a blister pack of ibuprofen and a bottle of water. She watched him pop four tablets out and swallow them. He closed his eyes and breathed in deeply.

Miller took the opportunity to stand up. She hated him towering over her. She wanted to run, didn't want to hear his story. She wanted out of there.

'Sit!' he yelled, and immediately brought both hands to his head. 'I've told you to sit down already. Just do as I ask so I can tell you my story.'

Miller backed away from him and sat leaning against the far wall, a fireplace to her right and the kitchen to her left.

Jay leaned against the opposite wall. Silent.

'So it was you,' Miller said. 'You killed Margaret Hughes and the three women here in Lentford.'

'Well, good on you. Margaret Hughes.' He gazed across at her. 'My first. No, that's not right. My second. How did you work it out? Or was it your boyfriend, Detective Parata?'

'I know Karl Taylor, your grandad.'

'Old Grandad Karl!' Jay shouted, slapping his knee and smiling. 'He used to be shit-scared of me, you know. How is Gramps?'

Miller ignored the question. 'He recognised the identikit. I went to see your mum.'

'My mum's dead,' he whispered.

'Your adoptive mother,' Miller clarified. 'She had a coin, seemed like a bit of a lucky charm. She held onto it the entire time I was there.'

'Margaret's bracelet,' Jay said, rubbing his temples. 'That was a bit of a slip-up, I guess. She struggled when I hauled her into the truck down the road from her house. I think that's when the bracelet broke but I didn't realise, leaving one of the coins in Gary's ute. When I buried her out at the dairy factory, I took one of the coins. Lesson learnt, though.' He held his hands in the air as if surrendering. 'Don't take souvenirs from the victims, it'll always come back and bite you in the arse. I gave it to Mum as a gift. She loved it. And I don't need some keepsake to remember what I did to Margaret.' He tapped the side of his head. 'I've got a pretty good memory.'

Jay slid down the wall, sitting, bringing his knees up to his chest.

'I used to sit right there.' He pointed to the middle of the room. 'The TV was set up in the corner there.' He pointed to the other side of the fireplace in the corner. 'The night it happened I was playing Sonic the Hedgehog. I'd gotten really good at it.' He smiled at Miller and then turned back to where the imaginary TV was.

'One of my mum's boyfriends had given me a Sega console a few weeks before. The night he gave it to me he told me I should call him Uncle, and then later he came into my room and slid into my bed.' Jay's lips curled up in disgust. 'I remember his breath hot on my bare back like he'd just been for a run, but all he'd done was drag his fat, drunken arse from Mum's room to mine. I felt his hand moving down my back and decided right then that it wasn't going to happen again.' Jay looked at Miller, his eyes wide. She had to turn away.

'I grabbed a pencil from my bedside table and turned and attacked. I was scared, but god I had to laugh when he rolled out of bed, shouting and screaming.' Jay laughed now, the sound loud and manic as he remembered. 'Uncle Terry left that night.

Mum beat the shit out of me. The damn jug cord left bruises all over me for days. But it was worth it. Uncle Terry was gone, and I got to keep my Sega. But I knew this wouldn't be the last of it. Mum had a knack for attracting these sickos.

'So, back to that night. I wasn't supposed to be up. The neighbours had their music blasting so I didn't hear Mum's footsteps on the path outside. The first thing I heard was loud voices on the doorstep. I shut down my game when I heard the front door open. I didn't have enough time to get down the hallway to my room – she would've seen me. So I hid in this closest here.' Jay got up and walked to the closet, situated between the lounge and kitchen. He opened it, peered in, then closed it again.

'I could see through the slats.' His fingers running up and down the wood created a clunky melody. 'They were fighting, Mum and Lauren. Over a client. I knew all about what Mum did. Lentford's a small town. The kids at school had fun teasing me about my mum's "hobby". Lauren was getting stuck into Mum, telling her she stole one of her clients. Demanding money. Mum yelled back saying the guy had chosen her. I was thinking how I was going to get back to my bedroom when Lauren pushed Mum so hard she fell over, right here.' Jay pointed at the floor by the closet.

Jay laughed again, recalling it. His bouts of laughing scared Miller most of all. She knew he wasn't in his right mind, and there was a possibility he wasn't going to let her go after this. She adjusted her position, thinking if she knelt she'd be able to get up quicker if she needed to.

'Stop moving!' he yelled.

'Okay, okay,' Miller said, desperate to placate him. 'Sorry. Go on.'

Jay started pacing back and forth in front of the closet, the floorboards creaking under his weight.

He stopped and stared at the floor, pointing. 'Lauren straddled my mother before she could get up again. Slapped her a few times.' He looked up and smiled. 'I remember wanting to jump out of the closet and join in. Mum was struggling under Lauren's weight. And then I remember Lauren's hands wrapping around my mother's scrawny neck.'

Jay walked towards Miller and knelt in front of her. He was staring at her, but Miller felt he couldn't see her.

'I watched as her hands squeezed tight around Mum's neck. I watched Mum struggle and then go still. Lauren hauled her fat arse off Mum. I watched her grab Mum's handbag on the couch.' He pointed to the wall he'd been leaning against as if the couch was still there. 'She tipped everything out and grabbed the notes that fell to the floor. Then she was gone.'

God, he saw his mother murdered.

'I came out of the closet and went over to Mum. Her eyes were shut. But her chest was still rising and falling. I grabbed her scarf from the couch. She always wore one when she went out. I slipped it around her neck.'

Miller closed her eyes, realising what was coming next.

'I kept on tightening it. It was easy.'

Jay reached out to Miller, as if in slow motion. Miller pressed herself up against the wall, nowhere else to go. Jay's hands encircled her neck. 'I remembered all the times she hit me.'

'Jay! No,' Miller shouted, her voice quashed as he applied more pressure.

'She put me down, brought home those sick men to do whatever they wanted with me.'

Miller clawed at Jay's hands. Slapping at his body.

'The happiness and relief I felt as I watched her chest rise and fall for the last time was out of this world.'

Jay refocused and looked at Miller. He dropped his hands.

'Sorry,' he mumbled, backing away. 'I didn't mean to do that.'

Miller doubled over, struggling to breathe, her eyes watering. Jay carried on talking as if he hadn't just tried to kill her. 'About five minutes after that I rang 111. A couple of cops arrived and then there were more. Detectives and people in overalls. I talked to a nice policewoman. She made me a Milo with the kitchen door closed.' Jay looked up where a wide space now led into the dining room and kitchen. 'Used to be a wall and door here,' he observed.

'She asked me what happened. I told her I was asleep in my bedroom, woke up hearing shouting and then quiet, and then a door slamming. I told her I got up and went into the lounge and saw Mum, the scarf around her neck. I told her I saw she wasn't breathing and that's when I rang the police.'

Jay looked up at Miller. 'And that's why I am what I am. That's my story, Miller. Well, the start at least. She was a horrible person. I killed her. I admit that. But the world was a lot better off with her not in it. You do understand that, don't you?' He came and stood in front of Miller, who cowered, trying to move away from him.

'She always said I wouldn't amount to anything. Always said I was nothing, a waste of space. But what I've done will show her. By doing this, people will know who I am. Even when I'm not here anymore, people will always remember my name. Remember what I did. Remember that for a short time, I was *someone*.' Jay took a deep breath and exhaled.

The knock on the front door was sudden, breaking the eerie calm that had descended after Jay's story.

'Police! Open up!'

'What did you do?' Jay said, looking at Miller's phone in the centre of the room. Still recording. 'Who did you ring? When did you ring—'

'I haven't called anyone,' Miller said.

There was more banging on the door. Jay grabbed his backpack and ran through the kitchen and out the back door.

Miller ran for the front door, unlocking the deadbolt and wrenching it open. Ash was standing on the doorstep, hand raised, ready to strike the door again.

'Miller?' she said, confused.

'He's gone out the back!' Miller shouted. 'Get him!'

Miller could hear shouting at the back of the house. Ash stepped inside and ran to the back door with Miller close behind. Jay was on the floor in the kitchen. Bull had one knee on his back and was handcuffing him. Jay was yelling and shouting, incoherent.

Ash took Miller into the lounge. 'We got a call from a neighbour. They'd got up to get a drink and saw a light on here. They knew there was no one in the house. Thought there might be squatters or teenagers up to no good. Are you okay?' Her forehead creased as she glanced at Miller's neck and took in her shaking form. 'Here, sit down.' She helped Miller to the floor.

'It's Jay... He's the Scarf Killer,' Miller said.

'Detective Parata filled us in this afternoon. I'll call him now.'

'Sarge!' Bull bellowed from the kitchen.

Ash glanced at Miller and they both ran through to the kitchen. Jay, hands cuffed behind his back, was yelling in pain. He threw himself onto the floor from a sitting position, his body tense, mouth settled into a grimace, neck tendons taut, eyes shut tight.

'He's having a seizure. Call an ambulance!' Ash yelled and knelt by Jay to remove his handcuffs.

Chapter 43

Miller walked along a maze of corridors at Waikato Hospital with Kahu early the following morning. Her neck ached and was already coming out in pale-blue bruises. She had rested only briefly at Lentford police station before Kahu had rung, asking for her.

'He wants to speak with you,' Kahu said between gritted teeth.

'Why me?' Miller asked, dreading seeing Jay again.

'The doctors have informed us he has an inoperable brain tumour. He's known about it for the last year or so. Doctors say he hasn't got long.'

'He's going to die? When?'

'Could be today, could still have months left. They don't know.'

'You going to be okay?' Kahu asked as they stood outside Jay's room, a uniformed officer in a chair by the door. 'He's been read his rights, plus he knows this conversation is being recorded. We've told him he needs a lawyer present, but he's declined, numerous times. Says the only one who really needs to hear this is you.'

Miller nodded.

'Come on. Let's get this over with. He refuses to say anything unless you're here.' He opened the door and Miller followed him in.

Jay was sitting up in bed. His eyes were closed; his tanned skin was pale, his face drawn. He looked peaceful, at rest, which maddened Miller. He opened his eyes and smiled at Miller, waving a hand towards a seat next to him. She stayed standing at the foot of the bed. She would treat this like an interview. No emotion. Get it done.

'I'm so glad you could come.' He looked at her neck. The grin was fleeting, but Miller saw it. 'I'm sorry about last night. That got out of hand. Did the detective tell you? I don't have long to live.'

If he's expecting sympathy, he's looking at the wrong person.

'Detective Parata here is *dying* to know what I've been up to for the last month.'

Kahu's jaw was clenched, his lips compressed.

'I'm sure you have questions.' Jay looked at Miller. 'Ask away.'

Miller could tell Jay knew he was in control. He had the choice of what information to divulge and when and knew it was driving Kahu mad.

'Margaret Hughes,' Miller said. She'd already filled Kahu in on what thirteen-year-old Jay had done to his mother. For Cassie's sake, she needed to find out how it had come about.

'I'd been working for Gary Vogel for a few months. We'd been working at Margaret's next-door neighbours. I'd seen her once there, and a couple of times out walking when I was leaving work for the day. She'd caught my eye. Attractive woman, I guess, but the reason she'd caught my eye was she walked every day and almost every weekend from her house to that place up the road that sold fruit and vegetables. The road wasn't busy at all. It was a no-exit. The road finished at the farm that had the shop. There were probably four or five other houses on the road, all with a lot of land, all rich as shit, their fancy houses blocked from the road by massive hedges. I hadn't really planned it. No, that's a lie. I dreamed about what I wanted to do if I ever got the chance. I'd finished up at this house one morning and was driving along the road when I saw her. I pulled over, wound down my window and got her over to my side of the truck. I grabbed her head, punched her in the face, then jumped out and rammed her head into the side of the truck. It was easy.'

Jay rubbed his dry hands together, the sound like sandpaper on wood. *He's enjoying this.*

'I put her in the back seat of the truck and got the hell out of there. I knew Gary would be pissed off. He needed the truck. Can't remember what I told him in the end.'

'You told him your mother was sick,' Kahu said without looking up.

Jay shook his head. 'You guys.' He grinned. Miller remembered how much she'd liked his smile. 'You're on to it.'

'Why Lentford?' Kahu said.

Jay smiled his even, white smile. Miller put her hands on the bed frame and squeezed tight. Never in her whole life had she wanted to hurt someone more.

'Lentford is home,' Jay said. 'I'm sure Miller filled you in. Anyway, I came across the old dairy factory. By this time it was mid-afternoon. It was quiet around there, no one else in sight. But I didn't want to get her out in broad daylight. She came to an hour later, started clawing and fighting. I'd jumped into the back seat. There was a bit of a struggle—'

'Did you sexually assault her?' Kahu asked. Miller found herself wishing, praying that he hadn't.

'What kind of sick fuck do you think I am?' Jay said, his face screwed up in disgust. 'As I was saying, we struggled. Maybe that's when the coin came off and rolled under the seat.

Anyway, she managed to get out of the truck. She was fast, for what she'd been through. I'll give her that. I went after her. I had a knife. Didn't want to use it – I hate blood. But she was so much stronger than I thought she'd be.' Jay looked directly at Miller. 'I stabbed her. To stop her, really. Stabbed her quite a few times. It was messy.'

He hunched his shoulders, his neck disappearing into the pale-blue hospital gown. 'It was still light but I hadn't seen any-one in hours so I dragged her behind one of the big vats and left her there. I used Gary's shovel in the back, dug a shallow grave. The grass was over a metre high, her body was totally hidden. Figured no one came out there anymore. And, boy, was I right. I mean, I thought it would take a while for her to be discovered, and by then I'd be off overseas. But fourteen years! And only then because a few property developers were looking around. It could've been a lot longer!' He laughed, happy how it all turned out.

All Miller could think about was ten-year-old Cassie tucked up in bed that night, wondering where her mother was.

'And what about your name?' Miller asked.

'Karl Taylor,' Jay said, smiling again and then wincing. He closed his eyes and breathed deeply. Miller was glad he was in some sort of pain – just not enough. 'You know Karl Taylor was my grandfather. Not my real one. My name, before I was adopted, was Jason Martin. I was adopted by Mum and Dad – Amanda and Grant Taylor – and changed my name when I was fourteen to Jason Taylor.'

'Why did you tell everyone your name was Karl Taylor when you were working in Tauranga?' Kahu asked.

'It's what I did when I went somewhere new. You need to understand, this was always with me. The need to take a life. I'm not stupid, you know. I worked cash jobs, didn't let people get too close. And it all paid off with Margaret. I did the deed and I disappeared.'

There was silence. Miller wanted to be out of this room, out of this hospital, but she knew there was more. 'How did you get into my house?' she asked.

'You still haven't figured that part out? I had a clear plan from the beginning. The letters, you, the victims, how it was done. I go out to The Oaks sometimes. You know, the treatment facility for the crazies – depressives, suicidal, druggies, alcoholics. They use me for all their advertising stuff, brochures, business cards, educational posters. I thought that was a good a place as any to find who I needed. I'm a quiet guy. Unassuming. I was part of the furniture there. They knew my face. They trusted me. The things I would hear.' He shook his head, disbelieving. 'I was in the staff room organising a bunch of brochures, and there were a couple of the counsellors in there. This was back in September. They were gossiping, as a lot of them do, about their colleagues and the patients. Apparently one of the patients, a female, was having it off with the boss lady, Fenella. They were having it off in her office every day for the last few months. Anyway, the boss lady got a fit of conscience and decided to call it off. The patient wasn't happy and goes at her with a letter opener. Cuts her forehead and her arm before being pulled off.'

Jay laughed. 'Bloody females. No charges were laid as this Fenella didn't want the authorities to know she was banging one of the patients. Anyway, I decided right then, I've found my girl. I get into one of the counsellor's offices on the pretence of delivering some brochures. I knew her first name and I looked her up on the computer. Again, very lax, didn't even need a password. She was in for drugs, violent outbursts etcetera. I approached her carefully, not wanting to scare her off. I brought her drugs, and when she was let out last month we met, talked. She didn't take much persuading. I introduced the idea to her slowly, in a roundabout way, didn't want to freak her out, but she was all in, said it sounded like "fun". She's sick in the head,' Jay said, without a trace of irony.

'Who are you talking about?' Kahu said.

'Her name's Tiffany. Tiffany Winslow.' Jay smiled when he saw Miller's reaction. 'And, get this, she bloody hooked up with Cassie Hughes while she was at The Oaks. I couldn't believe that part. Nothing to do with me. I guess it was all Fate, kind of like serendipity, like it was all supposed to be.'

'She got you into the houses,' Miller said. She turned to Kahu. 'Cassie!' Where was Tiff? What was she doing now?

Kahu whispered to the other detective standing behind the video camera, then left the room.

'Women living alone don't generally let guys into their homes. I wasn't a stranger to those women but if I came knocking late at night, sure as shit they weren't going to let me in. The plan worked brilliantly. You opened the door to her. Madi did it, Tamara did it and Emmeline did it. Tiff and I could've got through the whole female population of Lentford.' He laughed quietly. 'She gets let in, then she asks to use the toilet and I'm normally out the back. She lets me in through the back door and I go hide while she's chatting away to them. She used to do the "my car's broken down and my phone's dead" act so she could get in to use the phone. Or say that she was being followed and needed somewhere safe to ring a friend. Perfect plan. No break-in, nothing. I had the police stumped,' Jay said proudly. 'Of course, I checked out their houses beforehand. Noted the back door, where the lounge and bathroom were, that kind of thing.'

Miller retraced what Tiff had done when she was at her house the previous evening. She'd asked to use the toilet and would have gone into the kitchen and opened the door for Jay. 'She let you in and you went to hide in the wardrobe. Why the wardrobe?'

Jay was silent, as if waiting.

Miller nodded. 'It's all like your mother.' She remembered Jay's story of hiding in the cupboard, watching as Lauren assaulted his mother.

'My mother,' Jay said. 'I told you, Miller. She made me like this. It's her fault. After Mum, I went into foster care in Hamilton. I had just turned thirteen, shy, quiet, a bit of a runt. The two people who fostered me ended up adopting me – Amanda and Grant Taylor. As I said, I changed my name to theirs after they adopted me. When I moved back to Lentford I started using the surname Martin again, figured everyone had forgotten about the old slut who was murdered by her friend and the kid that got shipped off to foster care – and I was right. Plus, Martin's a common enough name. Anyway, I tried to move on and forget what happened, but it had awoken something inside me, and I was forever changed. I was violent at school, beat up kids younger than me. I strangled a boy at school once. Nothing serious. He was left with a bit of bruising – I wasn't going to kill him. I got expelled for that. My parents were understanding. I remember overhearing them one night after I'd been suspended. Mum – Amanda – she was asking Dad if the way my real mum had died and how I'd found her had fucked me up somehow. I was on my best behaviour from then on. I buried it deep for a long time. Not deep enough, I guess. It was always in the back of my head. Like a scratch that needed itching. And for a long time, I was good. Kids thought I was weird, and I did have a bit of a temper. But apart from that, I was okay. But then, before I killed Margaret, there was this realisation that something was missing. I didn't feel happy or satisfied. I felt like a failure.

She always said I'd amount to nothing.'

Kahu had come back in. 'Who did?' he asked.

'My mother,' Jay said, frowning at Kahu. 'The last time I felt truly happy was that night. The night my mother left my life.' He held his hand to the side of his face. 'When I found out about this thing growing in my head it was a sign. I needed to make my mark on the world before it was too late. And so it seemed obvious what I had to do. So that's the story you're going to tell, Miller. People will feel sorry for me. I'm damaged goods. My life was over before it began. My mother, those men, never gave me a chance.'

'Your adoptive parents did,' Miller said.

'It was too late then. The damage was done.'

'All excuses. You had the opportunity to turn your life around, but you chose not to.'

'Do you really think that?' Jay asked. 'Tell my story, Miller. Wait and see what the public think.'

'The scarves,' Kahu said. It wasn't posed as a question, but Jay began to speak.

'I took two things with me the night that nice police officer took me away from that dump. My Sega and Mum's scarves. I remember the police officer looking at me with big, sad eyes. I don't really know why I took them.' Jay looked honestly stumped. 'But I slept with them for a long time, till her smell was gone from them. I never got round to throwing them away. They came with me wherever I moved to, the countries I travelled to.'

'And you used them to strangle your victims,' Kahu said.

Jay nodded. 'Poetic, don't you think?'

'And the lipstick?'

'It's what she used to wear. The same colour every day, whether she was going off to work, or going to the pub, or doing other... stuff. I had to get the scene right, Detective, don't you see that?' He looked at Kahu and then at Miller, waiting for some reaction.

Does he think we're all of a sudden going to agree with him? Understand him?

'And what about their stories?' Miller said. 'Margaret's, Emmeline's, Madi's, Tamara's?'

'You look at them and think their stories have been cut short, don't you?' Jay's voice had become quieter and his speech sounded slurred, laboured. 'But don't you see? They've become a part of *my* story. They were nice women, but nothing special. People don't need to know about them, really. They've become public figures because of what I did to them. Wrong place, wrong time. Whenever I'm mentioned – and that's going to be a lot over the coming years – they'll be mentioned too. They will live on through me.'

Jay's smile turned into a grimace and he screamed in pain, clutching his head.

'Shit.' Kahu moved to the head of the bed and pushed the emergency button.

Jay's body bucked in his bed once and then he was still, eyes screwed up tight. Two doctors and three nurses raced into the room and Kahu ushered Miller out. They stood in the hall listening to the doctors trying to save the life of a man who had taken so many.

Chapter 44

Kahu stood on Miller's doorstep later that morning. 'He's dead. An acute haemorrhage into the tumour tissue, the doc said.' He looked as bleary-eyed as Miller felt. 'I need to get going. Press conference in Hamilton this morning. No doubt word is out in Lentford.'

'Have you talked to Cassie?' Miller asked.

'She's next on my list,' Kahu said checking his watch.

'So that's it? After all that, he gets away with it?'

'There won't be a court case, no. There'll be a coronial hearing at some point which will close the case. But the guy's dead. Not sure if that's getting away with it.'

'You know what I mean, Kahu,' Miller muttered, head down.

'You heard the confession, Miller. The story's all yours. A scoop.'

She looked up at him to make sure he wasn't angry.

He smiled. 'Tell the story. Tell them who he was, what he did. They need to know that seemingly average Joes like Jay are walking around their towns and cities. Not all evil, on the surface, is ugly and menacing. It doesn't always lurk in city centres after dark. It mows your lawns, frequents your local pub, takes its kids to school and contributes to communities.'

Miller nodded. That she could do. 'And Tiffany Winslow?'

'That's being taken care of,' Kahu said, turning to look out across the park. It was a Saturday, another beautiful day. Two days before Christmas, and the park was packed already.

'She'll get charged, won't she? She can't get away with what she did.'

'We're bringing her in for questioning this morning.'

'And?' Miller joined Kahu on the step, watching a toddler inch her way down the slide, the dad at the bottom waiting, arms splayed.

'And nothing. We'll see what she has to say for herself.'

'She was at my place last night,' Miller said. 'Jay explained exactly what they did.'

'We need evidence though. We lifted a lot of prints from the victim's houses. We'll be getting Tiffany's to compare. Keep this to yourself. Nothing's been released about her,' Kahu warned.

Miller nodded. 'You know that true crime tour I did with Logan?'

Kahu grunted. She knew his feelings on the subject.

'Logan took us to Jay's old house. Where I was last night. Where Jay murdered his mother. Jay, at thirteen years old, lied to the cops, sent a woman to jail for sixteen years. Then thirty years later he comes back and murders women the same way he murdered his mother.'

'Full circle,' Kahu said. He shook his head and walked back to his car.

Chapter 45

It was just past midday and the Kowhai Cafe was full to capacity. Word had got round Lentford that the Scarf Killer was Jay Martin. The whole coffee shop was in discussion, but Miller didn't hear Tiff's name mentioned. She ordered coffees for her and Cassie, and they eased their way into the corner by the window to wait.

Tables had been pushed together to accommodate a large group of people, obviously meeting for the sole point of discussing the latest news. Others were talking to neighbouring tables. The whole cafe buzzed with conversation about Jay, some of it true, some of it not. But it didn't seem to matter. Logan Dodds had been replaced with a whole new monster.

'Where is he now? Is he still here? In Lentford?' an older woman said, sitting at a table next to Cassie and Miller, her hand fluttering to her chest.

'Probably taken him to Hamilton,' someone offered up.

'I'm so glad he's not here anymore. Finally, we can get on with life. Go back to normal.'

'Just think what those poor girls went through. Sick bastard,' a man in his forties said to the long table in the middle of the room. 'He's been pretty much running Gavin Lexford's printing business. He's helped out at the schools. Given tours of the printing press to the kids. Probably a bloody paedo as well.'

Others muttered their agreement. 'I heard he even went out Tamara. They actually went on a date together.' People muttered their disapproval.

As if going on a date with Jay and then being killed by him made it so much worse, Miller thought.

'Don't you think she would've known?' the older woman said to Len as he brought over coffee and cake to the table.

'You'd think so, wouldn't you?' Len said. 'I mean, you have dinner with someone, chat for a couple of hours. Did she go home with him? You've got to wonder.' Len raised his eyebrows, implying that Tamara had done something wrong.

'She didn't go out with him,' Miller said, knowing it was pointless. Half the cafe turned towards her, eager for more. 'He asked her out, but she refused.'

'Still,' Len said and walked away.

Still what? Miller thought. There was always someone who wanted to fan the flames.

Miller took the takeaway coffee cups from the woman behind the counter, which made her think of Li – she was never far from Miller's mind. Cassie hadn't said a word since they entered the Kowhai. 'Let's get out of here,' Miller said.

Cassie nodded and they left, voices following them out the door. 'You know, Jay's lived here not even two years. He's not truly from Lentford,' someone said, as if that gave the town a pass. They didn't realise that the name Lentford would ever be synonymous with Jason Martin.

'I'm a bit surprised no one spoke to me,' Cassie said as they crossed the road and turned left and walked towards the river.

'As good as the grapevine is in Lentford, I don't think word's got out about your mother yet,' Miller said. 'You might want to brace yourself.' She sipped from her coffee. 'Kahu's told you what happened, right?' She was unsure of what Cassie knew.

No one back there knew about Tiffany or the fact that Jay was dead. It wouldn't take long, though. Miller gave it till the end of the day, and hoped Kahu had filled Cassie in.

'Detective Parata tracked me down this morning. He was outside my house when I got home. I stayed in Hamilton last night. He took me to the Riverview for a coffee, explained everything.'

Miller wondered if everything included Tiff.

'He's dead. Karl Taylor's dead.' Cassie shook her head. 'Jay,' she corrected herself, 'is dead. It's hard to reconcile the Karl Taylor I obsessed about, with Jay. I've been serving him in the pub for the last few weeks. It's like Karl Taylor was a phantom after all these years. I honestly didn't really expect to ever put a face to the name. Do you think he knew who I was?'

Miller remembered Jay's glee at finding out Tiffany and Cassie were together. 'I'd say so,' she said.

'Just another part of his game, I guess,' Cassie said as they stopped down by the river.

'Do you feel any kind of relief?' Miller asked. 'Closure?'

'Yes, to both,' Cassie said. 'But I also feel ripped off.'

Miller nodded.

'He's never going to get his day in court. People aren't going to hear about what he did. They won't get the chance to hate him as much as I did for all those years.'

'People hate him already,' Miller said.

'They hate him but they also want to know him,' Cassie said. 'And, hell, I kinda want to know him as well. Why did he do it? What made him do it?'

'I can tell the story,' Miller said. 'I can tell the whole world what he did to your mum, the women in Lentford. I can tell you and the rest of the world who he was and why he did it, but I won't write anything that excuses his actions.' She thought of what Jay had told her about his mother, his childhood, his so-called reasoning for taking the lives of others, intent that their names be forever intertwined with his. She had a feeling, whether she wrote this story or not, Jason Martin would be re-membered for many years to come, just as he wished, no matter how she reported his story. She crossed to the rubbish bin and deposited her empty cup.

'So trial by media then?' Cassie said.

'It's often a lot harsher than that of a courtroom.'

Cassie looked out to the river. 'I have a feeling that even if he had gone to trial, went to jail for the rest of his life, it would never have been enough for me. He took my mum from me all those years ago, and nothing will ever make that feeling of hopelessness and loss disappear. *Nothing.* So I should be glad he's not in this world anymore.'

'Have you seen Tiff since yesterday? Made up with her?' Miller asked, dancing around the subject, knowing she was on fragile ground.

Cassie visibly tensed, her coffee cup buckling in her hands. 'I haven't seen her since yesterday morning.' She touched the pale bruise on her cheekbone.

She doesn't know. Kahu hasn't told her. What if she's in danger, though?

'I love her. But I'm not sure what I'm going to do. I'll cook her dinner tonight, and we can talk. We might be able to work something out.' Cassie turned towards Miller. 'Her dad told me a lot of stuff. I'm just not sure if I want to be a part of her life. She can be really destructive.'

Miller wanted to yell and shout, grab Cassie by the shoulders and shake some sense into her. But Kahu had warned her not to speak about Tiffany.

Chapter 46

Cassie got back from the supermarket just before six. The front door was wide open and music was blaring from the lounge. Her stomach somersaulted knowing she was about to see Tiff. She called out as she put the groceries in the kitchen. Devilskin screamed out of the speakers, and she turned it off while taking in the state of the lounge. A suitcase was lying on the floor, clothes were strewn over the couch. Tiff's pipe was lying on the coffee table next to a small bag of white powder. Cassie rolled her eyes, wondering where the night would take them.

Tiff walked in from their bedroom with a pile of clothes and dumped them in the middle of the floor.

'Tiff?' Cassie said, walking up to her. She looked at her dilated pupils. 'Are you high?'

'Of course I'm bloody high.' She picked out clothes from the pile and threw them into the open suitcase. 'Where have you been?' she asked, not looking at Cassie.

'I stayed in Hamilton last night. With an old friend.'

'A woman?' Tiff asked.

'Yes, but it's not like that. I just needed some space to think, after what happened yesterday morning.'

'I went looking for you. I went to Miller's. I thought for sure you'd be there.' Tiff sat down on the couch and then stood back up again. 'I think we should leave,' she said. 'Me and you. Head down south or maybe go up to Auckland.' She went into the kitchen and rifled through the bags Cassie had left on the bench.

'Okay,' Cassie said uncertainly. 'You don't want to stay in Lentford anymore?'

'You know I don't. It's a hole. We really only ever stayed for you, for the whole Karl Taylor thing.'

'You know they've caught someone, right?'

Tiff was silent, then joined Cassie back in the lounge.

'You know Jay Martin? Came into the pub a bit. Worked at the printers. Jay's the Scarf Killer, Tiff. And he killed my mother.'

'What? He killed your mother!'

Cassie was surprised at her shock.

'I didn't know that.' Tiff got up again and headed to the kitchen.

Cassie sighed and followed her. It was almost impossible to talk to her when she was like this. Tiff got a bottle of wine from the fridge and busied herself opening it. Her hands were shaking.

'Why would you?' Cassie said.

'I... No reason.' Tiff grabbed a coffee mug from the dish rack and poured the wine, slopping some onto the floor.

'Tiff, you're shaking. We're all a bit shocked. I mean, we knew Jay, sort of; knew who he was. I still can't believe he killed those women. Killed Mum. I'm glad he's been caught, but it's all a lot to take in. I heard from Len—'

'Lentford's resident gossip,' Tiff said, half the wine was gone in one gulp.

'Apparently Jay had someone helping him.'

'What do you mean?' Tiff refilled her glass.

'The papers always reported that there was no evidence of a break-in, that the women had let the killer in. They thought maybe they knew him. He probably did know them, but not well enough that if he came knocking on the door late at night they'd let him in. So they think he had help.'

Tiff walked towards Cassie, her mouth a thin line, stained red from the wine. She reached out and caressed Cassie's bare arm. 'Do they know?' She knocked back the rest of the wine. 'Cassie, do you know something? Is there something you're not telling me?'

'What do you mean?' Cassie gulped, the sound loud in the silence.

'You were always such a bad liar. Too innocent and good, that's your problem. Have the cops got to you? They told me they wouldn't say anything. I haven't been charged with anything.'

'What are you talking about?'

'God! I'm so sick of this. Of you.' Tiff refilled her mug with wine and took another gulp.

'What do you mean?' Cassie said.

'What do you mean?' Tiff mimicked, her voice high. 'This privileged life you lead. You're so spoilt, you don't want for anything.'

'Tiff, you know that's not true.'

'Fine, you lost your mother, but you still had a family who loved you, money, a dad who gave you whatever you wanted.'

'And you had the same, Tiff. A loving family who would do anything for you – even now.'

'What are you talking about?'

'I visited your dad yesterday,' Cassie said, unsure it was the best idea to tell Tiff.

Tiff was silent. 'Whatever. I don't care. He probably sucked you in. Told you lies about me. You're really just like them.'

'Like who?' Cassie asked, making sure there was enough distance between her and Tiff in the small kitchen.

'The only reason he chose them was because they lived by themselves, but I knew them. I'd talked to all of them before.'

'Tiff—'

'Don't fuckin' pretend you don't know what I'm talking about. Those women. They had it all. Parents who loved them – you should've seen the photos in their houses, fuckin' every-where. Happy families – they had good jobs, money. I spoke to Tamara a lot out at The Oaks. Got to know her. She was always whingeing about her boyfriend. Didn't realise how good she had it.'

Tiff stopped and stared at her. Cassie tried to arrange her face into an expression that didn't show how horrified she was.

'Stop fuckin' acting like you don't know what's going on!' Tiff shouted. 'You act so bloody innocent. Speak up! Go on, Cass, tell me what's on your mind. Who's been whispering in your ear? That fuckin' black bastard Parata? It was him, wasn't it? Whispering shit in your ear about me helping Jay.'

'Tiff—' Cass could feel herself flush with fear.

'Look,' Tiff said, leaning against the bench, her right side pressed up against Cassie. 'The police questioned me today. I admitted to an affair with Fenella. And the assault. I admitted that too. But she wanted to call things off and I got upset. She was still in the bloody closet, started getting all precious about what people would think. I shouldn't have done what I did. It was wrong. I didn't mean to hurt you. She means nothing to me.'

'Jesus, Tiff,' Cassie said. 'I don't care about Fenella. But you assaulted her.'

Tiff sighed. 'What do you want to hear, Cass?' She leant down to Cassie and nibbled her ear lobe and whispered. 'Do you want me to say I helped Jay? Do you need a confession?'

Cassie felt the tears run down her cheeks. 'Enough,' she said.

'Enough?' Tiff threw her head back and laughed. 'No, Cassie. Not enough. You want the truth from me? We love each other, right? So we need to be honest with each other. I did it. I helped Jay. I helped the man who murdered your mother! How's that for a surprise?' Tiff was giggling now. 'It's not funny, I know.' She took a deep breath, trying to control herself. 'But Jesus, Cass. I had no idea.'

Cassie found it hard to stand, her legs failing to support her. She grabbed hold of the bench. 'If you had known he'd killed my mother, would you still have helped him?'

Tiff was silent for a while. 'Yeah, probably.' She looked at Cassie, a smile tugging at her lips.

Cassie stepped around Tiff, heading for the lounge. She needed to get out of here.

Tiff reached out and grabbed her hair. Cassie screamed and Tiff brought the half-empty wine bottle down on her head. 'You're not going anywhere, Cass.'

Cassie lay on the floor in the kitchen, staring at Tiff's bare feet. She reached for the side of her head and brought away a bloodied hand. She felt it, hot and thick, running into her ear. 'You won't tell anyone about this, right?' Tiff said, bending down to speak to her. Her voice had changed from hard and angry to soft and sing-song, belying the words coming from her mouth. 'For starters, no one will believe you. You don't have the best track record. Losing your mother all those years ago, your obsession with Karl Taylor and then being committed to The Oaks. Plus, you've just found out who's murdered your mother and you're all over the show.'

'Tiff...' Cassie said.

'We're done, Cassie. You're too weak. I'm outta here.' She got up and left the kitchen and Cassie heard her putting clothes into the suitcase.

Cassie pulled herself up, wondering if she'd done a good job, wondering where they were, and then there was loud knocking and Detective Parata barged in with a mass of people behind him.

'About bloody time,' Cassie said as he knelt down next to her, yelling for an ambulance.

There was a flurry of activity as a paramedic checked Cassie out. She sat up, leaning against the cupboard as the paramedic checked her wound, shone a torch in her eyes and asked her questions which she only half heard. Tiff was in the lounge, shouting obscenities. A detective walked towards her, backing her into the far wall by their bedroom. Tiff kicked her legs out and growled at him like a wild animal. Another detective helped restrain her, and even when the handcuffs were on she kept struggling.

Tiff caught Cassie's eye as she was dragged out of the house. 'This was all a lie!' she shouted, her eyes bright. 'What we had? Remember that! I never loved you. All of this – what I did – it was so much bigger, more important than you!'

Twenty minutes later the house was quiet. Detective Parata had told her she'd done a perfect job, that they'd heard everything that was said. Cassie sat on the couch, a mug of tea in her trembling hands. The victim support officer sat on the couch beside her, a hand lightly on her back, as she cried.

Half an hour later Cassie was ready to go forward. Without Tiff. Without her mum.

Chapter 47

Miller walked into the Royal on Christmas Eve with Ash. There was a *Lentford Leader* get-together and Miller assured Ash she would be welcome. Every table and leaner were taken, smokers congregated out back, there was a line for the pool tables and people were three deep at the bar. The air smelt of cigarette smoke wafting in from outside and the roast of the day, which seemed to have been ordered by half the pub. Miller had just come from Cassie's house where she was packed and waiting for her father to pick her up. Cassie was still in shock, sporting stitches on the side of her head where Tiff had hit her with a wine bottle.

'Detective Parata tracked me down yesterday morning when I got back from Hamilton,' Cassie had said. 'He told me what had happened, that Tiff was at the police station. He said they didn't have enough to arrest her. They bugged our place, had it under surveillance all of yesterday. All I had to do was try and get a confession out of her. She was out of her mind. But that's no excuse. That was Tiff, I'm beginning to realise.'

'You obviously had no idea what she'd been up to,' Miller said, amazed at what Tiff had almost got away with.

Cassie shook her head. 'I often worked nights at the pub. If she'd gone out, like she said, knocked on those women's doors and got inside I'd never have known anything about it. And if

I did get home and she wasn't in she just told me she was out scoring drugs.'

'What will you do now?' Miller asked.

'They offer the same childcare course in Tauranga. I'm going to move in with Dad. It's funny. I so desperately wanted to get away from him for such a long time and now it's the only place I want to be. I feel like all of this... I had to go through it. Karl Taylors, Tiff, The Oaks... I had to do all that before I came right.'

'That was a lot to go through.'

'I know, but without it, I wouldn't have had the same outcome. If I hadn't started obsessing about Karl Taylor I wouldn't have ended up in The Oaks, if I hadn't gone to The Oaks I wouldn't have met Tiff, if I hadn't meet Tiff I'd never have stayed in Lentford, and if I hadn't stayed in Lentford I wouldn't have met you. The article wouldn't have been written, Jay's grandad would never have seen it, you'd never have met Amanda. See? Full circle.' Cassie nodded, happy with her conclusion.

'A pretty traumatic full circle,' Miller said. 'Are you going to be okay, Cassie?' Miller asked, a hand on her arm. She always seemed so innocent. There was always a need in Miller to protect her.

'Yes,' Cassie nodded. 'For the first time in many years, probably since before Mum died, I can say with all certainty I'm going to be fine.'

'Miller!' Cody shouted, arms flailing in a drunken semaphore. 'Over here!'

Miller waved back and weaved her way to the table where Cody and Hine sat. 'No Eric?' she said, feigning disappointment. They'd arranged the get-together before the paper had split up for the holidays. An issue would be put out in a couple of days; all the content was ready to go. Ngaire had told Miller to hold off on her article about Jay. 'Leave it till the new year. I want as many people as possible to read it.'

'You just missed him,' Cody said. 'Scrounged our drinks and then left.'

'And Ngaire?'

'I got a text from her last night. I think she hates Christmas as much as you. She's taken a last-minute trip to Sydney. She wishes us all a Merry Christmas and will see us in the new year. I'm in charge of getting the files off to the printers. Apparently old man Lexford is coming out of semi-retirement to print it for us because...' Cody tailed off, unable to put it into words.

'Because his last employee was a serial killer,' Hine said, appearing at the table, handing Miller a Coke and pouring Ash a beer into an empty glass from the pitcher on the table without asking what her preference was.

'He was a spree killer, not a serial killer,' Miller said before she could stop herself, remembering what Logan had said on the tour.

Miller saw Lou and Maggie at a table close by with two other couples. Aubrey was at a table with four other women, all talking over each other. Johnno and Tane were manic behind the bar. Every now and then Johnno's sullen face lit up as he served a woman.

'There's a lot of chat round here,' Hine said. 'About Jay. God, to think I fancied him.'

'You fancy everyone,' said Cody.

Hine playfully pushed him, and he almost fell off his seat. They erupted into laughter.

A man next to them was telling anyone who would listen that for the last couple of years Jay had printed all his firm's business cards and calendars. 'Fuckin' freaks me out that I sat in an office with that sicko. Shooting the breeze, talking business.'

'Yeah, bro, I don't think you were really his type. You were safe.' There was a roar of laughter.

'Bit early for jokes like that, isn't it?' Hine said, sipping her beer.

Bull walked in a few minutes later and a crowd gathered around him. He had become known as the one who would offer up information when all the other cops kept tight-lipped. Miller was sure it had got him into some trouble, but by the looks of it, he loved the attention too much to keep quiet.

The group of men jostled Bull into the middle of the room, and someone handed him a beer. The place quietened enough to hear what Bull was saying.

When he realised he had the attention of everyone in the bar his voice grew louder. 'Jay Martin died yesterday morning. Had a brain tumour.'

Miller noticed Ash stiffen in her chair. 'He can't help himself can he,' she said to Miller. 'I've given him a verbal warning, about talking about open cases. I've told him the next one will be in writing.'

There was an immediate uproar:

'What the fuck?'

'Are you fuckin' serious!'

'Piece of shit gets away with it then.'

'Dead in the ground, exactly where he belongs.'

Bull motioned for quiet. 'Tiffany Winslow has also been charged as a party to murder. She was Jay's accomplice. Got him into the women's houses. She knew exactly what she was doing and knew what Jay planned. She'll get a hefty sentence.'

'Who's Tiffany Winslow?' Cody asked.

Miller looked at Ash who nodded. 'Word's going to get out sooner or later.' She took a gulp of beer and Miller quickly explained.

'Holy shit,' Cody said, shaking his head, putting down his

beer. 'Poor Cassie.'

Bull's voice pierced through the throng again. 'Logan Dodds has confessed to the murder of Li Chen and has been charged with—'

He was cut off by someone giving him a shove, his beer spilling down his front. Beatrice and William Dodds stood at the open door of the Royal with another couple. All talk halted, and Miller felt the hatred emanating from everyone in the room. William backed out, head down. Beatrice cast her eye across the room, meeting Miller's for just a second, then walked back out.

'Shit,' Hine said. 'They honestly thought it would be a good idea to come out for a meal tonight? Makes you wonder how they're supposed to live in a town this small after their son did what he did.'

Miller shook her head. She had no answer. Logan had taken Li's life and in doing so ruined her family's. But he'd also ensured that his parents' lives would never be the same again. Hine was right. Logan would be gone for some time, safe from the stares, snipes and gossip. It would be his parents who were punished for his actions.

Miller had had enough of the noise and talk. 'I think I'm done here,' she said, leaning into Ash so she could be heard.

'Me too.' Ash rose and said goodbye to Hine and Cody.

'Have a lovely Christmas, guys.' Miller stood and gave Cody and Hine a quick kiss on the cheek.

By the time she had made her way to the front door, Bull was in deep conversation with a group of women, including Aubrey, eager to know the workings of a murder trial, and the rest of the pub had gone back to talk of Christmas Day and New Year's plans.

'My place, tomorrow, for lunch. Yes? Save Zach from spending the whole of Christmas Day with his mother,' Ash said as they stood in the parking lot of the Royal.

Miller hesitated.

'Nothing fancy. Nothing too over the top. I hate to think of you alone on Christmas Day.'

Which is exactly what I want to be.

She promised Ash she'd think about it and they said their goodbyes.

Miller pulled into her driveway, noticing the For Sale sign up outside Li's house. Li's murder almost didn't seem real. Miller knew it was because there was no family around, no one left to remind people what had happened. There had been no funeral. After the autopsy Li's body had been flown back to China.

Miller sat in her car and wondered how they got the blood out of the carpet in her bedroom. Stupid thing to think about. She wondered who would buy it, whether it would sit empty for months or years. Everyone in Lentford would know it was the house where 'that Asian woman' was murdered. And it would be the same with Emmeline's, Madi's and Tamara's houses. Three more homes that would forever be tarnished with a horrific story.

Miller unlocked her front door, stopped and listened. Silence. Of course. But she knew that someone hiding in wait made no noise. One more sleep till Christmas. One hundred and eighty-nine days sober.

Chapter 48

Miller woke with a start on Christmas morning to a shrill scream and then crying. She rolled herself off the couch, which had been her bed since Jay had broken in two nights ago, and peered out the window. Greg, her neighbour, was picking one of his kids up off the footpath outside her driveway. A bike lay on its side and a thin line of blood ran down the girl's grazed leg. Greg picked his daughter up and gently brushed away the small bits of stone and grit embedded in her knees. She watched his mouth move, no doubt telling her she was okay, telling her to be brave, that it was all right because he was here. He folded her into his arms to quieten the sobbing. Miller turned away, ashamed and confused at the anger she felt.

It was still early but she was awake now. She inhaled, her body shuddering. She let the tears fall for Li. She thought of her mum and dad, the Christmases they used to share, often disastrous because of her drunken father, but there were enough good memories there to make her realise how alone she was now. She thought of the Christmases she and her mum had, just the two of them, but such happy times. Making mince pies, decorating the tree (Miller hadn't even bothered putting one up this year), going to church on Christmas morning to whichever church they fancied just because her mum enjoyed it – she wasn't religious but to her there was 'just something about

Christmas' so they'd sit in a pew at the back and sing 'Away in a Manger', 'Come All Ye Faithful' and 'Silent Night'. Then go home and eat a small lunch of ham and salad and at least three desserts – pavlova, Christmas pudding with whisky sauce, and trifle. They'd take a walk, have a nap in the afternoon then watch a movie, usually a classic like *It's a Wonderful Life* or *Miracle on 34th Street*. At night, they'd sit outside eating dessert for dinner.

Miller blew her nose and rubbed her eyes. She pulled the curtains across, blocking out the street's frivolity. She walked to the kitchen and without thinking about it reached to the back of the pantry. The bottle of wine was still there, the one she'd bought after discovering Li's body. She opened the cap and put her nose to the bottle and inhaled, the fumes making her dizzy, casting her back to long dinners with friends and exes, nights in with Nat, a shared bottle or two with her mum before she got sick, and then nights alone, after she was gone. She took a quick swig without another thought. The liquid hit the back of her throat and ran down into her stomach, quenching what felt like a decade-long thirst. She picked up her coffee mug and filled it to the brim. Avoiding her mum's photo on the windowsill, she grabbed a screwdriver from the laundry and went into her room.

She would sleep in her own bed tonight. She took another drink and put the mug on her drawers. Walking up to her wardrobe she started on the first set of screws. It was easier than she thought. She finished the first set of three and was about to start on the next when there was a knock at the door.

She picked up her mug, taking another drink. It had gone to her head and she felt better already. How could this possibly be a bad thing?

She put the screwdriver under her arm so she could open the door.

'Kahu,' she said, suddenly deflating.

'Hi,' Kahu said, looking first at Miller and then to the cup in her hand. 'You okay? You look upset.'

'I'm great,' Miller said, her voice forced, strangled. She turned her back on Kahu and walked back into her bedroom. She took another drink and went back to the last set of screws.

Kahu followed her in, peered inside the mug sitting on her drawers and watched her. The last screw came out and she expected the door to fall away. She gave it a yank, but it didn't budge.

'Let me help,' Kahu said, stepping forward.

'I don't need your help,' Miller said, still tugging at the door.

'I know. But let me.' He eased the door out of Miller's hand. He gave it a few tugs and it came away, leaving unpainted wood beneath.

'He— That was where he was,' Miller said, pointing to the wardrobe, a mess of shoes and clothes. 'He sat there, waiting for me, just like he did with Emmeline and Tamara and Madi.'

'I know,' Kahu said.

She reached for the mug and Kahu took it from her.

The guilt came then, and she wondered if Kahu had manifested it or if it would've come sooner or later. She followed Kahu into the kitchen, guilt and embarrassment turning her face red. She sat at the table and didn't fight him when he tipped the contents of the mug and bottle down the sink. The whole room smelt of fermented grapes. Kahu opened the doors out onto the deck and indicated for her to follow. They could hear yelps and laughter from across the fence. Kids trying out new toys in the backyard.

'When she died, my life fell apart. I am the ultimate cliché,' Kahu said. 'And that kind of embarrasses me. Trina made me strong. She was responsible for a lot of who I was – am. And when she died ... I didn't know who I was without her. I don't know if it was the right decision to leave Castle Bay, all of our friends, all the memories we had made. But it's done now. I feel like I'm coming out the other side. I know I've been difficult. But I couldn't bring myself to speak about her. It hurt – a lot. Like it physically hurt every time I remembered her. It didn't conjure up happy memories, just pain. But that's not me. I don't shut out friends and family. I don't give my life up for my work. Just like that, in there,' he tipped his head towards the kitchen, to the empty bottle on the bench, 'isn't really you.'

He said it with such vehemence that Miller believed him.

'Come on, get changed. Shoes on. Clean yourself up. Be in the car in five minutes. We're due at Ash's for lunch at eleven. If we want to get a game in we need to get moving.'

'You were invited too?' she asked.

'Yep. You're not the only one on their own this Christmas.'

It was said in an off-hand way, but the comment made her stop and think. She'd been so involved in herself and her own problems these last few weeks she hadn't been looking out for her friend.

'But come on, first I want to whip you at basketball. I'll wait for you outside.' He ushered her inside, locked the back door and left before she had a chance to protest.

Half of the court at the high school was taken up by a young boy on a new bike, learning to ride. Miller and Kahu watched for a few minutes as he wobbled his way around it, his mum following behind him, his dad holding a phone in front, recording and cheering at the same time.

Kahu bounced the ball a few times. He smiled at Miller, feinted left then darted to her right. For the next half hour, they pounded up and down the court. Miller, sluggish at first, found her rhythm, her need to beat Kahu overriding anything else she had going on in her head. As the sun rose higher, they were forced to retreat under the shade of an oak.

'I won,' Miller said. 'Just to be clear.' She lay down, staring up at the thick foliage blocking the sun and the never-ending blue sky. 'I've been going over it in my head,' she said as Kahu sat down next to her. 'I ask myself, is it better that Jay's dead? That there's absolutely no chance he will hurt anyone again. Or does that seem a cop-out? A lucky break? Would it have been better for Cassie, those women's families, me, to see him rot in jail? And Logan, he's in jail, where he should be. But then I think they don't rot in jail, do they? Logan will be out again at some stage. He'll probably be in his early sixties but one day he'll get to breathe in fresh air, take walks, eat what he likes, do what he likes.'

Kahu reached over and grasped Miller's hand. 'Women are dead. Families are destroyed. From where I stand there's never going to be a perfect outcome, so you need to stop trying to create one.'

Miller sat up. 'So now what?'

'You know you have a good thing going on here. Lentford, your job, your friends.'

At the mention of friends Miller thought of Li. The pain was physical. 'I know,' she said.

'So maybe it's time you looked at your move to Lentford as a positive instead of as a punishment.'

'After what's just happened, that's kind of hard to do,' Miller said. She could still feel the tang of wine on her tongue.

'So maybe you try to stop outrunning your problems,' Kahu said quietly, as if expecting reproach. 'They'll follow you wherever you go, and this seems a good a place as any to face them.'

'And how about you? You ran from Castle Bay, memories of

your and Trina's life together.'

'Yeah. I did. It didn't help.' He stood up and looked down at her. 'There's such a thing as starting over, second chances. I believe that.'

Miller wondered how many chances she'd get to make good.

'So now, we start over.' Kahu reached out his hand to her. 'We don't forget. We just start afresh.'

Miller nodded, grabbing his hand and hauling herself up.

Start afresh. She was good at that.

Acknowledgements

Writing another book featuring Miller was never really on the cards after I finished *Nothing Bad Happens Here*. It was always going to be a standalone book. So it is with many thanks to the people who contacted me and spoke to me about their love for Miller after reading *Nothing Bad Happens Here* and wanting to know what was next for her. It was fun meeting up with Miller and Kahu again and creating the community of Lentford.

As always, there is a long list of people I need to thank who helped me get *The Murder Club* off my laptop and into your hands.

To Nathan who was my go-to for any police procedure questions. Thank you so much for answering email upon email of questions from me. Any errors made in police procedure are, of course, my own.

Tina Shaw, thank you for assessing a very early draft of this novel and as always your advice and suggestions always sent me in the right direction.

To editor extraordinaire Stephen Stratford. Thank you for always putting a hundred percent into what you do. You unfailingly turn my manuscript into something so much better.

Thank you to my proofreader Kathy Swailes for doing such a thorough job.

There is a long list of people I contacted with questions I had about certain parts of the book. Even if it made up only one sentence of the book, thank you for your contribution: Kate, Anna, Casey, Cathy, Zealand Tattoo, Sarah, Claire, Tania and Bron.

To my agent Vicki Marsden. Thank you for all your support and help. It's lovely having someone who 'gets it', who I can talk through things with. You were privy to my very first thoughts for *The Murder Club* and your enthusiasm for the story gave me the confidence to write it.

To Mum and Dad, thank you for giving me access to your excellent LP collection, which became Miller's.

As always thank you to my family and friends who are so enthusiastic about my writing. It means a lot to have such a wide group of supportive people around me.

Lastly, thank you to Simon. There aren't really enough words to thank you for your support and all the hard work you put into helping me get a book out into the world. And to my two girls Cate and Abbie (who have been waiting patiently for a book dedication). You're the ones who, after many years, sparked my imagination again – yes, writing fairy stories and writing crime thrillers are worlds apart – but you're the ones who got me writing again and for that I will be forever thankful.

If you enjoyed *The Murder Club* please consider posting a review on Amazon or Goodreads.